PLIGHT OF THE GATEKEEPER'S SON

REVELATIONS PATH

KYMBERLY HASTINGS

COVER ARTIST: VIRGINIA MCKEVITT

ISBN
978-1-959314-99-8 (Paperback)
978-1-960197-00-9 (eBook)

PLIGHT OF THE GATEKEEPER'S SON

By Kymberly Yvonne Hastings

Kiev, The Ukraine, 1982
(G00D COPY) March 21, 2022

WE SHALL HAVE ORDER! *The German people were informed by their leaders at the beginning of the Second World War*

**Bringing to mind that in ancient times,
the Gatekeepers were responsible for maintaining this order**

Dedicated to the Gatekeeper's Son

Whose struggle against the hatred and prejudice he received for the sins of his father was a darkness with which he was forced to contend...Yet, this son developed into an extraordinary human being who urged people not to cry for him, but the six million who had suffered and died. Then a distant time beckoned him, the same as it later did me, and this Gatekeeper's son became involved with ancient civilizations...Places modern people, with their prejudices, weren't as in tune with as they were the present, since they weren't alive when these civilizations flourished.

His life has been a been a gift to the world. A role model who overcame and contributed to the peoples of many nations.

Revelation's Path
Has Echoes Of A True Story Laced With Fiction

TABLE OF CONTENTS

PART 1

EXPECTATIONS

CHAPTER ONE

Kiev, in the Ukraine
May, 1982

As he waited outside the door of his father-in-law's office, Valery Savin opened the envelope and removed the note inside it that the chief office secretary had shoved in his hand upon his arrival.

It read:

"You are to become friends with Arina Pavlik, the young violinist who plays at Laskin's Lair, Kiev's favorite nightclub. Then, charm her and if necessary, bed her."

"What!" Valery exclaimed, followed by a pause of disbelief. *And from my fatherin-law, of all people.*

Marek Falin, his widowed father-in-law, kept a mistress. He was a high-ranking, Soviet military and state official who'd arrested and deported countless numbers of people. *'Clearly a man to be feared,'* were the whispers circling Kiev.

And although Valery was also a high-ranking state official, and a man to be feared, his status was nothing compared to his father-in-law's. "Even though if the things I've been forced to do for Falin—who's an extremely brutal man—often sicken me," was the excuse he'd written in the notepad crammed inside his coat pocket. However, when a man's impoverished like I was, he does what he must to get ahead in the world."

Since even if he should meet some innocent person he was expected to impress, and this person dared to challenge him with a question about some of the terrible things he'd done for the Soviets, then he at least had a valid comeback...like he suspected this Arina Pavlik would be asking him about when he spent some time with her. So he needed to arouse her sympathy and inform her that he had been a thirteen-year old orphan born during the war, whose parents had injuries from it, which eventually lead to their deaths.

Scribbling in his notepad, he added: "In the orphanage if one of us did something wrong, we all got twenty licks across the bare butt, leaving me no choice but to run away and eat out of garbage cans. Eventually, however, I found myself cleaning boxcars for the railroad...I worked hard with many jobs I don't like thinking about because they still disturb me."

"That should be enough to arouse Arina Pavlik's sympathy, should it not?" he remarked, thinking aloud. *But then, in case she didn't believe me, perhaps I should add that my hard work impressed the right people, and they saw to it I ended up with a university degree.*

★★★

For nearly a month Valery had been going to Laskin's Lair to see Arina. A gorgeous violinist with an oval face and amber-gold curls, which were the same color as her eyes. She was a cultural icon in the city. *'A violin virtuoso,'* her fans would say, leaving him mystified. Was there really no male figure in her life? Apparently not if Marek was asking him to court her. And though he was forty and his marriage to Marek's nineteen year old daughter, Mila, was still one of convenience, it was sad. Because Marek had made sure the love of her life took a trip to the wall.

Naturally, Mila would never forgive him, but it didn't stop Marek from being angry with her and beating her shoulders and back, whenever the opportunity arouse. *'She refuses to let you take her to bed, Savin. So why don't you force yourself on her?'* Marek would yell.

'Because it's not in my nature!' I daringly would inform him. *'And besides Mila will come around sooner or later.'*

I should have lied and said I did take her to bed, but her anger at her father would have made her probably contradict me...'I refuse to let him win after what he's done,' were Mila's words.

So, trapped in a marriage like that has made it easy for me to develop a schoolboy crush on Arina. Which certainly makes the idea of having an affair with her darkly intriguing.

Valery's attention was suddenly diverted when the door to his father-in-law's office swung open, and two frightened-looking, Red Army soldiers exited. '*Wonder what they'd done to incur Marek's wrath?*' was something he'd have loved to asked him, but knew better.

"Why do you need to see me, Valery?" his stout father-in-law snapped.

"This—" He handed him the note. "Why are you asking me to do this?"

"Because Arina Pavlik seems to have put her life on hold until she can learn the whereabouts of Wallenberg," was Marek's answer.

"The prisoner who's been dead since *1947*?" Valery asked, having difficulty believing it. Somewhere there was a record that Josef Stalin had ordered him executed. Although who could be sure, since another public record stated Wallenberg had died from a heart attack.

Marek's bushy, dark brows rose. "If the man's alive it's on a need to know basis. Since reports continue to circulate he's not dead. With many saying that in the beginning he was taken to the Soviet military headquarters in the city of Debrecen, east of Budapest. Then by train through Romania to Moscow." He gave a small shrug. "At first, it was believed he was brought there to possibly reveal the defectors in Sweden... but who could really be sure."

Valery listened with bafflement. "Not a very strong reason to take Wallenberg."

"It isn't." He exhaled deeply. "And it's a reason that one way or the other, the Israelis are determined to find out, the same as those SS Nazis in Argentina and Paraguay, who fled there after the war.

"They're hunting Wallenberg, so they can hang him like the Israelis did Adolph Eichmann."

"Revenge," Valery replied, recalling that Wallenberg was reported to have saved over a hundred thousand Jews...an act that inspired the Israelis to put up monuments to him and name roads after him.

The Israelis were intent on finding out the truth and never failed to ask world leaders whenever they'd visit the Soviet Union, to try and learn from Soviet Premier Tikhonov, what had happened to their noble-blooded *Swedish Schindler*—as Wallenberg had come to be called. A real mystery. But would anyone ever be able to uncover it after all these years of nothing? Or was there possibly something that had come to light recently? *If not, then why am I being encouraged to have an affair with this Arina Pavlik?*

"Tell me about this gorgeous violinist, with the poise of a cinema star, that I love to hear play," Valery encouraged Marek. "What's she got to do with Wallenberg?"

"Nothing—other that she's believed to be his daughter."

"His daughter? "Valery's dismay caused his breath break slightly. "But Wallenberg wasn't married and didn't have any children."

"I know," Marek replied. "But this letter our lovely violinist was trying to smuggle out of the country states otherwise." He pointed at a folder.

"Interesting." Valery touched it. "Though what about this man you moved to the political prison here who claimed his name was *Wallenberg?* Though, in reality was discovered to be, Vilmos Langfelder, Wallenberg's Hungarian driver. Does he know anything?"

"Are you joking?" Marek chuckled. "After having been a political prisoner, in another of our political prisons for thirty-seven years, it's said he's confused. But he's not Wallenberg because he speaks poor Swedish, poor German, and poor Russian. Languages Wallenberg spoke. Though it doesn't seem to matter, since this Langfelder man is in our political prison nearby because of Arina. With rumors continuing to circulate she's Wallenberg's daughter. And now with this copy of a small painting in her letter, we've learned belonged to Wallenberg, it's always possible a light might come on in this Langfelder's brain, and he'll recall something about it."

Marek handed Valery the folder which contained Arina's letter. "Read it. She wrote these pages in German, and gave it to a friend to take to a Berlin newspaper and publish it under a false name. But when this friend's luggage got ransacked by one of our airport guards, Arina's letter was confiscated and sent to me."

"And her letter was about *what* exactly?"

"A recount of what her mother, Jamella, had told her before she died. Which you'll need to read before you leave here."

Valery quickly removed the letter from its large envelope, appreciating Arina's neat, legible hand as he began reading it.

May, 1982

Dear Friend,

It was reported before Wallenberg left Budapest to meet the Russians, that he remarked, *'If my luck holds, I'll be a guest. But if it doesn't, then I'll be a prisoner—'* He also had this strange painting that was on heavy paper and not canvas. And though a piece was missing, he loved it and had it framed, but somehow the frame got broken. The painting was small. About one-fourth the size of a newspaper sheet, making it easy for him to keep in his coat pocket, whenever he did some traveling.

"Strange painting?" Valery questioned.

"It's this." Marek reached for another folder on his desk. "Our violinist friend has the original that her mother re-framed. And she was gracious enough to allow me to photograph, both front and back."

Valery had to squint to see the fading picture. Clearly a painting from the early part of the century, with a weathered looking farmhouse on a hill in the distance that was difficult to make out. But it appeared to have a red, twisted chimney, which was something you didn't see very often...with the exception of a few having been along the Russian-Finnish border during this same time period. But looking closer, Valery noticed the bottom part of it had been torn off, which raises the question where Wallenberg got this painting? Did his partial amnesia—as Stalin claimed he had—not let him remember? Could be? But did it really matter? Because the important thing about the painting was a large rock on a hill covered in petroglyphs? However, it was the lower right part of those glyphs which had been torn off.

Adrenaline spiked Valery's blood as he looked over the next part of Arina's letter, before resuming his reading:

> "My mom suspected part of this painting was missing because of my father being shot by the Russians. And the strange writing on the back of the painting read: SHOULD YOU GET LOST, THEN THIS PAINTING WILL ALLOW YOU TO FIND YOUR WAY BACK.

Back to where? A statement that instantly aroused Valery's curiosity.

Marek took the photo of the painting from Valery. "No one could identify the place where the artist possibly painted the picture, any more than archeologists could read the petroglyph writing."

He handed him a note from an archeologist: *"Are these writings possibly some kind of message to future generations? A pity if they are. Since more than likely, thick brushes are now covering the rock on the hill making the glyphs impossible to see."*

"And Wallenberg's supposed to be living in this place nobody can find?" Valery asked. "Which could be in Sweden, the Balkans, Finland, or the Soviet Union."

"That's the story, with no petroglyphs that match the picture being found in any of those countries...but finish reading what Arina wrote." Marek urged, his eyes twinkling mockingly. "So that way you'll see how she came to be."

Valery disliked his innuendo, but nevertheless, gave him a strained smile before returning to her letter.

"When I came of age, I was told by my mother that the Russians took Wallenberg to our farming community to execute him, instead of Moscow, which was quite far away. The rumors voiced on street corners in Budapest said he was doing the driving. With his Hungarian driver friend, Vilmos Langfelder, in the back wearing the expensive coat and fedora he'd given him. So, thinking Langfelder was Wallenberg, the Russians immediately took him prisoner and shot the driver.

These Russians were in a hurry, so they buried the man they believed was the driver, quickly and shabbily before they left. But it didn't take long for Moscow to realize that Langfelder was the driver and not Wallenberg, who was dead according to the Russians who'd shot him. But then, where was his body? These Russians had made the mistake of detouring to some rural community with which nobody was familiar. And for that, they ended up being executed. And Langfelder, being a Hungarian outsider, hadn't a clue as to the where this rural community might be. So, the Soviets eventually left him alone.

But getting back to our farming community. Several hours passed before someone there noticed a hand sticking up in the ground. A wounded man was attempting to rise. Two farmers, eager to help this unknown man, carried him to my mother, who was known for the medicines she made from the herbs she collected.

The man had amnesia and couldn't remember his name. Although, later he said he thought it was Wallace. A Gaelic name my mother found odd for this part of the world, but then my mother's name, Jamella, was from a Caribbean novel.

Her husband was ill, and their only son had been killed in the war. So, when this man got better, he helped around the farm anyway he could. Nine years passed and when my mother's husband became bedridden, she had an affair with Wallace…I was born in 1955, and a month later, her husband died.

'I loved Wallace, and he loved me—' which pleased my mother. He loved the farmhouse too. *'Home is where the heart is,'* he declared, *'because having a daughter, and living with the wonderful lady who gave her to me, makes it that way.'*

All seemed to be going well until I turned six. It was then the Russians burst into our house and took Wallace from us. Tears spilled down my mother's cheeks. *'Why had they done this?'* she sobbed, as various reasons surfaced. Was Wallenberg OSS? Or maybe he was a Nazi? He'd certainly entertained people, like Adolph Eichmann, claiming it was bribery. Or was it something else? The Russians declared Wallenberg had helped a lot of fascists escape the Nazis. So could these be the possible reasons for arresting him in 1960, when word finally got out he was living in hiding with us? But who could really say Wallace was Wallenberg?

Shortly afterwards we moved to Kiev because we didn't want to hear the neighboring farmers' gossip that Wallace was really Wallenberg. But how could that be? Wallenberg had supposedly either died from a heart attack in 1947 or been executed by Stalin…A mystery that continued, with many questions not answered…Why did the Israelis not believe Wallenberg had died in 1947? Again, there seemed no real proof. The other mystery concerned Wallenberg's relatives in Sweden. They were financiers and industrialists who'd been doing business with the Russians for many years before the war. And when it ended, the country needed money badly…Also, a number of Wallenberg's family members were scientists. With one in particular being an outstanding physicist who later—so it was rumored from 1960 to present day—happened to be helping the Russians get closer to developing teleportation and invisibility.And these relatives all loved Wallenberg and spent twenty-two years searching for him, but to no avail.

'It's blackmail,' the well-known gypsy or Romani psychic, Madam Abilita Carnet, informed us when she'd visited Kiev. *'The Soviet Special Services needed Wallenberg. So in November of 1944, he requested a meeting with them and asked to go to Moscow in January 1945. The Soviets didn't view the Jews like Wallenberg did, who had been known to suggest they wanted them evacuated to Siberia. But even so, Wallenberg felt he should go over the financial support plan he was*

developing for the surviving Russian Jews. Something that immediately the Soviets recognized as a tool with which they could do business cheaply with Wallenberg's people—plus get valuable information from the scientists in the family, who were believed to have been ordered to keep up the pretend hunt for him. Only for twenty-two years it was a real hunt, until his hiding place in your farming community was finally discovered.

'This Swedish Schindler would be treated well with attendants to see after his needs. And at certain times his relatives would be able to visit with him, under guard, on very small ships dropping anchor in various Soviet harbors.'

'And his daughter, Arina?' my mother had asked this Berlin psychic. *'What about her?'*

But Madam Carnet simply shook her head and said, *'It's been my experience the Russians love to be mysterious—part of their act. So they probably told Wallenberg not to tell anyone he had a daughter.'*

'Then the deal with the Russians has been was struck!' I remember hearing my mother say. *'And is Wallenberg in poor health now?'*

'Yes,' Madam Carnet answered. *'And if he dies they'll probably replace him with an imposter.'*

'Sadly. But where's he's living?' my mother asked.

Madam Carnet referred to the painting with the petroglyphs. *'Here most likely. A place no one has a clue as to where it might be.'* Though she did tell my mother she'd meditate on the problem and should have an answer for her the following week...Although, when my mother returned to the place where she was staying, she couldn't be found. *'Went back to Berlin,'* remarked a man at the house.

So that ended that.

My mother and I weren't unhappy living in Kiev. She worked in a laundry and dealt out medicines on the side...In the beginning we struggled. Though, when I was in the third grade I was overcome with joy, when she announced she'd made enough money to pay a man to instruct me in violin. In better times when my mother was growing up, her family was fairly affluent and a cousin had willed her his violin. Something that made me determined to become a violinist.

Sincerely yours,
Arina Pavlik

"Interesting," Valery said, putting Arina's letter back in its envelope and placing it on Marek's desk. "More questions than answers in her letter...

but why these questions now? If Wallenberg is alive he'd be sixty-nine. So what's awakened this sudden urge to find him after all these years? Has someone seen him or something? And after such along passage of time, would he be able to be recognized?"

"My position doesn't allow me to divulge anything," Marek reminded. "But it is worth noting that from my point of view Wallenberg's anonymity continues to be an asset to us Soviets. Remember that! And should word get out he's alive, we'll be in deep trouble if we don't get a handle on the situation."

"But is he alive?"

"If I knew I couldn't answer. However, should it be revealed he is alive, then promise me you'll contradict it anyway you can."

"Which I will." Valery assured him, wishing he could add, '*So it's no wonder Madam Carnet left Kiev, when she said Wallenberg's family was being blackmailed by the Soviets.*'

Marek handed Valey a bound book with some recent clippings from Berlin newspapers in it. "You wanted to know what's got this stuff about Wallenberg coming to light after all these years. Well, take a look at the picture of the young man in one of these clippings. He's a former news reporter, with an outstanding reputation for being honest in his field."

A lengthy pause followed with Valery trying to recall where he'd seen the young man's face. He was a handsome fellow with dark curly hair and blue eyes. Had he been in a movie...? He didn't think so.

But then it hit him like he'd been punched in the stomach by a prizefighter. The young man's picture last week had briefly flashed on a television screen...This fellow was Gerado Gerhart Behl, the youngest son of Otho Behl, who'd helped Adolph Eichmann organize the holocaust that had killed six million people.

Eichmann had been in hiding for almost seventeen years, and apparently so had his good friend Otho Behl. A man the Israelis were just as intent on capturing as they'd been Eichmann. And they were in Paraguay chasing him in his stolen Buick when he'd crashed into a large, truck that was hauling gasoline.

Immediately, the car caught fire and exploded, talking the life of Behl. But not the lives of those thugs in Paraguay, who were part of a Nazi terror cell that later burned Jewish shops and synagogues.

Valery uttered an expletive. "Behl and his offspring!" his voice boomed. "Wouldn't you know one of them would end up a neo-Nazi news reporter—"

"O-oh *no*." Marek quickly let it be known. "Gerado Behl or rather Gerado Gerhart—his newspaper name—is not a neo-Nazi like his two older brothers. And he *backed* the building of a new Germany and showed this support by doing time in the German army in his teens. Though he could have done it because if another holocaust happened, his military training would enable him to protect this Jewish couple, who'd helped to raise him...However, it would have been better for *us* if Behl had been a neo-Nazi. Because *Senor* Gerhart, *Herr* Gerhart, or *Signor* Gerhart—who goes by all three titles—has a great remorse over his father's actions. And knowing how after all these years many of the Israelis still refuse to believe Wallenberg is dead, Gerado Gerhart, is determined to uncover the truth about him. 'The least I can do for the Israelis,' he said in an interview. 'After what my father did to them.'

Marek then proceeded to explain that apparently this Berlin newspaper where *Herr* Behl worked had no clue as who he really was. In fact, it was well known he'd been raised, in part, by a wealthy Jewish lady, Isabella Wurtz Swanda, that he called godmother. And her husband, Antonio, he called godfather.

"Isabella was living in Italy," Marek continued. "Though her parents were from Germany and had moved to Paraguay between the wars. And the fact she was Jewish, was the main reason none of the members of the newspaper's staff where *Herr* Behl had worked for several years, suspected he was one of Otho Behl's sons—especially since he was such a popular reporter. Then, an assignment came for *Herr* Gerhart or Behl to go with two other investigative reporters to Israel, to interview people Wallenberg had saved—"

"Bad decision," Valery broke it.

"It was. And he was looking forward to it when, somehow, the Israelis got wind of who he really was. 'The son of war criminal, Otho Behl, is never to be allowed to visit Israel,' was what the Israelis informed his Berlin newspaper. And it seemed this newspaper agreed, because the next day *Herr* Behl found himself without a job."

God—what the hell...! It took Valery a moment to find his voice and make a response. "Which must have been sad for *Herr* Behl, knowing how the world looks for heroes. Something he was thought to be, with all the admirers he was said to have."

"Like a large fan club." Marek frowned, like he hated to admit it. Then, he drew a breath. "Some interviews then followed from a rival newspaper, with this murderer's son stating that one way or another he was determined to learn what had happened to Wallenberg. "If he's alive, I'm going to find him" he'd told them.

A statement that caught Arina Pavlik's attention, who sent a letter to him, stating she was Wallenberg's daughter."

Valery was swept with disbelief. "Now that was daring."

"It was. With *Herr* Behl answering it the very next day. "If your father's alive, then I'll help you find him.""

But what really attracted everyone's attention was when *Herr* Behl informed Arina Pavlik that he and his godmother, Isabella, were coming to Kiev to meet her. And they would be there by the end of the following week.

"Great goodness!" Valery's thoughts were whirling. "If there really is a Soviet blackmail scheme concerning Wallenberg, then I'm surprised after what Arina wrote she's not in a Gulag camp."

"Her musical talent makes her one of Kiev's cultural icons," Marek remarked, like he wasn't exactly proud of it. "So at present, a forced-work camp isn't for her. Though, with the newspapers now involved, it could stir up some problems for us. Which is why we need to appear laidback, and the reason I'm bringing you into it. Since women, with the exception of my daughter, flock to you...'His handsome face is deliciously appealing,' I've heard them say. And they love your sable-colored hair and blue eyes—"

"Which are similar to *Herr* Behl's." an annoyed Valery pushed himself to complete.

Marek looked him up and down. "Behl is muscular like you, and though you may be forty, you two resemble each other enough to be brothers. Have you looked in the mirror lately?"

"Oh yes!" Valery said, before muttering an expletive. "And I could have gone a lifetime without hearing I resemble a Nazi war criminal's son."

"And I could have gone a lifetime without learning that in 1945 the Americans had Behl in a detention camp, and he escaped. Although, if he hadn't escaped Gerado Behl would have never been born...but that's really not the point. I've checked, and Arina has no lover or sweetheart in her life. However, with *Herr* Behl also playing the violin and being twenty-seven—her same age—she's apt to have one. With my sources telling me *he* has no lover or sweetheart either."

A moment passed before Marek added, "Something that could complicate things for us. So, *woo* her and take her to bed, before anyone else can come into her life."

"Certainly short notice with *Herr* Behl arriving next week."

"It is. But you can do it." An expectant pause followed with Marek offering him a slightly amused smile. "Just don't fall in love with her."

"Something I'll certainly try hard not to do," Valery declared, feeling like he was hanging from a precipice during an earthquake. When it suddenly struck him. Since his time to *woo* Arina was short, and she wanted to publish her letter in a Berlin newspaper, then why not send it to *Herr* Behl now? With no one being the wiser, should this news reporter re-write it later under his newspaper name…"An Interview With Psychic Madam Abilita Carnet About What Happened to Wallenberg," was what it could be titled.

A lot of people discredited these psychic fortune-tellers; so the Soviets would undoubtedly dismiss what she had to say.

"If Behl's coming next week to talk with Arina, then plans have to be made right away," Valery said beneath his breath. *And I'll put a note in with her letter that will let him know she can have her story published without being sent to a Gulag camp. But will this impress her enough to crawl in bed with me?*

And if this talented, gorgeous lady does, then will I fall in love with her—if I'm not already? I can't take my eyes off her each time I listen to her play the violin. A scenario that continues to needle me, muddling my thoughts. Because if the truth be known, after the arrests, deportations, and trips to the wall in which I've participated, I'm not much better than Otho Behl.

CHAPTER TWO

AN ITALIAN VILLA OUTSIDE ROME

May, 1982

The shrill sound of the alarm clock made Gerado raise his head and groan. *Damn!* If he hadn't had that nightmare again; the one he'd periodically had ever since he was seven years old…The one that had made him come straight up out of bed the first time he'd had it. *Not pleasant. With my father appearing to me each time I have it. He's in hell, because whenever he comes to me a sheet of fire is behind him. Enough to freak a person out. But then, he hands me a crushed swastika, which actually burned my hand the first time I had the nightmare. So I quickly put it on my nightstand, where it left a mark that's present to this very day.*

Gerado didn't want to tell Isabella about his nightmare. She knew when he had it that he always awoke uptight and trembling. Since when he was a kid, her bedroom and her husband Antonio's was next door to his. And any time this terrible dream occurred, they'd rush in to comfort him.

Never mind about telling his housekeeper mother. A woman who was fastidious and worked extremely hard for them in an impeccably starched apron, wrapped around one of her floral printed dresses.

'It's like she's trying to forget everything that happened in Germany and Paraguay,' Isabella would say. *'And she does all this canning. Things I've never required a housekeeper to do. But if it keeps her from being depressed, then I don't say anything. And when I offer her more money for doing it, she refuses. So I slip extra money in her bank account that she thinks is interest.'*

'*We take care of all her needs and wants, along with Gerado's,*' Antonio would *add,* '*and if her money's never spent, it'll end up being some money for Gerado—in addition to the trust we set up for him. Besides, he loves his mother, and she loves him. Always kissing him good night.*'

'*Sadly, she didn't know about her husband at the time,*' Isabella would point out. '*And the terrible things he did. But she certainly heard about them afterwards. Which is why when she's not canning or doing housework, she's in prayer...Especially for her two sons who were in the SS in their teens and flaunted a variety of pictures wearing this terrible clothing...One of which, is next to her Bible—*'

"Trying to heal the wounds to her soul," Gerado murmured, not needing a mirror to know his face was dimmed with sorrow. "And I pray everyday for the souls of the millions who died. But even so, I probably had that nightmare again because *me,* a Heidelberg University graduate, just lost my newspaper job in Berlin and, under the circumstances, thought it best, to give up my apartment."

And yes, I had money in trust funds, but I kept it safe-guarded...Especially considering I took pride in being independent and earning my own money as a news reporter.

The painful memory of his job loss continued to haunt him, and he fought to shove it away...but without much luck.

"I've been described as being an outstanding journalist with great confidence—who *goes* for it when the need arises. Making it easy for me to carry on with my life, despite my wounds."

Yet, here I am without out a job because my father helped organize the killing of six million people...Why in the name of God, had he done it? A question that makes me tremble each time I pray for an answer.

The plausible explanation given in many history books was that in 1920, the year of the depression, Germany was paying for the mistakes it had made during the Great War. With the German people feeling they had no future since the Jews, with their money, had the top jobs. So when the *Fuhrer* came along the German people extolled him. And they believed him when he said the Jews needed to be killed. Clearly the inability to know right from wrong. Because the Jews had no weapons with which to fight back. And those who dared to question the *Fuhrer* about it, got taken down along with them.

Gerado's stomach knotted as his thoughts flashed back to his father; a shadowed figure who never ceased to haunt him. Something, if possible, he needed to do about that before his Kiev trip.

He peered at the alarm clock again. *Time for breakfast.* He didn't like being late, so he hastily through on his clothes and headed downstairs to the patio.

It never ceased to amaze him he'd grown up in such a stately place, with parquet floors in the foyer and Aubusson carpet in most of the other rooms.

Inhaling deeply, he enjoyed the pleasant smell of fresh-baked bread that filled the air as he crossed the living room to the patio where Isabella was seated at its table with her coffee cup.

"Did you sleep well, Gerado?" she asked as he planted a light kiss on her forehead.

"I tried...but why do you ask?"

"Because I thought I heard you cry out."

"I did." he confessed, wishing she hadn't heard him.

Isabella stirred her coffee. "Your nightmare again?'

"What else? It got worse after your Antonio died. Who, as you know, was like a father to me. But then it left for a time—"

A solemn look stole into her expression. "And now it's come back."

"No doubt because I lost my job."

He reached in his pocket for Antonio's gold, cigarette lighter and lit a table candle on this bright sunny day in memory of him. And though he didn't smoke like Antonio, he always carried it. *So something of him is with me. Even if I know better than to take it to Russia, since it's apt to get confiscated.*

Of course few people realized the Soviet Union was not really Russia. It was created by four socialist republics: Belarus, Russia, Transcaucasia, and Georgia. Something he'd written about in a news article last year that had aroused a good deal of curiosity.

People loved his writing, which made him enjoy being a journalist. Although, when something unpleasant happened to him, it always seemed Otho Behl invaded his dreams. *Why? Because when I was five years old I still can't shake the terrible memories I have of him.*

And he cringed each time he remembered what he did to him the night before he was killed.

'The Israelis are coming for me like they did Eichmann!' he'd shouted over and over.

He was drinking heavily, and when my mother mentioned I was friends with Isabella Wurtz, he blew up. 'A Jewish bitch when the Israelis are coming after me? No son of mine does that!' And before I knew it he had torn off my shorts and was whipping me on the bottom with his razor strap.

I screamed and cried, but my mother couldn't stop him. Because each time she tried, he'd slap her. Abuse that neither of us were ever able to forget.

In the hopes of forgetting about last night, Gerado poured himself a cup of coffee and was attempting to swallow the despair in his throat, when the maid suddenly appeared. "Some slices of fresh-baked bread, sir, and your oatmeal."

He thanked her. And taking his spoon, he put a small portion of it in his bowl, fearful that if he ate more it might make the tightness in his gut worse.

Isabella gave him a loving pat on the arm. "Things will get better for you, Gerado, once you meet Arina Pavlik. With something telling me that being Wallenberg's so-called daughter, she can't help but have a wealth of written information about him tucked away in a journal that should be quite valuable for you—"

Gerado grinned briefly. "Which as your brother, Manuel, would say, will be like finding an ancient jewel hidden inside a valuable relic."

"An archeologist talking. Who, by the way, phoned again last night."

"He's worried about us, like I am about him," Gerado said. "With my two neo-Nazi brothers—who unfortunately have made money in their business endeavors—now spending six months in Berlin and the other six in Paraguay."

Isabella shivered. "Something that puts me on edge when I think about Manuel recently taking that archeology teaching position at Berlin's *Freie University*—"

"—he's sixty years old but declares he can still go on digs."

"Which I'm sure he can. Although, since you've given him the recent pictures of your brothers you found in a newspaper that are similar to the ones you gave me earlier, I'm sure he'll recognize them if they show up."

"Did Manuel say anything else?"

"Only to remind us to bring gifts for Arina, since he suspects she'll have gifts for us."

"A Kiev custom I've never heard of," Gerado admitted with a shrug. "But, nevertheless, I've bought something expensive for her."

"Same as me."

He grinned anew, hoping to develop a close friendship with this delightful-looking young woman.

When suddenly the doorbell chimed, prompting the maid to hurry up and answer it.

"I got our Kiev plane tickets yesterday," remarked Isabella. "So I wonder who it could be?"

"Then I guess I'd better find out," said Gerado, rising and heading for the door.

"A delivery for you, *Signor* Gerhart," announced a man standing on the porch. He handed him an envelope with no return address.

"What is it?" asked Isabella, joining him.

"This." Gerado passed it to her, before giving the delivery man a tip. "Doesn't say who it's from." He felt a sudden tenseness. "I don't like mysteries."

"Then, breakfast aside, I guess we'd better open it."

"Definitely."

Isabella pulled her chair closer to his, as a copy of a picture with petroglyphs on a rock fell out. And on the back was written, "Where my father might be. As my letter will explain." Signed, Arina Pavlik.

Also on its back in small print was the name *Valery Savin*, Soviet official.

"Our contact man," Gerado remarked. "Who appears to be trying to help us."

Isabella glanced at the name. "But can we trust him?"

"A Russian, who knows?"

She took the picture." I'll get this picture express-mailed to Manuel's apartment before we leave. And I'll also have Arina's letter copied and mailed with it."

"Good idea. Since hopefully he'll be able to decipher some of those glyphs in this picture."

"Hopefully—or otherwise that picture's not the greatest clue when it comes to locating someone."

They began reading Arina's letter together. And when they got to the bottom of the page, Savin had written in German that this was an original letter, a friend of Arina's was attempting to smuggle to a Berlin newspaper. However, it had been taken by a guard at the airport and given to Soviet military official, Marek Falin... "But we'll talk about it in private when you arrive, *Herr* Behl," Savin's note had ended.

Gerado sighed and shook his head. "Arina should have known better than to try and smuggle something like this letter out of the Iron Curtain."

"True. Although it is interesting this Savin's attempting to help her."

"I suspect it's because this picture of her she's enclosed, shows her to be one the most gorgeous women I've ever seen. With long, golden waves brushing her shoulders, and amber-gold eyes, which you can fall into, and keep plunging and plunging," He hesitated before confiding, "Something that makes her capable of spiking a man's blood with fire. And if the truth be known, staring at her picture makes me feel like I'm already in love with her."

"Love at first sight," remarked Isabella with a broad smile. "So there must be something to it, considering how you've had plenty of beautiful women chasing you."

"Part of my job so I'm told. But none looks like Arina. "A delightful shiver of wanting ran through him each time he thought about her, and the pensive shimmer haunting her eyes. *Beautiful but not flirtatious.* "In fact, I wouldn't be surprised if Arina's not Valery Savin's mistress."

"And you mentioned he's a married man." Isabella said. "But what about this Berlin psychic, Madam Abilita Carnet, Arina wrote about. Didn't you interview her?"

"Once. Since a lot of her gypsy relatives had been killed in the holocaust. Which she was quite informative about. And I was impressed that my article would remind the world that Romanies were killed along with Jews at places like Auschwitz. So before I left, she told me I was going to have two sons." He gave his head a hard shake. "Whenever, under the present circumstances, I can't imagine."

"She's supposed to be quite good at what she does. Yet, she can't find out about Wallenberg?"

"Which certainly raises some questions, doesn't it?"

"Indeed it does."

"But look at this." Isabella held up a postcard of their hotel. *The International.* It was attached with a paper clip to the back of Arina's letter. "And this Valery Savin writes on this postcard that he'll be meeting us at the airport, so be sure and bring your swimsuits since our lovely hotel has a new pool."

"An idea I like, considering this Russian state official will probably see our luggage is not ransacked—"

Isabella looked up from the postcard. "He seems to be helping us in our attempt to locate Wallenberg. And it surprises me. But are you packed?"

"I threw some things together last night," he said, recalling the clothing he'd put in his bag. "Though in light of Arina's letter I feel there're some things I need to add, and others I need to remove."

"Then do what you must because don't forget, we have a six a.m. departure tomorrow."

"How could I forget any of it," he said, rising again. "It's my first freelance assignment as a news reporter. With a voice inside my head warning us to be careful, because a frightening adventure lies ahead."

"Same thing a voice is telling me."

"I realize that like us, a good many Russians are now fluent in German and English but even so, have you brushed up on your Russian for those who aren't?"

"Manuel and I are talking in Russian. And I've been playing those language records we bought for you years ago."

"They certainly helped me when I studied the language at Heidelberg."

"And I'm glad. Because it does help a German news investigator to speak Russian."

"Quite true." Unmoving, he stood beside her chair. "Which as you know in my profession—like Manuel's, reading Russian is just as important as speaking it. And I've said it many times that I wouldn't have been able to do any of this if it hadn't been for you and Antonio." Once again he kissed her on the forehead. "My angel godmother, " he murmured, before turning on his heel and heading up the stairs to his room.

He'd left his suitcase open with his camera in it. And he frowned as he asked the question—*What do I need to take out? Certainly not my blue jeans and denim jacket. Perhaps some of my fancier shirts in exchange for some of my plainer ones. Even though I might be playing my violin? Probably so, with the Soviets—after confiscating Arina's letter—hovering over us...An act that definitely draws attention to our Wallenberg hunt. Though regardless, I'll take my tuxedo, since my instincts tell me Valery Savin is planning on hosting a champagne supper for us.*

He knew more about Arina than he'd expected to know about her, before they met. "She's a wounded soul like me," he said aloud, like he was preparing a speech. "So why not show her this journal-like article about my life that I'd hoped to edit and publish in a magazine some day? Something I very much wanted to do. until I decided that people might feel sorry for me. Which they shouldn't."

If they have to feel sorrow, then it should be for the six million who died. "However, if Arina reads this—which I'll put in letter form—then she'll know something about me, like I do her. So it'll be easier to get on with our business. Especially since Wallenberg was half-Jew, and I'm Otho Behl's son. "

He reached in his desk drawer and removed what he'd written the previous year. It was neatly typed in a purple folder Isabella had given him. 'Am I royalty?' he'd asked her.

'*To me you are,*' she'd said, giving him a hug. '*Because you're an exceptional human being who's always struck me as being spear brave—like your name.*'

'*As long as I don't take after my two brothers, Hermann and Vaiter, who like we know, are Nazis,*' Gerado recalled he'd told her.

'*Which you won't,*' she'd assured him.

A rival Berlin newspaper had wanted to do a book about me; obviously one that would shed tears.

But repeating my thoughts, I told them if you're going to do a book, then do it about the six million who died... '*That's where your tears need to be shed.*'

So, settling back in the chair at his desk, he began thumbing through what he'd written about his life.

Some of what he remembered and some of what he'd been told later.

May, 1982
My Dearest Arina,

The day I turned *five*...that's when it really began for me. My parents had moved from Germany before I was born and settled in Asuncion, Paraguay, the country's capital. With my father, a salesman for a radio company, using his middle name, *Hoffman*, for a last name. He didn't make much money, but my mother, Sudie, helped out by being a part-time worker in a flower shop near our house.

When I grew up I learned from her that my father had explained to my two grown brothers that I was a *late child*—something that should never have happened. '*And your mother could have stopped her pregnancy, but she'd refused.*'

I have clear memories of my brothers calling me, *Late Child.*

Especially at siesta time in Paraguay's afternoon, but still, there were times my mother couldn't get away from the flower shop. So she'd ask my two brothers—who worked in a garage—to borrow their boss's old, but well-cared for lender car, so they come get me and take me home. *'That way you can have a nap,'* my mother told me. Several times I refused to go with my brothers, but she'd insist. So, with glee on their faces they'd put me in that lender car as tears ran down my cheeks.

Once at our house, they'd open a drawer, remove a picture, and shove it in my face. *'See our black Schutzstaffel uniforms,'* they'd say. *'We were in the SS when we were still in our teens.'*

I had no idea what they were talking about, but I'd begin to cry because I knew what was coming next. They each wore belts with metal buckles, and took great pleasure in whipping me with them. Taking turns to see who could strike me the hardest. *'Got to learn to toughen up if you're gonna be in the SS,'* they'd inform me.

Then, they'd tell my mother when she returned, that I'd fallen and injured myself. *'Are all late children this clumsy?'* they'd ask her, pretending to be surprised.

I knew better than to say anything because I feared I'd get more beatings from them.

My mother was concerned about my injuries and said she asked my father what she should do. But he didn't seem interested. *'He's overactive. So paddle Gerado, hard, with a large ruler. And if he doesn't settle down, then I'll scorch his bare bottom with my razor strap...'* Though—thank goodness—he only used his razor strap on me one time.

'Something I tried to keep from happening,' my mother informed me when I was older, and we were living in Italy. Adding, *'Your father didn't appear to be concerned about hurting you, any more than he was about the things he did during the war. And I didn't know what they were then, because he believed a husband shouldn't be having a conversation with his wife about his war experiences...Besides, he told me, he was in his office mostly during the war. And as far as your two brothers being in the SS in their teens, they got transferred from Hitler Youth, and even if it was late in the war, Otho Behl was watching over them.'*

When my father was home he rarely said two words to me. And when my brothers would visit they would frighten me. So the only person I had was my mother, who always seemed to be busy.

Then Isabella came into my life and gave me the comfort I needed. Another lifetime, I later came to think of it. So I'll share the stories she and my mother told me when I reached my teen years, about that dreadful time when I was so very innocent.

'*You have such trusting eyes,*' Isabella was always telling me. '*Which lets me know that if I hadn't been around, your teen years might have been a very dark and depressing time for you.*'

'*Which I'm sure they would have been,*' I agreed.

The first time I saw Isabella was in the flower shop. She was quite beautiful with dark hair and green eyes. And she was getting a lot of attention from the shop's owner and my mother. '*You're our best customer,*' my mother said. My two brothers were also there, waiting impatiently to take me home for my nap—and that's when I begin to cry.

'*Now don't cry,*' said Isabella, '*because your eyes are the lovely color of blueberries and don't need to be filled with tears...But what's your name?*' she asked me in her silky voice.

'*Gerado.*' My mother answered for me.

Isabella then took my hand. '*What's the matter, Gerado, don't you want a nap?*' But I shook my head.

I was wearing shorts, with the marks from Hermann and Vaiter's belts on my legs. And suddenly she appeared quite concerned.

'*Did someone spank you?*'

I nodded.

'*Who? Your mother or your father?*'

I didn't answer, but pointed at my brothers.

A fearful look crossed her face, '*God help us,*' she muttered. And turning to my mother she said, '*I live with my parents and they, like me, love children, so why not let me take Gerado to my house for a nap? And on the way we can stop for an ice cream.*'

A faint smile flitted across my face as my mother quickly agreed.

Isabella's home was like a Spanish castle. And she liked living there and being a secretary for her financier father.

'*Wealthy bitch,*' my brothers were heard to mumble.

'*Seems Late Child's got himself a Jewish girlfriend,*' said Vaiter.

Isabella stopped. "*I was a late child too.*'

'*A Jewish late child,*' said Hermann.' *Which might not have happened if we'd exterminated more Jews.*'

Isabella's hand was trembling as she held mine and put me in her fancy Buick. Though as she started toward the driver's side, my two brothers blocked her. *'Tell us,'* said Vaiter, *'what happened to Manuel, that older, archeologist brother of yours who was in Budapest with Wallenberg briefly?'*

'He's out of the country on one of his digs,' she answered, fear in her eyes.

'You know,' said Hermann, *'my father's good friend, Adolph Eichmann got your Aryan looking brother—with the help of our father—to identify some of Budapest's wealthy Jews. And they gave your brother money. But our father never saw any of it, because soon afterwards, Wallenberg helped Manuel disappear. So what happened? Did Wallenberg give the money to two Palestinian Jews, who used it to smuggle Jewish children to London? Our father—the exceptional Otho Behl—later heard?'*

Isabella appeared to be astounded at hearing the name Otho Behl. And told me she wasn't sure how she did it, but she managed to get in her Buick and drive off with me…Later, when she returned to the flower shop, she drove my mother and I home, so we wouldn't have to ride the bus. *'Did you not know Gerado's two older brothers are putting those marks on him? And he's afraid to tell you?'*

My mother was shocked. *'His father thinks he gets hurt because he's probably overactive, and he's encouraging me to paddle him with a very large ruler or otherwise-he's taking a razor strap to him.*

Isabella was equally shocked. *'Have you paddled him, with a ruler?'*

But my mother shook her head that she hadn't.

'You'd better not,' she warned. *'Because Gerado has the makings of a fine human being that you'll destroy if you do. So let me take him for lunch everyday, and I'll see he gets his nap afterwards,'*

And to my great relief, my mother let her do it.

My father didn't seem worried about having been a war criminal. After all, he and his good friend, Adolph Eichmann, had managed to escape from the Americans when they'd put them in a detention camp. And now, over seventeen years had passed since that time and all was going well. Until Eichmann, in Argentina, was taken prisoner by the Israelis.

That sparked a great fear in my father as it did my two brothers. *'They're coming for me—I know it!'* he would say.

And sure enough, when Isabella brought me through the doors of her Spanish castle, her father immediately asked, *'Whose child is this?'*

'Otho Behl's.'

'The Jew killers'son? And we're entertaining him?'

'*You'd better know we are,*' Isabella said sternly, '*because he's a battered and abused child that I'm claiming as mine.*'

'*All right. But I'm making some calls to some Israelis in Argentina and urge them to come here quickly. Or otherwise, our world stands a good chance of being torn to shreds.*'

'*That it does,*' Isabella agreed. '*So tell your friends in Argentina we're in dire need of them.*'

Which her father did.

Upon their arrival, Hermann and Vaiter received word from a wealthy, former SS *kommandant*, living in the city, that word had it their father's house was being watched by the Israelis. '*How the hell am I supposed to get out of here without a car?*' Otho had asked his sons. '*You know they got Eichmann off a bus, but if he'd had a fine car things might have been different.*'

'*How about a late model Buick?*' Hermann piped up.

'*Would be perfect if it weren't such an expensive car.*'

'*Never mind, we'll get it,*' said Vaiter—

The persistent knocking on the front door of her house surprised Isabella and her parents, prompting her father to call the police. But before he could reach them four men, armed with submachine guns, burst into the house: Hermann, Vaiter, and two of their Nazi-thug friends. '*Give us the keys, Isabella, to that fancy Buick you drive!*' Vaiter demanded.

'*T...they're upstairs,*' she gasped, panting in terror.

"*Then we'll follow her, Hermann, while she gets them,* Vaiter said. "*Because she's apt to have a gun up there.*'

Their two Nazi friends held their submachine guns on her parents, and the two servants who worked for them, while Hermann and Vaiter followed Isabella.

Panic-stricken, she was shaking from head to toe when she reached the top of the stairs, so she just stood there...Of course the keys were in her purse, but she was so frightened she couldn't remember where she'd put it.

'*Where are they?*' Hermann asked, slapping her hard.

'*Probably in her purse,*' Vaiter anwered, spotting it on a table in the hall.

And emptying it quickly, he grabbed the keys and whatever money she had in it.

'*Well we've got the Jew bitch now!*' Hermann smiled, giving her a push that caused her to lose her balance and tumble down the stairs.

Isabella was taken to the hospital the minute Hermann, Vaiter and their Nazi friends left. The police never caught them, leading Isabella's father to suspect these law men had been given money by some of the wealthy SS in the city, with orders to back-off.

Turning to the next page of his article, Gerado looked at the sentence. "The night that followed was the one I remembered as being the worst of my life. Something I talked with Isabella about when I was older. And she agreed...mentioning the razor strap with which my father nearly finished me off."

When the pearl light came the next day, my father deemed it was a good time to get away. So without saying a word to us, he grabbed his suitcase, the Buick keys, and took off.

I was bleeding and my mother's face was swollen from the slaps he'd given her, but it didn't stop her from wrapping me in a blanket and taking me to the bus stop. 'And as I recall,' she told me.' we had to wait twenty minutes for a bus, with me crying. And it was slow, dropping us off two blocks from Isabella's home.'

She rang the doorbell several times before a servant answered. 'It's Gerado. He's hurt and needs a doctor.' But my mother said this servant acted like she didn't want to help us, until Isabella's appeared. 'And when I showed him what your father had done to you, he immediately took us to Isabella.'

She had just returned from the hospital, and the doctor was with her.

He said it was a miracle she'd survived that shove down the stairs. However, when she saw me, she immediately burst into tears. 'See after Gerado and his mother—then me,' she ordered the doctor, who was horrified at the beating I'd received.

'Who would do this to a child?' he asked.

'Otho Behl,' replied my mother.

'Whom I intend to kill!' Isabella shouted.

But she didn't have to because an hour later, it was on the news that Nazi war criminal, Otho Behl, in a stolen Buick was being chased, by what a news reporter insisted were the Israelis. *'He was driving much too fast and crashed into a large truck hauling gasoline. It caused the car to catch fire and explode...killing him.'*

'You take Gerado and see that he grows up to be a find young man,' my mother told Isabella.

But she refused. *'You're his mother. So don't break his heart and leave him. I'll be his godmother and my soon-to-be husband in Italy his godfather. We'll all keep our Paraguay citizenship like Manuel. And Gerado will grow up under your supervision—but with our care—in the Italian villa my father has given me as a wedding present... You'll also be our housekeeper living there, with a nice salary from us. And I know it's gossiped that Eichmann's family will be getting some money from the Israelis, but they never had custody of your husband. So go back to your house with the bodyguard my father hired yesterday, and one of our maids. And they'll help you pack your things, and then bring you back here. Where you and Gerado will remain, until I get strong enough for the three of us to leave for Italy.'*

Isabella had a massive bed, and she insisted my mother sleep in it, with me between them. *'It should give my godson a degree of comfort, before we leave...'* Which it did.

My mother was so endeared with Isabella, the two became best friends.

Antonio Swanda, an older man, had left for Italy six months ago to open an expensive gift shop there.

'After that tumble down the stairs, the doctors don't think I'll be able to have children,' Isabella told him.

'But you do,' he said, giving me a welcoming hug and a kiss. *'And something tells me this little fellow's going to turn out to be a great young man.'*

Antonio was an amazing individual, who'd take Isabella with my mother and me, to visit her parents in Berlin. They didn't have much money, so he'd always give them some while we were with them, and make sure we shared some fine meals.

All went well until my late teens, when I was in the German army. My mother was dying and they gave me leave. And as I sat beside her bed, her last words to me were, *'God instructed an angel to drop you in my womb. And this angel will watch over you, as you struggle to find your healing path...with Isabella always being there for you.'"*

Most sincerely yours,
Gerado Gerhart Behl

He closed his purple folder, his eyes misting each time he read that part in his article about the angel.

Clearly, the hunt to find Wallenberg would be difficult, but recalling his mother's last words, it gave him a degree of hope.

CHAPTER THREE

Kiev
** A week before Gerado and
Isabella's arrival**

Arina was planted in a chair next to Valery Savin, The chair needed a paint job badly, as did the other chairs at their large table.

It was a good thing this table was in the back, with this cafe being dimly lit for early afternoon. There were few customers. Which didn't surprise Arina, since this out-of-the-way cafe told her that married, high-ranking Soviet officials, who risked their careers keeping a mistress, probably dined with them here. A good many were like this Valery Savin, who held a high-rank in the military and also one in the Russian Military Industrial Complex.

Arina was shocked to be here with him like this. Last night at Laskin's Lair they'd waltzed...he in his steel-toed boots. And today as she finished her violin practice, he'd come by in his car and offered to take her out to eat. Why was he doing this? And why was she accepting? Savin was a recently, married man. Something that made her nervous and not want one of the two vodkas he had a waiter bring to them. "Now, how about something to eat?" he asked her.

"Not hungry," she declared flatly, struggling to find the courage to break free from him. *Valery's attentiveness says one* thing; *he's planning on taking me to bed.*

The secret police were quite merciless if married Soviet officials got caught cheating on their wives. And one such official, so she'd heard, had ended up making a trip to the wall. Yet, here was this Valery Savin who, daringly, was appearing to do the same thing.

He was forty years old, but still dazzling looking, even with the silver streaks on his temples. So why was he taking such a risk? In the past he'd undoubtedly had a flock of good-looking women seeking his attention... Had they vanished now that he was married?

'Just leave me alone,' Arina was about to say. When he took her hand and his blue eyes, glistening like stained glass, made her heart do a turnover.

"I have to tell you something, Arina. I married Marek Falin's nineteen year old daughter, Mila, after he'd just ordered her sweetheart executed for the simple reason he didn't like him. He planned to marry her off to someone he approved of. And she said that if this future husband forced his attentions on her, she'd kill herself. And that's when I stepped in. My parents, who were good people, died when I was eight, causing me to be sent to an orphanage. Which was a dreadful place where we got whippings for the slightest offense. So when I turned thirteen, I took off."

His gaze held hers. And that's when Arina noticed the sadness in his eyes and was certain she saw a tear in them.

"I was angry at the human race," he continued. "And had no bones ordering people shot or sent to a Gulag camp. And since Mila's father had a great deal of money, he'd taken from the wealthy before ordering them killed, I offered to marry her for her money. Promising her we'd start slow, and I'd never touch her unless she wanted me to. And she agreed...so we sleep in separate bedrooms."

"With obviously no uh—" Arina stopped, trying to extricate a word which, under the circumstances, she deemed appropriate."

"Sex," he completed. "Something I haven't had in quite awhile." He paused to extract a cigarette from his jacket pocket. "However, the problem's not about that, but about that letter you were trying to smuggle to that Berlin newspaper—"

"—that Marek Falin ended up with?" she finished.

"Yes. And I sneaked around and copied it, then sent it to *Herr* Behl."

She was surprised at the way Valery's appeal was growing on her. "That's commendable of you."

"I'd like to think...Though, in your letter you mentioned Madam Carnet had said sixty-nine year old Wallenberg had been held hostage for years, as part of a Soviet blackmail scheme. *'So if this* is true as is gossiped,' my father-in-law said, 'We can't risk Arina Pavlik and this, Gerado

Behl—who's considered to be such an excellent reporter—uncovering Wallenberg's whereabouts.'"

Valery's eyes met Arina's fleetingly, as if he were waiting for her to respond. But when she didn't, he proceeded. 'Falin then advised me to make you my mistress. So I'd be able to keep track of what was going on."

"And you're telling me this why?" Arina questioned, finding his honesty to be such a beautiful thing that warmth seeped into her every pore. Never in her wildest dreams could she imagine hearing something like that from such a high-ranking Soviet official.

"Because the older I get the more remorseful I get over the things I've done," said Valery. "Work for the Party. And I'm beginning to have difficulty reckoning with it."

Arina now feared she wouldn't be able to control her emotions where he was concerned.

Why of all times is this happening to me? He seemed to be trying to help her, but also trying to steal her heart. If that was his intention, he surely knew it took time to do that with most women.

In the past she'd had two male friends; though none had managed to steal her heart. And now, Valery was arousing her sympathy. That had to be it. Something that was always a danger to her, making her wonder if she didn't inherit these sympatric urges from her father. *Is it because I'm lonely in these troubled times, with so much pain in this city?*

He took her hand again, only this time it jolted her, making her feel like she'd been struck by a bolt of the rarely seen red lightning '*Red is the color of desire,*' is what Madam Carnet had been quoted a saying in a newspaper article.

"So if I don't become your mistress, then what's going to happen?" Arina asked him, impaled by his steady gaze.

"Nothing. Because we're going to pretend we care for each another."

For some peculiar reason she didn't like the word *pretend*. "And if we didn't pretend?"

"I refuse to do that to you. Considering I'm a married man and probably will be for the rest of my days. Since if we did develop strong feelings for each other, it wouldn't be fair to you because we could only be together for a very short time." He stopped to take a gulp of vodka. "Arina, I must confess I fell hard for you awhile back, which is also the reason I've asked you out. And unfortunately, I've even thought about getting you in my bed by saying things that would arouse your sympathy for me. But that's wrong. So I'm being open with you."

Such words from a man known in Kiev as a person who took what he wanted, without seeming to care how he hurt someone. "Something that arouses my sympathy even more," she blurted, amazed at how touched she was by his frankness. Was it because of the neediness she sensed in him that made him seem vulnerable? *If that's the case, then you'd better watch yourself, Arina, since you're vulnerable too.*

"Which makes me regret my openness with you," Valery admitted, looking straight into her eyes. "Because my darker side wants to lure you into my bed. "His voice verged on a whisper—' *I order you to Woo her and take her to bed before anyone else can come into her life—*'

"Who said that?"

"M father-in-law. And I'm telling you all this because I want you to trust me."

He was being so honest with her that she lacked the strength to turn away from him. *More than I can deal with.* And against her better judgment she said, "Valery, let's go to my apartment."

"There's nothing I'd like better, as long you understand that all we can hope for in our relationship is like having a few pieces of chocolate from a very large box. Would you willingly forego the chocolate altogether or enjoy only the few pieces?"

Their eyes locked as he pressed his hand against her heart, causing her pulse to quicken. "I'd enjoy the few pieces."

"Even if we can never share anything between us but a brief degree of happiness that will last no more than a week? Because that's what it'll mean. Which brings me to a promise I want from you—"

She fidgeted nervously, wondering why it seemed it was almost like he was being the devil's advocate, the way he was asking her to barter? *Or is my imagination being too hard on him?* "Which is *what* promise?" she asked after an awkward silence."

"I've studied this fellow, Gerado Behl, who's coming to help you find your father," said Valery, removing a picture of him from his pocket. "He's spoken of as having a compassionate nature and being an outstanding journalist. And from what we've learned not involved with anyone. So you and I will be parting when he arrives, in order for you to get to know him. Especially since he's twenty-seven, your age, plays the violin, and is a wounded soul the same as you."

She stared at Gerado's picture in utter disbelief. *Valery's obviously forcing me to make a response Something I find difficult doing on the spur of the moment.*

"And—" he continued, "if you marry him, I'll make the arrangements so you'll be free to leave the Soviet Union, or Iron Curtain—as western journalists often call our country. And then you'll be able to move in with him and his godmother in their lovely Italian villa. Which is another world which will allow you to look forward to a great future."

Words she certainly wasn't expecting to hear. "Gerado Behl has a beautiful face, and is a trim, muscular fellow like you."

"In my younger days possibly, but now?"

She tensed, then paused. "You're still devilishly handsome. Though if I should become involved with *Herr* Behl would it be because of the resemblance you share with him? Something that's not right, any more than marrying him to get out of the country. Especially if I find my father. Because if he can't leave then I won't either—"

Valery held up his hand to ward her off. "Don't worry. Things will have a way of working out for you."

"Perhaps." She felt a little off-kilter. "But if I were to end up with Behl, then what will people say if Wallenberg's daughter marries the son of a Jew killer?"

"Not much. Even though, some western newspapers will report that it's just another affirmation of how misguided the people behind the Iron Curtain are."

"That it is." Arina shrugged, caught by the thought. "But if Gerado and I do find my father, what will happen then? Will one of your high-ranking Soviet officials be sending us to a Gulag camp.

"You should know I'd not let that happen. So trust me. And remember it was I who managed to get that letter you wrote out of the country." The recollection made him smile. "Though as far as what happens if you and Behl do find Wallenberg—which I doubt—with that twisted chimney painting not telling us much, then we'll cross that muddy river when we get to it."

★★★

Except for the small kitchen in the corner, Arina knew her apartment looked like one room in a cheap hotel. Its furnishings were simply a folded-out sofa that made a bed, and a table with four dining chairs. Valery laid his cap on the table.

There was also a clothes rack with a locked suitcase under it. A pinkish-green curtain fluttered in the window above it."

"The communal bathroom is down the hall, I presume, "he said.

"It is."

"Something I don't like," he remarked, frowning. "Because I'm having a problem believing this is the apartment of Kiev's cultural icon." He went over to the clothes rack. "Almost no dresses. One sweater. A winter coat. And flat shoes that don't appear to give you much support."

"I entertain in those shoes."

"And winter?"

"My galoshes. I wear over my wool socks if I have to walk to work." She gestured at them on the opposite side of the rack.

"Too far," Valery shook his head."

"No it's close."

"It's a wonder you don't catch you death. Which makes me ask why you're living like this."

"Playing the violin, without connections in Moscow, is not a lucrative vocation. And I've refused to give into some of those single, high-ranking Soviet officials who've gone out of their way not to make it easy for me, because I won't sleep with them."

"Yet, you're planning on sleeping with me."

"I know. But just keep things secret until we find my father. Otherwise, we might attract attention from some of these other high-ranking Soviet officials I've refused to let bed me."

"It's possible, even if Marek is pressuring us to get together," he said, stepping closer to her.

"Though I really regret we can't go to my villa. Since it shocks me you're living in such a depressing place." He continued to frown at her living quarters until he remarked in a brisk tone, "This apartment is another good reason for me to defy my orders and encourage *Herr* Behl to enter your life."

"Well, don't be in a hurry." Arina cautioned. "Since even if I barely know you—strange as it is—I'm really beginning to like you. And defying orders, could get you a trip to the wall."

"Just let them try it!" he challenged.

"Maybe things would be better if I'd given myself to some of Kiev's, arrogant, single Soviet officials."

"Which you're about to do."

"But not to get money and move to a better place."

"Still, I'm amazed you'd even consider me, when I'm offering you so little." He removed a condom from his pocket. "I hope my need doesn't offend you since, like I've said, I'm overdue for a woman."

"If it offended me, I'd have treated you like I'd done other Soviet officials."

"But thankfully you didn't." He encircled her in an embrace before claiming her lips with his tongue. A ravishment that sent shivers of hunger darting through her, making her impatient for them to be joined.

Passion overwhelmed the core of her body as they helped each other shed their clothes. "I feel like a school boy of fifteen," he whispered, before they fell on the sofa-bed.

"With my feelings for you defying reason," she whispered back, inhaling the intoxicating musky scent of his body.

Gently his hand circled her breast, with her nipples firming under his touch. They were gentle which surprised her. But when he tantalized her buds with his tongue, flames exploded inside her.

He might be a high-ranking Soviet official, but any previous doubts and fears, disappeared when she welcomed the beauty of his male strength into her body.

An exquisite harmony bound them. And her breath froze as she dissolved against him.

The ecstasy drowning her was more than she could imagine, flooding her with a tidal wave of joy.

"O-oh-my." She soared higher and higher with his urgency matching hers, until she cried out in release, a moment before a surrendering moan of delight came from his lips.

★★★

Afterwards they slept for half an hour like the satisfied lovers they were. But as the late afternoon sun crept into the apartment window, Arina awoke. *His warmth was certainly unexpected.*

Valery was already awake, his hand on her head which was beneath his chin. And like her, he seemed to be enjoying the sensation of being under the blanket they shared."

"What time do you have to be at work this evening?"

"Nine."

He rose slightly. "You're right about accepting those few pieces of chocolate. So we need to enjoy them while we can."

"Definitely."

"Then if you're up to it, let's take advantage of the time we have left."

"I'm clearly up to it." She smiled, as his magic hands rolled her excited, quivering body under his.

"I still marvel this has happened between us," he murmured afterwards. "Since it's almost like we're soul mates."

"Only explanation. With my feelings for someone never being like this before."

"That's great, my sweet, because I feared you might be angry with yourself for not being able to control your emotions...since you don't like high-ranking Russian officials."

"I don't. Although, the neediness I saw in your face plucked at my heart like a violin string—"

"—that allowed you to hold *my* heart in the palm of your hand," he completed."

"To attempt it at least."

He'd been so tender and gentle she couldn't keep from asking, "We have only a week until Gerado arrives. Which makes me curious how you'll survive without a woman after we part?"

"Drink and smoke in the evenings in my solitude, for a month or two."

"That's not good."

"No. However, make no mistake about it, Gerado is like a box of chocolate dropped in your lap. And even if you two don't find Wallenberg, then take advantage of the opportunity that's headed your way. In fact,

Gerado and his godmother will be staying at *The International.* Kiev's finest hotel, with its gorgeous pool. And since I've read Gerado loves to swim, I'm going to suggest when he arrives that the two of you spend some relaxing time at the hotel's gorgeous pool. Where afterwards, you'll have lunch there at my expense."

"But I don't even own a bathing suit," she pointed out.

"No matter, I'm buying you a deep, raspberry colored one with a matching lace cover meant to compliment it and you."

"Still, Gerado's indicated in a telegram I received yesterday that he wants to play his violin with me at the Babi Yar memorial ceremony that evening. And my hair will be mess."

"Not if I make arrangements with the beauty salon in the hotel."

A smile flashed briefly. "You've got it all planned, don't you?"

"To the last detail," he said, bowing and making a sweeping flourish. "Anything for my beautiful lady."

CHAPTER FOUR

The week passed quickly with Valery, to his great sorrow, realizing Gerado Behl's and Isabella Swanda's flight would soon be touching down.

Marek was angry over Gerado having a swim with Arina at the hotel. "Damnit, Valery, why 'd you encourage it? Behl and Arina—who'll be in near-nothing attire—are apt to go upstairs and have a good romp in the bedroom after their little swimming adventure. Something's that's sending the message to me that you and Arina aren't getting along."

"Oh, but we are," Valery assured him, stifling the urge to inform him that, sadly, last night was the end of things between them. "Arina and I are in bed every chance we can get."

"Well enjoy her while you can," Marek advised, as if aware of his uneasiness. "Because yesterday afternoon I received a message from Moscow notifying me Wallenberg, who's been treated for amnesia, is living in Minsk. And all that needs to happen is for Arina, Behl, and his godmother—accompanied by you—to fly to Minsk tomorrow morning, and verify he's her father. And since Behl represents the press, he'll write it up, and the story will end...With Arina most likely moving to Minsk."

Valery's eyes held Marek's for a moment. "Do they know they'll be flying to Minsk?"

"I telegraphed Behl and Arina last night and informed them all about the situation."

Several questions spun through Valery's head. "Interesting this man who claims to be Wallenberg is turning up on the day Behl and his godmother are arriving."

"Indeed it is."

"So if Arina moves to Minsk, then why would it be a bad thing if she and Behl got together?"

"Because Behl's a well-known, investigative reporter who could become a loose cannon. And possibly create an international incident if something goes wrong."

"But if this man is really Wallenberg—"

"Which I feel certain he is—" Marek stalled, before proceeding, "He's told doctors he is. And though I realize he's nearly seventy years old and doesn't look like he did when he was thirty-three, there are still ways of identifying him."

"Like what?" Valery asked. "Without this developing DNA testing, which will probably be used in court cases beginning in 1985."

"Don't forget we have artists," Marek reminded with an air of confidence. "Who're able to take a young face and draw it the way it would look when it's old. And one such artist has taken Wallenberg's thirty-three year old face and drawn it like it looks now."

"And you're certain this artist hasn't laid eyes on this man who claims to be Wallenberg?"

"She's signed a document stating she hasn't."

"I'll discuss the trip in depth with *Herr* Behl and his godmother when they arrive," Valery said, sensing Marek was lying. It seemed too much of a coincidence finding Wallenberg on the day these people were due to show up.

"And by the way, tell Arina she doesn't need that painting any more now that we've located Wallenberg," Marek remarked.

"Will do," Valery said, surprised at how well this Wallenberg *lie* was falling into place. Something that clearly took some manufactured, advance planning.

★★★

"It's disgusting," Valery murmured, running late when he picked up Arina to take her with him to the airport. And if that wasn't enough, it worried him when he saw her standing outside her apartment waiting. The breeze had the typical chill for a May morning, and she was wearing only a beige sweater for a wrap. *Regardless of what she says, I must get her a leather jacket like mine, before we fly to Minsk*, was what came to his mind.

"Are you ready to go to Minsk tomorrow?" he asked her.

"Naturally, after getting your father in-law's telegram last night." Her eyes were distant for a fleeting moment. "It's just I'm not sure what to expect."

"Neither am I."

Dressed in civilian clothing, Valery had chosen to drive his own car to the airport. Something that clearly surprised Arina, "B...but," she sputtered.

"I didn't want Marek's chauffeured, Soviet luxury car," he said, refusing to elaborate.

"Marek will probably be angry with me for not using it and dressed like I am—but too bad. *It just doesn't feel right...like my having to fly with you, Behl, and his godmother to Minsk tomorrow to meet this man I strongly suspect is a Wallenberg imposter.*"

He gave Arina a hug before holding open the passenger door.

"You didn't come last night after I finished work."

"No. Our last night together, and I couldn't bear it. So I took several strong drinks and before I knew it, I was passed out cold."

"I don't know what to say because—"

"Say nothing." He leaned over and gave her a quick kiss.

"B...but Valery—"

"Gerado will say it all, Arina."

Tears trembled on her eyelids, so Valery quickly changed the subject. "You mentioned you hadn't seen the airport in awhile, which means I'd be interested in knowing if you like it or not...now that parts of it have been remodeled."

"I'll definitely let you know," she replied, blotting her tears.

With the traffic being heavy it took them awhile to reach the airport, but when they finally pulled up to it, Arina pointed at some of its glass windowpanes."

"They've been added to emphasize its curved, oval roof," Valery said, trying hard not to think how they would never again belong to each other. *Never be in bed together.* And as the years came and went, just a ghost from his past. So he continued to make small talk. "And if a glass dome were on top of that roof, what would it remind you of?"

She blotted her eyes again. "A...a gigantic crystal ball."

"Good description."

Both inside and outside, the building was surrounded with policemen, marching up and down its many corridors, as soldiers with rifles inspected everyone's papers.

When a soldier stopped Valery and asked him for his, he held up a laminated copy of his badge, since he'd left his original one at his house.

Immediately, the soldier saluted him...something that wasn't necessary—but no matter. He didn't bother to ask Arina for her identification papers.

As they made their way down a long hallway to the arrival area, they were halted at various checkpoints. And each time Valery flashed his laminated badge, they would either salute him or click their heels and bow.

"They treat you like you're a Russian prince," Arina observed. "A Romanov resurrected from the shooting at Ekaterinburg in 1918."

He grinned faintly. "I doubt that." He was holding her arm as he headed toward a spiral flight of stairs. "An architect recently wrote that if this airport had a glass dome with these winding steps leading all the way to its top, it would appear like a stairway connected to the galaxy—"

"Or a huge snake with the power to suck the life from us."

"That's not pleasant."

"No it's not." A brief silence followed as he attempted to cloak his despair over his soon-to-be separation from her glorious body. They'd fit so well together and made such beautiful love...like being surrounded by violins. "I don't think I mentioned it but Marek has a large, pet snakc..." A change of subject with unexpected words. Something badly needed.

"Goodness," Adrina begin as if weighing the distaste of it. "That sounds about like him."

"And this snake gives him trouble. Since when he feeds it a live rat, the rat will make sure to bite both him and the snake, before it gets swallowed whole. And I've advised him to feed it dead rats, but he won't here of it. So the rats continue to bite him.

"Then he gets what he deserves, but not the poor rat."

When they stepped from the stairs into another long hallway, Valery informed her the waiting room where Gerado and his godmother would be after disembarking was directly ahead.

"Mustn't keep them waiting."

"Definitely not. With Gerado being your ticket to a better future."

"But if this man in Minsk is really my father, what then? I should stay with him, you know."

It was the second time she'd brought it up since they'd become lovers. "If your father has any sense, then he'll encourage you to get the hell out of this country that's imprisoned him for what you maintain is twenty-two years—" Valery paused to remove a cigarette from the pocket of his leather jacket. "And marry Gerado Behl so you can do just that."

"Something that remains to be seen—"

A plane taxied on the runway, with people sitting in chairs watching it in front of a huge glass window. Valery looked beyond it into the distance. *Nothing I can salvage. I have to let go of Arina, with a haze of pain gripping me, that's like a kind of death...But at least that way, she'll be able to live.*

He bowed his head each time he thought about it...like they were caught in the middle of the Second World War, and the Germans were forcing them apart—only to die miserably.

He stood close to Arina as she waited for Gerado and his godmother to disembark.

They were easy to recognize. Behl with a jacket thrown over his arm carrying a violin case, and his godmother with a designer satchel looped through her forearm. *Still a great beauty even if she is in her middle years,* Valery was quick to note.

"Welcome to Kiev," he greeted, trading handshakes with Gerado.

"My godmother and I have certainly been looking forward to this," he said, his gaze focused on Arina. "And I'm certainly honored to be playing a duet with such a talented young woman, at the Babi Yar memorial ceremony this evening."

"As I am with you," she said, smiling.

"And I'm sure if you got my father-in-law's telegram," Valery said, "you know we're flying to Minsk, the capital of Belarus, tomorrow morning."

"Certainly unexpected,"Gerado declared. "But we're looking forward to it. In fact, Isabella phoned her brother in Berlin, and he'll be joining us there."

"Ah—yes, the archeology professor," Valery recalled.

Isabella focused her attention to Arina. "We each have a gift for you," she interjected, reaching into her satchel and removing a jewelry box with an exquisite, gold violin pin inside it.

"W...why my goodness!"Arina exclaimed as she handed it to her. "It's gorgeous."

"It's real gold." Isabella smiled, pointing at the mark on the pin.

"I've never had anything that's real gold."

"Then it's about time you did," she replied, pinning it on her dress.

"And this is also for you." Gerado said, removing a bottle of expensive French perfume from the inner pocket of the jacket he'd thrown over his arm.

She leaned forward and planted a light kiss on his cheek. "Something else I've never had. And I thank you."

Valery was disgusted with himself. Why hadn't he bought her something like that? He patronized several of the expensive import shops in this town, so it should be easy for him to slip a bottle in the pocket of that leather jacket he was buying her.

"And don't forget, you also have something for our guests," Valery reminded Arina, her eyes still wide with surprise at her lovely gifts.

"Their gifts are right here. "She reached into her purse and removed two Ukrainian, waffle-woven sashes. "They're the wide, Cossack style, which wrapped around the waist, makes an attractive belt. "

She handed Isabella one in shades of red, and Gerado one in a rhythm of brown-beige colors.

And they each thanked her.

"Since we'll be working closely with each other would it offend you and your godmother if we called each other by our first names?" Valery asked Gerado.

A response was *no* from both of them. So, Valery then summoned an attendant to help with their luggage when it arrived. And since there were not many on the flight, it didn't take long.

"Did you bring your swimsuit?" he asked Gerado, as they headed toward the car.

"Yes." He smiled. "And I'm looking forward to a swim after that bumpy flight we had."

"Too bad you didn't have a pleasant flight."

"I've had worse."

Valery flicked a glance at Isabella. "And will you be swimming?"

"Hardly. Gerado's the swimmer. So I'll be making arrangements for the flowers we'll be taking to the memorial this evening."

"With which I'll help you," Valery volunteered. "But not before we've had lunch at the fine restaurant, where my wife and I often dine. And don't worry about Gerado and Arina, because I've authorized the hotel to let them have whatever they want off the menu at my expense."

"Something I'm sure Arina, like me, appreciates," Gerado admitted with a grin.

Valery reminded them they had a tight schedule to keep, so after a swim and lunch Arina would have her hair done in the beauty salon at the hotel. And then, they would meet in the lobby no later than two p.m. "My wife, Mila, who has her own car, will be meeting you there since I have business at the ministry. Still though, I'll be there to introduce you to her before she drives you wherever you feel you need to go."

★★★

The International Hotel was as elegant as its pictures. And once Gerado and Isabella had checked into their adjourning rooms on the tenth floor, they proceeded to go about their business. Gerado offered his bath to Arina so she could change into her swimsuit, and afterwards he did the same.

She complimented him on his deeply tanned body as they boarded the elevator to the indoor pool.

Damnation! Was she ever gorgeous, Gerado marveled, generating a yearning in him that made him want to hold her.

The raspberry-colored swimsuit she was wearing was going to make it extremely difficult for him to keep his hands off her but somehow, he'd manage. And if he got lucky, and Arina liked him, then it should just become a matter of choosing the right moment. He was particular about the women he took to bed, so there wasn't as much sex in his life as he would have liked. What he needed was to be married and get those two sons on the way that Madam Carnet told him he was going to father.

He took Arina's hand when they got to the pool. And after exchanging smiles, they wasted no time in getting in the water. Where they swam, laughed, splashed each other. Frolicking like they were still in their teens. Time passed quickly, with their afternoon commitments beckoning them. "Lunchtime," he said, getting out. They dried each other off with the hotel's plush towels. And then, he began massaging her shoulders.

Smiling anew, she turned to him. A sure indication she was enjoying the feeling of his hands on her.

"More?" he asked.

She nodded, lightly touching the swirls of dark hair on his deeply tanned chest. "And by the way, I love your soft-spoken voice."

He returned her smile. "Glad you do."

This time when he finished, he planted a light kiss on each of her shoulders. "We'd better order lunch so you won't miss your salon appointment." He handed her the menu on the small table next to their lounge chairs.

"How about fried fish sandwiches, Russian fries, and a bottle of white wine?" she asked him.

"Excellent choice. And a few of those pasties from that rolling tiered cart, the waiter's offering the guests"

She flashed an eager glance at it. "Would be quite a treat."

They ate quickly, then took the elevator back to the room to change. "While you're under the hair dryer, read this letter I wrote you about my life," said Gerado." Since I received the letter from Valery about yours." He handed her the purple folder in which he carried them both.

"Something I'll look forward to doing." She beamed, sliding it in her large purse.

While she had her hair done, Gerado waited in the lobby, wondering about this man who claimed he was Wallenberg, they would be meeting in Minsk tomorrow. Would he recognize Arina if he really was her father? He doubted it, since too many years had passed. Besides, this man was likely an imposter, who was conveniently making his presence known the day of their arrival, in the hopes of getting some money...*And as for her painting with the petroglyphs. Now that was something indeed.*

The staff at the salon must have worked quickly because it wasn't long before Arina joined him. "You look fantastic," he told her, his jaw falling open at the glossy gold of the wavy curls, swinging around her shoulders.

"I don't get to the beauty salon much, but when I do it always gives me great pleasure."

"Then you should go every week."

"I would if I could, but it's expensive."

Gerado reached into his pocket and handed her some money. "Will this cover today?"

"It will. However, a friend paid for today, so keep your money." She attempted to hand it back, but he stopped her.

"Keep it for next week."

"But we might not he here next week."

"Doesn't matter, just hang onto it in case we are." He tilted his head a fraction as he gazed at his purple folder she carried. "Tell me, did you have time to read it?"

"Every bit. And the way your father and brothers treated you brought tears to my eyes."

"But no one ever treated me like that again," he assured her, reflecting on the ashes of his past that at times he imagined were the ashes coming from a crematorium." Isabella respected me and so did Antonio…like I respected them. And they didn't believe in punishments like Hermann. Vaiter, and Otho Behl. So if you're going to feel sorry for someone, let it be Isabella, and the way they treated her."

"She's certainly a lovely lady."

"My second mother."

"The brief time you spent in the German army in your late teens impressed me."

"I did it because—should the need arise—I wanted to be able to protect the people I love. In addition, to showing my support for the new Germany."

"And Isabella was in favor of it?"

"She and Antonio were surprised. However, when I explained I considered it part of my education before attending the university, I got no argument from them—but about tomorrow. Are you puzzled by this sudden appearance of Wallenberg on the day we arrive?"

"Very." A look of bewilderment crossed her face. "And this age-regressed drawing makes me distrustful."

"It does me. With drawings like that done a lot, since DNA testing won't really be out for several more years."

"But there're some other ways, aren't there?"

"Well," Gerado pondered it. "If Wallenberg got shot, a scar from a wound would show. Do you recall his having one?"

"A crease on his scalp, my mother said was from a bullet."

Gerado allowed a long moment to pass as he continued to ponder it. "If the Russians placed him in a shallow grave, then more than likely he did have a head wound. And pictures show Wallenberg as losing his hair at an early age. So what we need to look for on this fellow in Minsk is a crease, like an off center hair line part, that's maybe four or five inches long."

"My father had a lot of hair, but only because my mother had a formula she created so a man, if he was losing his hair, could grow it back. And I do remember the men in our community flocking to her to buy it."

"Do you have pictures of Wallenberg with all that hair?"

"We didn't own a camera," she replied with a downcast expression. "But a neighbor took some pictures."

"And do you have one or two?" he continued to probe.

She gave him a sideways glance. "If there were any, my mother had them in a book with her formulas, which she sold to a man here in Kiev."

"And that's been how long?"

"Five years. My mother was dying and couldn't work, so we were surviving by *my* playing the violin on the street."

"And this man?" Gerado asked, trying not to act impatient. "Where is he now?"

"My mother mentioned a street that sounded like *Staffin*. But I was so unhappy over her selling her notebook of medical formulas because we needed money, I went out of my way to try and forget she'd sold them."

"Something we'll need to find and visit once someone arrives to pick us up. Because a sixty-nine-year-old man—unless he's wearing a toupee—usually doesn't have a lot of hair." He paused. "But what about our violin practice?"

"We'll work it in some way, because Valery and Isabella should be arriving soon."

CHAPTER FIVE

Gerado noticed when Valery entered the lobby with Isabella, that Arina closed her eyes, like an anguish was searing her heart. An attractive, dark-haired young woman with a peculiar-looking bruise on her face had her arm through his. She was quite thin, but walked with an air of confidence that only a few, select females in this country appeared to have. "Meet my wife, Mila, who'll be your driver," Valery introduced her. "With she and I both having the military car phones." He turned to Arina with a sudden brightness. "My wife is a great admirer of your violin music."

She remained where she was, but Gerado stood up. "Our pleasure," he said, admiring Mila's blue eyes and the way her dark hair was styled like Arina's. *But that bruise?* He continued to wonder about it.

"Did you have a nice swim?" Isabella asked him.

"Very. And a wonderful lunch thanks to Valery."

"We had a nice lunch too. With Valery's lovely wife joining us."

"And by the way, I'm having a champagne supper tonight." He glanced at Gerado. "With your godmother telling me you brought your tuxedo, so bring it along. And after the memorial service we'll change at my place, since I'll be in uniform at the service."

"A tuxedo goes well with a champagne supper."

"Especially with our lovely ladies in their flowing gowns."

"Then I'll leave you in good hands with my wife." He kissed Mila on the cheek, then surprised everyone by clicking his heels and bowing at them. Something Gerado couldn't recall having ever seen a high-ranking Soviet state official do in a situation like this. *Surprise, yes.* And he was just as surprised at Arina showing such a silent, unfriendly reaction.

Mila waved her hand in the direction of her car. "I'm parked in front because my husband's allowed to park whatever he pleases."

"Must be nice," Gerado said, attempting to hide the hint of sarcasm in his voice.

"Just tell me where you want to go." Mila said.

"Is there a street that sounds like *Staffin*?" he asked.

"There is."

"And is there a herb and spice shop on it?"

"Are you reading my mind? I took morphine the doctor gave me this morning to relieve my pain. But since it's returning—and I prefer natural medicines-I was thinking about going there."

Gerado took Isabella's hand. "Do you want to come with us or wait here?"

"Why I'll go with you." She grinned, giving him a warm hug and whispering in his ear, "And you should know by now, that one of the greatest shows on earth for me is to watch you in your persistence to learn the truth." Her grin widened. "So naturally I'll be coming along."

He returned her hug. "Having you around always makes things better."

Arina listened but said nothing, until they arrived at the shop.

"I'm in a hurry, so excuse me," said Mila, darting into the place before Gerado could open the passenger doors for Isabella and Arina.

"She must be in a lot of pain," said Isabella, a flash of alarm in her eyes as she headed toward the shop. "So I'll see if I can do something for her."

Gerado offered his arm to Arina to loop through his. And the two walked up the porch steps to the shop's open door.

A gentleman with blond hair and a curling mustache introduced himself as the manager and asked Arina if he could be of help to her. But before she could answer, she pointed at two black-and-white photographs, side by side, in a single frame propped against a small lamp. "Wallenberg."

Gerado reached for them. "Certainly looks like him. With hair and without it."

"Put the picture back," the manager ordered, surprising them. "The police were here two days ago and stole my other two similar to it—"

"Where did you get those photographs?" Arina interrupted.

"From a lady who had formulas in a book from the old days. And these formulas showed how to treat many of the ailments we're all suffering from today…Although, the best thing in the book was a formula for how a man, who was losing his hair, could grow it back."

"And these photographs were tucked inside the book?" Gerado asked.

"There were six in all. And this lady wanted to keep them, but I told her I needed them for examples."

Arina gestured at one of the photos. "Did she tell you who this man was?"

"I didn't ask her. But those policemen that came here were certainly interested. Which is why they up and stole two of my photographs."

"That doesn't surprise me in the least," said Gerado, having no qualms about admitting it. Though, what if they come back and take these two?"

"I still have two more, but that's it. And I need them."

"Will you sell these two photos to me?" Gerado gently pressed, holding them up.

"I thought I told you not to touch them!" he snapped. "So put those pictures back down!"

"How much do you want for them?"

"They're not for sale—"

Gerado reached in his wallet and removed a one hundred, American dollar bill." Not even for this?"

The manager was aghast. "Where'd you get that?"

"I'm a Berlin news reporter."

"Well then, please—you're welcome to take them."

Amazement rolled over Arina's face. "I've never seen so much money in my life."

"And you're apt to see more with the donation Isabella's planning to make for that larger Babi Yar memorial."

"Gerado! Come quick—"Isabella's voice startled him.

"What's wrong!"

"Mila's in a lot of pain."

He turned tentatively to Arina before exiting. "Anything you want here, have the gentleman put it on my bill."

Mila was in a back room with a lady whose specialty was cosmetics.

"I'm sore all over, and my head's throbbing," she told Gerado.

"And you didn't take your morphine the doctor gave you, did you?"

"I said I liked natural medicines."

"But right now you need the morphine. So where is it?"

"In my purse."

"And I have it," Isabella said, handing it to her.

"There's water right here," the cosmetic lady said, pouring her a cup.

Gerado looked closely at the bruise on Mila's face. "How did this happen?"

"My father. He had *my* sweetheart, Nicky, framed for a crime and executed, because of what he declared was my reckless desire for him… My first thrust of love. But the truth was my father considered Nicky's people beneath me and didn't want me near them." She gulped hard, tears choking her. "And then he forced me into a marriage with Valery…A marriage which hasn't been consummated because I've threatened suicide if he touches me. And my father's so angry about it that when I showed up in his office two days ago, he nearly beat me to death."

"Marek Falin." Gerado shed a sigh. "But what about that kiss Valery gave you before he left the hotel?"

"He maintains we have to keep up appearances. Which we probably do. Though nobody ever forgets their first love. And Nicky was mine."

Gerado recalled his mother having said the same thing, adding, *'Even if other's follow'*…And Otho Behl, unfortunately, was one of the others who did.

"My godson gives a good massage, so let him rub your neck and shoulders where the pain is," Isabella advised.

Mila didn't object. And Gerado, pulling a stool over to her, sat down and began kneading her neck and shoulders. "You want children, don't you?"

"Sometime."

"So why don't you and Valery try to bond?"

"How?"

"Well—" He paused, giving it some hard thought. "Like possibly taking a nap together the times he's home in the afternoon. Since it doesn't appear Valery's aggressive with you."

"He's not."

"Then figure out several more ways the two of you can bond."

"I suppose I'll have to if I'm ever going to have any children." She frowned, like she didn't really have a choice.

"I doubt you'll be sorry."

"Maybe not." It took awhile for the morphine to be effective, with Mila checking her watch several times before she said it was time to leave. "Next stop is where?" she asked on their way out.

"My—" Arina stopped, staring at her with a sullen expression before answering "I have to get the music for the evening as well as my dress."

"Then we'll get them.

As they pulled away from the shop, Gerado said to Isabella in a suffocated whisper, "I think we were right about Arina being Valery's mistress. And as we've heard, it's dangerous because the secret police love to catch high-ranking officials cheating on their wives—"

"*A honey-trap,*" Isabella interrupted. "With this security protocol established because they found the honey-trap highly successful in obtaining top secret information from compromised, male officials—"

"Claiming married men," Gerado added, "more often than not, having a better opportunity to be compromised. And usually, they end up taking a trip to the wall."

"Those damned secret police are waiting to make trouble for anyone they can." was Isabella's angry reply.

Arina's apartment wasn't that far. And when Mila parked the car, she pointed at a red brick building a block away. "I'll be down at that cafe, which is sometimes called a pub. So come and get me when you finish."

Gerado got in the middle of Isabella and Arina and had them hook their arms through his, so he could help them up the steep stairs leading to her apartment.

"You didn't find anything for me to buy you in that herb and spice shop, did you? "he asked her.

Her face was full of mixed emotions. "Those photos of Wallenberg were more than I could ever expect...and I still can't believe you spent all that money."

"A necessary evil."

"I didn't get a very good look at those photos," Isabella remarked.

A grin overtook Gerado's features. "But you will tomorrow on our fight to Minsk, because I need you to study them, as I will later."

Arina asked them to wait at the top of he stairs while she unlocked the door to her apartment. "I want to warn you before you come in, that it resembles a room at a cheap hotel."

"We'll try not to take note," Isabella assured her. "But since we're leaving early for Minsk, I can have an extra bed put in my room at the hotel, so we won't have to come back here to pick you up."

"That's a great idea, "said Arina, with a smile that let them each know she was basking in the knowledge of its comfort. "As long as I can have a warm bath in a large tub."

"You can."

"So gather up what you feel you'll need for tonight and our trip," Gerado suggested.

Which she wasted no time in doing...emptying her suitcase and putting some clothing and cosmetics in it. Then she flipped through the music sheets that had been in the suitcase, making selections from what was said to be the lost World War Two Yiddish music of the thirties and forties.

When she got to the first sheet, she removed the small, framed painting with the petroglyphs and though bulky. And though bulky, she slid it inside. "This is for your brother tomorrow," she told Isabella. "Since I'm sure the copy you sent him in Berlin is not as good as my original."

"He mentioned something last night about copies not being as good as originals."

Gerado reached for her suitcase, and after Arina locked the door, they headed back down the stairs.

The café in the next block was closer than it looked and when they got there, Mila was seated at table near the bar with an elderly man. "This is Ustin Dimitri, a retired, *spetsnaz* instructor, who was the uncle of my friend who died. And his brother manages this cafe. However, Ustin is here as a volunteer in order to maintain a military presence, should the need arise."

He acknowledged Isabella and Arina. Then shook hands with Gerado and remarked, "You're the news reporter, aren't you?"

"I was working for a newspaper in Berlin but was forced to resign."

"Because you Otho's Behl's son." It was a statement not a question. "Who reportedly has two brothers, Hermann and Vaiter Behl,who operate a Nazi terror cell in Paraguay."

"Part of my family with which I have no contact."

"Still, keep an eye on them because my instincts tell me they're up to no good."

"I've never thought otherwise."

"They have a strong neo-Nazi support team in Berlin backing them up," Ustin informed him."

"That they do. However, so far I've managed to avoid it."

Ustin's gaze drifted for a moment, as if reflecting on the neo-Nazis in Berlin. "That brief time you did in the German army was commendable, *Herr* Behl."

"Something I did to become proficient with their military weapons and their manual of arms. Since who knows, I may be called on to protect those close to me."

"Wise thinking—"

"Hate to break this up, but it's time to go," Mila said, cutting into their flow.

Gerado glanced at his watch. "Yes it is."

So he, along with Isabella and Arina, extended their pleasure to Ustin at having met him, before heading to the car with Mila.

"That man participated in special operations, didn't he?" Isabella asked Gerado, keeping a low voice.

"Supposedly. And he's a man to be left alone, from the reports I've read."

Mila waved them toward her car. And once they'd climbed in it, she put her foot on the accelerator and quickly drove them back to the hotel. "Remember I won't be at the memorial because I'll be overseeing the chef as he prepares our champagne supper."

"Then we'll look forward to joining you later," Gerado said.

"Think the hotel will mind us practicing in my room?" Gerado asked Arina on their way up, to the tenth floor.

"They shouldn't...In fact, the guests will probably enjoy it. With word being passed around that you're quite an accomplished violinist."

"I don't know about that, but I do enjoy playing my violin."

"All it takes."

Their practice didn't take long, and soon Isabella and Arina were dressed in their flowing mid-calf gowns.

Arina's gown was purple with a short, matching jacket. And Isabella's was black with a short, green jacket.

As advised by Arina, Gerado wore a blue shirt and casual slacks. The tuxedo, he brought for later was in a plastic bag. And he hung it in the silver Volga; the chauffeured, Soviet luxury car that had been arranged for them.

Inside it, he along with Isabella and Arina, each held an armload of flowers to place around the Babi Yar memorial marker over the gully. Which had once been a huge grave for the murdered.

It was a deep ravine outside the city, and when they arrived the sun was setting. *A burning sky.*

A fairly large group of people were already seated in folding chairs in front of the speaker's stand where Rabbi Feinstein would speak. And a short distance away were the music stands where Gerado and Arina would be playing their violins.

Isabella sniffed. "This massacre happened on Yom Kippur. September the twenty-ninth and thirtieth in 1941. And not only Jews were murdered but Russians, Gypsies, Ukrainians, and other nationalities."

"And sadly my father was one of those who oversaw it, "Gerado replied in a choked voice. "And I later read in a history book that a woman held up her baby and begged him to spare it. But he didn't. And afterwards another baby that the bullet missed, kept nursing on its deceased mother's breast."

"A terrible tragedy," Valery remarked. He was dressed like the state official he was, in a highly decorated uniform. "But just remember that in the end, it was *we* Russians who tore Hitler's Germany apart—and got back our land."

Arina handed Valery her violin case and reached over and gave Gerado a hug. "Calm down now," she murmured.

"Do you think someone will recognize me?" Gerado asked.

"No. But just in case I'm going to buy you one of those billed caps that woman over there is selling.

"NOT FORGOTTEN, is written on them." She pointed at a small, folding table in the vicinity of the folding chairs. "And some of the money she gets goes to the larger memorial marker over the ravine that's being planned for later."

Gerado blotted his eyes with his handkerchief. "I'll pay for this cap."

"Absolutely not," she insisted. "After what you paid for today."

Isabella opened her satchel and handed Arina some money. "Here, buy one for all of us."

Rabbi Feinstein approached, and when he stepped up to the speaker's stand he shook Valery's hand. "This is our man who does outstanding work for our beloved Mother Russia," he announced to the audience.

Whistles and shouts followed as everyone present stood up and applauded.

Then Valery, along with Isabella, Arina, and Gerado took their seats behind the speaker's stand.

Isabella, treated as an honored guest, after having made a substantial donation toward the future's larger marker was snapping pictures. In the past the ravine was called the *old wives gully*, where the bodies of the murdered had fallen. And their bodies had remained there until 1943, when the Nazis exhumed and burned them.

Rabbi Feinstein began talking. "Over thirty-three thousand people were slaughtered—night and day—with the machine guns never stopping... Blood gushed in every direction, and their pain will be with us forever. I know because my wounds sent me home from the Russian Front." He stopped to wipe his eyes. "I was quite anxious to see my wife and little daughter. For they were like two roses I carried in my heart. Yet, when I returned I learned, to my horror, that Nazis had killed them." He wiped his eyes again. "I felt like my roses had been torched and turned to ash. But strangely, even though fire still surrounds them, these two roses bloom to this very day...We have our memories. We must not let them fade." Then, he bowed his head and said, "Thanks to our outstanding Russian leaders, we defeated the enemy, and the Germans will never set foot in our land again."

Another explosion of applause followed as the people in the audience rose. The rabbi then motioned at Valery to stand beside him as the applause continued, with shouts praising the dedication of the Soviet warriors.

When the excitement finally died down, Gerado and Arina took their positions in front of their music stands, placed their sheet music on them, and began playing their violins. Solemn, but beautiful lilting music with precise notes, floated through the air.

Each piece echoed the tragedy, until their last one: the Soviet national anthem.

More shouts and applause followed with Gerado and Arina bowing to each other, before bowing to their standing audience.

"We're weeping," Arina told Gerado in a soft-spoken voice.

He removed his handkerchief and blotted her eyes, and she removed hers, and blotted his.

Rabbi Feinstein commended them for their performance, shook Gerado's hand, and hugged both him and Arina.

"The rabbi has another engagement or he'd be joining us," said Valery. "So let's go to my place and get some champagne." He motioned Arina, Isabella, and Gerado to follow him to the silver Volga.

'Which will take us to what I suspect is Valery's villa, where discoveries, like this luxury car, await us,' Gerado considered saying.

CHAPTER SIX

Gerado marveled at Valery's gorgeous villa as he, Isabella, and Arina entered it.

Mila, in an attractive black and gold floral outfit, stood at the door welcoming them.

Valery directed Gerado to follow him so they could change into their tuxedos. And when they returned fifteen minutes later, waltz music was playing in the background.

"I guess, in truth, this villa is what I expected," Gerald told Isabella in a cool tone. "But what I didn't expect was it looks like its decor has been influenced by Catherine's Palace."

"This villa is rococo grandeur at its best."

The wallpaper in the main room was the traditional blue and white of the palace. And the arched windows had a gold décor that matched the other gilded details in the room.

"Don't suppose we could get a glimpse of the amber room," Gerado teased Isabella.

"Afraid not."

He feigned an affronted sigh, bordering on a huff. "Only a good socialist can live like this."

"Now, now," Isabella scolded, "You're being sarcastic."

"Indeed I am."

They exchanged smiles.

Arina, standing back, looked a trifle miffed at the luxurious surroundings.

"Do you like it?" Valery asked, stepping over to her.

"No," she answered. "I like my apartment much better. Which looks like a room at a cheap hotel. Plus, the communal bath that never has any hot water."

More sarcasm. Gerado shook his head. *And from such a lovely lady. But who could blame her.*

"Our newsman here will take care of everything, Arina," Valery declared, with a certainty that implied he knew he'd do just that. "So try not to worry." He gestured at Mila. "My wife likes to waltz—something I never knew. So I'll waltz with Isabella before we have our champagne—"

"And I'll waltz with Arina," Gerado cut in. "Considering I've just been designated to take care of everything concerning her."

If he sounded miffed, he really wasn't. And a vitality zinged through him as holding her snugly, he swept her toward the small, dancing space.

"You look great, Gerado, in your black tux with its bow tie," she said, a smile accompanying her approval. "The same as Valery. But what things, concerning me, has he designated you to take care of?"

"Getting you out of the Soviet Union." His open lips lightly brushed hers as he spoke.

"He has some good intentions for me, but he can't seem to understand that with my father living here, I wouldn't leave."

"I think you can trust him to do what's right for both of you. And if think your father is a prisoner, and you stayed with him, then you'd be a prisoner too."

"Quite possibly."

He spun her around several more times until Valery, with a warm glow on his face, boldly cut in.

Mila then stepped over and took hold of Gerado's hand. "Let's waltz."

"I'd be honored." He grinned, bowing. "Dancing is an excellent way to bond. Did you think that up?"

"I did. And Valery and I waltzed before he left for the memorial."

"Then good for you."

As Gerado waltzed with Mila, he caught glimpses of Valery and Arina. And he couldn't help but notice the despair in their eyes, and the neediness on their faces. They were obviously in love, with his holding her appearing to calm her down from her earlier bitterness. But again, who could blame her? Valery was living in an exquisite villa, and she was living in the slums of Kiev.

And then, there was Mila with her marriage to him being one of convenience.

The music stopped suddenly when a waiter rang a silver dinner bell, and another began passing around glasses of *Dom Perigon* champagne.

"Dinner is served," Valery announced.

Fueled with eagerness, his guests scrambled to their seats at a round table covered in a white linen cloth, with lace trim around its edges. Silverware glistened next to white china trimmed in gold. And in the middle of the tableware were four arrangements in small, crystal vases filled with multi-colored flowers.

"Mila is an outstanding decorator," Valery said, nodding at her.

"Definitely." Gerado agreed.

As food began appearing on the table, everyone brightened. First there was the cavier spread on small pieces of a fluffy bread and served on a relish tray. Then, there was the traditional borscht soup and Olivier salad, followed by beef shashlik, chicken Kiev, and stroganoff. And although not in season, the chef made Kiev's tasty Easter bread. "What I've always wanted to try," Isabella exclaimed, a bright smile on her lips.

Dessert was a chocolate crepe suzette, accompanied by the traditional, sweet *Pierogis* rolls, for anyone who wanted something more.

Gerado was now on his fourth glass of champagne. When he'd arrived at this lovely villa, the waltzing had taken his mind off Babi Yar, but now—things were different. Shame burned through him, and he drew in a sharp breath. The champagne was returning him to the ravine, where people were screaming and crying. And for a moment it was like *he* was his father...oblivious to their pleas, as he gave the order for the machine guns to keep up their firing.

How could he do it? How could he keep signing papers that gave orders for the deaths of over six million innocent people. *Oh God! My blood is tainted, and the blood of my children will be tainted too.*

"Gerado!" Isabella said, giving his arm a shake. "What's wrong?"

"I was at Babi Yar giving orders for those people to be shot because my blood is tainted—"

"—no it's not."

Grief threatened to crush him. "It was like something inside me had died and the devil was there to take me."

"Hush." She pressed a finger to her lips. "You've had too much to drink."

"I want to be standing with those people being slaughtered," he burst out." So my tainted blood will never be able to harm anyone."

"I know you're trying to identify with these people, to ease what you believe to be your tainted blood. But it's not going to help them." She motioned at a waiter. "Would you please bring us some coffee?"

"It's on the way."

"My beloved, Isabella...a Jew," Gerado said, practically in tears. "Yet, you took me in and mothered me. The son of one of the greatest murderers of your people in history. Not to mention my two Nazi brothers who pushed you down the stairs and nearly killed you. Something to this very day I have difficulty dealing with."

"You were just an innocent child in great need." She placed her hand over his." And if I hadn't taken you in, I'd have been no better than your father or brothers."

"All I can do is find Wallenberg for the Israelis. And then I'll disappear and give the credit to Arina, since she's his daughter."

"Even if she his daughter, you're helping her. So we'll see about that."

The coffee arrived and soon everyone at the table was enjoying a cup.

"Don't forget, Gerado, I was standing at the foot of your mother's bed as she lay dying. And I heard her last words. 'God instructed an angel to drop you in my womb. And this angel will be there for you as you struggle to find your healing path—'

"With you, my extraordinary Isabella, also being there for me," he acknowledged. "Because something's telling me I'll need all the help I can get. Since I don't really see how that painting's going to lead us to Wallenberg." He tossed his napkin aside, allowing a brief stretch of time to lapse before continuing, "It's practically an insurmountable task. And as far a Madam Carnat, and this painting she maintains is where Wallenberg is supposedly living, then if I can't find him, it'll end up being my plight— along with the Israelis."

Isabella reached inside her satchel and removed the painting Arina had given her earlier. "Do you think this picture could be somewhere other than Europe?"

"What makes you ask?"

"Manuel. He showed his copy it to a friend who thought he'd seen those glyphs in the United States somewhere—"

"May I see that painting?" Mila broke in.

Isabella passed it to her. "Do you recognize anything?"

"That house with the twisted chimney looks familiar."

"And you've seen it where?"

Her gaze remained pinned on the painting. "At an art gallery several weeks ago."

Overhearing her, Valery and Arina's eyes widened in surprise.

"Certainly unexpected," Gerado replied, struggling to keep his tone even. "So if I give you some money, Mila, will you buy it for us while we're in Minsk?"

Isabella opened her satchel again, but Mila stopped her. "If it's still there I'll buy it, and you can pay me later."

"But if it's not there then what do we do?" Gerado asked her.

"I'll slip the art dealer some extra money if he'll give me the name of the person who bought it. And tell me where he or she lives."

"And I'll reimburse you if it comes to that," Gerado said, continuing to wonder if that painting would really help them.

Poor evidence. Any good journalist would know that. And if Wallenberg was alive, and this painting was the only clue Arina had, then it was clear the Russians didn't appear to be taking it seriously.

The evening was drawing to a close, so Valery suggested that those going to Minsk needed to get some sleep. "It's an early morning flight, meaning we'd best get to bed."

Something they all agreed was the correct thing to do. And soon Gerado, Arina, and Isabella were in the chauffeured Volga heading back to the hotel.

When Isabella got to her room, Arina turned to follow her but Gerado, taking hold of her hand, stopped her. He searched her eyes. "I enjoyed your company tonight."

"As I did yours...a lovely camaraderie."

He framed her face with his hands and his lips descended on her peach-colored ones, caressing them more than kissing them. But when they parted, she pressed her open ones to his.

An electric current raced through him, quickening his pulse. She was easy to adore, and he wanted her badly, with a hot ache growing inside him as he ravished her warm mouth with his insistent tongue.

Something that was almost more than he could take. "Once I get going, I get carried away. Making it difficult for me to stop. Which means we'd better quit now before we end up in bed together. And then you won't get that hot bath you want, and I won't get the cold shower I need right about now."

"That's true."

He kissed her on the forehead. "I know you're having trouble getting over what I'm calling your *first love*. And, sadly, it doesn't appear you're ready for someone else to follow."

"He *is* or *was* my only real love," Arina replied. "Which may sound strange, considering I'm twentyseven."

"Well, in case you've forgotten, I'm also twenty-seven," Gerado said. "And I've not really had what I'd call a first love. Something that makes me suspect we're both particular."

"That it does," she admitted before turning and going inside.

'My lips will tingle for the rest of the night,' he yearned to say, but didn't.

There'd been a neediness on her face and Valery's when they were waltzing, making him wonder long had they been together? Not long, he suspected.

BERLIN—8 p.m. May, 1982
Another Supper Party

Hermann and Vaiter, Gerado's older brothers, were mottled faced men whose official business name was Behl Brothers. "We're verbal couriers for the neo-Nazi SS," they were known to brag to the right people.

These two brothers were also known for the parties they threw. And tonight, at the large house they rented in West Berlin, they were throwing one.

A glistening chandelier dangled in the living room, where a piano, violin, and accordion player flooded the house with their Mozart and Wagner music. All guests listened intently as Hermann and Viater's wives, two voluptuous women, began serving the food they'd prepared: German style pot roast or rather *Sauerbraten*, smothered in bacon and onion gravy. "A German feast," Vaiter boasted, gesturing at the red braised cabbage, mushroom spaetzles, crispy potato pancakes, fresh baked rolls, fruit, cheeses, and pastries.

Glasen, Danner, and Ackert, three men who'd been *kommandants* of Nazi sub-camps, were seated at the dining room's round table. And each of these men had a patch on their ties that resembled the collar patches of an SS officer.

Hermann and Vaiter were seated together at the table. And on the left side of them, sat their two adult sons. Each with a heavily made-up female friend. And these two women were wearing matching, low cut dresses designed to call attention to their large breasts.

"Our sons always show good taste in women." Vaiter laughed heartily. "Because there're plenty like them in Paraguay."

Sitting on the left side of Hermann Behl was Ernst Weir, a nineteen year old student studying archeology at the prestigious *Freie University* here in Berlin. This copper-haired fellow usually played the piano at the supper parties Hermann and Viater threw, but tonight he was an honored guest.

Hermann stood up. "My fellow SS brothers, our special guest tonight is, Ernst Weir, who works at the university in the office of Professor Manuel Wurtz, the archeologist Jew. And this professor was married to Ernst's aunt, Eva Wurtz, with the three of them living together at one time."

It was an explanation clearly meant to gain conviction from his guests about why Ernst was sitting with them. "And ordinarily this young man here is our piano player," Hermann explained. "But when I learned he was the professor's office assistant, things began to galvanize into action for my brother and me." A deliberate pause." Ernst has a graduate-school scholarship at a Canadian university near Quebec, and he'll be moving to Canada in September. It's expensive there, and he's told me he needs to stockpile some money. And playing the piano isn't bringing in that much. So that's how we come in—"

"Let me finish the story," Viater interrupted, rising.

"Go ahead." Hermann shot back, his brows slanting in a frown.

"When Professor Manuel Wurtz was a young man he stole money from my father and gave it to Wallenberg to help get Jewish children to London. So this professor's got to pay," he stressed, in a voice bridled with anger. "He has *two* twenty-five hundred year old Etruscan bullas on loan to the university, but they're in a display case with an alarm." He held up a photo of them. "They're quite valuable. And Ernst volunteered to help us steal them if we'd cut him in. And we agreed—"

"But that was before Ernst stumbled onto this," said Hermann, rising again. He held the copy of a petroglyph painting in one hand and in the other, a copy of a letter sent to Professor Wurtz. It's from Arina Pavlik, who confirms the rumor floating around, that she's Wallenberg's daughter.

"And she and our young brother, news reporter Gerado Gerhart, that we refer to as *Late Child*, have managed to get together and go on a Wallenberg hunt. Something my brother and I've been trying to do for years. But since Wallenberg's in the Soviet Union, we've been unsuccessful. Now Professor Wurtz—who calls himself *Late Child's* uncle—wrote in a newspaper letter that it was important the Jews know the truth about what happened to Wallenberg. And he commended his nephew, now free lancing, for using his investigative reporter skills to help Wallenberg's daughter."

Vaiter then, produced a paper he'd written, and began reading some of the things that had happened to his family because of Manuel Wurtz:

"Otho Behl was driving Isabella Wurtz's Buick—we'd stolen from her——when he crashed into that large truck. We took the Buick because he had no money to buy one of his own. Yet, it was Isabella's father, we later learned, who alerted the Israelis to Otho Behl's whereabouts...And you know how her father found out? Take a *guess.*"

A silence passed as he as his three SS friends swapped looks.

But when no one answered he began to read again:

"It was our sorry, five year old *brother, Late Child*. He should have been aborted but my mother wouldn't hear of it. And he bothered us because he cried a lot, like the spoiled brat he was. And Isabella, who was a customer at the flower shop where our mother, Sudie, worked, took pity on him...If you ask me *Late Child* needed the shit beat out of him for all that crying he was doing. However, our mother let Isabella take him. And that's what led to our father's death. That Jew bitch somehow found out Otho Behl was our father and insisted her father contact the Israelis."

Ernst's eyes were huge. "Wow!" He breathed, before quickly taking a gulp of burgundy from his crystal goblet. "My aunt's always looked up to Isabella, but she's never said anything about that. And I've been around Gerado or *Late Child* only briefly...But what do you know about this woman who handed your father over to the Israelis?"

"Well—"Vaiter drew in his lips thoughtfully, then turned to Hermann. "You tell 'um. Since you like to do most of the talking."

"Be glad too," he replied, with an undeniable tinge of sarcasm. "Isabella took our mother, Sudie, and *Late Child* to Italy. Where she and her husband Antonio Swanda, worked her like the Russians worked their serfs—"

"And *Late Child*?" Ernst asked. "What do you think about him now that he's such a well known news reporter?"

"That he became one of them," Vaiter replied.

Ernst looked taken aback. "Like a Jew?"

"No," Hermann spoke up. "Because the newspaper said they wouldn't let him visit Israel." He glowered at him. "Didn't your aunt ever tell you anything?"

"Very little. I didn't pay much attention to her when she and Manuel talked." He reached for a pastry. "Besides, my aunt's always saying Jews aren't really bad people."

"What!" Vaiter exclaimed, his eyes as round as the moon at its fullest. "You tell your aunt, that when she married that *damned* Jew, Manuel, it told me she didn't know the difference between shit and wild honey."

That brought crafty smiles from the three, former SS *kommandants*, now citizens of Paraguay.

"But tell us more about this picture, Hermann," *Kommandant* Glasen implored him. "And that letter from Arina Pavlik."

"It's all in this 'photo copied letter' here." He removed it from a folder. "And later, you can read it for yourselves. But basically it's saying this Arina Pavlik's mother had a reading in Kiev from this West Berlin psychic, Madam Carnet—"

"Who's just a cheap, gypsy fortune-teller," *Kommandant* Danner, butted in, frowning.

"She's more than that," Vaiter interceded. "She has Swiss citizenship, and people from all over swear by her...especially several high-ranking Russian officials. And besides, our beloved *fuhrer* was heavily into the occult."

Danner's frown deepened. "Unfortunately he was. Which just might be why we lost the war."

"His psychic wasn't any good," Hermann informed him. "However, if someone who had Madam Carnet's ability had been working for him, we wouldn't have lost it."

"And besides, psychics have been know to solve murder cases," Vaiter reminded. "Plus, during the war the SS asked several psychics not to reveal any secret information about our battle plans. So they promised to simply say, 'In the fall and in the spring,' which was clever of them."

"If this Madam Carnet's that good, then why in hell can't she tell us where Wallenberg is?" asked *Kommandant* Ackert, clearly exasperated.

"She's afraid," replied Vaiter. "Because if she does, then those Russian secret police in East Berlin are apt to slip over the wall and grab her."

"Even if I could, I wouldn't go to East Berlin," said Ernst. "Since my aunt had a friend from the states who went there to buy some white angels. And those guards at the gate made her put the East Berlin money she didn't spend in a special box. *'For you know—'* she asked me? 'To use—*you know*—with that kind of women they crawl in bed with.' And—"

"But switching subjects to something more relevant," Hermann cut him short, with a flare of annoyance. "Ernst gave us a copy of another letter from Isabella to Manuel, who appears to be doing everything he can to find out about this copied picture with the glyphs and twisted chimney. So I'm passing it around as Glasen reads us the underlined part of Isabella's letter she expressed-mailed to her brother before leaving Italy for Kiev."

Kommandant Glasen cleared his throat before beginning. "I expect to hear soon that you've found something out about that picture—"

"And Ernst is standing by to let us know when it happens," Vaiter remarked. "So let's give him a toast."

Immediately, everyone at the table tipped their shiny goblets in Ernst's direction.

"And once we find Wallenberg," Hermann continued, "we'll take him to Paraguay and hang him like the Israelis did Adolph Eichmann. *Our example!*"

That brought a round of standing applause from each guest.

"But what about Wallenberg's daughter?" Ernst stupidly asked.

"Arina Pavlik," Hermann mused, rubbing his chin. "A good question, considering *Late Child's* helping her. Which means she's more than likely his girlfriend. And *you know*—one of those kind of women."

"Then we'll hang her too," Vaiter said, laughing darkly.

"*Sieg Heil!*" shouted *Kommandant* Danner with a proud expression.

Another round of applause followed.

CHAPTER SEVEN

Off to Minsk

A plane was rolling toward Isabella and Gerado as they gathered their belongings and prepared to step out on the tarmac. He felt an uneasiness as he boarded the flight to Minsk, and he suspected Isabella shared his feeling. Earlier Valery had given him a letter from Marek Falin stating he expected him to bring his camera and write a news story that confirmed the man in Minsk was Wallenberg. "And it puts me in a fluster," Gerado told Isabella, "because I suspect this man is an impostor. And I refuse to lie and write this story that's certain to have some terrible repercussions."

Isabella placed her hand against her heart. "Something I don't like thinking about."

Arina was walking with Valery in her flat, open-toes shoes. And she looked great in them and the leather jacket, he'd draped around her shoulders earlier. "There's a bottle of French perfume in its zippered pocket," Gerado heard him tell her.

Isabella's gaze shifted between the couple with an amused look. "Valery's not about to let you out do him with that perfume."

"No he's not. And Arina may not realize it yet, but she's coming back with us because I'm marrying her."

"What!" Isabella stopped where she stood.

"It may be a marriage we have annulled later if she wants," Gerado explained. "But she deserves better than living like she's living, with my gift to her being that of a new life."

"Which she certainly needs."

Their plane was now at the gate. So Valery motioned them forward, since the only luggage they had were just some large, canvas tote bags with the extra changes of underwear in them they'd been advised to take, plus a few toiletry items.

Arina took her seat beside Gerado, and Isabella took hers beside Valery, who was behind them. "It's a short flight so we should be there in no time," he assured them.

"It's my first flight," Arina told Gerado.

He took her hand. "Then hang onto to me, because our early morning silver sky seems to have been replaced by some storm clouds. Which can only mean one thing...we're going to experience some turbulence."

"I'm looking forward to meeting Manuel," Arina told him.

"He's like my uncle. And when I was a kid whenever he'd return from his foreign trips, he'd always made sure we had some good times together. That continued later in our days when I was a news reporter in Berlin. We'd have lunch together and get into some heated, but good-natured, political discussions."

"Do you think he's discovered something about that painting?"

"If he had Isabella would have heard." Gerado gazed out the window at the sky which was now dark as lead. "My flying experience tells me our flight'sArina swallowed hard."

Trembling, Arina swallowed hard. "I...I'll try."

The sudden rising and falling of the plane made her shift closer to him.

"Easy now," he said softly, interlocking his fingers through hers in an attempt to calm her."

"I guess you've flown a lot."

"Had to as a journalist. But the worst flight I think I ever had was the one where we flew over the Bermuda Triangle—"

Arina gasped. "Weren't you afraid with all those disappearances?"

"Not really. Even if the flight was so bumpy, we didn't get anything to drink until we landed."

"That's terrible."

"Better than disappearing into some unknown world. Because if I had, I'd have never met you."

"Really now." She eyed him with a gleeful expression. "Gerado, you're as sweet as a sugar rabbit."

"A sugar rabbit?" he questioned. "I've been called a lot of names but never that. So just what the hell is a *sugar rabbit?*"

"When we'd sneak and celebrate Russian Easter, my mother would always make me a sweet in the shape of a rabbit. Which she called my sugar rabbit."

"I hope it was good to eat."

"O-oh it was."

Valery tapped Gerado on the shoulder, just as a sudden burst of turbulence caused the plane to shake. "It's rough, then calm, then rough again," he remarked in a disgusted tone. "But is Arina all right?"

"We're practically in each other's arms."

"Good. Although, what I need to talk to you about is that painting. Do you still have the original?"

Why was he asking? Gerado wondered. *Usually he didn't mind answering Valery's questions. But today, with this Wallenberg man they were meeting, he suspected he was planning on showing him the painting. And if he did, would this man have a response?*

That painting is clearly a mystery which I doubt this Wallenberg man knows anything about. Unless he's been coached to say something. And I'll question his motives like I'm beginning to question Madam Carnet's motives.

Did she really know something about that painting? And if she did, then why didn't she give Arina's mother a clue? Would that have flagged the East Berlin police? Probably not. And besides, Madam Carnet had claimed she needed to mediate on the problem—then, left Kiev. Was she frightened? Or was it just her way of handling a question for which she had no answer?

Gerado's hesitation in not answering Valery's question brought a response from Isabella. "I express-mailed the painting to Manuel, because he needed the original to better study those glyphs."

A statement Gerado immediately recognized as a lie. *She'd dropped it in her satchel before they left, to slip to Manuel. Something Arina and I encouraged her to do.*

"So all we have is a copy?" Valery asked her in a challenging tone. "And you don't think Manuel will be bringing the original?"

"One of his archeologist friends is viewing it," Isabella quickly answered. "But why do you need the original?"

Valery looked quite distraught." Marek Falin has ordered me to bring him the original when we return tomorrow," he explained, in a voice sharp as a Cossack's sword.

"And he needs it *why?*" Gerado dared to ask. "If this man in Minsk is Wallenberg, then Marek Falin will have no need of it."

But when Valery didn't answer, it confirmed what Gerado already suspected. *This fellow they were going to meet was an imposter. And Falin's request for the painting was just another rock added to a pile that was getting larger and larger.*

★★★

It was ten in the morning when they arrived in Minsk, the largest city in Belarus and located on the Svilach and Niamiha rivers.

A chauffeur driving a Soviet Volga dropped them off at the Edwardian-style house where they were to meet Wallenberg.

The house had survived the Second World War, yet surprisingly its prewar facade still had an air of grandeur. Its windows looked to have been repainted, and its wooden floor had a waxed brilliance that shone like the ocean under a full moon. Arrangements for this visit had been made with what appeared to be great care.

The communal room was quite attractive with colorful flowers in crystal vases, on each of the room's two small tables. On one of the tables was a photograph of Wallenberg at age thirty-three, wearing a hat, and beside it, the framed pencil drawing of Wallenberg at his present age of sixty-nine. However, on the other table was the photograph of the half-bald Wallenberg at age thirty-three, while next to it was the photograph of him with a full head of hair.

"I know where those came from," said Arina.

"Kiev's Herb and Spice Shop," Gerado acknowledged, snapping pictures of them with the expensive camera he and Isabella owned. "Pictures the police stole in an effort to convince us that our man here, is Wallenberg."

An ancient-looking beige church chair, with gold-colored feet and legs, had been placed in front of a window with the curtains drawn. The chair resembled a throne. "

"Was Wallenberg royalty?" Gerado asked Isabella. "If he was I never heard anyone mention it.

"His father had *von* in his middle name—"

"Which can or cannot signal royalty," She reminded her.

"True."

Six green, wing-back chairs in a semi-circle were in front of the throne. "I assume they're meant for us," Gerado told her.

"Appears like it."

A high-ranking, state official in a dress uniform like Valery's came over and greeted them. He and Valery apparently knew one another. "Leonid Devin, "he informed Gerado as they shook hands.

A servant, dressed in coattails, appeared with a tray of crystal goblets, each filled with champagne. While another, following him, offered *hors d'oeuvres* and pastries from a silver tray.

"A little early for champagne," Isabella remarked reaching for a glass.

"Not for a state occasion." Gerado murmured satirically. "So enjoy it. Since all this showiness looks to me like an *intimation* factor."

Manuel had arrived an hour earlier. "Your brother's silver hair and expensive suits always give him an exquisite touch," Gerado told Isabella as they waited outside the dining-conference room for him...When he saw them, he gave them each a hug. And they returned his hug. Smiling, Isabella slipped Arina's painting in his large pocket, before introducing Arina and Valery to him.

"Kato Orman is here, and the two of us were discussing Wallenberg," said Manuel.

He nodded at a dark-haired fellow in a gray suit. "He's a Hungarian, and he and Wallenberg were good friends. But unfortunately I haven't seen Kato since I left Budapest."

Kato gave him a bright smile. "Though somehow we always manage to write letters to each other at the beginning of every year."

Valery and Gerado exchanged handshakes with Kato and expressed their pleasure at meeting him.

"Maybe you can visit us in Italy in the not too distant future," Isabella suggested.

"I'd love to but—" He regarded her with a solemn look. "My family and I live in Israel, and it's hard for me to get away unless it's business. So why don't you come and visit us?"

Isabella smiled at Gerado and Arina. "The three of us are planning on doing just that."

"We *hope*," Gerado countered.

"And I'll be coming too," Manuel interjected. "Since now being a university professor makes it easier for me to get vacations."

"Don't mean to change the subject," said Arina. "But tell me more, *Herr* Orman, about Wallenberg."

"Be glad to. Budapest was being invaded, and I was going off to help the Palestine Jews smuggle children to London. Though on my last visit to the Swedish embassy I warned Wallenberg about the dangers he was facing with the Russians and Germans fighting...But he had financial paperwork ready to help the surviving Jews, and he needed to talk to Moscow about it. Surely they'd understand—but *no*. "Kato's voice suddenly dropped to a whisper. "Even after what the murdering Germans had done, the Soviet Union still didn't feel the way about Jews like Wallenberg did."

Tears fogged Arina's eyes. "My father's heart was too big. And in the end, that's what did him in."

Gerado put his arm around her. "Why don't we sit down. Our man should be appearing soon."

Kato joined them, taking the chair next to Gerado. "You're the news reporter who writes under the name Gerado Gerhart, aren't you?"

"I worked for a Berlin newspaper, but I'm not working for it now."

He gazed at him with a detached curiosity. "Why not?"

"Didn't you hear? I got fired when they learned I was the son of Otho Behl."

"The war criminal!" Kato exclaimed. That clearly struck a nerve because he bolted from his chair and took a step backward.

War criminal's son. Words which were enough to shatter Gerado's heart.

Karo stared at him the way he would have stared at an SS officer who'd just given him a death sentence. "*You*, Gerado Behl," he remarked, shaking an admonishing finger, "have poisoned blood—"

"Not on his life!" Arina protested.

Isabella sprang to her feet. "Gerado Behl is my godson!"

"That I look on to be my nephew," Manuel added, raising his voice. "Since I'm divorced, because my wife discovered archeology didn't make for a good home life. And Gerado would have been welcome to live in my apartment in Berlin if my second bedroom hadn't been turned into a library."

"Then please accept my apologies," said Kato, his face turning a bright red. "Because I'm here on behalf of Israel."

"Just you'll know," Isabella flared. "Due to his evil father, Gerado's life brings tears. Though, he doesn't like me to say his father gave him a hard time, and he's always telling me, 'Save your tears for those who suffered and died.'"

"And my kind and comforting *godmother*—" He put his arm around her. "Who got pushed down her stairs, by my two Nazi brothers, causing an injury that robbed her of her ability to bear children."

Kato's gaze was now intent on Isabella's face. "A terrible tragedy—"

"—please." Without warning Valery lifted his hand in the theatrical manner of a melodramatic actor, and closed it over Kato's shoulder.

"Everyone is requested to retake their seats," announced Leonid Devin. "Since our guest here is with Wallenberg's physician, Dr. Vald Litvak. And the kind lady, Madam Sana Petulengro, who took Wallenberg in after she found him eating from a garbage can. He kept saying he was *Wallenberg*, and since they were both in need of money, it was she who approached Moscow… At first the officials were not terribly impressed, because another man in the past, in a Russian political prison, kept insisting he was Wallenberg. Although when the proof finally surfaced, it was discovered he wasn't."

"More than likely it was Wallenberg's driver," Valery clarified.

"Probably," continued Kato. "But then an official had an artist take Wallenberg's picture when he was thirty-three and regress it to how he would look at sixty-nine. And without seeing him, the artist did a remarkable job in duplicating the way he looks today. Which you'll see, after our musicians and choir have finished performing for us."

"Musicians and choir?" Gerado repeated. "Now that was certainly unexpected."

"They're coming through the front door as we speak," Valery pointed out, gesturing in their direction. Heads turned as several musicians in dark coats entered the communal room with their instruments.

They were followed by five young girls in their teens, proudly waving small, Soviet flags. They each wore a white blouse and navy skirt. School uniforms.

"Are we ready?" Devin asked, once the girls and musicians were assembled in front of the communal room's fireplace.

"We are," answered the maestro.

The choir then began singing the Soviet National Anthem, and everyone present rose.

"I wonder what this man we're meeting—who's been imprisoned for God knows how long-thinks about this?" A bewildered Gerado whispered to Isabella.

"That it's clearly a mockery."

More songs followed with each one praising the Soviet Union, until the last one. Which to Gerado and Arina's surprise was a Ukrainian folk song, *"Minka"* or in English known as *"Marie."* It was a bride's song about the loss of something, with a lively melody which made it popular in many primary schools—especially in America.

When the singing finally stopped the girls bowed, and everyone applauded.

Devin came forward and thanked the musicians and girls before one of the helpers in coattails escorted them to the door. "The doctor has informed me that *Herr* Wallenberg is ready to make his appearance. And Dr. Vlad Litvak and Madam Sana Petulengro will be accompanying him in case there're questions you need to ask concerning his amnesia. The good doctor has been dealing with such cases for many years, and is a great authority when it comes to lapses of memory."

Gerado took Arina's hand in comfort and understanding. "I know this is difficult for you, but just remember we're in this together. So try not to get upset if you don't get the answers you're expecting."

The green curtains parted behind the throne-looking chair, and a gentleman wearing a blue shirt and jacket came forward. He was followed by a man carrying a medical bag, whose bourbon-colored hair shown like a burnt halo in the noon sunlight. A woman, who looked to be in her fifties, stood beside him. "It's a pleasure for me to present Dr. Litvak and Madam Petulengro," said Devin.

The woman had shiny black curls and bright red lips and was wearing a colorful bolero and skirt that accentuated her silver necklace and dangling earrings. *Clearly one of the Romani people,* Gerado mentally acknowledged, finding her attractiveness impressive.

The doctor stepped forward and handed each guest a sheet of paper about Wallenberg and his condition. "This is the information we have on him. So read it before I present him.

And quickly taking it, Gerado immediately began doing just that:

"When the Soviets took Wallenberg prisoner, it was believed he was working for the OSS or Office of Strategic Services. However, no one in Europe or America would acknowledge it. He escaped from the Russians when they arrested him and his driver. And a good many years passed before the Soviets found him in a farming community, where they took him away at gun point.

Sadly, even if he was well-treated, he remained in a political prison for many years. Then a gas leak caused an explosion in the prison that almost killed him. And he was in such bad shape that he was immediately taken to a Soviet hospital...He could not remember his name and had no idea why he was in a hospital. But as time passed and his memory failed to return he was put in an asylum near Minsk. Although gradually, so it seemed, bits and pieces of his life returned. Even if there were still many blank spots and often complete lapses of memory. One of which was that he did not respond to his name, but only the name, Sergey...Was he frightened to be called by the name Wallenberg and found it hard to keep his courage? Perhaps he felt it was an encouragement of his vulnerability. Then a nurse, who acted like his friend at the asylum, found an old magazine with his picture in it. 'It says here you're Wallenberg,' she declared. 'An when we call you *that*, you refuse to respond. So please try harder for me, because that's really your name.'

It was shortly afterwards that he began asking for his family in the Soviet Union...However, it is interesting to note that he never once mentioned Sweden, nor spoke any Swedish...It was like he'd forgotten his native language.

In an attempt to find his Soviet family, he escaped from the asylum, with no idea where to look for them. But he reasoned that since many gypsies or Romanies were able to locate things as well as see the past and the future, he would find one who could do just that.

Still, it was difficult being on his own in Minsk, and he had no luck at first. Then he saw a nightclub advertising gypsy performers, and it was there he met Madam Petulengro, who took him in."

★★★

When Gerado finished reading the paper, he folded it." What do you make of it?" he asked Arina and Isabella. But appearing at a loss they simply shook their heads.

Finally, Manuel replied," We'll just have to wait and see."

Arina closed her eyes a moment before the curtains parted again and the man, believed to be Wallenberg, entered. It was an emotional moment. Everyone in the room's attention was pulled to him as Madam Petulengro pointed at the throne-like chair and urged him to take a seat.

He was a bony man, with a full head of brown curly hair which came as no surprise to Gerado. But what really caught him off guard was the startling resemblance in the eyes, to the younger Wallenberg. *Unbelievable. If Moscow is backing this claimant, like I believe they are, then he's an excellent choice since everyone's supposed to have a double.*

But could this man really be Wallenberg? A lengthy silence followed as Gerado, astonished, envisioned a current as strong as a riptide extracting his doubts and dropping him in the bottom of the ocean...or maybe it was more like these doubts of his were being thrown under a train and crushed.? Any way this man was certainly not what he'd expected.

And Arina, now standing, looked as overwhelmed as he felt. "Is this possibly my father?" she murmured.

"I know time has passed, Arina," this Wallenberg man began. "But don't you recognize anything about me?"

"Y...your voice," her lips quivered as if torn by conflicting emotions. "It has a gentle softness that touches my reverie."

"It's taken me so very long to learn where you were. And I wanted badly to find you and your mother, but I was in prison. And after that explosion I experienced many years of lost memory in the asylum."

Arina was tearing up. "Easy now," Gerado whispered, his arm locked tightly around her waist.

How he yearned to crush her to him. *In the brief time we've been together, I'm clearly in love with her. Which means I'm right to believe in love at first sight, even if there're many who deny it.*

"I've lost everything I ever loved," the man remarked in a voice full of feeling. "And even now after that terrible accident and my time in the asylum, I sadly have only a few memories."

"It's a terrible thing to be without comfort," Arina replied. "And it's something I think of as living in a shadowed world, where you're never able to catch a glimpse of sunlight."

A look of melancholy passed over the man's face. "It has taken me such a long time to find you. And learn to my sorrow that your mother, who was the love of my life, has passed."

"She died five years ago...a tragic loss that often makes it difficult for me to resume life."

"O-oh but you must," he insisted. "For *me* if no one else."

"And him." Arina's eyes drifted up to Gerado. "Who's giving me the support I need for now."

'And later.' He wanted to add...*If only this man was really Wallenberg and not an illusion. How easy it would be for them all. But this conversation was not moving them forward. With a serious question that needs to be asked if I'm to do a news story verifying the man is Wallenberg.*

"Arina." Gerado squeezed down on her hand. "We need to know if this man has a scalp scar?"

She turned to this man with a tinge of concern. "But he looks so much like Wallenberg."

"I know. Still though, you've yet to ask him a question about your childhood."

"Would it do any good, considering he often suffers from a degree of amnesia?" she asked. "When his scalp scar is all the proof I really need."

"Probably not." Gerado shrugged, his eyes on hers.

Arina stood there for a few moments, her hand covering his as she appeared to ponder this Wallenberg man's scalp scar. "I...it's just that since you're the journalist, I think it would be better if you asked him about the scar."

Gerado swallowed back a feeling of self-reproach. It was obvious Arina was hoping against hope, this man was Wallenberg. *And I can't blame her for it, because it would certainly be wonderful if he was. And we'd met up with him the day after Isabella and I arrived in Kiev. But I know better. The Israelis have been hunting him since 1945. But with no luck.*

So after a long pause, Gerado approached the man. "I'm Gerado Gerhart the journalist," he introduced himself. "And I'm supposed to write an article about this. So I'd like to see your scalp scar that Arina mentioned she saw as a child."

"Which means I'll need to remove my toupee," he said, touching it lightly.

"Stop!" Devin yelled. "We told you not to do it, don't you remember?"

Isabella and Manuel were now standing beside Gerado. "Either he removes his toupee, or I'm not doing the news story," Gerado informed Devin. "And I know you probably think it's simpler for me to agree at this point, but you're wrong."

Madam Petulengro was now standing beside this man they called Wallenberg. "I don't have a scar on my scalp, Sana. You should know."

She took his hand in a loving manner. "Of course you don't, because I would have seen it."

"I never saw one either," Dr. Litvak told Devin. "So what harm would there be in letting those see that he doesn't have one?"

"He doesn't have a scar because we Soviets don't shoot men like Wallenberg. So *write* your story." Devin told Gerado in a terse voice.

"No!" Gerado bristled."I refuse to do a news story that's a lie. Even if some high-ranking official expects me to do one." There was defiance in his tone that he meant as a challenge to Devin, should he dare to bring some of these high-ranking friends into this matter. *'If you Russians persist then there're other things I can do,'* Gerado considered telling him.

Devin waved an arm at Valery. "Savin, you brought this journalist here, so it's your responsibility to make sure he does what he's supposed to do—"

"As you know, I represent Israel," interrupted Kato Orman. "So let me present my side of the matter. Since many of my friends who live there believe, like me, that if Wallenberg survived after being shot, it was probably a head wound. Which would mean he'd have a scalp scar."

It was now Arina's turn to speak. "My father had a scalp scar from a bullet wound. I remember it clearly because even if he was middle-aged he had very little hair. And my mother knew how to make a hair-growing solution that would give him hair when he wanted it." She paused as if recalling it.

"Though after two months it would fall out. And my mother would offer to rub her solution into his scalp again.

However, if it was summer, he'd refuse. 'Since in this weather it's more comfortable to be almost bald,' he'd say."

"And how old were you then, Fraulein Pavik?" Devin asked her, in a cynical voice. "Five? Six,"

"I was attending primary school."

"A little young to remember much, I'd say."

Gerado had now moved past them and was standing so close to the throne chair that the toe of his shoe was pressing against its golden foot.

"How about this?," he asked, reaching into his wallet and withdrawing a one hundred American dollar bill. "If you take off that toupee, I'll give you this."

Madam Petulengro's eyes were suddenly as round as a bicycle's wheel. "Why that's more money than I've ever seen in my life." she gasped, staring at it in utter disbelief.

Kato moved forward until he was standing only a few feet from the throne chair. "You'd better take it, Wallenberg," he encouraged him, grinning. "Or else your Madam Petulengro's apt to give you a *good* scalp scar."

It was obviously meant to be a joke, but no one smiled.

"I would never strike this poor man," she replied angrily. "And if he doesn't want to take this money, then he doesn't have to!"

"But I want to, Sana," he quickly said. "Because we need it."

Relief swept through Gerado; the decision had been made. "Arina." He waved in the man's direction. "Have a look."

Her reaction was immediate. "He's removing the toupee. So I'll check for the scar." She looked from Gerado to him. "And that toupee is expensive. Which tells me he got it from our Soviet friends."

"Without a doubt."

The man was nearly bald, making it easy for everyone present to see there was no scalp scar.

In the background, a furious Devin shouted at Valery. "Didn't you know better than to bring these people who weren't going to confirm he was Wallenberg?"

Valery shifted one foot then the other, like he was restless.

"His vexation is evident from being shouted at on what appears to be a state occasion." Gerado told Arina in a subdued voice.

"Father-in-law or not," Devin snapped at Valery. "Marek Falin will hear about this and take action!"

'*What action?*' Gerado started to ask, turning around and glaring at Devin.

Arina was too upset to pay much attention to their conversation. Her hand was holding this Wallenberg imposter's and for a brief moment it seemed she was pretending he was her father.

"Sana treats me well, but I've been without love and family for a terribly long time." His face mirrored the ache in his heart as his hand in Arina's, trembling. "I wasn't meant to be taken by the Russians and suffer the prison—the asylum, the loss of memory, and the emptiness. It was a tragic scene of despair for me after all the people I saved."

His words appeared to have a disturbing effect on Arina, who dropped to her knees and kissed his hand; the desolation in her eyes now similar to his.

Gerado knelt beside her to remind her—as he had done previously—that she was not alone...*My love for you is strong, Arina. And hopefully a joy will open between us that will carry you, along with me, into a brilliant light.*

"I'll say nothing to try to convince you I'm Wallenberg," the man said. "But I would like a moment to touch your hair, your dress, and hear your voice again before you leave." He looked down. "Write to me. Sana has our address." His eyes filled with tears of obvious frustration. "And all I ask is that if you're not my daughter don't ever tell me."

Isabella and Manuel were apparently so moved that each handed Sana an American fifty dollar bill."

"M...more?" she questioned, appearing so grateful it was like the word stuck in her throat for a moment. "What we want is to leave this country, that's made it so difficult for us to exist here."

Arina's eyes were bordered with tears as she appeared to relive the pain of her lost father. So Gerado whisked her through the dining-conference room door where, in this private space, they wept jointly.

His tears mingled with hers as his protective arms pressed her tightly against him. He was sobbing the way he was doing as a child, when Isabella had first approached him.

And suddenly, she was once again there for him, along with Manuel. "I know it's painful, Gerado," he said, giving him a hug, along with Arina.

It was clearly not the end; someway, somehow, Wallenberg would be found.

The the communal room was missing some people when they returned...with Sana, the Wallenberg imposter, Dr. Litvak, and Devin having mysteriously vanished.

"You and I will find Wallenberg," Gerado assured Arina, now more determined than ever.

If he'd had doubts earlier about the painting, and Madam Carnet's hesitation to confirm Wallenberg was alive, he didn't have them any more. The pieces of the puzzle were beginning to assemble.

The Russians had maintained they'd found Wallenberg on the day of his and Isabella's arrival in Kiev.

Yet, their man had turned out to be an imposter, with no scalp scar, because the Soviets claimed they didn't shoot men like Wallenberg…Then, there was Marek Falin who'd demanded Arina hand over her father's painting to him.

"Madam Carnet is right. Wallenberg is alive," Gerado quickly wrote in his notepad. "Even if that painting—without any clues to its whereabouts—doesn't appear to offer us much hope."

"If there was *only* something we could do for this Madam Sana and that man who called himself Wallenberg," Arina told Valery, returning Gerado's attention to the present as they rejoined him.

Overhearing her, Kato Orman stepped over to Gerado. "That gypsy woman wants to leave the country with this Wallenberg man. So maybe I can help them."

"How?" Gerado asked, having his doubts about it. "It's a proven fact that it's not easy to get anyone out of the Soviet Union—"

"Not necessarily," Kato countered. "There are those here, and in other Soviet countries, who've been known to hand over Jews to Israel for money. And Wallenberg was part Jew. And this man has a strong resemblance to him, so maybe…but that gypsy woman?"

"What about her?" Gerado asked in a curt tone. "The Romanies were treated as badly as the Jews. So, if this man gets the opportunity to go to Israel, then she should go with him."

"I'm in agreement with that."

"Then do it soon if you can, because I'm anxious to hear," said Gerado, heading toward the front door.

"You can rest assured I'll see it's done," Kato promised, giving him a pat on his arm. "But right now I have a plane to catch, which doesn't give me time to make the necessary calls." He shook Manuel's hand. "Just know it will happen. And you, along with your family, enjoy the rest of your day. And we'll talk soon."

"You're an outstanding journalist, Gerado," Valery complimented him on their way out. "But be careful. You saw Mila's bruises. Which should tell you that my father-in-law is not an easy man to go up against."

CHAPTER EIGHT

Gerado found Valery's unwelcome frankness to be disturbing. A man such as Marek Falin beating his daughter like he'd bet Mila, was capable of anything. And knowing that Gerado, once again, had concerns about what his intentions might be. Would Falin stop him from finding Wallenberg by forcing him to leave the country?

Quite possibly. And what would happen to Arina? Would she be imprisoned in a forced-work camp for saying the man wasn't her father? She might if Valery wasn't around to come to her aid.

Gerado knew he'd defend her. After all, she was his mistress even if it might cost him his high-ranking position in the Soviet military.

A long afternoon awaited them, so Valery suggested they have lunch at a small cafe several blocks away. "I don't know about you, but I'm starving. That champagne and those hors d'oeuvres don't seem to have gone very far."

Isabella and Manuel agreed. The weather was pleasant so they sat at a round table with five chairs, on a summer terrace. There was a balcony above them with *Leopard's Bane* blooming in a box.

"They look like sunflowers with their orange and yellow coloring," Isabella remarked.

Arina glanced at them. "They're of the same family. Although these are also used for medical purposes."

A waiter brought wine and Valery began filling their glasses. "What shall we have, good people? I hear this place has excellent goulash."

"Then let's have it," Manuel replied, as everyone held up their wine glasses and clinked them together.

When the goulash came they devoured it, praising Manuel for his encouragement since they claimed it was the best they'd ever had.

After they finished Valery suggested that since they had no luggage, they take a short walk with him. "There's a place I want you to see, where you'll probably prefer to stay rather than at a hotel."

Their curiosity piqued they were eager to go with him and see this place, which was three blocks away. So amid the clattering noise of streetcars and other vehicles, they crossed each street with caution until Valery, stopped in front of the driveway of another pre-war Edwardian styled house. "Does something about this place look familiar?" he asked, his index finger pointing skyward.

"My goodness!" exclaimed Manuel, his gaze shooting up to the house's roof. "It has a twisted chimney like the one in Arina's painting. And I know there're different kinds of twisted chimneys, but this one certainly bears a close resemblance to the one we're searching for."

"It was an ordinary chimney that was re-built after the war." Valery explained. "Only this time with a coiled, serpentine look—you're calling *twisted*—that some of our more superstitious people living here believed might frighten the Germans should they ever return."

All eyes were focused on this red-bricked, picturesque chimney stabbing the sky, which was as blue as the swimming pool in their Kiev's hotel.

Isabella snapped a picture of the chimney."How tall would you say it is?"

"I've heard eight meters, and forty-eight meters," said Valery. "Depending if your measuring from the roof or the fireplace. And its bricks, so I was told, were tinted by hand."

Gerado couldn't take his eyes off it. "And we'll be staying here?"

"If you like. The house looks a lot like the place we just came from. Although, many of its apartments are vacant, so there's plenty of space."

"Where do we have dinner and breakfast, Valery?" Arina asked him, looking around.

"A place we just passed. Which is a block down the street on the opposite side. There's a cafe with a very small sign that I'm told serves excellent food. And a cobblestone walkway with the cafe's garbage cans, runs alongside it making it easy to find. Especially, with the street across from it having a large billboard praising our Russian workers." Valery reached in his pocket and handed everyone a flyer.

A well known musician, Andre Goslin, would be performing at the cafe tonight with his Ukrainian Trembita or Balalaika. "Which, in case you don't know," Valery said, "it's looked on as a Russian three-string guitar. Which is considered to be the most Russian of all folk instruments. And was made in Kiev from spruce fir tops, with its wooden body being hollowed-out."

Arina's eyes lit up. "I know this musician who's playing tonight, and he's excellent."

Gerado stroked her hand. "Then we'll have something to look forward."

"Indeed we will," Isabella and Manuel remarked simultaneously.

Valery pivoted toward them. "Then be ready around six, and we'll all go together."

A dark car making the murmur of a powerful engine darted in and out of Traffic, with its unpleasant sound catching everyone's attention.

"Let's go inside," Isabella suggested, turning and heading toward the porch steps.

Gerado and Manuel were preparing to follow her, when this car made an abrupt stop in front of the house. It had tinted windows and no license plate. "I...is that—" Manuel muttered uneasily.

"—the secret police," Gerado replied, dread seizing him.

He along with everyone else stared, as a heavy man with a mustache got out of the car and shot Valery an intimidating look. "You're Valery Savin, are you not?"

"I am." His voice grated harshly. "So tell me, what's going on."

The man leered at Valery in his dress uniform as if he were a criminal. And starting to get angry, Valery remarked in a belligerent tone that was so inflamed, it scalded the air, "I don't like your attitude, so why in hell are you approaching us?"

"There're suspicious people in the area, and we're canvasing it. Which means we'll need to see your identification."

Valery showed him his I.D. but the mustached man and his people didn't leave.

"Is he one of your people?" He pointed, frowning at Gerado.

"I've been assigned to watch after him and his friends."

"The secret police are after Valery," Arina murmured.

"They certainly seem to be giving him a hard time, " Manuel replied, stiffening like he was quite concerned.

Isabella whitened, her hand shaking. So Gerado put his arm around her. Naturally, he loved her as much as he'd loved his mother and didn't like to see her frightened. And it upset him to see her closely watching this mustached man, whose steady gaze was impaling each of them.

It's difficult for her to take it all in, Gerado lamented. *The same as me.*

An uneasy pause followed. It was obvious from the way these secret police were acting, they were up to no good.

"Do you have the painting?" the mustached man asked, his eyes probing Valery with an icy stare.

"None of your business," he replied in reckless anger.

"Next question then," the man remarked in an authoritarian tone, "Which of these people refused to do the news story?"

"I did," Gerado responded, before Valery could answer. It was now quite clear to him that Marek Falin had Valery rise in rank in order to use him as a tool, in his power base in his ministry.

Gerado's pulse began to beat erratically, as a cold, dark silence enveloped him. *Someone will soon be headed to a Gulag camp.* And he wondered if it would be Valery or him—*or perhaps both of us.*

When the car finally sped away, Valery directed everyone to follow him into the spacious house.

"I need to call my father-in-law, his secretary, and my wife," he told the receptionist.

She was a pleasant lady who was waiting to escort anyone, who asked her, to his or her room.

Isabella and Manuel took her up on the offer, but Arina and Gerado hung back.

"Use the phone on the desk in the communal room," the woman said, before starting toward the staircase.

Arina went over and stood beside Valery as he made the calls. But, strangely, neither Marek or his secretary could be reached. Mila, however, was easy to reach. Though, like him, it appeared she was unable to contact neither her father—nor anyone on his staff.

Valery then gave Mila the phone number of this house where they were staying.

"Call me as soon as you make contact with someone," Gerado heard him say, watching him closely as a paralyzing fear appeared to sweep through him.

'This is an unfairness that defies human decency,' he thought about telling him *'And all this is because of my refusal to write that news story, and not hand over that original painting.'*

He was consumed with apprehension for Valery, since like it on not, he'd become his friend. *And these damned secret police are jealous of high-ranking men like him. Whether it be they're married with a mistress or otherwise...any excuse to haul them off to Gulag camp would do just fine.*

"Gerado." Arina stepped up to him. "It appears Valery needs our help."

"Definitely. However, there're only two ways we can do it. One is you can give him the painting, or the other is I can lie and write that news story."

"We've already said we don't have the painting."

"And I've already said I won't write the news story—" He stopped, allowing his hesitation to stretch a moment, before he continued, "Seeing that Manuel has your original painting is more important than my lying and writing the news story. So if worse comes to worse, I'll write an outline Valery can show Marek."

"No, Gerado, don't do it!" Arina warned, staying him with her arm.

"Yes—hear me out. If Marek threatens to send Valey to a Gulag camp, then my outline can be a bargaining chip with which he can work. Since my writing style is well-known and if anyone else writes under my name, it'll be obvious that it's not me. So I'll agree to write the story as long as they'll release Valery...and as far as your painting goes, my research indicates that Marek is a man not to be trusted. Which tells me he has a personal reason for wanting that painting—"

"Like what?" she asked with an inquisitive glance.

"Who knows?" Gerado gave his head a sharp shake. "Maybe he believes there's buried treasure in that twisted chimney house."

She shrugged nonchalantly. "I suppose anything's possible."

Gerado focused his gaze on the wall clock. "It's been a deplorable day, so why don't you go check on Isabella, and the two of you take a nap."

"Maybe—but what about you?"

"I'm going to search this place for a typewriter and work on my outline."

"Don't over do it because you need rest too."

"Don't we all."

★★★

As they waited in the communal room preparing to leave for dinner, Gerado became aware that no one from Kiev had telephoned Valery. So he handed him the outline of the news story he'd done earlier.

"But it's a lie, so don't write it," he urged, appearing to have difficulty masking his uneasiness. "Since you're known for your honesty as a reporter."

"I try. But this outline is a bargaining chip to see you don't get in any trouble. Which indicates you'd better hang onto it because I consider you a friend—but we'll talk more about that later."

"I'm flattered you consider me a friend, even if I wouldn't have thought—"

"We're in a different world now, "Gerado broke in, squeezing his arm. "So, detach yourself from the way we people from the West feel about Soviets. And on this journey we've seen the thoughtful ways you've treated us, letting me know it's our obligation to treat you the same."

That said, Valery gathered the group and they began walking toward the café. It was a pleasant place. A red-and-white checked oilcloth covered the table, with salt and pepper shakers to match. Two bottles of white wine had been placed at each end of the table.

They ordered the fried trout, the thick Russian fries and Bulgaria's well-known Shopska salad, made with cucumbers instead of lettuce. Fresh bread in a basket had been placed on the table with a *carafe* full of olive oil beside it.

"Attractive," Gerado observed. He wanted to enjoy the evening, even if his mind kept wandering back to their earlier encounter with the secret police, and its possible effect on them.

It made it difficult for him to pull himself together. And his head swam as sunk in thought, he stared at the table's candle with its flickering flame that came and went. *Like waves on a beach. Or was this flame more like the pain darting through a wounded, fluttering fairy?*

Looking forward to a fish dinner, everyone seemed to make a point of engaging in lively conversation, with their talk even bringing some laughter as they waited for their fried trout.

It came sooner than expected, their lively conversation suddenly ceasing as they admired the way their filleted pieces had been placed in the center of a paper plates cut in the shape of a fish.

"Very creative. "Isabella remarked, folding the fish's paper tail in an upward position. "With lots of possibilities."

"Why this trout is a good as the tilapia—or rather St. Peter's fish—my mother used to fry for us." Gerado exclaimed, holding a forkful of the trout over his plate. And savoring its taste, the concerns plaguing him earlier seemed to vanish for the moment.

Isabella turned toward him."Your mother was a great cook, even if she refused to eat with us. 'Cooks don't eat with the people they cook for,' she would say. 'So let Gerado sit with you.' Which she knew we wouldn't have had any other way."

Dessert, a hot chocolate cake, surprised them. And since it was so delicious they quickly devoured it.

"I'll have them bring some more," Valery offered, but they declined.

The accompanying musicians were gathering on a small stage next to the bar with their instruments: one had a tambourine, another an accordion, and the third a keyboard.

Andre Goslin appeared, his sandy hair the identical color of his balalaika; although, before any music began he went over to Arina.

She rose, and he gave her a hug, bringing curious stares from Gerado and Valery.

"Who do I thank for allowing me to entertain Kiev's lovely violinist tonight?" Andre asked her.

She nodded at Valery in his uniform. "We're acting as guides for some guests from Italy and Berlin." And extending a hand to Isabella, Gerado, and Manuel, she introduced them.

Andre bowed and said he was honored to meet them all. Then chuckling, he returned his attention to Arina. "I'll never forget that story you told me about those guests from the U.K. visiting Kiev—"

"And that balalaika...*Mercy!*"

"Tell us," Manuel insisted. "I'm sure we'd all love to hear it."

"It's a silly story—"

"Doesn't matter," Gerado cut in. "I think we could all use a good laugh tonight."

"Guess I have no choice," Arina replied, a vague smiled touching her lips. "The story happened in a Kiev alley with shops on both sides. And these guests were on a cultural tour and not a shopping one. With one lady getting furious with the guide for not allowing them to at least have some brief shopping. But he refused. They needed to be at a certain place at a certain time. Then, another lady on the tour saw a balalaika in a shop. And that was all it took. She paid the shopkeeper, grabbed the balalaika, and hurried out with it. The amazing thing being she never once fell behind with the tour. 'Did you see that!' cried this angry lady, who wanted to shop. 'I'll see our guide gets fired!' But, luckily, she wasn't able to do it."

Andre grinned. "A tale that certainly shows how attractive Kiev's balalaika's can be." He put his hand on Arina's arm. "But tell me, what can I play for my lovely violinist who's visiting us tonight?"

She started to answer but before she could, Valery spoke, "It's getting late, and we're going to have to leave soon. So we can only stay for one or two pieces."

"Then how about *"Midnight in Moscow* and *"The Flight if the Bumblebee?"* In honor of our lovely violinist, sitting here, who plays both pieces so beautifully?"

Valery agreed just as the bartender, waving a phone in his direction, caught his attention. "I think it's your wife, who claims you gave her our number."

"I did." He hurried over to the phone. Not minding the musicians were now playing the relaxing, jazz instrumental, *"Midnight in Moscow"* with its faint tinkling-like sound in the background.

It wasn't loud, making it easy for Gerado to hear Valery ask, "Is that you, Mila?"

They talked briefly before he hurried over to the table.

"We need to leave!" he said, a shadow of alarm touching his face as he quickly dropped some money in a small bucket on the stage for the musicians.

The face-paced, *"The Flight of the Bumblebee,"* was beginning, and Andre took the liberty of stepping off the stage with his balalaika and going over to Arina, to indicate it was being played in her honor.

"We'll leave the minute's it's over, Valery," Gerado whispered to him. "And we shouldn't be far behind you."

But to his dismay, the music lasted longer than anticipated, making him uneasy, the same as it appeared to be making Arina. Who fidgeting nervously, buttoned two buttons on her leather jacket in the wrong holes. When he pointed it out, she corrected the mistake, leaving the jacket open.

He was about to suggest they leave anyway, and already had some money in his hand for Andre, when the café's door crashed open with a loud bang.

Immediately, Gerado's eyes assessed the two men who entered. One was large, with a powerful set of shoulders, while the other, smaller man had muscular arms.

Their hair was short but well-trimmed, as were their fingernails. And they were dressed in civilian, well tailored clothes, the same navy blue as their polished shoes.

"They're arrogant, overly confident men who have a military bearing," he told Arina in a low voice. "Which tells me they're Red Army."

"True." She shuddered. Her face now the eggshell white of an unpainted canvas as these soldiers' eyes stared at Gerado, like he was a wolf in a trap waiting to be shot.

"Bring us vodka and make it quick—" they ordered the waiter.

Which he did, watching, as each man swallowed his in a single gulp.

When the music finally stopped, Gerado sprang to his feet "Sorry, but we have to make a hasty departure, "he told Andre, quickly stuffing some money in his pocket.

Concern, etched the musician's features as he gazed at Arina. "Thank you. And you two be careful."

"What we're attempting to do," Gerado said, grabbing her arm before dashing off.

A terrible sense of danger aroused him when he noticed the sudden absence of the two Red Army soldiers. Were they in the men's room or outside waiting? One mistake could be costly.

Preparing to make a run to the house, he and Arina barged out the door and into the night's chilly breeze with a non-stop urgency.

★★★

A threat to smash us. They were in such a hurry Arina failed to see one of the cobblestones not far from the lamp post overlooking the café. And she tripped on it, stopping briefly to look at the crimson smear on the top of her big toe. "*Ambush!*" she cried, her world on the verge of falling apart.

In one swift movement the larger of the two Red Army soldiers stepped out from the shadows of the alley and grabbed Gerado.

The soldier him roughly around, before giving him a right hook in the stomach. A frenzied action that threw him off balance and knocked the breath out of him.

Instantly he fell to the ground, striking his head against the cobblestones.

He groaned several times at the terrible pain shooting through him. And he gasped as this large man, with a hate-filled expression, gave him a violent kick in the ass. "Punishment for the sins of the father!" he shouted.

Arina's heart leaped.'*Gerado*!' She opened her mouth to shout, but her lips refused to move.

Time was of the essence, telling her she had to do something and *quick*! So taking a step backward, she grabbed a garbage can lid and struck the smaller soldier on top of his head.

"You bitch! he yelped.

She struck him again. And in retaliation his muscular arms slammed her against the brick wall, ripping the top of her dress and camisole.

Her body throbbed with apprehension at the tearing sound of her dress and undergarment.

"Look what we have here!" said the soldier in a gleeful tone. His eyes glistening with excitement as he gazed at her exposed breasts.

The larger soldier turned to see. And when he saw her breasts, the expression on his face brought to mind a snake preparing to swallow a frightened rabbit.

Panting in terror, Arina's pulse quickened as fearful images of these dark and ugly men built in her mind.

CHAPTER NINE

Gerado mentally exploded. *She will not be raped nor tortured!* Fury raced through him with a cry for vengeance, and in a sudden rush of adrenaline he quickly rose from the rough cobblestones.

The larger soldier was so distracted by Arina's beauty that Gerado, on his feet, had no problem hitting him in the throat, crushing his larynx, and cutting off his breath.

Seeing that, the smaller soldier attempted to remove his pistol from its holster when Gerado, his emotions out of control, caught him off guard. Which put the soldier, in a mental fog that made him unprepared for Gerado's retaliation.

A hesitation followed, with Gerado hitting the bridge of his nose with the heel of his right hand—a chop that temporarily blinded him.

"Did you think attacking me would be like a walk in the park?" he asked, grabbing the pistol from his hand— "Well for you, soldier, it's more like a stroll through valley of the shadow of death."

And taking Arina by the arm, they sped to the safety of the house.

Valery, Isabella, and Manuel were sitting in the communal room waiting, and when they saw them, their mouths flew open.

"What happened?" Valery asked, rushing over to them. "Like me, Isabella and Manuel were ahead of you." His hand touched Gerado's shoulder and rested there. "But from the looks of it, I'd say you've been beaten with a stick and thrown in a ditch."

Gerado's voice trembled. "T...that's more or less what happened." He handed Valery the pistol. "Red Army soldiers in civilian clothes attacked us."

"Did you kill them?"

"No, but came close to it. So they'll probably need to visit the military hospital here."

"I like this silencer on this pistol," Valery said, examining it. "And it's a good thing you were briefly in the German army in your teens because it's obvious, seeing Arina's torn dress, it was the reason she didn't get raped."

Isabella's arm was on Gerado's, and she was sobbing. "We've got to get a cab and get him to the civilian hospital at once!"

Manuel's hands were around Isabella's arms in an attempt to calm her. "Easy now, I'm calling one."

"No need," said the receptionist. "One's on the way."

Valery took Arina in his arms. "Were you hurt?"

"Just my toe. Though the important thing is Gerado kept me from being raped."

"For which I'll never be able to repay him," Valery replied. "But Mila was right when she told me on the phone her father was up to something—"

"There's a cab down the street, waiting at a light," Manuel interrupted, now on the porch. "So that's probably it."

"If it is, it was quick," said Arina."

"Yes indeed."

"My head's spinning," said Gerado. "And I'm having a sinking sensation."

He was coughing so badly he collapsed on the sofa. "M...my rush of adrenaline's leaving me," he gasped, his breathing labored. "And this weakness spreading through me is making me feel a lot of pain." He also suspected there were ugly marks on his body, since he felt like he'd been cut with a whiplash.

Deep sobs racked Isabella as she took his hand. "When you were five years old and your awful father beat you with that razor strap, I vowed no one would ever beat you like that again—but I should have known better. With those evil Red Army soldiers and the secret police hovering over us."

"Easy," Gerado soothed. 'I'll be all right. But what about you, Arina?"

"I'm fine except for my toe."

Isabella stared at her. "And that's another thing, young lady, you have no future in this god-awful country. So one way or another we're getting you out of it."

Valery held up the small service pistol Gerado had given him. "Did you recognize it as a Soviet Makarov?"

He nodded. "It's the official sidearm issued to various Soviet agencies. And something the *inside* Russian departments, often make good use of."

"Which is why I'm keeping it."

"The wise thing to do," Gerado admitted.

"A cab just pulled up in the driveway," Manuel hollered at Valery. "And it looks small, so Arina will probably have to sit in your lap."

"Won't bother me at all."

★★★

They were in the hospital's emergency waiting area. "And it's crowded like the rest of the hospital, " Gerado's dizzied senses heard a nurse say. "And he'll be put in a ward after his recovery exam."

It didn't bother him, but it bothered Isabella who wanted him in a private room. "I'm determined to leave on the plane in the morning with you," he told her. "So I can surely spend one night in a ward."

"And I'll stay with him through the night," Arina volunteered.

"But not in a chair," Valery interceded. "In the cot I'm paying for."

"Let me pay for some of this," Gerado insisted. "Those sorry bastards ripped Arina's dress, and she has to keep her jacket fastened. So is there any place we can find her a dress at this hour?"

"Yes. "Valery smiled as if guarding a secret. "After the nurse takes care of her toe, I know a shop that will open after hours for an emergency. And I'm paying for clothes for all of you. It's *my* gift." He patted Arina's hand. "So I'll need your dress and slacks size."

"And her shoe size," Gerado added. "Since she needs a good pair of boots and some sturdy shoes."

"Which she hasn't let me buy her," Valery explained, his frustration obvious. "But now she has no choice...especially since I have a strong idea what she likes."

A faint frown of protest appeared on Isabella's face. "You don't have to buy clothes for all of us, Valery."

"But I do," he insisted. "Since it's my appreciation for the efforts you've made here—so *hush*."

"And we thank you," said Manuel, flushing.

★★★

Arina waited in the lobby, while Gerado was taken to recovery for his exam.

Valery, Isabella, and Manuel were gone for a lengthy amount of time, and when they returned, they held several boxes of clothing, plus a suitcase. But Gerado, to their despair, had still not been released from recovery.

Isabella's brow was creased with worry. "Have we heard anything?"

"The doctor was just here," said Arina. "And he told me that so far all seems to be fine, though a few more tests are still needed."

Valery opened the suitcase. "Then we'll look at your clothes." He removed three dresses, a pair of dark slacks, and a white blouse. There was also a pair of blue jeans, a denim jacket, and tennis shoes in a separate bag."

She picked them up. "Blue jeans are often hard to find and expensive."

"Doesn't matter. This seller had some imported items" He nodded at Manuel. "He's holding the box that has your boots and shoes in it, and they should go well with these dresses."

The first dress he held up was a rose colored one with a matching jacket that would be perfect for her violin performances. "I love its shiny fabric." She smiled, stroking it. The second dress was a floral, black one with white flowers scattered over it. A pleasant contrast. But the third was the most gorgeous of all...a gray, silk dress with spaghetti straps and a black-and-white houndstooth jacket that complimented it.

"And your shoes and boots are taupe," said Manuel, opening the box. "A color Isabella assures me goes with everything."

Arina was so touched tears rose in her eyes. "I can't thank you enough." She told Valery. "And Manuel and Isabella are wearing leather jackets that look similar to mine."

"Gerado got one too." Valery beamed. "Along with a robe, pajamas, slacks, and a shirt Isabella picked out for him, that are in the bottom of the suitcase."

"I saw them," Arina said.

"I knew what to do for him because I always helped my husband put his wardrobe together," Isabella responded. "Prompting Gerado to insist I help him too. Since he's in the public eye and needs to look his best." A pause. "In addition I helped his mother when she was alive, who only wanted to dress up when there school events, recitals, or trips to Berlin. Then, I'd see she went to the beauty salon, where she'd get her hair and nails done. And afterwards, I'd help her make-up. She wanted to look good for Gerado. And at these events we'd introduce her as his mother and my husband and I as his godparents."

Arina slipped on her new shoes. "You're a great lady, Isabella, I could tell that the minute I met you. And I love these attractive shoes you picked out."

"I did too...though the important thing is if they're comfortable."

"Very."

"Then I'll show you the restroom where you can change your dress," Valery offered. "So pick one." She chose the black dress with the white flowers and looped it over her arm.

"This way then." He motioned.

When they got to a hall that was deserted, he stopped and put his arms around hers. And she drank in the comfort of his nearness. Her heart was still aching for him, the same as she sensed his was doing for hers, making her feel for a moment she was his again.

Reclaiming her lips, he covered hers hungrily. And trembling she clung to him until he stopped.

"Like a crumbling ember," he muttered.

"O-oh, Valery." She sighed. "You're still so very hard to resist."

"Kissing you was a comfort I couldn't resist in these turbulent times."

"The same as me, even if sadly—"

"—we have to move on," he completed, pressing his hand against her heart, "You're fortunate enough to have two men who love you, when most women only have one."

★★★

When they returned, Gerado was being taken to the ward on a stretcher. "He's doing well," the doctor assured everyone.

"Yes indeed," Gerado said lightly. "Considering I got poked and prodded anywhere they could find a hole in me."

The doctor grinned. "However, we'll keep him overnight just to make sure, since he tells me he's flying out of here tomorrow."

"In this hospital gown." He chuckled. "If Manuel doesn't help me change into those pajamas and robe, he says Valery bought me."

"Which I'll be happy to do." Manuel assured him, reaching for the pajamas in the suitcase. "I have a class to teach tomorrow, so considering I have a very early morning flight to Berlin, this will be my goodbye."

"Just make sure to be careful with that painting I saw Isabella slip you," Valery warned.

"God! You saw it?"

"I suspected you'd end up with it."

"My colleagues and I are onto something," Manuel said, helping Gerado into his pajamas. "And if we had that painting's missing piece, it might surprise you what we're able to confirm."

His sinking sensation returning, Gerado had difficulty drawing a clean breath of air in the stuffy hospital. "Mila's supposed to have bought a painting she saw, that has a twisted chimney exactly like the one in painting. Did she mention she bought it?"

"We had other things to discuss, Valery said. "Like the sudden absence of her father."

It was getting late, so Manuel said his good-byes.

"We have an early morning flight too," Isabella reminded, giving Gerado a kiss." So Valery's insisting we need to go back to the house and get some sleep."

"Then do it," Gerado urged.

He waited until they left before asking Arina if she wouldn't be uncomfortable sleeping in her pretty, new dress.

But she shook her head. "This material doesn't wrinkle, so I'll be fine."

They talked briefly, with him telling her about Manuel's fondness for German Shepherds. "He couldn't take a dog on his digs, so Isabella would keep it, saying, 'That way Gerado will have a dog too.' making me quite happy."

"She's certainly been good to you—"

"The same as she was to my mother before she died."

Arina touched his forearm. Her amber-gold eyes shimmering with light as she adjusted his bed covers. "You've done so much for me I feel I owe you. Although, not having any money there's only one way I can repay you—"

"Let me guess." He flashed his trademark smile. "You're offering to let me take you to bed."

"Exactly."

He paused for breath. "Make no mistake, as lovely and big-hearted as you are, no man in his right mind would ever be able to get enough of you—"

"Then you'll do it?"

"No!" he insisted archly. "What kind of man would I be if I demanded you repay me with your body? And besides you're still in love with Valery."

"Our arrangement was we'd break apart upon your arrival. Which we did."

"But you didn't know him very long, did you? So it should have made it harder."

"I'd known men, he'd known women, yet we viewed each other as being our first real loves. Which amounted to just a brief happiness for us. And he was honest with me and told me I needed to marry you to get out of the Soviet Union."

"Which even if it's in name only, I'm hoping you'll do." Now sitting up, Gerado took her in his arms. "So does that make it easier between us?"

"When I think of the effort you've made to help me find my father, it makes it harder not to be in love with you." She kissed his forehead. "I know this doesn't make much sense, so let's pretend I'm a woman who takes help from a man only because she has plans to pressure him into having sex with her."

For a long moment Gerado just stared at her. "I've never heard of that." He chuckled, shaking his head, dazed. "But are you saying what I think you're saying?"

"That you're obligated to have sex with me," she replied, a suggestive grin on her oval face. "Because I allowed you to give me all that help."

"Well now," he said, pretending to give it some thought. "That's certainly an original twist."

"I'm demanding you repay me by making love to me."

His brows flickered inquiringly. "Then I guess you leave me no choice," he said, his grin matching hers. "But when's this supposed to happen?"

She put her head on his shoulder against his pajama top "When you get to feeling better."

"Makes sense."

They exchanged hugs and kisses, holding hands before they fell asleep. And he dreamed a dream—no a nightmare!

He was in a concentration camp, in striped pajamas with his head shaved, as an SS officer announced to a guard. "Gerado Behl is Otho

Behl's son, and he's a Jewish sympathizer. So his father's ordered us to knock some sense into him."

Which they did. First stripping him naked in the snow and whipping him. Then forcing him to do heavy labor in dangerous places where bullets flew between the Germans and Russians. And afterwards, they'd force him to watch the SS, in their black uniforms, beat people with batons until they dropped dead...*their blood covering the ground.* It made him wish he could die too.

For food he never received anything more than watered down soup and was often forced to use snow for his water.

Gunfire echoed daily across the camp, with prisoners being shot for the slightest offense.

Then, with a sudden start, he opened his eyes. Arina had her hands on his shoulders, giving them a shake. "You were having a nightmare. Was it about that beating you received earlier?"

"No." He tried to focus. "I was in a concentration camp and people were suffering."

A tear rolled down his cheek as he closed his eyes again.

CHAPTER TEN

When Valery returned from Minsk, he had orders to report to Marek Falin in his office at once. Which, covering his uneasiness, is exactly what he did. He suspected Marek had plans to punish him in some way for not forcing Gerado to write that news story. Well he at least had an outline from him, and like he'd said, it was a tool with which he could bargain, if not now, then perhaps later.

Marek's hazel eyes were bloodshot and his breath reeked of alcohol. The same as his uniform which was stained in places. A good indication he'd worn it last night, when he'd been drinking with Olga.

"You're my son-on-law!" he shouted at Valery. "Who's living in a fine villa, and being groomed to take my place, should something happen to me. Yet, you can't do the two things I've asked. The first is retrieve that painting. And the second is getting that war criminal's son to write a newspaper article." He thumbed through the papers scattered on his desk until he found the written complaint from Leonid Devin. "This came in on the plane this morning." He shoved it in Valery's face. "And he's writing me about your inefficiency—"

"Try to calm down," Valery suggested, taking a step back. "Since the painting's in Berlin. And as for Gerado and his newspaper article, I can talk him into writing it...just give me some more time."

On the floor he saw that he and Mila's wedding picture, once in a gold frame, had been ripped it two. Glass covered it.

"Manuel's colleagues are working hard to uncover something about the missing piece of that painting," he explained. "And if they can figure it out, then they maintain they'll have a good idea as to where that house with the twisted chimney once was."

"And no petroglyphs?" Marek shouted, his rage growing.

Valery knew he had to come up with something and quick. "There's speculation those glyphs might be in another country."

"Another country." Marek yelled. "You think I'm stupid?" He came around from his desk and putting his hands on Valery's shoulders, shoved him against the bookcase. These were books Marek never read but kept to look intellectual...The shelves hurt Valery's shoulders and his back, and he stumbled as he struggled to regain his balance.

"Those glyphs are *here!*" Marel exploded, his rock-hard features paling with wrath. "In the Soviet Union."

His father-in-law's aggressive act shocked him. When was the last time anyone had done him like that? *At the orphanage maybe? Which was nearly twenty of thirty years ago.*

Anger and humiliation thundered through him, causing him to come close to exploding with his need for vengeance. And he struggled to contain himself as he glared at Marek, enraged.

Their eyes were pinned on each other, motivating Valery to daringly, ask the question he'd been tempted to blurt when Marek had demanded he retrieve the original painting Arina had been so carefully guarding. "Are you seeking this painting, Marek, because Manuel and his colleagues are getting close to learning where the Soviets are hiding Wallenberg? And if they are, then why in hell can't he be moved? Is it because he's elderly and ill, or is it feared moving him might kill him?"

He didn't think Marek would put his hands on him again. He might be drunk but even drunk, he was usually able to keep his cool to a degree. The only time Valery had ever known Marek to show physical violence to anyone was to Mila. But then she was a woman, and her pig-headed father didn't respect women the way he did men.

O-oh but I should have known better—Marek's a vicious son-of-a-bitch.

With the violence he meted out, making Valery imagine for a moment he was being struck with a crowbar, as Marek punched him in the belly with his fists several times. " I think of my fists the way I do asteroids from outer space," he could swear he heard Marek brag. "Powerful enough to wipe a man out quickly."

Then he began slapping his face until he was senseless. Darkness threatened to engulf him, and he might have fallen had he not grabbed the edge of Marek's desk. Where he stood, paralyzed, for several moments to keep from toppling to the floor. The urge to slap his father-in-law was strong.

If anyone else had treated me like this they'd be dead. Though where Marek was concerned he knew better. If he fought back it would mean either a Gulag camp or more than likely a trip to the wall.

There were other ways he could destroy Marek and destroy him he would. *For Mila's sake as well as mine.* The trick would be on finding the way to do, leaving no trail as to who had done it. *The perfect crime.*

Valery reached for his handkerchief and pressed it against his mouth and nose in an effort to stop the bleeding. It didn't feel like he'd lost a tooth or that his nose was broken—but they hurt like hell.

Most of the slaps had been across his cheeks. With Marek's violent nature slamming them so hard they burned like a scorpion's touch. Until finally, this evil man stopped.

Immediately, a terrible hush filled the room, accompanied by the painful throbbing Valery was beginning to feel in his jaw. *How long before it goes away? Probably more time than I care to think.*

He had nothing to say to Marek, and couldn't if he'd wanted to, considering the battered shape of his mouth. So, he simply turned and left.

★★★

Earlier, when Mila had met them at the airport she was shocked to learn that Red Army soldiers had attacked Gerado and Arina. They discussed what had happened in Minsk. And afterwards, she informed him she had an appointment this morning with Ustin Dimitri, the retired *spetsnz* instructor…*I can't image why,* Valery pondered. *Even if it does sound intriguing.*

She'd learned the artist who'd painted the twisted chimney was deceased…probably the reason it has been sold. But even so, Mila had managed to bribe the gallery manager into giving her the address of the person who'd bought it. A woman, who raised farm animals in what was deemed a virtual wilderness, a good distance from the city.

"Where we're going is a densely forested area, which many describe as being downright spooky," Mila informed Valery. "And I've been given directions to the woman's house, but have no way of contacting her.

"Though regardless, if Gerado feels well enough, then we'll leave this afternoon and show up at her house unannounced."

Gerado assured her, that even if he did hurt, he'd be able to go. Lamenting, that due to his head injury he was not allowed to take morphine. 'I'm learning to tough it out," he told her with a grin.

"Which is bad," Isabella said. "The same as that nightmare Arina told me you had last night, where you were beaten in a concentration camp."

He took his godmother's hand. "But I recalled how you'd eased me once, when you once said, 'this too will pass.' And praised me for briefly joining the German army, even though you and Antonio had reservations about it. Especially, when my training would have us young soldiers sometimes sleep on the grass in a bedroll. Something Antonio certainly didn't like."

Isabella closed her hand over his. "Your army experience is what saved you and Arina in that cobblestone alley."

"Which I felt certain it did."

And then, she'd given him some of the natural medicine that Mila had given her for emergencies. "This should help a little, though you really need something stronger."

"I agree."

★★★

Valery was pleased Mila had volunteered to meet them at the airport and return Gerado, Arina, and Isabella to their hotel. *The morning moved along quickly and pleasantly.*

But after Mila dropped them off, Valery had her drive him to their villa so he could get his car.

"Still no words from your father?" he asked her.

"None whatsoever,"

"Then I'll go see about him."

It hadn't taken him long to reach Marek's office... *Which, recalling later, was clearly a mistake because of the terrible beating I received from him.*

He knew he should have called Mila immediately and told her about what her father had done. Though for some peculiar reason, he couldn't.

He also needed some of her natural medicine. But right now she had her own problems with that trip to the country she and Gerado were getting ready to make..Exactly what were they expecting to learn from that farm woman who'd purchased the painting?

He doubted very little. And suspected this journey they'd be making would end up being a disappointing adventure.

"We have so little to go on, Valery, that we can't rule out anything." Gerado had explained earlier.

And he'd agreed.

Looking back at their departure from the airport—*before Marek beat me*—he recalled a conversation in the car between Isabella and Arina. She wasn't working tonight, and Isabella had made plans to hire a cab and return with her to her apartment and help her pack the things she wanted to keep. *'We'll then take them to the hotel, so you'll be ready to go to Italy with us, when we leave the Soviet Union.'*

Mila was anxious to leave for the country and promised to phone him from the car, when she began her journey back to Kiev. "That way, Isabella, and Arina will join Gerado and I for dinner tonight at the hotel around nine o'clock. So please try to be there."

It sounded good. As does the fact I have a pistol with a silencer that no one, except Gerado, knows I have...And I trust him. Though hidden away, I do have other pistols with silencers that not one human being on this planet knows about.

★★★

It was mid-afternoon before Gerado and Mila left for the country. And feeling restless and uncomfortable, he continued to wonder like Valery, if they could really learn anything about that painting from the person who'd bought it?

He put a pillow on his seat before he got in Mila's car." My butt's sore because that sorry Red Army son-of-a-bitch kicked me in the ass...but what about you?" He stared at the bruise near her temple that was slowly fading. "You had a head injury like me, yet got morphine. So how does that work?"

"I got slapped *once*. Not really a head injury. It's just that this deepening bruise is slow to heal." She paused. "My real injuries came from the ones on my back and shoulders, when me father threw me on the floor and kicked me more times than I could count."

"Your father sounds like a real winner."

"He's a beast who needs to be locked up," Mila said, making a turn onto a cobblestone street.

A momentary apprehension swept through Gerado. "Looks like that damned alley in Minsk."

Mila made several more turns at intersecting boulevards before the noisy streetcars and cheaply made cars began to thin out."

"In Czechhoslovakia, for a news story, I rode in a cardboard car that ran quite well."

"I've ridden in one too. And it amazes me that something like that could run as well as it did."

Blocks of gray apartment buildings began showing up on both sides of the road, as farther down from them, some manufacturing plants appeared.

This continued until they turned onto a two-lane highway with fields on both sides of it. "Wish we could have two-lanes all the way." She sighed. "Because where we're headed will require us to travel on a one-lane, dirt country road."

"Something that won't be easy if we end up having to go back to Kiev in the dark."

"I've done it before, so I can do it again."

A plane flew overhead, then another. "Appears the airport's nearby," Gerado remarked, watching as two more planes roared behind the first one. This time, flying lower, they looked for a moment like they were preparing to land on the highway.

"Those low flying planes, where you can read that sky-blue, Russian writing on the underside of their wings and it makes me shudder."

Gerado grinned." Interesting your eyes, my eyes, and Valery's are the same blue as that writing."

She returned his grin. "I hope it doesn't mean they're coming for us."

"From the way I feel, I think they already got me."

"Let's hope not. "

She stopped at a traffic light before making a turn at its crossing, and Gerado looked up at the gray clouds forming. "Let's just hope it doesn't rain, or else we're apt to have a big problem traveling on a muddy, country road."

"I'm not worried." She glanced up. "The weather report's good. Even if we've been advised to expect a few sprinkles."

"As long as you can handle it," he said, attempting to re-adjust his pillow in the hopes of easing his pain. "I've driven in a lot of places, but the Soviet Union's not one of them."

"Don't worry, we'll be fine," she assured him, reaching over and patting his hand. "At the next traffic light there's a wide intersection, which is the other turn we'll take in order to get us to the country."

And she was right...with it not being long before some wheat fields began to appear.

They continued for several miles before Mila made another turn. This time it was onto a winding dirt road flanked with spruce trees.

"We're definitely in the country now," she remarked in a somewhat cheerful tone.

"I've read the Ukraine's one of the Soviet Union's outstanding grain-growing regions," Gerado said. "Which impresses me."

"Me too. Because we don't need food shortages like they had in 1930, when people starved to death."

"One of the Ukraine's great tragedies," he said sadly.

As time passed a great many fields and farmlands began appearing, stretching out before them as far as their eyes could see.

"Has anyone ever told you, Gerado, this area is haunted?" she asked.

"I've heard it described as being one of the three witch hotspots in the world," he remarked. Adding after a long contemplation, "All those trees so close to each other do seem to give it an eerie look."

"My friend took a picture of a ghost here. A German soldier. Which really spooked me."

"Yet, you're not afraid to venture out here after that?"

"I have my pistol."

"Pistol!" he exclaimed, shock hitting him like a baseball bat. "I take it you can shoot it."

"I've had excellent training but no one, not even Valery, knows. So please keep it a secret."

"I most surely will," he promised, reflecting on the strong connection she appeared to have with Ustin Dimitri, when she'd introduced him at the cafe two days ago.

"Speaking of scary things, there's a witch cemetery not far from here that would make an interesting news story."

"I'll keep it in mind."

She stopped the car for a moment to glance at some directions she'd written. "We're not far—maybe three more sharp turns."

"To the witch cemetery or the woman's house?" Gerado teased her.

She laughed. "To the witch cemetery, of course. We'll simply call up one of the witches and ask her to tell us where Wallenberg is."

"Now, Mila." He chuckled. "You know that's too high a price to pay."

"It is," she agreed. "But it would be interesting if someone dared to do it."

"Have to be someone crazy."

"Believe me, they're plenty out here who are."

She made two more sharp turns, then stopped again. Only this time in front of a spruce-log house that looked to be only two rooms. Which most likely had one bedroom, with the living, dining, and kitchen areas combined.

"A rustic setting, indeed," Gerado commented. "Which doesn't fit the image of someone living out here and buying a painting at an art gallery in Kiev." *Something quite surprising. Like the way things, at present, appear to be going in my life.*

CHAPTER ELEVEN

The house's roof had split spruce shingles. And there was a water tank, woodshed, and small henhouse not far from the place. A wooden fence with chicken wire circled the yard, and a gravel path led to the porch.

A barking, black dog was at the gate. And several chickens were wandering around loose in the yard.

"I'm supposed to have made three turns," Mila said, studying her notes. "But I've only made two and this house fits the description of what I wrote down."

"Only one way to find out," said Gerado, getting out of the car. He groaned and clutched his back the minute his feet touched ground. "That damned pain just won't go away, And it's worse standing."

"Then get back in the car while I go to the door and knock."

But he shook his head. "Might be a witch in there instead of the lady we're seeking," he joked. "So even with a pistol, I can't allow you to fend for yourself."

"If all goes well, I'll rub your back before we leave, like you did mine."

"Which would certainly put me in your debt."

The barking dog was now at the gate. "He's either there to greet us or bite us." Mila commented, her sky-blue gaze focused on him. "But, don't worry, knowing nearly all the country people have a dog, I brought some meat." She reached into her pocket and tossed him several chunks she was carrying in a small paper bag.

"Comrade, stop that barking!" yelled a large woman in a red dress, standing on the porch. She eyed her visitors. "What can I do for you?"

"I'm a news reporter from Berlin," Gerado quickly said. "And I'd like to interview you about a painting you recently purchased."

"The one with that strange-looking chimney?"

"That would be it."

"Then come in."

When they stepped through the door, she pointed at it hanging on the wall above a small table.

Gerado then introduced himself and Mila, and the woman invited them to have a seat on a sofa.

"And I'm Zella Kolodynski and very pleased to meet you."

"I know it's four-thirty in the afternoon," said Mila, "but we didn't have time for lunch. So, I bought a picnic basket we'll be happy to share with you."

"Why that's wonderful," Zella said, her voice rising in surprise." I didn't have lunch either...but find a seat at the table, while I brew us some tea."

"We'd love that," Mila said. "Since it's been my experience that you people out here brew the best Russian tea I've ever tasted."

"One of the few pleasures we have out here." She got up to brew the tea.

"You live alone?" Gerado asked her.

"Ever since my husband passed away three years ago. But my two sons live down the way, and they're here every other day to help me with the animals."

"I'll go get the picnic basket," Mila said, rising.

Gerado also rose. "Need me to help?"

"Just stay where you are. I'll be back before you can snap your fingers."

He thought it best not to mention the painting again until they began eating.

"I've got cucumber sandwiches with Russian dressing, some cheese, and four bottles of fruit juice,"Mila said, setting the basket on the table. It was covered in a floral red cloth that matched the window curtains hanging over the kitchen sink.

"Cucumbers are always good," Zella said. "Even is we did have a tour guide from Switzerland visit us, who complained that all his people had to eat on their two-week tour of the Soviet Union was beef, potatoes, cabbage, and cucumbers. I didn't see anything wrong with it, but he kept saying his people wanted some chicken once in awhile."

The tea kettle whistled, and Zella jumped to tend to it. "It's hot so be careful," she warned, bringing three cups and a tea pitcher on a tray to the table.

As they ate their sandwiches and sipped their hot tea slowly, Gerado complimented her on it, deeming it was the right time to ask her about the painting. So, reaching into his pocket, he removed his copy of Arina's and handed it to her.

"W...why by golly!" her voice broke. "That's it!"

"*It?*" Gerado questioned.

"Yes. It's the painting that man in the Vladeti Prison described to my brother-in-law."

Mila gazed at her with a curious expression. "What man?"

"Well. "She hesitated, appearing to give it some thought. "There was a Hungarian political prisoner who called himself *Wallenberg* because that was the name of a man he drove for. But his real name was something like Vil...um...or Vilmos."

"Langfelder?" Mila questioned.

"That's it." She jabbed a finger at the painting. "I remember hearing my brother-in-law say it several times."

"And your brother-in-law was who?" Gerado asked, removing a small notepad and pencil from his pocket.

"A guard who lived at the prison in order to have the time he needed to do his paintings. Because in case you haven't heard, these elite political prisons aren't brutal like our regular ones are—"

"I know that's right," Gerado cut her short. "Because I've done a news story about how brutal some of those prisons are in this country."

Zella looked from Gerado to Mila, then lowered her voice, "I maybe shouldn't tell you this, but my husband loved reading those magazines from the states, that a friend of his smuggled in. He could read English quite well, and he'd say those descriptions of county clubs in the states reminded him of that political prison where my brother worked—"she stopped for a moment. 'Which is like a country *club* with a gated community,' were the words he used."

"Don't quit now," Gerado pressed, keeping his fingers crossed she'd continue. "We're here to learn all we can from you."

She reached for a photo album on a small table next to the larger one at which they were sitting.

"My sons were so interested in these pictures that they wrote extensively about my brother-inlaw and his friend, Vilmos," she reveled. "And my sons made sure the names of the people in the photos were written beneath them—like a book with pictures. And in addition, there's some writing from my brother-in-law about that chimney picture he painted. And Vil, also wrote some stuff too."

Everything was written in Russian, but since Gerado read Russian, it didn't matter. So, he quickly opened the album. And since Mila was sitting next to him, it made it easy for them to view the pictures and read the writing.

The first photo in it was the artist; a chubby, ruddy-cheeked fellow by the name of Yuri Kolodynski. A photo of him was followed by eight photographs of paintings he'd done.

Some writing followed, in which Yuri described his painting of the twisted chimney.

"One of the many interesting things Yuri made notes that he claimed he owed the painting to his friend Vil or Bill—the English translation of his name," Gerado read, copying some of his notes, though putting many in his own words:

> "Bill had been in political prisons for thirty-seven years, but appeared to have adjusted and didn't seem unhappy. And, surprisingly, had even learned English from Hollywood's western movies—not reading *the* Russian, but listening to the English. And many of these movies featured Hopalong and Topper—inspiring Bill to call himself, *Cowboy Bill from Texas*. With everyone in the prison coming to love him—This small group of political prisoners did things to occupy their minds and keep them busy, since a happy prisoner is not a trouble maker. And Cowboy Bill loved to cook, and even talked the prison administer, Abram Evanoff, into letting them have popcorn for their movies. To be in a Russian prison for many years, these prisoners didn't seem to be unhappy. Something that was credited to the camaraderie they'd developed with the other prisoners and the guards. ONE OF THE MAIN REASONS BEING BECAUSE OF OUR FUN-LOVING, COWBOY BILL…was printed in large lettering at the bottom of one of the album's pages."

Gerado flipped to the next page and sure enough—there he was. Cowboy Bill, a brown-haired, portly fellow with a grin wide enough to connect the Rhine River to the Thames, like they'd been centuries ago.

A note beneath it read:

> "Cowboy Bill knows all about that small painting with the twisted chimney, since Wallenberg had shown it to him many times. It wasn't on canvas, but some kind of heavy paper. And it had been torn, but taped together. Wallenberg kept it in his coat pocket. And when they were burying him, Bill, in a hurry, had quickly attempted to take it out of Wallenberg's pocket, causing its bottom, patched piece to get torn off. Unfortunately, the Russians had shoved Bill away, so the larger piece remained in Wallenberg's pocket as they buried him facedown...Cowboy Bill was quoted as saying, 'I was able to keep the small piece since my captors viewed it as trash. Also, there was some peculiar writing on the back that has faded as time has passed. Something I knew would, so I memorized it.'"

A cry of excitement broke from Gerado's lips. "By God, we've struck gold!"

Mila was equally astounded. "This is better than finding a witch!"

"We can't thank you enough!" Gerado told Zella.

"And I'm much obliged."

"But look—" Mila pointed, having turned to the next page. "There's something about the chimney here."

It was some more writing discussing a talk Cowboy Bill had with Yuri about his wanting to become an artist, in order to re-create Wallenberg's picture. He'd even done a sketch...which was strange looking.

"The house, with that peculiar-looking chimney was supposedly in back of a hill," Yuri wrote. "And it had glyphs all over a rock in front of it. But since nobody could draw the glyphs, I only drew the house with the twisted chimney...I needed money, and Cowboy Bill knew it. So, he told me to sell it and keep the change–something that brought a laugh from everyone."

The delight morphing on Mila's face was as bright as sunshine on a hay field." It's all coming together," she exclaimed.

But they'd stayed longer than intended, with darkness beginning to fall. "Think we should go?" Gerado asked her.

"A darkening sky with a dark cloud cover—so *yes*, we need to go."

"She has to drive on that one lane country road," Gerado explained to Zella.

"Then you'd better make haste," she urged. "Because it can get real dangerous in the dark."

Gerado glanced at his watch. "One last thing. What do the men do for women in this country club prison? Anything?"

"Most have wives who were considered to be accomplices, so they're in an elite prison down the road. And they visit at least once a week. And those who don't have wives." She rolled her eyes. "There're some other women, like prostitutes, who get paid."

"Interesting but unexpected." Gerado smiled, slipping her some money.

"Mercy!" she exclaimed." I wasn't expecting this."

"You've earned it."

"You folks are always welcome here. So please do come back."

"We'll try," Mila said. "But we have some difficulties facing us."

"Then I'll make a wish for you to overcome them."

On their way out Gerado tried to repay Mila for the bribe money she'd given the gallery manager, but she refused. "Let's go," she said, starting the car. "I'm just sorry we have to hurry and time hasn't allowed me to rub your back."

"You can do it at the hotel."

It was surprising how dark it was getting by the time they turned onto the one lane road. A heavy cloud cover hid the moon and stars, making it extremely difficult to see.

"I'm glad this Cowboy Bill's in a political prison and not a regular one," Mila said. "Because if he'd been in a regular one for thirty-seven years, he wouldn't have survived."

"I'm sure you didn't read my article, but are you aware that most Russian prisons—especially the Danil Prison, its name meaning *judge,* are terrible—"

"Yes. And judge they do," she interrupted.

"Which as I'm sure you know, the scenic, Russian Republic of Karelia, refuses to give up some of its old ways.

"I know about that prison," said Mila, stealing a quick glance at Gerado. "But I don't get to hear much talk about it. So tell me more about what you wrote in your article,"

"That the land is politically divided between Russia and Finland. And that this Russian prison—with its white nights—is sitting close to one of the most beautiful spots in the Soviet Union."

"Odd for a prison to be in such a scenic place."

"I agree. With one of the things that's really bad is having six male prisoners living together in a barracks. They're in a fairly large barrack, but even so, it's *the male prisoners* who end up getting beatings from the guards—"

"With the women not getting them?"

"No. Because almost every night these male prisoners are allowed to go to the female quarters and have sex with the woman assigned to them, when she first arrives. This woman they picked is usually their mate as long as they're in the prison—like was done in Siberia after the Second World War."

Mila gasped, the thought appearing to tear at her insides. "It's enough to make a woman kill herself."

"I think it's allowed because the Soviets don't want their male prisoners to become homosexuals."

"That figures," she huffed.

"Bedding their female prison mate almost each evening, is the only perk these prisoners get—but these beatings those men undergo with riding crops are exactly like the way the SS did prisoners. Gerado's expression shifted. "Have you heard about that?"

"Just a brief mention of it. And it's sad to know that for every six group of prisoners if somebody in the group does something wrong, they're all are punished. Which the guards will never admit to the prisoners what the wrong doing was...nor who did it. Then, two guards, on each end of the six prisoners, whip each man's back with a riding crop twenty-four times."

"And each man is stripped and made to kneel," Gerado affirmed, "his head on the floor. And when they finish the whippings they strike everyone's butt with a baton several times." He tensed. The painful memories of the abuse he'd received at the hands of his brothers and father never failed to hammer him with old fears and uncertainties. "And the prisoners cry like frightened children."

He took a breath of the chilly night air, as his mind flashed back to the sketch someone had done of their torture, which accompanied his article. "I'm stunned the prisoners can do any work after that."

She breathed a heavy sigh, "I don't know how they do it. But at least the guards give them some cream to rub on their cuts, and allow them to do upholstery work for a week before they go back to their hard labor."

"And the women?"

"Their job is to make clothes before they participate in the night's sexual activities."

The disturbance Gerado saw in Mila's eyes shattered their conversation for a moment.

"The Soviets do that in orphanages too..." Her tone drug as she stopped the car for a moment and blotted her eyes, "They're clouding with more anguish." She sniffed. "But anyway, the kids are divided in groups. And if someone does something wrong in that group, they all get whipped. I know because that's why Valery ran away from the orphanage when he was thirteen."

"A terrible way to control people."

"It is. Though, unfortunately, it does seem to work." Another minute passed before she asked, "Who told you about that Danil prison?"

"A colleague at a news conference in Spain," said Gerado. "He was a Russian who devised a way to get out of the Soviet Union." Then, after a contemplative moment passed he added, "his brother had been a prison guard there."

"A terrible job to have," Mila said, her hands tight on the wheel as she made the first turn.

This dark country road was narrowing, so it was more difficult for her to make the two additional turns. "How do you do it?" Gerado asked.

"By pretending my fingers are glued to the wheel."

"Good thinking."

The vegetation got denser, and the line of trees on each side of the road were so close, it made it difficult to see.

"You love Arina, don't you," Mila piped up suddenly.

"I do, "he answered, the mention of it unexpected.

"I know about Arina and Valery."

"You do?" he asked, trying to mask his jolt of surprise. "How'd you find out?"

"The looks they exchange. Which is the real reason he's working with you to find her father. But then again, despair squeezes my heart each time I think about my Nicky—the love of my life. And how my cruel father ordered his execution for a theft someone else committed."

They talked at length about it with Gerado confiding the marriage of possible convenience Valery wanted to occur between Arina and him was also something he'd wanted for her. 'Get her out of the Soviet Union,' were his words.

"She really should go." Mila said, her voice hardening. "And this idea that even if you do find Wallenberg, she'll be fortunate if she can be with him for only a few minutes."

Gerado now began to worry. Earlier he'd doubted the painting could lead them to Wallenberg. But if this Cowboy Bill had the missing piece that Manuel's colleagues declared they needed to confirm the location of those glyphs, then they stood a good chance of finding him. And if they did, what would happen to Mila and Valery...? Gerado knew instinctively that Marek Falin would probably have Valery executed if he found Wallenberg. And Mila? What would happen to her? From the way Falin was treating her, it wouldn't surprise him if he had her executed along with Valery. *So much to think about. So much to consider.*

He was about to discuss the matter with her when suddenly, he looked up and saw a huge light, the size of a car, hovering above the treetops. Mila slammed on her brakes. "Look at that!" she exclaimed. "What on earth is it?"

"An orb," Gerado answered, dumbstruck. "I know because I've interviewed a good many people who claim to have seen one."

Mila's voice appeared to flee for a moment as if struggling to find the courage to ask him, "Where's it from?"

"Nobody knows. UFO's...Angels...to name a few of the things people believe it comes from."

Then as quickly as the light came on, it went off. "Like a giant flashlight," Gerado murmured.

Fear threatened to smash Mila. "We've got to get out of her!" And putting her foot on the accelerator, she would have taken off had the car's engine not died. "No!" she screamed. "This can't be—"And that's when the man appeared. At least eight and a half inches tall, he was wearing a suit that shone like quicksilver.

"Have you ever seen anyone that tall?" she asked Gerado.

"Not that I can recall."

Her blood was obviously running cold. "B...because he's an *alien!*" Her hands trembled, and her voice shook in desperation. "You and Valery are tall, but this man's height defies description."

Gerado opened the car door. "I'll see what he wants."

"No!" Mila cried, grabbing his arm. "I have a pistol."

"Put it back, I'll be fine." He went over to he man and shook hands with him. "I'm Gerado Gerhart Behl."

"I know who you are, "the man said with a kindly look. "But what can I do for you?"

"We're having some car trouble. And being out here on this one lane road isn't a very good place to be stuck."

"Don't worry. Just get back in, and you'll be fine." He glanced at Mila, who looked like she was waiting for the blow to come.

"You have a painful bruise that isn't healing like it should," the man told her. "So if you'll allow me to touch it, then I'll make sure it does."

She turned her head tentatively, either not wanting to believe him or not able to find her tongue.

Finally, in nervous burst," she said, "G...go...uh ahead."

He pressed an index finger against her bruise, and a tiny gasp escaped her as her eyes widened with astonishment.

"Is it gone?" he asked.

She opened her mouth to answer, but whatever words she tried to form, fled from her lips as quickly as a mouse being chased by a cat.

Gerado scooted closer to her. "Your bruise is gone, Mila, and I'm not in pain any more." He looked up at the tall figure in the silver suit. "I somehow get the impression we've met, but I can't remember anything about it."

"It was a very long time ago, and you were quite young."

"I suspect you brought Isabella to me—"

"She *was* and *is* a gift." The man took Mila's hand. "You have a great sense of loss. And you're sad. But your husband is trying to atone for his previous actions in the past. So be good to him. He needs you. Particularly tonight." He pointed at a small, first-aid kit on the floor near her large purse. "If I can hold it for a moment, it should help him when you return to Kiev." His face was bright with encouragement.

Mila was still in such a daze, she just stared at him, transfixed. Prompting Gerado to hand the kit to him. And gazing at it as he held it, he watched it glow pink, then silver, then pink again, before it returned to its original tan color. Then, he handed it back.

Moonlight now flooded the trees, and a few twinkling stars as bright as Christmas ornaments were visible. Gerado smiled when some of the dark clouds began to lift which, to his astonishment, revealed a star-studded sky. "Can you believe all these stars?" he uttered. "When there was just a handful only a moment ago.

Mila, jerked from her daze, stepped from the car. "I think I should do this," she said, putting her arms around the man and giving him a hug.

He lowered his head to hers. "The goodness in your soul will allow you to overcome the sorrow you are feeling," he informed her in a gentle voice.

Gerado, also stepping from the car, went over to the man, and shook his hand again. "What you've done here—"

"—is what I was meant to do.

The words struck Gerado's heart.

"You're a good person," this man continued. "You are loved. You are kind...things that matter." He glanced skyward. "But just remember...when the time comes, you must let go of things that aren't meant to be."

He started to ask him a question, but before the words could form, the man disappeared...*like the fading image of a dream.* And then, the car started.

"W...was that an angel? "Mila asked, her gaze drifting to the front of the car where the man had first appeared.

"I do believe it was."

"Then that explains the sprinkles of gold I saw in your hair, when you were talking with him."

PART 2

PATHS

CHAPTER TWELVE

Thinking about all that had happened, Gerado waited until Mila had turned onto the two-lane highway, before he asked her. "If Valery's in need of a first-aid kit, do you think he's been injured."

"Could be." She slammed on her brake at a traffic light she came close to running. "And I phoned him before we left the hotel, but he couldn't be reached."

"We're supposed to be back at the hotel by nine tonight for dinner," Gerado reminded, watching the intersecting boulevards pile up with traffic. "Do you think Valery will be at the hotel waiting?"

"He should be."

"Why don't you call him on your car phone?"

"Too risky with all this traffic. "

"Then let me."

"I'd have to stop and hand it to you. And that'll slow us down."

He redirected his eyes to the traffic. "Probably will."

Twenty minutes passed with the traffic getting worse and worse. But the good thing was when they arrived at the hotel, Mila parked in front of it like her husband did.

Immediately, the doorman came over. But when she flashed one of Valery's badges at him, he simply said, "I'm so very sorry, Madam."

Gerado followed behind her as she dashed into the lobby, where Isabella and Arina were waiting in comfortable chairs near the door. In the background the radio played some mood-moving, gypsy music. Arina's favorite, since she maintained her finest violin teacher had been part of a gypsy family that Wallenberg had kept from being sent to Auschwitz.

"Where's Valery?" Mila asked.

"We haven't seen him." Isabella replied, her face gravitating toward the door.

Mila shot a glance at the reception desk. "Then I'd better try and call him right away."

She started toward it, when Valery suddenly appeared in the doorway... Purple shadows were under his eyes, fissures on his upper and lower lip, and bruises, the size of apricots, on each cheek.

Clearly stricken, Mila burst into tears. "What happened?"

"You have a father—I have a father-in-law...whose anger can be as vicious as a dragon's wrath. Which *today*, slammed me with its raw fury."

"Isabella and Arina gazed at Valery, astounded. "Have you seen a doctor?" they chorused.

"QuicK—Mila!" Gerado shouted."Get out that first-aid kit you shoved in your large purse, that our friend said you'd need."

Blinded with tears she had trouble gripping it, so Gerado grabbed it for her. It was glowing a faint pink and not tan, when he handed it to Valery. "Hold this for a minute, and you should be fine like me."

"And me," said Mila. She pointed at her temple. "Look. My bruise is gone—"

"H...how's this possible?" Valery gasped, touching her healed face, then his.

"An angel...we met an angel."

"An angel!" He gave her a look of utter astonishment.

"Could something like this happen any other way?"

"I...I can't think of any." He hesitated, baffled. "And I know angels aren't supposed to be discussed in the Soviet Union, but who gives a damn. The way I feel tonight, this country can go to hell!"

Clearly touched by what had happened, Isabella and Arina were in tears. "Easy now," Gerado said, giving them each a hug and a kiss. He stroked Isabella's hand. "This angel mentioned you, like my mother did before she died."

More tears flowed, until Mila burst out, "If this experience wasn't otherworldly enough, then wait till you hear what else happened. Which, after I tell you, you'll realize we have a full day ahead of us tomorrow. So we need to eat something *now*, or otherwise we're running the risk of collapsing."

"Then follow me to the dining room," Valery said, hooking his arm through hers.

"When that man appeared, I was so afraid I had my hand on my pistol."

"Your pistol?" he questioned. "Do you even know how to shoot one?"

"Yes I do—thanks to your friend Ustin Dimitri's teachings. He's turned me into an expert shot and have papers to prove it."

"Another reason for surprise. Can my world be knocked any further off-kilter by all I'm hearing tonight?" Valery asked, holding the edge of a dining chair to steady himself.

"After my beloved Nicky died, Ustin also taught me "Taekwondo, French Syvette, Karate, and Judo," Mila proceeded to inform him. "Because sometimes you need a combination of several in a fight."

"No wonder I never forced myself on you." Awareness continuing to shock him. "I wouldn't be standing here if I had."

"I'd have never harmed you."

"No, but your father harmed *you*. So why'd you let him?"

"Ustin said some things were best kept secret."

Gerado stared at Mila in awe. "Arina and I could have used you in that fight we had with those Red Army fellows in Minsk."

"Ustin said you did an amazing job."

"Arina helped me."

"Not really." She looked embarrassed. "All I did was hit one of those soldiers on the head with a garbage can lid—"

"Doesn't matter," Isabella replied, her eyes filled with praise. "You ladies are fantastic and if I were younger, I'd be following in your footsteps."

"One, two," Valery counted on his fingers. "Is this all the surprises we have for tonight, Mila?"

She didn't answer but directed them to take their dining seats and order. "We have a long day tomorrow."

At the waiter's suggestion Valery ordered wine, soup, salad, and smoked chicken with roasted potatoes. Dessert would be a Russian version of *apfelstrudle*.

"A pleasant addition." The waiter smiled.

When it was finished, Valery ordered another bottle of wine for the table. "Something tells me we're going to need it for whatever's coming next."

Mila rose as did Gerado. "Our cue to drop the thermite bomb," she announced.

"Thermite bomb?" Valery questioned, staring at her like she'd lost her mind. "Is this some kind of a joke? I know I burn papers for Marek in that large drum in back of our house, and in forty-five seconds they're ash. So what the hell are you talking about?"

"The missing piece of that painting." She lifted her chin with an air of self-confidence. "Gerado and I know where it is."

That was enough to make Valery, Isabella, and Arina stare at her, tongue-tied.

But before any questions could be asked, Mila began explaining how this piece had survived.

"Wallenberg's driver, Vilmos Langfelder, now called Cowboy Bill, managed to retrieve part of the painting when the Russians shot Wallenberg. Something they viewed this broken off piece as trash. So Cowboy Bill was been allowed to keep it. Which makes it easy for us, since he's now in the political prison close by we'll be visiting tomorrow."

"I know Abram Evanoff, the administer of that prison," Valery said. "And I've done some favors for him, so now it's his turn to do some favors for me."

Arina's eyes glistened with emotion. "D...do you think this Cowboy Bill will let us have his missing piece?"

"Without question." Valery didn't hesitate to assure her. "That man's been in prison for thirty-seven years. And all because he was the driver for a man who was coming to ask the Russians to give some financial help to the Russian Jews after the war—"

"How soon before you can get him out," Isabella broke in lightly.

"Tomorrow."

She shot a disbelieving look at him. "Won't he need papers—"

"—and a passport and plane ticket, which I'll get him. "

Valery's confident mood stymied Gerado for a moment as well as Isabella, from the look on her face.

"Where's he going?" Mila blurted.

"To Berlin, with Isabella."

The waiter was now refilling everyone's wine glasses. "Finding that missing piece of that painting is something none of us were expecting,"

Valery said, rising. "Which is why we should propose a toast to finding Wallenberg, in the hopes he'll get to spend the rest of his years with his lovely daughter."

"To Wallenberg and Arina!" repeated Mila, Isabella, and Gerado together, like a choir. They clinked their wine glasses and raised them in Arina's direction.

"Is this really happening?" she asked after a moment.

Gerado's hand covered hers possessively. "It is. And make no mistake, we *will* find your father."

Isabella peered at Valery. "But what time tomorrow will I go to Berlin with Wallenberg's former driver?"

"If our luck holds—as I feel certain it will—I'll have plane tickets for tomorrow afternoon."

A silence billowed between them as she appeared to give it some serious thought. "If this driver hasn't been out in the regular world for thirty-seven years, how am I supposed to handle him?"Isabella asked, scooting closer to Mila. "What if he breaks and runs, once we arrive in Berlin?"

"The lady we visited said he was a very good-natured fellow who calls himself, Cowboy Bill. So I don't see a problem," Mila replied.

"Then he can live in my vacant house in Tuscany," Isabella remarked without question.

"Let me elaborate," said Valery. "This Cowboy Bill's been in several of our political prisons. But he was transferred to Vladeti Prison, here, because of the rumor circulating that Arina was Wallenberg's daughter." His eyes focused on Isabella. "In the beginning he called himself Wallenberg, because he was playing that role. Since it's believed Wallenberg was driving when the Soviets took him."

"A convoluted mess." Mila shook her head, followed by a sigh.

Valery shifted his attention to Gerado. "At his first prison everybody believed he was deranged because he kept calling himself Wallenberg. But even so, they thought the day might possibly come when he could reveal something about Wallenberg...Was he shot in the country and had died? Or had be been rescued and was in hiding?

No one had an answer, but eventually words from a greedy neighbor in the country close to where Wallenbeg was living, informed the Soviets as to his location—"

"And they swooped down on him like a hungry pterodactyl," Arina recalled.

"A flying dinosaur." Gerado remarked, shaking his head. "That figures—"

"—with no one we know of, ever seeing her father again," Valery disclosed. "A reason that makes me suspect this Cowboy Bill was kept around, just in case some questions might arise. Which now, they have. And all because of a piece of a painting nobody considered anything more than trash."

After a long silence, Isabella beamed a little. "Vilmos Langfelder befriended Manuel. So he'll probably hang around to be with him."

Leaning closer to Isabella, Gerado whispered. "Even with Manuel in Berlin, I can't stop worrying about your being there...With my two crazy brothers and their SS friends in the same town."

"Manuel will look after me."

"I know he'll try, but he's quite busy these days at the university. The same as he and his colleagues, who're trying to locate information about that painting."

Gerado tightened his grip around his wine glass. "Just be careful," he warned. His brothers were like two snakes in a freeze frame looking for a way to strike, but as yet had been unable to do so. *But how can I help Isabella and Bill?* Then, in a flash it came to him. "You have copies of pictures, Isabella, in your satchel of my brothers in their SS uniforms when they were in their teens...along with a recent copied picture of them from a newspaper. So make sure our Cowboy Bill also has some copies."

"I'll have some made before I leave here." Gerardo smiled at her, and she smiled back.

"Certainly something to think about if this Bill's playing cowboy."

"It is. Because you can tell him he has a new assignment as sheriff and needs to keep a lookout for my two wicked brothers."

"Good idea. Although it would help if he had a cowboy hat and boots—"

Gerado frowned. "Something I'm afraid I don't have."

"No, but Manuel does. A colleague gave him a hat and boots, but they're too large. So, hopefully they'll fit our cowboy."

"Which should help solve our problem if they do."

Before Mila and Valery left, he instructed everyone to meet them here in the morning at six a.m. for breakfast. "That way we'll have the early start we need in the Volga to Vladeti Prison. And bring your violins. It's only a small group of prisoners at this place, but they'll enjoy hearing you play."

"If we take the Volga, won't it signal my father where we're headed?" Mila asked.

"I could care less." He put his arms around her, and she gave him a light kiss on the brow. "I think when he sees how I'm healed, he'll be in for a shock. But any more questions from anyone?"

"That outline I gave you," said Gerado, feeling the need for some enlightment. "Did you get a chance to show it to Marek?"

The look on Valery's face was expressionless. "I chose not too."

Gerado stared at him in stunned despair. "After what we went through?" He inhaled deeply. "For God's sake—that was your bargaining chip. Which, if you'd chosen to use, Marek might not have knocked you around the way he did."

"I know. But if I'd used it, you could have easily ended up having to write an article, confirming that our Wallenberg imposter was the man Arina believed to be her father...That was the main thing he wanted. And of course, the other thing was that painting Manuel took to Berlin."

"Hard to believe you'd risk yourself like that," Gerado replied, continuing to be swept with a deep sense of awe.

"Don't worry, I can handle it," Valery ground out. "But Arina—she's gone through a lot of agony over the years—"

"I gathered that."

"Then you understand how she must feel. Wallenberg committed no crime, yet we Soviets have had him for a little over twenty-two years. With Israel begging them for information about him. Information I'll make certain to give them when we find him."

"But won't that be risky?" Gerado asked.

"No matter. For Arina's sake, I'm taking matters into my own hands." He made a broad, courtly sweep with his arm.

Instantly, a concern for their safety tore through Gerado. *Terrible risk he's taking.* And he simmered in frustration as the thought resonated in his brain: *Only God knows how Valery must love Arina.*

★★★

Later, hearing sniffling in the hallway, Gerado swung around. Isabella had her hands on Arina's shoulders attempting to console her.

"What's the matter?" he asked her.

"Just some bad memories when the Soviets took her father."

Arina wiped her eyes, though her tears continued to rise. "I'll tell him about it, Isabella. So get some sleep since you've got a flight to catch tomorrow afternoon."

Gerado hugged Isabella. "We'll be up directly, but how about we three wear our blue jeans and tennis shoes tomorrow, when we meet Cowboy Bill?"

"That's a great idea. And I'll call Valery and Mila when they get home, and see if they want to do the same. But first, I'm sending a telegram to Manuel about the missing piece of that painting."

"He certainly needs to know."

After she left, Gerado took Arina's hand in his and escorted her back to the lobby. "Now tell me everything about what happened to your father."

She stared at his hand in hers, and then at him, as she sat down stiffly on the lobby's white sofa.

She often sat like she was on alert, ready to bolt up. *Waiting with eagerness for someone to appear...Wallenberg, undoubtedly. A habit she'd probably developed as a child after he'd been taken.*

She then began recounting what had happened. "It was 1960 before the Soviets finally found my father and came to arrest him. A neighbor, who was his dear friend, knocked on our door. He warned us the Soviets were just a few farmhouses away. We were scared and my mother and I began to tremble, with my father ransacking our small house trying to find a place to hide. But in the end, there was only our one closet. So he resorted to the old trick of straightening our footwear on the closet's floor and hiding behind its clothing. His boots would show, but the position he was in, made it look they were just part of our footwear."

Gerado tightened his grip on Arina's hand. "It was a clever thing to do."

"My father was a very clever man. And when the knocking began, Mom and I tried to act calm. The knocking continued, getting louder and louder, with demands to open the door. But we didn't comply until we were certain my father was so well-hidden in the closet, no one could tell anything was in it but clothes and shoes.

"My mother then started toward the door. But before she could open it, they broke the lock, and three men in uniform stomped in. 'You're husband's under arrest!' they shouted at her. 'So you'd better tell us where he is!' She told them he'd gone to town to make some purchases and had no idea when he'd return. However, they were welcome to search the place. And search they did—with no results. I suspected they were about to grab my mother and I, when one of the soldiers stopped suddenly, 'I just remembered a hiding game my son used to play.' And turning abruptly he want back to the closet and began going through our clothes. In seconds he found my father. 'My son used to hide so good, that if people saw his shoes, they'd think they were just closet shoes,' the soldier bragged. 'Never suspecting he was actually wearing them.'"

Gerado 's eyes were downcast. "I can imagine how you felt, "he replied, in a tone bleak with sorrow, "They stole his life."

"My mother had her medicines, and I had my violin I was attempting to learn to play from my music instructor in my primary school. These two things were what kept my mother and I from falling apart. And after she passed, my violin was all I had until Valery showed up."

Up until now if Gerado had sensed a distance between him and Arina, but he'd ignored it. Though now it appeared to be widening. So, he had to face it and ask the question, *What had the angel meant by letting go of things not meant to be? Was he talking about this relationship I crave between Arina and me? Even if she acts like she and Valery are growing worlds apart, with each passing day. Probably so, because it's becoming quite obvious they're still close.*

"It's good you and Valery shared a little happiness. And I know you'll always love him but—"

"I do want to make love to you, Gerado." She emphasized his name. "Regardless of what you may think."

What could he say? How long had it been since he'd had a woman? Too long. And he'd adored her from the beginning. No—loved her...It was getting quite difficult for him to hold back. Especially after her offer. *But if she loves me, it's not the same emotional feelings she continues to show for* Valery.

A sobering thought. Does she really want me, or am I just the best she can do?

Tonight was clearly not the right time for them. Yet, she needed some warmth and comfort after reliving that horrible time, when the Soviets had torn the door down and arrested her father.

"We're emotionally drained," he told her. "And tonight is not the good time for us."

Then he began to think about the idea he'd suggested to Mila about bonding with Valery. '*Sleep together in your clothes.*' Certainly worth a try with Arina. "Considering the missing piece of your painting this Cowboy Bill allegedly has, tomorrow can either be a good day or a bad day...We're both on edge. So how about if we comfort each other by sleeping together in our clothes? You need some good sleep. And having someone to snuggle with can be an easy way to get it."

"You're right there," she quickly agreed, making him suspect she knew all about it from Valery.

★★★

Gerado telephoned Isabella once Arina was in the bath in his room. "She's staying with me tonight—but don't get your hopes up. She's still very much in love with Valery, so we're sleeping together in our clothes."

"Damnit!" was Isabella's word before hanging up.

When Arina returned from her bath, she'd put back on the navy dress she'd worn at dinner.

Why was he deluding himself? What was he expecting...? That she'd throw on one of those fluffy white robes reserved for guests, over her naked body? He knew better, but it didn't stop him from dreaming.

He was still wearing his shirt, denim jacket, and blue jeans, and probably should have showered. But after that angel touched him, he'd felt so clean it didn't seem necessary.

Arina seemed eager to get some sleep, so when she crawled in bed with him she placed her body against his, spoon-fashion. Her way of deliberately snuggling closer? Although, what really surprised him was the light kiss she leaned over and placed on his forehead. For a moment he was excited, until he recognized it as an apology kiss. *Like the one my mother gave me after my father beat me so violently.* And it surprised him, that as young as he'd been, he could still remember it.

CHAPTER THIRTEEN

Gerado looked forward to viewing the Vladeti Prison, a name that meant *rule*. '*It's like a country club with a gated community,*' he recalled Zella saying.

He'd been in country clubs in the states, but this was the Soviet Union. "A prison that's sure to make a good news story with or without Cowboy Bill," he told Isabella.

This detention center for select individuals was in a wooded area, a good distance from the city on a secluded estate. "The average person would give up his liberty to live in a place like this," Valery remarked, smiling.

"I can imagine," Gerado said, admiring it. "Because I've never seen a prison like this before."

"Which you'll probably never see again."

Two prison guards opened the iron gates for their luxury Volga, with Valery flashing his badge at them before the car headed down a winding, paved road toward a two-story house. It had huge, white porch columns. "Looks like something you'd see outside Atlanta before the Civil War," Gerado commented.

"It had once been an elaborate two-story house owned wealthy Jews," Valery explained, gazing out the car's window. "But after Stalin passed, the architect, who was as obsessed with the film *Gone With the Wind* as Adolph Hitler had been, turned it into a southern-looking plantation house."

Gerado's expression became one of concern. "I hope this architect didn't get in any trouble."

"He didn't. Because he kept insisting that we Russians could build a house like that too—but much better."

The place had a manicured lawn. And curving stones, set in cement, lined a wide sidewalk leading to a porch with a balcony. There were some comfortable-looking lawn chairs on the porch behind the white columns.

Large signs hung from the columns, directing prisoner and guests toward a golf course, pool, garden, and a roasting pit for smoking.

The prisoner administrator must have been watching, because when the Volga pulled up, he came out of the attractive front door with ornate, filigree work above it. He and Valery shook hands, before the introductions began. "Abram Evanoff, and I pleased to meet you," he announced.

He was a tall man with gray hair, and eyes as brown as cultivated-earth. And his face broke into a smile when he saw Gerado. "I'm honored to have such a well-known news reporter visiting us, plus Kiev's lovely violinist. Which is one of the reasons we're having an early lunch for everyone. With beef and chicken kabobs already being smoked in the roasting pit."

"And the other reason?" Mila asked.

"When Valery phoned and said Cowboy Bill would be leaving, we here were all overcome with grief. Everybody loves Bill, and there was never any trouble with any of the prisoners, with our good boy, Bill, always around to cheer them up."

Mila's face brightened. "What I suspected."

Unfortunately, we have a problem that demands you release Bill," Valery said. "So if you can help me with this paperwork in my briefcase, I'd be much obliged." He gestured at Isabella, adding, "Considering time is of the essence since she and Bill have a three p.m. flight today."

"We'll get right on it," said Abram. "But in the meantime, Bill's in the communal room waiting to meet everyone. So after introductions, your friends can talk with him while we work on getting his release papers and passport."

Abram led them into a large reception area. The room had slated marble walls with an overstuffed velvet sofa and matching chairs, next to a fireplace.

Acting excited to meet them, Bill got up from the sofa and dashed over. "I'm so happy you fine folks are here," he said, pumping Valery's and Gerado's hands. "And I'm told you all speak English which has become my first language—'cause it's the way the cowboys talk. And even with all them translations on the TV screen, I didn't read 'um, but just listened to the cowboys."

"You're wearing blue jeans," remarked Isabella, surprised.

"A gift from the good people who work here. And believe me, they weren't cheap."

"But you need some boots and a cowboy hat...and believe *me*, when I say my brother Manuel has some that will probably fit you. In fact, I'll phone him and have him bring them to you at the airport when we arrive in Berlin this afternoon."

"That'll be we real nice, Miss Isabel, 'cause Manuel and I go way back. And you can't imagine how happy I am that we're gonna be together again."

Valery and Abram encouraged everyone to have a seat." They've some important questions for you, Bill," Abram said, before he and Valery left.

Mila took a seat on the sofa beside Bill and Arina sat on the other side, so he was sandwiched between them. "I find it hard to believe I'm sitting next to Wallenberg's daughter." His eyes glowed as he took her hand.

"And I find it hard to believe I'm sitting next to someone who has the missing piece of my painting."

"Pull up your chairs," Mila encouraged Gerado and Isabella. "That way you won't have to strain to see it."

Arina waited until they had, before she reached in her purse and removed a copy of the painting. "Manuel has the original, but this will have to make-do until you get to Berlin."

There was a folder on the coffee table in front of the sofa. "It's in here", he said, opening the folder and removing the small piece of the painting he'd managed to keep for thirty-seven years. Your father loved this painting, and I did too. Which is the reason I kept this piece, even if I was told many times that it was just trash...But you couldn't fool me. I knew who'd owned it. And I used to dream that one day I'd be able to tape it back with the original."

Mila took out a notepad and pen form her jacket pocket, the same as Gerado was doing. "There's writing on the upper part of the painting. And I'm told there was some on the lower part, which you memorized before it faded," hc said.

"That I did."

"We're thankful you remember it," Mila said, preparing to write.

"The Soviets thought I had amnesia, but I fooled 'um," Bill bragged. "But what the writing said was:

"IF DARKNESS FALLS, AND YOU CAN'T FIND YOUR WAY. THEN THOSE WHO LOVE YOU WILL FIND A PATH USING THIS PAINTING, THAT WILL GUIDE THEM BACK TO YOU."

Shocked and thrilled, Gerado stood bolt upright. "That's exactly what we're been wanting to hear!"

Arina's eyes gleamed. "Because my father's expecting us."

Seeing her so happy soothed Gerado's heart.

Isabella wiped her eyes. "Those words bring tears to my eyes."

Mila tore off a page from her notepad and handed it to her. "I wrote what Bill read so you can give it to Manuel and his colleagues."

"Have we any tape?" Arina asked, holding up the copy of her painting. "If you don't mind, Bill, I want to attach your missing piece to my copy."

"I don't mind."

"I'll get some tape from Valery," said Mila, rising—"

"No wait." Gerado stalled her, retrieving his seat. "Bill's about to show us the missing piece of the painting, so don't go anywhere."

"Are we ready?" Bill asked.

Everyone nodded.

He took a deep breath, then released it, before taking his part of the painting and turning it several ways. "Gives ya'll a very good look."

For an endless moment they all appeared to be in such a state of shock that no words were exchanged.

"W...why it's a giant's hand." Arina finally said, mesmerized.

Gerado stood back up to get a better look. "And it seems this six-fingered, giant's hand is pointing westward."

"I knew it!" Isabella exclaimed. "Manuel mentioned something about a colleague claiming to have seen some pictures with glyphs and a giant's hand in North Carolina."

Gerado continued to stare at the picture as he asked Bill the question—that to date—no one had been able to answer. "Do you have any idea how Wallenberg got this painting? Apparently, due to his partial amnesia as a result of his head wound, he was never able to remember."

Bill looked at Gerado in confusion. "I never asked him, but he did tell me a strange story about it before his head wound. "

Arina went completely still. "Was it near the Finnish border?"

He ignored the question but proceeded to explain how Wallenberg was nine years old and on vacation when he received the painting. He was in a forest with an older cousin who liked to bird watch. When, suddenly, in the darker part of the forest they saw a very tall man. His cousin joked that he didn't see a problem such a tall fellow would have bird watching... And this man must have heard him, because he came over to Wallenberg. 'This is for you, little man,' he told him, handing him the small, framed painting. 'So keep it close and don't ever lose it.'

And then, this tall fellow seemed to vanish before his very eyes.

"He was obviously an angel," Mila blurted.

"Obviously." Gerado agreed.

A silence passed before Isabella stood up. "I need to phone Manuel and read him the faded part on the back and inform him this missing part of the painting confirms what his friend said."

"Then follow me," said Mila. "I have to go to the office and tell Valery. And also, get Arina some tape.

While they were gone Gerado handed Bill, a *before* and *after* picture of his two wicked brothers living in Berlin. He told him what they'd done to Isabella and warned him to keep a lookout for them, in case they showed up.

"Outlaws are my specialty," Bill said proudly. "And I've no objection to shootin' an owl hoot in the back if they try to mess with Miss Isabel and Manuel."

Arina's eyes snagged Gerado's. "Where will he get a pistol?" she asked him.

"He won't have one. So let's hope the need doesn't arise."

A few minutes later Mila and Isabella returned. "Manuel is teaching, but he knows we'll be staying at the Hotel Metropolitan. However, his student assistant, Ernst, the nephew of my brother's ex-wife, Eva, took the message about the cowboy hat and boots for Bill. I explained to Ernst, that Bill had been Wallenberg's driver, and this was important. The main reason being the missing piece of the painting he had, appeared to confirm the information Manuel's friend from the states had given him. Then, maybe I shouldn't have done it. But I read Ernst the faded message that was on the back, and he wrote it down for Manuel."

Valery appeared shortly afterwards. "We're certainly better off now, than we were. And thanks to you, Cowboy Bill." He went over and shook his hand again. "But are you all packed and ready to leave with us after our lunch?"

"We're got your passport, release papers, plane ticket, and Valery and Mila's phone numbers in this," said Abram, handing him a folder. "Have you got a bag to put them in?"

"I'm only taking a canvas tote bag. And it's down here." He pointed at the floor. "I left most of my stuff for my friends here, who were always saying they wanted something belonging to me."

"Let me put that folder in my satchel here," Isabella suggested. "And I'll also put that copied painting with it's taped missing piece on it, in here. Since I consider this satchel to be my luggage."

"Be glad to." Bill reached down and handed the folder to her, and Arina handed her the copied painting.

"Bill's making a short speech and saying good-bye to his friends before lunch," said Abram. The expression in his eyes clearly showed a pang of regret at Bill's departure. "Valery brought a bottle of champagne he kept iced down in the back of the Volga, and he means for us to have a glass before lunch."

Abram motioned at two waiters standing in the doorway. One had the bottle of champagne, and the other a tray of glasses.

Valery waited until everyone's glass was full before he stood up and announced, "Last night Mila and I became official husband and wife."

Everyone, including Arina, applauded, even if she did have a downcast expression on her face.

Glasses echoed against one another, with Valery taking Mila in his arms and kissing her. She returned his kiss. "I regret that I didn't realize it sooner, but I'm very fortunate to have Valery for my husband. Even if he did tease me after we married, that I didn't need to do anything but see the beds were made."

"We're being summoned,' said Abram. "The prisoners are waiting in folding chairs for Bill to speak. And afterwards, Valery tells me that Arina and Gerado are going to play a few pieces on their violins. So follow me."

Outside was a podium with twenty-five chairs for the prisoners, and a few for the guests.

And when Bill took his place behind the podium there was standing applause, with every prisoner appearing to be shedding tears.

Bill explained his deep sorrow at leaving everyone, but duty called. He had an assignment to go up against the neo-Nazi SS who were said to be creating quite a disturbance in Berlin. "So don't be so miserable looking, since I must do what I must do, to protect the innocent." That brought such a thunderstorm of applause the other prisoners got out of their chairs and went up to the podium. They lined up so they could each give Bill a hug. "And by the way," he continued, "at my suggestion, our fine prison administrator, Abram Evanoff, is bringing in some emotional therapy dogs that should give you plenty of comfort."

The prisoners thanked Abram with applause, who nodded graciously at them, before waving Arina and Gerado to come forward with their violins. "And now some music from two very accomplished musicians," he announced. "So resume your seats."

Applause followed as they took their places and waited for the signal from Abram for the music to begin.

A few moments passed, with everyone settled comfortably back in his chair, before Abram waved his hand at them. Arina glanced at Gerado, and they exchanged grins as they slid their bows over their strings.

Within seconds one of several perky, gypsy songs began livening the air. *Sheer magic*. Gerado's breath caught. *My heart is beating to the pulse of the music*.

At the conclusion of their performance the dinner bell rang, and everyone was directed to line up at a table with plates and cutlery near the roasting pit. Two waiters served them and when their plates were full, they took their seats at tables scattered across the lawn. Three additional waiters put large bottles of wine on each table.

There were seven seats at a round table where Valery sat with his group and Cowboy Bill, along Abram. Everyone complimented the beef and chicken kebobs, as well as the side dishes accompanying them: compote-filled fruit bowls, potatoes, stuffed cabbage rolls, and homemade bread. But the big surprise was dessert—vanilla ice cream, dipped in chocolate and covered in coconut. A *Snowball* it was called, and Russian tea was served with it to make it even more enjoyable.

Valery shook his head in disbelief. "What on earth did we do to rate ice cream, Abram?"

"Something we have on special occasions which, today, is one of them."

Bill asked if he could have a second, and being the guest of honor, his request was quickly granted. He was diving into it when Abram's secretary dashed up. "Just got a phone call from Ustin Dimitri. And he says to tell you Marek Falin's headed our way." She sounded frightened. "With possibly some company."

CHAPTER FOURTEEN

Gerado opened his mouth, then hesitated, their predicament hitting him like a boulder.

"I said my father would find out where we were when we reserved that Volga," Mila reminded, tilting her head in Valery's direction.

He gave a brisk smile. "And I told you it didn't matter. So let him come." He said it like a man who'd been emboldened to show no sigh of fear. "Though I do think it wise if Isabella and Cowboy Bill get in the Volga and head straight to the airport."

"And to think I was about to ask for a third dessert," Bill remarked. "But with outlaws comin,' a man has to put aside what's pleasant and to tend to business."

Since their personal effects were in large, cloth bags, and the Volga was parked on the driveway, it made it easy for Isabella and Bill to get up and head toward the Volga. She waved at everybody, thanking them. But Bill stopped a moment before loping off toward the Volga at Valery's urging.

Arina and Gerado followed behind them, stopping only when Isabella did. "Do be careful," he warned, kissing her on the brow. "Because as you know, it appears my brothers are staying in Berlin longer than usual. And I suspect they already know they can't find Wallenberg, unless they use us to find him...So, since their hellbent on hanging Wallenberg, they're probably keeping an eye on Manuel."

"That's true, and I'll be very careful" she promised, returning his kiss. "Because you'll always be my little boy."

She grabbed a hug from him. "And you'll always be my angel godmother."

"What about phone numbers?" Mila asked her. "

"Valery has Manuel's. And you and he will be getting mine as soon as Bill and I check into our hotel."

Mila patted Isabella's hand. "Phone us every hour or so."

"My intention."

Arina also patted her hand. And smiling, Isabella planted a light kiss on the cheek before climbing into the Volga.

"I hope they don't have any problems," Gerado told Arina, watching, as the car sped away.

Her hand squeezed his shoulder. "So do I."

When the car was finally out of sight, they went back to the table and picked up their violin cases, next to where they'd been sitting. Everything was strangely deserted. "Where is everybody?" Gerado asked Abram.

"In their rooms. I told them with Marek coming, it would be a good idea for them to stay out of sight."

"And us?"

"Why don't you spend a little time in the garden relaxing until Marek comes?"

"Good idea as long as Arina and I aren't very far from Valery and Mila."

"They'll be with me in the communal room," Abram said, "but let me take your violin cases." They handed them to him, and once Gerado's hand was free, he took Arina's and stoked it. "The garden has some colorful flowers and a large white bench where we can talk."

"Wait!" called Valery, rushing over with Mila. "Ustin's phoned again and his sources are telling him that seeing we're at the prison, Marek's called the prison Bill was in before he was transferred to Vladeti."

"Did he learn anything?" Gerado asked, trying to mask his trepidation.

"Ustin suspects the prison administrator mentioned something about that folded paper of the painting Bill carried around, with the giant's hand on it." Valery looked from Arina to Gerado. "But if you two don't feel safe here, then I'll arrange for a car to drive you back to the hotel."

Gerado lifted Arina's hand. "What do you say?"

"That we should stay with Valery and Mila."

"I agree. Considering the way they're doing all they can to lookout for us."

Valery took Gerado's hand. "I was an only child, but in the short time you've been here you've done so much for Mila and me, I wish you were my brother."

"No reason not to be,"Gerado said. "Blood ties don't make for brothers." It didn't matter he'd been Arina's lover, he liked Valery. And in the brief time he and Isabella had been in the Soviet Union, he was amazed at how Valery had done all he could for them. Something that seemed to be more than just wanting them to get Arina to Italy. *His actions have truly generated a feeling of brotherhood between us.*

Valery paused, and gave his forearm a pat. "Then I accept your very exceptional offer."

Mila gave Gerado a light kiss on the lips. "Having you for a brother-in-law is great!" She also took Arina's hand and smiled tenderly. "You're going to be happy with Gerado, like I am with Valery."

"So go spend some time in the garden," Valery encouraged, puffing on a cigarette. "And Mila and I will be keeping a lookout for Marek, and let you know when he comes."

"Did anyone ever figure out why Marek's so anxious to get this painting?" Gerado asked.

"Ustin believes Moscow's threatened to kill him,"Mila answered, adding,"should anyone under his watch, discover Wallenberg's whereabouts."

"I'm prepared to deal with Marek," Valery reiterated to Gerado. "So you and Arina go to the garden like you were planning."

★★★

Gerado inhaled deeply. The garden was a small square enclosed by a tan rock wall. And with the woods being near by, the branches of their tall trees made rustling sounds as they scratched against each other.

The air in the garden smelled like lilac, which appeared to be twined with rose bushes, bougainvillea, and numerous multi-colored flowers. It was a place of staggering beauty...enhanced by billowing pink clouds floating across a luminous blue sky.

Gerado was fortunate to be alone with Arina in such a place. *Does she want me or not? A question I continue to ask myself, with her body language giving me mixed signs. I can usually tell when people are lying, but right now it seems my emotions are creating a huge, stumbling block.*

Maybe talking more with her would close the distance. Since I'm anxious to know what she's thinking.

Was it her love for Valery, with whom she could never have, that was causing the mixture of sadness and pain in her face? Expressions Gerado doubted he'd never be able to forget.

Like him, as had been pointed out earlier, she was a wounded soul. But his wounds had been easier with which to deal because of Isabella and Antonio. So could he ease Arina's wounds like they'd eased his?

In the past he'd had some passionate love affairs with women: one a wealthy realtor, another a TV actress in a series, and several others with similar careers.

These women had found him handsome. *'Like a film star,'* they'd say. Yet, they'd been intent on advancing their careers and using his notoriety as a news reporter to help them do it.

"Tell me more about Valery," Gerado began, swallowing his pride. "Of course you know he and Mila's marriage is working now. And believe it or not I'm happy for him and her."

She gulped hard, tears sliding down her cheeks. "Although it's painful for me, but sweet for Valery. Since with the exception of my mother and father, Valery cared about me like no one I've ever never known."

Well, haven't I also cared about you? I've helped you financially in your effort to locate your father. And never asked for anything in return.

But her affair with Valery was over...a married man with wife problems no longer.

Once again she confided she'd known from the beginning their affair would be brief. Despite the fact Valery and Mila were two unhappy people forced into a marriage, from which there seemed no escape.

Gerado's thoughts swam as he contemplated what he might do for her. He'd certainly try to sooth her, even if he had no real proof she wanted him. A reason that made him wonder whether or not she'd listen to him? What was he to her, when she looked at Valery the way she did? *If only I could hold her like I did when I gave her that goodnight kiss.*

Something so wonderful it was almost more than he could bear. So why did he have to be the perfect gentleman and not take her to bed? *Was it because we'd just met? Or was it because of the looks she and Valery had exchanged at the champagne supper? I barely knew her, yet seeing her with him—his mistress—increased my despair. Especially, when I envisioned Valery holding her; an image that brought me more pain.*

At least, Arina had been honest enough to admit to me she'd promised Valery she'd make the effort to become involved with me when I arrived in Kiev. 'You have no future behind the Iron Curtain,' he'd imagined him saying. 'And I intend to protect you...which means getting you out of this country. Something I feel certain Gerado will help me do. And as for your father, you'll have to just visit with him briefly, since he'll be forced to remain here.'

So down deep, what does that really mean? Gerado questioned. *That Arina and I will just be friends? If it was, then why in the Minsk hospital, had she offered him sex when they returned to Kiev?*

He'd kept her from being raped, but he doubted it was her reason for the offer. It seemed too ionic...arousing his suspicions that she'd offered herself to him because of the money he'd spent trying to help her find her father. What else could it be? Why would she do it, when her heart still belonged to Valery?

Of course, feeling like he did about her, he wasn't going to refuse her in the bedroom. What man could get enough of a woman like Arina? 'None with a brain,' he'd said.

Then, another thought occurred to him. Did she need sex from him to help her forget about Valery? Possibly. *It's not exactly like she's exploding with love or concern for me—seeing the difficulty she's having letting go of her feelings for Valery.* It hung between them like a dark thunder cloud, stifling his urge to embrace her.

Gerado ran his fingers through his hair. *Damn it! Yesterday my world was spinning, but today it's splintering...a peculiar time.*

When Isabella and Antonio had come into his life, they'd made sure he was the master of his destiny. And if there had been reservations about his joining the German army they'd, nevertheless, respected his decision.

Isabella's arms, always there to embrace him, had helped ease his pain after his father's abuse. But regretfully, he couldn't seem to ease Arina's.

Suddenly, a Volga rolled up in the driveway, and an angry-looking man, not waiting for the chauffeur, opened the door and bolted out. "Marek Falin, has to be him," said Gerado, shifting uncomfortably.

He and Arina both rose quickly, heading toward the porch where Marek, smelling of bourbon, was yelling at Abram. "Bring the prisoner to me who has the rest of that painting!" he ordered.

"Can't because he's gone," Mila said, stepping onto the porch. Valery was directly behind her.

Marek's mouth opened as if to ask, 'gone where? ' When seeing his son-in-law, without a mark on his face, closed his mouth like a man paralyzed with numbness.

"Come in and have a seat," Abram invited. He motioned at the burgundy sofa before locking the door. "How about some coffee?"

Marek made no reply but pointed in the direction of Valery and asked him with a sneer, "What'd you do?"

He didn't answer, but Mila did. "An angel."

"Angel?" Marek spat. It was obvious the word upset him. "Soviets do not discuss angels, which is religion."

"Then give me your explanation about what happened?" Valery asked, refocusing the conversation.

"It's these damned space aliens who land in our country, because it's so big. Something that makes it easy for them to hide. And they often do, unless they get picked up on radar and shot down by our fighter pilots."

"It *was* an angel," Gerado spoke up. "I know because I'd met him before."

"Then that explains everything," Marek fumed. "These aliens are up to something no good because that prison official, where this Bill fellow was previously incarcerated, said the part of the painting he had was a six-fingered giant's hand pointing westward at something...Which means those glyphs on the upper part of the painting have to be some kind of alien language, since nobody's been able to read them."

Valery arched his brows. "If this is true then why is Wallenberg and this painting attracting these aliens?"

"Most likely it's a way of stirring up trouble between us and the Israelis." Marek scowled. "Who won't stop asking about Wallenberg. So, if they can get a war started between us, then I suspect these aliens will take advantage of it, and establish some bases down here. A necessary distraction."

"The Israelis aren't stupid enough to start a war with Russia—"

A sudden, furious pounding at the front door ended Valery's sentence.

"Are these the others we suspected might be coming?" Abram asked, glancing at the door **warily**.

"Has to be."

"Open up!" yelled a male voice.

The knocking got louder, followed by some angry shouts and cursing from another male voice.

"Better let um' in," Marek advised. "My men won't stop until you do."

Mila and Valery exchanged censured glances, with Arina and Gerado doing likewise. "Ill-disciplined troops, like those soldiers in Minsk," he reminded her.

Valery turned to Marek with a grim expression. "Knowing you the way I do, I'd expect you to bring company."

The louder the knocking got, the more fearful the look on Abram's face, like something bad was going to befall them.

A moment passed, then another. Although, Marek said not a word.

"Just silence punctuating his response," Gerado remarked with a quiet emphasis.

"Want me to open it?" Valery finally asked his father-in-law.

Still no answer.

'More company out there, like the secretary said,' Gerado considered reminding. "Which is unfortunate for us. "

"Who's out there, Val?" Mila pressed, stepping over to him.

"Two Red Army soldiers," he remarked, glancing out a window with a burgundy velvet curtain not far from the door. "And they're wearing khaki caps, that have a red and gold star sewn on them."

Mila looked from her husband to Gerado. "I feel certain these soldiers hid under blanket covers in the back seat of the Volga as it drove through the gates—"

"Let um' in!" Marek demanded.

"Go ahead, Valery," Abram urged. He shifted back and forth, making it obvious his fear was growing. "Our locks aren't that hard to turn."

"Guess they aren't, " Valery remarked stepping toward the door. "Because who'd want to leave this attractive place."

There were two locks, and he turned them twice before these soldiers—one bony and one wiry, paused in the doorway. They each had a pistol, their uniforms were smudged with dirt, and they smelled of bourbon.

"Most likely from some of my father-on-law's imported liquor," Valery remarked with a disgusted look.

The soldiers marched into the entry with an exhilarated triumphant that reminded Gerado of the SS soldiers he'd seen in movies when they tromped into houses, to arrest Jews. *The way my bullying brothers liked to act,* he recalled angrily.

"Please, all of you," Abram said, like he knew what was coming. "Let's have some coffee and pastries.

Like a good host it was obvious he was trying hard to be pleasant, gesturing for the soldiers to be seated.

But they ignored him. And instead the wiry one picked up a silver, serving tray on the coffee table, and the bony one a silver vase. Their icy features stared at Marek. "You said we could take what we wanted," the bony one reminded.

"Anything but my daughter," he said.

"Who happens to be my wife," Valery reminded. "And not just in name only. In fact, there's a chance she could be pregnant."

Words that appeared to shock Marek.

Gerado glared at him. Events were colliding. *What would Marek have these soldiers do? Some sign. Some indication—please!*

Arina shook like she was having a nervous spasm. "What's going to happen?" she asked in a hushed whisper.

Apprehension coursed through Gerado at the shameless, indecent way these two soldiers were eyeing her.

Suddenly Marek shoved a pistol in Valery's stomach.

Abram took a step toward them, but Valery ordered him to get back. "You're not involved—" Then his eyes met Mila's. *'Hold off on showing your marshal arts training or you'll get us all shot,'* was the warning he appeared to be telegraphing her.

Something Gerado was certain she knew, but nevertheless, a necessary reminder with the dangers facing them.

"I'm putting those two under arrest for stealing a painting!" Marek hollered, pointing a stubby finger at Arina and Gerado. "So take the woman! And no matter she's considered Kiev's cultural icon." He fixed his eyes on the couple. "And make sure, *Paper Boy,* here gets to watch."

Trapped in a haze of panic, Gerado and Arina's breathing quickened. And grabbing her hand he began edging toward the kitchen.

They were nearly at its door when the short, wiry soldier jumped behind them, blocking their path.

Gerado turned, his eyes darted alarmingly at the pistol the man held. *No time to react.* Arina's pulse, was racing the same as his—God! How pale she looked. Like someone on the verge of passing out. Disgusted by his inability to do anything, he put his arm around her and pressed her tightly against him.

Then came a sudden movement. Mila was undoing the buttons on her blouse and sliding it, along with her camisole, from her shoulders. Her breasts were in full view. "How about me, soldiers?" "You," they said in unison.

"Why not?" The bony one shrugged, the look in his eyes filled with a fierce sparkle.

That was all it took for Gerado to find himself holding the short, bleary-eyed soldier's pistol.

Mila was also holding a pistol, but it was the bony one's. And Valery, looking as astounded as the soldier, was now holding Marek's. "But she's my daughter," he pointed out, a certain formality in his voice.

Valery released a pent-up breath. "Thanks, Mila, I could never imagined—"

"—that I'd do whatever I could for you, Gerado, and Arina?"

"I...it's just the way—"

Mila pulled up her camisole. "Things had to be."

The bony soldier, drunker than the shorter, wiry one, appeared to be more aggressive. And balling his hand in a tight fist, he lifted it to slap her.

"Just try it you sorry piece of scum." And with her right foot, leg out, she kicked him in his left knee cap.

An anguished cry tore through the room as he fell sideways, his head hitting the floor.

A fast down and out...muscle memory...no emotion. With a *what-happened look*, on his face.

The wiry soldier's mouth opened in disbelief as the revelation appeared to slid up his spine that he was clearly unprepared for someone like Mila.

Her mouth was tense as she shoved him, kicked him, and spun him around several times, before smashing his head against the marble wall.

"Want me to finish the job?" she ground out.

Heavy breathing, groaning, and curses followed. "Bitch!" he spat.

"Get to the porch," she ordered. "Your uniforms are smeared with blood."

But neither man could rise.

"I've got help coming to move them," Abram intervened. "Just stand by."

The drunk Marek, disoriented, staggered from the door toward the Volga. But not seeing the small rug on the porch, he tripped on it and struck his head on one of columns.

Abram rushed out. "Do we need an ambulance, Valery? He's unconscious or—"He looked around before asking in a whispery voice, "Does he go to his special doctor with his small hospital?"

"The special hospital, so Moscow won't find out."

"In that case I'll loan you a car," said Abram, reaching for some keys in his pocket.

"Something we'll need if following behind that Volga."

He quickly had a car brought around. "Want me to drive?" Mila asked. Valery nodded.

"If Arina and I are under arrest, then what do we do?" Gerado asked him.

"Nothing. Marek said he *was* putting you under arrest, which hasn't happened yet."

"But it will."

"No. When Marek's down, I'm in charge. And I'll have the doctor write it up. Besides, it was an embarrassing situation, and he probably won't remember he said it. But just in case—Ustin, Mila, and I will be keeping an eye on things...We're committed to you. So go to Isabella's room at the hotel and you and Arina stay there."

Gerado nodded they would.

They reached the small hospital sooner than expected, and Valery had them get out of the car so he could give them each a hug. "I'm sorry you had to go through this."

Mila also gave them a hug. "I am too."

"But you handled it well," Gerado said, putting things back in focus. "And I congratulate you."

Valery sighed heavily. "I'm trying—but just remember that in our Soviet world, you can never be sure about anything."

★★★

BERLIN

Ernst was elated when he hung up the phone from Isabella's call. The missing piece of that painting had been found. "What luck!" he said, smiling as he dialed Hermann. *With the way things are going it appears I'll soon have a nice stash.*

When Hermann came on the line, Ernst could tell he was elated too, as he began asking him for all the details.

Reflecting on his brief conversation with Isabella, Ernst made several jerky movements in an attempt to stimulate his brain. Then, he read him the writing someone remembered before it faded, that was on the lower part of the painting. It was followed by the mention of the six-fingered giant's hand on the rock below the glyphs, pointing west."

"Unbelievable," Hermann exclaimed.

"Isabella's flying in this afternoon with the missing piece of the painting," Ernst proceeded." And Manuel is meeting her. Though she'll be staying at the Hotel Metropolitan."

Vaiter must have been listening, because he came on the line. "It's in our favor that she's staying at the hotel rather than Manuel's apartment."

"I know. Because his second bedroom has been turned into a small library."

"That sounds like something the jerk would do," Vaiter countered in a chiding tone.

"He's a professor," Ernst reminded. "And it's been my experience professors do a lot of crazy things."

"If everything goes the way Hermann and I've planned, Manuel won't be a professor much longer."

"Give me back that phone, Vaiter," Hermann ordered in the background.

"Not yet—"

"The hell you say!" Apparently Hermann grabbed it because he came on the line. "Ernst, Manuel's got a lot to pay for. So don't get soft-hearted on me."

"Needing the money for my move to Canada the way I do, I can't afford to. But *Late Child*, what about him?"

"He'll probably hang with Wallenberg, like we've said."

CHAPTER FIFTEEN

BERLIN
Mid-Afternoon

When the plane landed, Isabella hurried to Manuel who was waiting with his ex-wife, Eva. He had the boots and a cowboy hat for Bill, with a souvenir sheriff's badge pinned on it. Bill was ecstatic, and he and Manuel exchanged several hugs before he put on the hat, grabbed the boots, and headed toward the nearest chair to change. "Excuse me, but I gotta have my boots."

They were a perfect fit, and he hugged and thanked Manuel again, before shoving his shoes in his large, canvas tote bag.

"Now that I'm not going on any more digs," said Manuel, "Eva and I have a healthy relationship, and we've talked about re-marriage but as for now, decided against it.

Isabella smiled. "When the right time comes, you'll know what to do." She recalled how Eva had been a beautiful woman in her younger days, but now she had her hair pulled back in a bun and wore no make-up.

"Here." Isabella said, reaching in her satchel and handing Manuel the missing piece of the painting. "What we've all been waiting for."

The enormous grin on his face as he slid it in his briefcase was a clear sign his pulses were racing. "One of the best finds ever."

"And this is for you," she told Bill, handing him an American one hundred dollar bill. "You can exchange it at the hotel."

Bill was flabbergasted. "Why, Miss Isabel, I've never seen so much money in my life."

"What everyone says...just don't spend it all in one place."

"You can bet your last dollar I won't."

Manuel smiled again. "I'm not sure, but I suspect Jesse James never had that much money, even if he did do all those train and bank robberies."

"Just so you'll know, I've taken it upon myself to protect you and Miss Isabel, from Gerado's two terrible brothers, Hermann and Vaiter Behl."

"Good luck if you can do it."

Eva's eye widened as she looked him over from head to toe. "He looks tough. So he just might surprise us."

"Thanks, Mam.'" Bill bowed slightly. "I think I'll make a good sheriff from watchin' all that TV."

Manuel was eager to get Isabella and Bill to the hotel. "I need to put this painting piece in my safe. Plus, I've got some calls to make about it. So, how about if we meet for dinner around eight at the hotel?"

They both agreed, with Manuel driving them to the hotel and getting them checked in a suite.

"A sofa bed for Bill will be in the living area," he told Isabella. "But I have to go." And he left in such a hurry, it resembled a dust-cloud *whoosh*.

***

Ernst was anxiously shuffling and filing some papers in Manuel's office as he waited for his return. *"What's taking him so long…? Hermann and Vaiter have promised to give me another thousand American dollars once I give them a copy of that painting's missing piece."*

In an effort to stave off panic, he heaved a sigh. All he could do was wait as the minutes ticked by. Until, finally, Manuel appeared with his briefcase. "Did you get it?" Ernst asked, rushing up to him.

"It's right here," Manuel said, opening the briefcase. He removed the original piece with the giant's hand and went over to his safe.

"Don't you need some copies?"

"No. I've already made some."

It looked to Ernst like he had three copies of the original and three of the missing piece. "Want me to tape them together?"

Manuel shook his head. "I'm doing it."

"Isabella's so nice that I'd like to spend sometime with her."

"When?" The request appeared to surprise him. "We'll be having lunch at the hotel tomorrow, but we'll be talking business."

Ernst's eyes narrowed at him. "What about tonight?"

"We inviting a guest and don't want to be interrupted," Manuel stressed, locking his briefcase. "So tend to your work here, and I'll see you tomorrow." He headed toward the door.

The office was quiet for a stretch before Ernst decided to shift his attention to the phone and see what the Behl brothers wanted him to do. Their phone rang several times before Hermann came on the line. Ernst swallowed with difficulty, confessing he'd been unable to get a copy of the missing part of the painting.

Hermann was furious as was Vaiter. "You'd better get it if you want your money," they'd threatened, sounding like a duet.

"But how do I get it when it's locked in a safe? And Manuel has copies locked in his briefcase." Ernst knew he had to come up with something fast. But what? His thoughts were tumbling like clothes in a washing machine, or was it a dryer? "He and his sister are having lunch together at the hotel tomorrow."

"And will he have the briefcase?" Hermann grilled him.

"He takes it everywhere."

"But it's unlikely he'll be going to his sister's hotel room—"

"Not unless you can figure a way for him to do it," Vaiter broke in with an agitated sigh.

"So think about it, Ernst, and call us back when you've got an answer."

A quick, disconnect followed.

Getting Manuel to Isabella's room was next to impossible. The good professor had a class following lunch. *So what to do?* Ernst reflected. *Surely there was something.* He sank down in Manuel's desk chair and closed his eyes, in the hopes something would come to him. Then, he opened the lower desk drawer where Manuel kept the notes, letters, and telegrams that came to him. Ernst had read and re-read them so many times, he knew them practically by heart. *Nothing there.*

One note that probably should have been trashed, read:

"Must remember to remind Isabella and Gerado to bring gifts for Arina, since she'll have gifts for them. A Kiev custom, a man told me, though I've never heard of it…Many of the people are poor in Kiev, leading me to suspect that most don't have money for gifts."

Gifts. The word attracted Ernst. When suddenly it struck him like a cannonball. "I'll have two large gifts delivered to Isabella's room. One for her and the other for Manuel."

Then he went on to plot. He'd be hiding in the hotel, watching. And when they finished lunch, he'd pretend to show up at the hotel with a message someone had left on Manuel's office door. It would read:

"Two large gift packages have been delivered to Frau Isabella Swanda's room. One is for her, and the other for Professor Wurtz."

And if they asked him who sent them, he'd say it appeared to be a surprise.

In the mean time, Hermann and Vaiter will be watching too. And when lunch is finished, Isabella and Manuel will then go to the room and start opening their gifts. There'll be looking for a card, but there won't be one.

Hermann and Vaiter, with masks on their faces, will then start knocking on the door. '*We've another package,*' they'll say.

Manuel will hurry to open the door. And that's when they'll shove a pistol in his stomach and demand he hand over one of his copies of the picture with that giant's hand taped to it.

"But there'd really have to be some nice presents in those boxes, "Ernst mused. "To attract them. "

And since he didn't want to spend any money, he considered things he could do. Then it struck him; only this time not like a cannonball, but a ripe apple dropped from a tree. His aunt had two new silver -plated serving trays. They looked expensive but weren't, with one shaped like a fish and the other a large shell. She'd bought them from a neighbor who was moving. 'I bought them because they'll make possible wedding gifts for some of my friends and family in the future.' Manuel had never seen them.

Perfect gifts. "And since I'm quite good at gift wrapping, I'll make them very attractive, heightening Isabella and Manuel's curiosity." Ernst said aloud.

He commended himself for being so ingenious. And picking up the phone dialed Hermann and Vaiter. They loved his idea as he didn't doubt they would, and he agreed to meet him tomorrow at the Hotel Metropolitan around noon.

★★★

BERLIN
Later that evening

"This *Wiener schnitzel's* delicious," said Isabella, seated to the left of Manuel at one of the hotel's dining tables. On her right was Manuel's good friend, the American archeologist, Pat Grisham. He had a visiting relative from the states and apologized, because he couldn't stay very long. So they were having an early dinner.

Seated across the table from him was Cowboy Bill, wearing his hat and boots. "My guest is going to be surprised when he learns who I had dinner with tonight," Grisham remarked, smiling.

"Does anyone want anything more to eat?" Manuel asked, reflecting his smile. "In case you've forgotten, it's all on me tonight."

But they shook their heads, with Isabella admitting her stomach had run out of room.

After wiping his mouth with his napkin, Bill scrambled to rise. "I've got the *Behl* brothers to keep a lookout for, so may I be excused?"

"What makes you think they'd be here?" Grisham asked.

"From stories we're hearing about how they're using us to help them locate Wallenberg. So why wouldn't they be—"

"They might," Manuel interjected. "Because my student assistant Ernst says that rumors are floating around they've got a copy of the upper part of that twisted chimney picture."

Grisham looked like he doubted it was true. "Now how on earth would they get that?"

"Ernst says there were two pictures that got smudged slightly when he was copying them in the copy room. He threw them away, but tore them up before he did. If someone knew how to tape well, they just might have been able to put them back together for money. Since I do get the feeling we have some neo-Nazis working at the university."

"And these neo-Nazis know you'd have something like that?" Grisham asked Manuel. "How?"

"Newspaper letters...Gerado, Arina...I'm related more or less. Which I suspect is the only lead those Behl brothers have—"

"Something else we find peculiar," Isabella intervened, 'is that Hermann and Vaiter, who are always six months in Berlin and six months in Paraguay, appear to be spending a full year in the city now."

"Have no fear," Bill blurted. "If they show up I'm on'um. So I'd best be startin' my night watch right about now." And turning on his heel, he headed in the direction of the reception desk.

Bill's departure appeared to strike a note with Grisham. "Night watch what?," he asked his mouth dropping open in confusion.

"Beware, Pat," Isabella joked. "Or I'm apt to stuff a tennis ball in that open mouth of yours."

"Better not." He chuckled. "But tell me, is this Bill fellow for real?"

"What do you mean by *real*?" Manuel asked.

"Is Bill a Texas sheriff or a Hollywood actor?"

Isabella laughed. "Both I suspect."

"Amazing he had that missing piece of the painting and claimed to know so much about it."

Manuel handed Grisham a photo-copy of the painting. "What do you make of that six-fingered giant's hand, Pat?"

"Old Testament. Fallen angels mating with the daughters of man. Nephilims they're called."

"My thoughts exactly."

Grisham appeared to study it. "This picture confirms what my archeologist friend in North Carolina believed we'd find." He opened his briefcase and produced a photo of the glyphs and giant's hand on a rock, this friend had express-mailed him. "See it's the same."

Isabella viewing it over his shoulder, rolled her eyes doubtfully. "But no twisted chimney."

"For what it's worth, the giant's hand is pointing west. The direction of faraway California and the Pacific. And at the time these glyphs and giant's hand were believed to have been put on this rock, there were no houses," Grisham stopped and stared at Manuel. "Do you have any idea who might have drawn the painting and written those cryptic messages on its back?"

"An angel," said Isabella, not giving Manuel time to answer. "According to the description Wallenberg gave Bill. Of course, Wallenberg was just a little boy at the time. Though I don't doubt it's veracity, because my godson, Gerado, recently had an experience with an angel. Which fit Wallenberg's description of the one who gave him the painting."

Grisham looked like he was ready to slide under the table. "I didn't hear about that."

"But you will sooner or later," Manuel assured him.

"You and Isabella must talk on the phone a lot."

"We do. No matter where we are or what time—unless I'm teaching."

"The main thing about the painting is that the house with the twisted chimney is in the distance *behind* the rock...which suggests it's possibly just a clue," Grisham remarked.

"Clue to what?" Manuel asked.

"This." He shoved a photograph at him of a house with a twisted chimney similar to the one in the painting. "The giant's hand is pointing at this house with a twisted chimney that's forward, not backward."

"Well, I'll be darn. When do you think this house was built?"

"It was built in North Carolina in 1904." He shoved several papers at Manuel. "But it was later torn down and replaced by a state museum. These papers, however, were copied from an old architectural journal with pictures of the house, because of its interesting story about a well-to-do Russian man, Bogdan Rodin, who was touring the states. There was a small painting of the house for sale with the twisted chimney and the glyphs, and it's belived Rodin bought it."

"Something a well-to-do Russian man could easily do," said Manuel. He stared at Isabella, and eager for an explanation, she tilted her head toward Grisham.

"This man visited the twisted chimney house in 1910 and was so impressed, he wanted to build one like it in Russia...He owned land near the Finnish border, which on the Russian side was close to the scenic Republic of Karelia. A place we know the tourists love...There were some twisted chimney houses in Finland, but the one in North Carolina was much more impressive, so Rodin claimed."

Grisham's tone was now a bit strong."Though sadly, it never got built." He reached for the journal article. "Bogdan Rodin had to return to the states for financing. But, unfortunately, he didn't make it because he was a passenger on the Titanic and went down with it."

Isabella redirected her eyes to the picture. "It's terrible he had to die."

"I realize it was a long time ago," Grisham said, pointing at the deceased man's name listed in the journal article. And in addition, it's also mentioned in this article that he talked of a spa from the seventeen hundreds, which was close to his land. Two things that should make it easy for your Soviet friend, Valery Savin, to have someone on his staff, locate grid information that will enable him to find coordinates.

"Which, hopefully, will produce a map which shows the roads to take leading to those coordinates," Manuel remarked.

"All this is really amazing," Isabella replied.

"It is," Grisham agreed, rising from the table. He gave Manuel a pat on the back. "Sorry to have to leave good company, but it's a little past nine, and as you know, my relative is waiting at my apartment. So I need to leave now. "

"You've been great, Pat," Manuel acknowledged, hurriedly writing down everything he'd learned from him on the back of one of one of the photo copies of the painting...Isabella was doing the same, on a copy he'd handed her.

"It's only an hour's time difference between Berlin and Kiev, with Kiev ahead," Manuel pointed out. "Yet, we've not had any calls from Mila, Valery, or Gerado. Which makes me fear they're probably having some trouble with Marek."

"That's another concern." She breathed in a shallow, quick gasp. "If Gerado says he's going to call me, you know he always does."

"Then we'll call Valery tomorrow and see what's happening," said Manuel, stuffing a copy of Grisham's journal article in his briefcase.

★★★

Cowboy Bill didn't waste any time getting back to his and Isabella's vast suite. "Got to find the copy room here and get some more of the *before* and *after* photos of Hermann and Vaiter Behl. Then, I'll put a *WANTED SIGN* above their names, and at the bottom, the sigh will read: *CONTACT SHERIFF BILL AT THE RECEPTION DESK.*"

He removed the photos from his bag and was about to start out the door with them, when he heard someone rummaging behind the bar. "Better show yourself with your hands up," he warned, turning around.

"'Cause I'm the new sheriff here." There was a hint of boastfulness in his voice.

A trembling, fair-haired boy, who looked to be about eighteen, stepped out from behind the bar with his palms raised. A bottle of whiskey was sticking out of his jacket pocket. "When did this place get a sheriff? My father's one of its owners, and he never said anything about it."

"As of today," replied Bill. "Which means you can't take my whiskey. "He reached for the opened, long-necked bottle in the young man's pocket and took a draw from it. "'Cause ever good sheriff needs a spark now and then. " He also took another draw from it. "But what's your name, Son?"

"A...are you gonna report me?"

"Not if you tell me your name."

"It's Max Ritter. And yours?"

"Cowboy Bill from Texas."

"Were you ever in a Hopalong movie?"

"Well—" He paused to give it some serious thought. "More or less, I'd say."

"A real movie star!" exclaimed Max. "*Oh my!*"

"But tell me, Son, why'd you want that whiskey?"

"Because I'm tryin' to throw a party my father doesn't know about— "He hesitated. A cloak-like shroud of sorrow falling between them before he added, "Though without any money, I don't see how I can do it."

"Now that *is* a problem." Bill pursed his lips. "And if I don't find a deputy, I don't think I can corral those Behl brothers very well. So, how about I pay you twenty American dollars and deputize you?

Max's features were suddenly animated. "Why that 'ud be great, just tell me what to do."

Bill handed him the *before* and *after* pictures of the Behl brothers. "These here are two bad hombres. And as you can see, when they were your age, they were in the SS."

"The SS," Max repeated with a grim expression. "And we're doin' what?"

"Copyin' this picture with my *WANTED SIGN* on it, and hangin' it all over the hotel—even in the mens' rooms."

"And then what?" Max asked.

"We gotta stop 'um from harmin' Miss Isabel and her brother Manuel—which means keepin' a close watch for Hermann and Vaiter

Behl." A pointed pause. "But without my six shooter I'm not exactly sure what we can do when that pair shows up."

Max appeared to give it some thought. "Have you got some money?"

He nodded. "Miss Isabel gave me a hundred dollars. But she told me not to spend it in one place."

"You won't, but I got some friends. And if you'll go with me, I can help you purchase some tier gas from a man in the military who steals it and sells it...And I also know a fellow who can make smoke bombs."

"How much do you think it'll cost?"

"Not any more than what you're giving me for the party." Silence fell between them before Max asked, "How long before you think those Behl brothers show up?"

"My gut feelin' is tellin' me those sorry bastards will show up tomorrow. So if you'll stick with me, and help with those smoke bombs and tier gas then when they show up, we'll be ready for them."

"I'd love to, since I've never worked with a real cowboy before." Max threw back his head and smiled. "Why it's just like being out west, where I've always wanted to be."

"I sense you'll make a good deputy. And if all I spend is forty dollars, from the money Miss Isabel gave me, then I'll slip you another twenty once we get the Behl brothers outta the way."

"I'd love that."

"Same as me. But here—" Bill handed him the whiskey bottle. "How about if we drink to it, Max?" "There's nothing I'd like better."

He took a big gulp from it, followed by Bill. "It's a shame to waste good whiskey. So let's finish it off, head for the copy room, and then start hangin' posters."

"I believe this is one of the best nights I've ever had." Max grinned, taking another large gulp.

"I know it is for me," said Bill, finishing off the bottle.

★★★

In the bar Isabella and Manuel were also doing some drinking. Their earlier decision not to phone Valery, Mila, or Gerado until tomorrow had been waved. Isabella was brimming with tears, so Manuel had given in. "No one's answering," he said, after putting the phone back on its rest.

"Because that damn Marek's arrested them!" she blurted. "And here we sit, with time passing like years."

Manuel put his hand on her arm. Unlikely. Considering Mila's, Marek's daughter and Valery his son-in-law.

Isabella remained silent before she appealed, "Marek Falin's crazy and capable of anything, so we've got to do something."

"I don't doubt the man's crazy," said Manuel peering at the door. "And to make matters worse those Behl brothers are apt to show up any time, for a copy of the bottom part of that painting. That some mysterious person, I feel certain, has informed them we had."

His words echoed her sentiments. "And that really bothers me when I think Bill and I have only been here a few hours."

"With the way things seem to be going, a mysterious person is certainly something we can't rule out," Manuel replied, cutting a glance toward his briefcase. "Which is now overflowing, with this pertinent information Grisham surprisingly uncovered for us—"

"—and you keep everything under lock and key too, don't you?'

"Have to. Because Ernst could be right about stuff he's torn up in the copy room, that some neo-Nazis pasted back together."

"Ernst," she ventured, allowing a moment to pass. "He does keep bringing up the question if you really trust him?"

"He's never given me a reason not to."

"Besides, you did help Eva raise him after her sister died."

"And we tried to do a good job."

"Is he still playing the piano with his group for parties?"

"Not as much."

"Doesn't he need the money?"

Manuel leaned back in his chair. "Ernst doesn't know it, but Eva does." His face lit up. "I'm giving him a large stash for his graduation present. So he won't have any worries his first year in Canada."

"I hope you can afford it with the way you spend money."

"I can. Because I'm getting ready to sign that book contract about why the various Egyptian temples were placed where they were." He appeared to mull it over. "Of course I'll have to re-visit Egypt, and Eva wants to go with me this time."

"Which is as it should be."

It was still early, and Manuel offered to spend the night with Isabella, but since Bill had the sofa bed she stalled, reflecting. "Since beds were scarce in Budapest didn't you and Bill have to sleep together some?"

"We did."

"So, if you sleep with Bill on the sofa bed, it should be like old times should it not?"

Manuel smiled, nodding his agreement. "That way I'll hopefully get someone in Kiev to pick up the phone."

"Let's keep our fingers crossed."

But she broke into tears again, after she and Manuel were in her room. Bill wasn't there, but she wasn't worried. It was Gerado's silence that was breaking her heart and continuing to mortify her. "What on earth could have happened to him and Arina?" she found herself murmuring over and over.

CHAPTER SIXTEEN

**Earlier in the day
** Gerado and Arina's afternoon
return to Kiev from Vladeti
Prison****

When Gerado and Arina got back to the hotel, Valery and Mila suggested they go to the bar and have a drink. It had a festive atmosphere and could lift their spirits with the energetic Russian music playing. One of the most popular things in the bar was a small, wooden bear. Its tail could be pulled down, and the handle tapped so the bar tenders could draw drinks for their customers.

Ustin was waiting for them. "Think we're going to have some more trouble from Marek tonight?" he asked Valery.

"I expect we'll have plenty of trouble when he returns tomorrow after his recovery. But tonight, I'm in charge, and Marek's doctor gave me papers to prove it."

"Still what if certain authorities chose not to honor those papers?" Ustin speculated. "Can we deal with it?"

"I've made plans—just in case," Valery spoke with confidence. "But what are you drinking? Vodka?"

He nodded.

"And we're drinking what?" Gerado asked Arina.

"Champagne."

That surprised him. "I'm for it. After all we went through with those ill-disciplined soldiers."

"Champagne sounds great," Valery said. "We should celebrate our victory."

The waiter was quick to serve them, and they lifted their glasses, tipped them, and clinked them.

Gerado and Arina would be spending the night in Isabella's room: a double bed and a single bed. She could have the larger bed, since he wasn't expecting anything to occur.

Valery turned to Gerado. "Ustin's keeping watch, so I think you and Arina should go to your room."

"I need to shower," Gerado told her. "And you can have the bigger bed, and I'll take the smaller one." Since after all, he wasn't expecting anything to occur. So why not?

But before they left he ordered some wine to take with them.

And seeming pleased, her arms circled his waist like she was emotionally drawn to him as they boarded the elevator to Isabella's former room. And when they got off, he smiled, before unlocking the door and ushering her inside.

Arina gestured at the sofa."Let's sit on it," she suggested, as he put on some soft music. "Even after the champagne, it seems we're still on edge over what happened."

"Nervous, I'd say. Which is why I brought the wine."

She drew a sharp breath." Valery's made plans to deal with whatever happens. And after that awful beating, I'm afraid for him. "Her mouth went slack. H...he's going against Marek, you know, who'll return tomorrow."

"And I've certainly prayed that Marek won't harm him."

"Same as me." Her continued inability to let go of the married Valery was disturbing...*Yes, Marek* is a *real threat.*

Gerado removed his notepad from his pocket and began reading silently what he'd written on his way back to Berlin:

"Maybe I'm being paranoid, but if Marek beats Valery again, it wouldn't surprise me if Arina stayed on and if possible, continued to be his mistress. And if that happens where does that leave me? I can take her to Italy, but if I can't make her happy like Valery, she'll be looking for another Valery. And I'll be looking for women who have bits and pieces of Arina in them. Golden hair. Violin players...And if she choses not to be mine, then I'll probably spend the rest of my days courting women like that. When all I want to do it take her in my arms, which I can't. Tears sting my eyes. My heart is breaking for her. "

"One of the things that bothers me," said Gerado, slipping his notepad back in his pocket. "Is that Valery doesn't seem to be worried."

Arina's jaw tightened. "They're liable to throw him in a Gulag camp."

"And there's no other way?"

"Other than a trip to the wall."

"God forbid."

He tried to take her hand, but she pulled back, sparking a fear in him. *Valery again. And if Marek kills him, what will happen to her emotionally?*

When she'd put her arm around his waist in the elevator it had seemed for a moment like she was trying to show she cared for him— but pulling away from him on the sofa was an indication she still loved Valery. *And isn't ready for me…It's certainly difficult to let go of her. Making me fear that if nsomething does happen to Valery she won't consider me. As I become more and more aware she's married to Valery in her heart, and always will be.*

Gerado reached for his notepad again and began reading some notes he'd made for a possible future article:

"Though some might find it strange, my attraction for Arina blossomed quickly, soothing my heart. Making it difficult for me to imagine what it would be like without her. And I pray that as the years pass, she will think of me as more than just someone who helped find her father."

"I owe you so much, I don't know where to begin," she said, returning his thoughts from his notepad to the present. "And I apologize."

"For what?"

"For not loving you the way you should be loved."

'*What a shocking admission*,' he also mouthed, anxiety spurting through him. "We're friends, Arina, and I don't hold anything against you."

"I know. However, it *does* matter to me when I think how much you care for me."

"I know you're not mine—it's just that we've got to stop pretending we can be a happy couple if you return to Italy with me. So I'm doing my best to understand and accept it," he admitted in a resigned tone.

He opened the wine and poured her a drink. "I can't change my feelings for you any more than you can change your feelings for Valery. But I assume you've already figured that out."

★★★

Arina stared at Gerado, bewildered. "If I'd never met Valery, then I could love you the way you deserve to be loved. So if I'm happy for Valery and Mila, why is that? When I can't break free of him?"

She swallowed the sob that rose in her throat. "Something I realize in inflicting pain on you, and saddens me greatly."

"You're unique," Gerado said after a few moments. "The fact you can love a man so deeply, is something I've not seen in a woman."

"Probably because the women you've known have been superficial."

"They have been." His head bent down like he was remembering "What is it Valery can give you that I can't? When he can't give you freedom like me."

"Maybe that's it. *Sacrifice.* We had no last night together before you came because he wasn't emotionally up to it. And if he'd come to me like he'd said, he'd look on it as an admission he couldn't stand—beautiful but painful memories. His marriage made it impossible to give me the kind of life I deserved, when I could have the best of another world. So the decision was either I remain repressed here, with little opportunity, or I leave the country. Something he likened to boarding a rocket ship headed to a magnificent world in outer space, where my life would be uplifted. But once there, I could never return to earth—where *he*, my love, was stuck...Confusing emotions torment me...Because in a way Valery was like my father, who believed if you truly loved someone you'd sacrifice yourself for them."

It was obvious to Gerado that Valery had been kind, honest, and respectful towards her—wanting the best for her. *Something that makes it impossible for her to deny her attraction for him and love me.*

"As much as I care about you," Gerado said, reaching for her hand. "Then you should know by now that if I got you to Italy, I'd let you go."

"I know you would. You've already done a lot, and Valery knows it. Making us both ashamed."

"And he hasn't said it, but I'll say it. He's used you to help me have a better life, like I've used you to help me find my father." Frustration appeared to seize her heart. "O-oh, Gerado, you're such a good and kind man, with such tender feelings. How could I exploit you?"

He refilled their wine glasses. "I can't answer that. But I can ask you if there's any chance your feelings could ever shift from Valery to me? Or is it still too soon to know?"

"Not in the least." She squeezed his hand." Someway this feeling that still rages in my heart for Valery has got to end."

"And you have no idea how to make it happen?"

"None. But we've got wine, so let's celebrate more than just getting away from those soldiers."

"How?"

"You and I have yet to go to bed—"She hesitated a moment before asking, "Do I need to finish the sentence for you to understand?"

★★★

"My God!" Gerado drew a startled breath. He couldn't believe what she was saying. Was she seeking solace? And did it matter at this point? Even so, he drew back a moment. "And you're really sure you want this?"

"Only if it's what you want."

"It is. As long as you remember you don't have to do anything to repay me. And by the way I do have condoms."

"That's good." Her hand tightened on his arm. " I'm doing this because you're my *sugar rabbit*, and too good to pass up."

Was she really saying all this—or am I dreaming? If he wasn't, then it was almost more than he could stand. *I'll give her so much pleasure she'll ache for the fulfillment of my lovemaking. And hopefully, never want anyone else.*

He released a deep sigh of contentment. "But before anything between us happens, I really need to shower." He glanced at a stain on his shirt sleeve. "Considering after rubbing shoulders with those drunken soldiers, I suspect I smell like a goat."

"No more than I do. Which is why I'd like to shower too." A pinkish blush blossomed on her cheeks.

"Only with you."

Swept with joy, he did a double take at her words. When was the last time he'd had an offer like that? Not any time recently.

"Even though we have a hand shower, your hair's so lovely I'd like to pin it up to keep it from getting completely wet."

"And I'd like you to, because if I do it some strands will probably get very wet."

Her words, *'too good to pass up,'* continued to excite him, even if they weren't exactly a declaration of *love…But still, it certainly sounds like we're getting there.* His heart swelled with feeling. And besides—he could always pretend she loved him as their bodies joined, and they soared to awesome heights.

After all, I'm her ticket out of this dreadful country. So, I'll hold her tight. Something she needs with her vulnerability so apparent. Even if Valery's devotion…to her and hers to him…make it pointless for her to deny her attraction for him.

Gerado raked a hand through her thick mass of golden curls, searching for hairpins. She didn't have that many, but he removed each one carefully. When he had eight, he put them on the table in front of the sofa, assuming that was all. Although, it didn't stop him from combing her hair with his fingers.

Gazing at her compassionately he took her in his arms, her head against his shoulder.

He savored the warmth of her cheeks, allowing a moment to pass, then another before he pulled back, drew her face to his, and cupped it. His spirits rose as his mouth covered hers hungrily, his open lips demanding a response.

★★★

Desire flooded Arina, and she moaned when he parted her lips with his tongue. Shivers of need raced through her, as their breaths blended and his tongue explored the recesses of her mouth.

Their earlier Russian world, with all its concerns, had fallen away for the moment, allowing the heaviness lodged in her heart to re-shape her former visions and give her the necessary faith…without the man she loved…to embrace a better future from this somber past. *A future that appears to be a beginning to re-shaping itself with Gerado—who's aching to share his dreams from a more peaceful world with me. He may not be my soul mate, but this has to mean we're right for each other. And me? Why have I had such difficulty admitting it? My heart continues to grill me.*

The strong hardness of Gerado's lips torched her with their sweetness, making her yearn to ease the growing need spiking her blood. She'd lost Valery, and the beauty they'd shared, but of course it was still a little soon for her memories of him to release her completely—or was it?

My mother never had another man after Wallace. Her reason being she could never get over him. Something I now understand perfectly. And it raises a mask of uncertainty with me, that if in the end, this will be the same for me?

Should Marek arrange for Valery either to be sent to a Gulag camp or making a trip to the wall.

When finally she and Gerado broke apart, his fingers thrust through her mass of thick curls, before reaching for her hairpins on the table. And taking them one by one, he began pinning her curls upward. But her hair was so heavy some strands fell against her shoulders, requiring him to wrap his hand around them as he pinned them.

Fueled with anticipation, once they were secured she removed her blouse and fell into his arms.

Smiling, she reflected on his good looks. *Valery's handsome, but Gerado's younger. And he looks as great in his blue jeans as he did in his expensive, black tux.*

Still, whenever his shinning blue eyes sift through me, it's a reminder of my separation from Valery.

Although for some reason, at this particular time, the pain's not as bad. Something I try to imagine is like being reborn. And this new existence is pumping life into me as never before...Like a calm river suddenly being awakened by rapids.

Gerado began unbuttoning his shirt, and she assisted him as he eased out of it. Her smile widened as she recalled the swirls of the gypsy-dark hair on his tanned chest from their swim. Inspiring her to run her hands over it several times.

★★★

'Nurturing. We both need nurturing,' Gerado wanted to say as he watched her unfasten the tiny buttons on her silk camisole. And the shadow across his heart, growing dimmer by the minute, disappeared completely when she opened the camisole and slid its shoulder straps down her arms.

Instantly, the rose-tinted, pointed tips of her breasts were revealed. "Such beauty." He marveled, pressing his mouth against them in the hopes of bringing her untried senses with him to life.

And sure enough, a tangible bond appeared to be developing between them each time her heart thudded against his. *'Is my magnetism potent?'* he wished he could ask her. When a surrendering moan slipped through her lips, as if nothing existed other than this golden wave of ecstasy flooding her with an uncontrollable delight.

At some point he removed her blue jeans, and panties, then his blue jeans and briefs. And kissing her cheeks, throat, shoulders, and breasts, he toyed with the idea of bedding her now and showering afterwards. But no, those damned soldiers smelled like goats, making him continue to suspect he probably did too.

So, sweeping her in his arms, he carried her into the shower and turned on the water.

It was a narrow space where they were barely a breath apart, with a surprising intensity from the hand shower's water pressure that quickly covered their fevered bodies. "This is like being in a thunderstorm." She grinned.

"That's drowning us with tears of joy," he replied, mirroring her grin.

"Which is a perfect description from my handsome journalist," she said as she touched his swollen manhood. "And if I were in a parade I'd strut my delight at being in such company."

He scrubbed her back, her chest, and her arms with a soapy sponge that made it easy to rub it up and down. And when he finished, she did the same to him.

Afterwards, he kissed her all the way down to her stomach, then stroked her cleft with his fingers, sliding them in and out.

She drew a shaky breath, as she clutched a handful of his damp hair. His manhood full and hard, prompting him to give her another ardent kiss. "Are you ready to make love?"

Her answer was a nod.

He padded into the bedroom with her, but stopped at the closet, where he reached for the fuzzy warmth of the room's two white robes. "You were hot in the shower, but out here you're got goose bumps. So we'll put these on and take them off—" He couldn't keep from smiling as he added, "Before we're holding each other, naked, under the covers."

The telephone rang, surprising them. "Do your suppose that's Isabella? Arina asked.

"It's little early." He picked up the phone. "Who's calling?" he spoke into it.

But no answer, followed by a sudden disconnect. "I felt like someone was there, but this phone doesn't appear to be working."

Her eyes snapped up. "Like the tourists say, 'Nothing works in Russia.'" She glared at the phone with disgust. "So maybe we should go down to the reception desk."

He took her in his arms, and she rested her head on his chest. "Valery said to stay in the room," he reminded, his lips lightly brushing her brow.

"And finish what we started?"

"No reason not too." He kissed her forehead again, fearing he might not be able to control himself if he held back. Something he knew he must do in order to heighten the fire he was building in her.

They went over to the bed and for a moment, after removing their robes, they lay side by side in their nakedness. His protective arms were wrapped around her, and her slender, silky legs were wrapped around him.

Neither moved.

Finding the experience pleasant, Gerado wondered how long they could stay like that before his impatience got the better of him?

Not long, with such a sensual woman.

He eased himself over her, aware her heart fluttered wildly each time he touched the pebble hardness of her swollen nipples.

"You're so beautiful, Arina," he murmured, struggling for control.

If his body could unlock some of the emotions she still harbored for Valery, then there was a strong possibility he might be able to help her ease her sorrow over losing him.

And impatient to do just that, Gerado's mouth returned to her naked stomach, with one kiss following another until he lowered his head between her thighs and, once again, began stroking the moist softness of her cleft with his tongue.

***

Arina's heart gloried in this shared moment as these surges of excitement, shooting through her body, stoked her growing fire. Gerado was not yet fully embedded inside her, though instead of his fingers, it was now his swollen manhood sliding in and out of her pleasure point, tantalizing her. She definitely wanted more of him.

When—suddenly—the sensuous delight developing between them was aborted with the ringing of the phone again. "I thought it wasn't working," he said, removing himself from her and turning his naked body around to stare at it.

Another ring followed, but before he could grab it off its rest, the ringing stopped.

Then a deadly silence—followed by a furious pounding shaking the door. "Put your clothes on, Arina! It appears we're in trouble."

"Certainly sounds like it."

"Police! Let us in!" came a shout resembling a command.

"We're getting dressed," Gerado shouted back, grabbing his blue jeans, shirt, and his and Arina's denim jackets.

She already had on her blue jeans and was buttoning her shirt, when the door crashed open.

Three male figures, dressed in expensive black-clad clothing entered. Each carried a Soviet Makarov, heightening their sinister look.

The taller of the three men, who looked to be the leader, asked Gerado, "Are you *Herr* Gerhart, the news reporter?"

"Yes I am," he replied sternly.

The man then turned to Arina with a cold look. "And you, Madam, are you Arina Pavlik?"

She blanched. "I am."

"Then the two of you are under arrest. So you'll need to come with us"

"Under arrest for what?" Gerado challenged him.

But the man, not answering, opened the room's door wider. "Hurry and get a move on or you won't like what we do!"

Alarmed, Arina's penetrating gaze darted between this man and Gerado. These were the secret police, and Valery was supposed to be protecting them, with Ustin and Mila standing by to back him up. So where were they? Had they also been arrested?

Marek was in the hospital and the doctor had given Valery papers, putting him in charge. What had happened? And who was trying to phone them earlier?

Was it Ustin trying to warn them? Maybe not? He hadn't come to their room. And he would have done it, would he not?

What had she and Gerado done to cause the secret police to arrest them? Surely it wasn't over her painting. Though Marek had wanted the painting, and by their not giving it to him his vengeful nature was surfacing...making it a crime against the state for not giving him the painting. Unfortunately, it was the only thing that made sense.

Still, Valery was in charge, and these secret police were apparently usurping him.

"I insist on talking to Valery Savin," Arina told the tall man.

But he just stood there, completely indifferent to her request.

"This is obviously a mistake," Gerado informed the man. "Valery Savin brought us here earlier, and we're not under arrest. So like, Arina, I demand to talk to him."

"You're coming with us or else," warned a man standing next to the room's open door.

'Or else what?' Gerado looked like he wanted to ask, but obviously knowing better didn't. "Stay calm," he whispered to Arina, putting his arm around her.

"We'd better go with them. Though the truth will surface before nightfall."

"Let's hope," she replied. The somber undercurrent in her tone giving it an ominous quality. "Or otherwise it'll be too late for us."

CHAPTER SEVENTEEN

This three-man team of black-clad bullies with their Soviet Malarovs, pushed them into the elevator. Gerado wasn't able to collect himself any more than Arina.

Though when they reached the lobby and saw Valery, Mila, and Ustin waiting, they weren't nearly as panicked.

"Thank God!" Gerado exclaimed, his voice rising an octave.

"I knew they'd come, "Arina said, brightening.

Valery extinguished his cigarette before stepping up to the tall man, with the written statement Marek's doctor had given him. "I'm in charge today. And these people have done nothing wrong. And are clearly not enemies of the state."

But unmoved, the man waved the doctor's statement aside. "This prewritten order, with which I was presented, was written by Marek Falin yesterday morning." He removed it from his coat pocket and handed it to Valery.

He glanced at them sullenly, like he wished he could tear it up. What the man said was true.

Marek had ordered Gerado and Arina's arrest, scribbling at the bottom, "A Gulag camp near Moscow would be the ideal way to twist their fate."

Valery passed it to Mila, who grumbled, "What I'd expect my sorry, son-of-a-bitch father would do."

She passed the statement to Ustin. "Theft. It mentions property of the state—a painting—was stolen by enemies of the state." There was a certain tension in his expression.

Gerado and Arina shook their heads. "But how can that be when the painting belonged to me?" she whispered to Valery in a pensive tone.

"*Shush*." He laid a finger across her lips and in a very low voice reminded, "You should know I won't let Marek get away with this—but for now." He gazed at the floor with a downcast expression. "There's nothing I can do—"

"—other than send us to a place from which no one ever returns," Gerado finished.

Before anyone could intervene, Mila stepped forward. "Since my father's causing this, I'm staying with you as a guard. There's an extra Soviet uniform in the car so I'll quickly change into. And my Val will give me papers to show for now and later. But right now, no questions should be asked."

"Ustin and I will be coming with Mila to see everything's situated," Valery informed Gerado in a low voice. "But then, you're probably aware we have important business to tend to. So we'll leave you in Mila's hands."

Gerado stared at him, unflinching. "Someone needs to call Manuel."

"I will," Ustin volunteered. "Although it'll be later when I know something."

"Manuel's got to be careful how he tells Isabella about us, so my godmother won't fall apart."

Valery touched his arm. "Something I feel certain he can handle."

The tall men resumed their custody of Gerado and Arina and drove them to a brownish-gray building with no windows, where they were ushered inside. Ustin was nearby, watching.

Following behind these indifferent-acting men, Valery flashed his badge at two guards, and they saluted him. "My wife, who's Marek Falin's daughter," he introduced Mila. And when she held up her guard-verification paper, they snapped to attention. "She's been summoned to see after these prisoners."

"Then everyone follow me," said one of the guards, waving them forward.

He led them to a dimly lit basement room that had four locks on its metal door, with three chairs, and a small table inside.

Even in the spring it was as cold as winter's barrenness. "Or worse," Valery murmured like one who knew from experience, "it's as cold as the despair of men forced to sign confessions for crimes they didn't commit."

"I can't say much now," Mila whispered to Gerado. "And If we talk it must be very low. Considering this place has peep holes" She leaned into him. "Still, if you have questions, ask me."

Marek's returning tomorrow. And if you're here when he does, you and Arina will be put on a plane to Moscow," Valery informed them.

"Which we probably will be," Gerado growled.

"Not if my plan works, and the transfer I'm arranging goes through," said Valery, his lips parting in a stiff smile.

"Transfer to where?"

"Just wait—you'll know soon enough."

"And if there's a cost involved?"

He put his hand on Gerado's shoulder. "Don't worry, I'm handling it. But Ustin and I have to go.

Time is running out."

"What about the restroom here?" Arina asked.

"It's oriental."

She sighed, her disgust evident. "Which means it's just a hole in the floor."

"That news articles say the prisoners here get to use it only one time per day," Gerado replied with contempt.

"Mila will help you," Valery interceded. "And if you need something to eat, it won't be much, but she'll slip you some food."

Gerado shook his head vehemently. "I don't think I'll need anything."

Arina shivered. "Me either."

"The important thing," Valery resumed, "is to stay calm and know that I'd give my life for you and Arina."

She and Gerado exchanged looks. "Something we don't like thinking about."

"Have faith. My plan will work."

Mila moved closer to them. "They'll probably give me papers for you to sign confessing to your charges of theft...but you'll refuse—"

Because it could mean a trip to the wall," Valery warned. "So you and Arina be careful."

They assured him they would be. "One more thing," said Mila, touching the gold violin pin on Arina's denim jacket. "I'd better keep this for you before someone takes it."

"Please do," Arina said, unpinning it.

"I promise it won't leave my side."

★ ★ ★

As Valery and Mila left the cell, the guard outside it, sprang to attention when they heard the door slam shut.

"What's your plan?" Ustin wanted to know, once he was in Valery's car.

Arina and Gerado can't go to some Gulag camp near Moscow, so I'm having them transferred to the Danil Prison near the Finnish-Russian border."

"That's such a brutal prison you should get no arguments from Marek about it." Ustin said, allowing a moment to pass before asking, "But why there?"

"Because if things go as I've planned, then they should only be there two days and a night at the most. But if my plans fail then that prison's close enough to the Finnish border where you can arrange an escape for them. And also, it's not that far from where we believe Wallenberg might be. However, if they do have to escape, they'll sadly have to forego finding Wallenberg."

★★★

Valery knew that if things were to go smoothly for Gerado and Arina, they had to be headed toward the Danil Prison before midnight. Which meant being flown from Kiev to St. Petersburg on a special military aircraft.

This city was the closest Soviet airport to the scenic Karelia, with the flight taking around two hours. And upon arrival at the airport, a military vehicle would be waiting to drive them to the Danil Prison.

"A three hundred and eighty-six kilometer drive that will put them there early the next morning," he reminded Ustin. "And Mila, with paper work stating she's their guard, will be with them all the way and afterwards, in an attempt to keep them from being abused."

"But she can only do so much." Ustin shuddered, like he hated to think about it.

"She can keep Arina from being raped, but not Gerado from being brutalized. Especially, with the word out that he's Otho Behl's son...Just pray nothing bad happens to him before I can get him out."

When he arrived at his office, Ustin offered his support to help him with his paperwork and the travel arrangements...*A God send.*

"Hopefully, Val, with both of us working everything will come together like we want ."

"It should." Valery checked his watch."Now I'll have time to phone Isabella and Manuel, without cutting them short."

"You've got talking to do about Marek," Ustin responded. "With outside listeners. So be careful what you say. Or better yet, speak in German, since not too many Russians speak it."

"It's good you reminded me," he said, absorbing his words with a light bitterness...*Damn the Soviets and the way they had to stick their nose in everything!*

★★★

The phone rang several times in the Berlin hotel room before Manuel was able to get to it. "Valery, is that you!" he burst out. "What's happened?"

Isabella, hurrying over, said into the phone. "My head's on Manuel's shoulder so I can listen too—but Gerado and Arina. What about them?"

"They're in my custody, but I can't talk."

"I knew it!" she shouted. "It's Marek, isn't it?"

"He was drunk and struck his head, but is being released from the hospital tomorrow—"

"—and he's probably made plans to arrest them over that painting they refuse to give him," Isabella flared.

"Don't worry," Valery attempted to sooth."Mila and I aren't going to let anything happen to your Gerado and his Arina."

"And if Manuel and I were to bring him the painting?" Isabella asked. "What then?"

"They'd arrest the two of you for theft."

"Probably would," she snapped. "But has that damn Marek made plans to ship Gerado and Arina off to Siberia?"

"I can't talk. Just trust me. Since you should know how dear those two are to me."

"But speaking of that painting," said Manuel, changing the subject. "Pat Grisham believes he's found the location."

"What!" Valery exclaimed. "Why that's such exciting news I nearly dropped the phone. But is it close to here we think?"

"Yes," Manuel, replied in a buoyant tone. "So grab a pen and notepad and write some of this down. "He then began reading his summary of Pat Grisham's notes:

"He told me the missing part of the painting confirmed that the house, with the twisted chimney, had been in North Carolina, and appeared to be what the giant's hand was pointing at...This house had been torn down years ago and was now a state museum Luckily, the museum had an old architectural journal with pictures of the house, that mentioned a Russian tourist, Bogdan Rodin, visiting it in 1910. He was impressed and owned land near the Finnish border, but needed to return to the states for financing in order to build a house like it. Though sadly, he never made it, because he died on the Titanic."

"So, Valery," Manuel concluded, "being in the Soviet Union should make it easy for you to have someone look up the grid location of Rodin's land, find some possible coordinates, and hopefully a map that shows the roads leading to it."

"And Ustin, standing here, is just the man who can do it," Valery said. " So I'm handing him my notepad. And when we finish talking, I'll put him on the phone."

"YaHOO," Bill yelled from across the hotel room. "My deputy and I are gonna get'um!"

"Is that Cowboy Bill?" Valery asked.

"Yes," Bill answered, grabbing the phone. "Only it's now Sheriff Bill, with my young deputy, Max Ritter, who's standing here beside me."

"Just what do you think you're gonna do, Bill?" Valery asked him.

"Max and I are gonna get those Behl brothers, which are due to ride in tomorrow—"

"How do you know that?" Ustin cut in, apparently listening on another office phone. It was obvious he was shocked from the way the words stuck in his throat.

"They got the top part of the paintin's picture and need the bottom part," Bill reminded." Which tells me somebody at the university, where Manuel teaches, is tippin' them off...Just don't be surprised when those Behl brothers show up here at the hotel tomorrow."

Valery came back on the phone. "Ustin and I have to oversee a plane take-off, so we need to get going. But tell Isabella we'll get back in touch with you as soon as we know something."

There was a click, indicating he'd put the phone back on its rest.

★★★

"It seems those Behl brothers appear to have a contact at the university," said Valery, tapping a pencil on his desk like he was disturbed.

"Then how about I get some of my friends in East Berlin to check around and see if they can't give us a name, from a person with whom they work in West Berlin?"

"Fine with me."

The special military plane would be taking off for St. Petersburg in less than an hour. And a seed of eagerness sprouted within Valery as he as he drove, with Ustin at his side, to the dull, brownish-gray building that served as a temporary prison. "While I realize Gerado and Arina are running the risk of being harmed at Daniel Prison in the short time they're there, at least we have some good news about Wallenberg's possible location we can give them. That should bolster their spirits."

"Which I'll start working on the minute I'm back in your office," Ustin remarked.

When they reached this very unattractive brown building and parked at it's front door, Mila was waiting for them. "You're late." She pointed at her watch.

"Late because we have good news," Valery said, smiling. "Manuel's friend has given us information based on the painting, that he feels is Wallenberg's location."

"Couldn't come at a better time...or worse."

"How are Gerado and Arina?"

"Not good. They just sit shivering in that dark, basement cell, even of they're wearing their denim jackets. And I've offered them food and water, but they've refused."

"Bring something for them on the plane. Maybe they'll eat then."

"I trust you, husband, but this sending them to Danil Prison is a little much."

"I have a plan, Mila, just pray it works."

"A plan," she repeated, her face conveying a certain disbelief. "You've said that. Yet, I don't have a clue as to what it might be."

"You're not supposed to know." His tone was a bit overbearing. "Not even Ustin."

"Clearly a big mystery." She sighed with a frustrated expression.

"That could possibly threaten you if you knew," he confided quietly. "Though just remember if worse comes to worse, Ustin will help you get Gerado and Arina over the Russian border and into Finland."

"If anyone can do it, he's the man who can."

Valery flashed his badge when a guard approached, motivating him to snap to attention and salute.

"I have papers transferring this male and female prisoner to Danil Prison." He motioned at Ustin, who held up the papers. "A special military plane is awaiting them, with my wife accompanying them to the prison."

The guard said nothing but indicated they follow him to the basement cell where the couple was being kept. "Get out!" he ordered when he unlocked the door.

Gerado took a deep breath, laced his fingers through Arina's, and they exited quickly. "If only we were free to go," he uttered.

Caution, like an easily damaged shell, crept into Mila's face, the same as it was doing Valery's and Ustin's. "Only two days and a night at Danil," Valery informed Gerado. "Then you and Arina will be free to go."

However, once they got to the car, Gerado, obviously unconvinced, exploded. "Why in hell can't you get us out of this mess, Valery?"

"Marek," he answered. "It's all because of Marek."

"I bet Isabella's upset."

"Manuel's handling her."

"And you can't let us go?" Gerado asked, shaking his head like he was struggling to identify the problem.

"You might not want to go after the information I just received from Manuel and his friend as to where Wallenberg is being kept—"

"And it's close to this prison," Arina cut him short.

"Not very far. Ustin's working on the coordinates."

"Now isn't that the irony," Gerado murmured satirically." We finally locate Wallenberg, but we're being sent to prison. The worst prison in the Soviet Union!"

"Just wait. You won't be there for long," Valery said, feeling a need to remind him.

"Then you must know something we don't know."

"My plan—like I've said."

"That we know nothing about, and if it doesn't work—"

"Then you and Arina will escape."

"Which means we'll never find my father," Arina put in.

"So close, yet so far." Gerado frowned as if weighed by the unfairness of it all." Which to me, is a heavy price to pay."

"Marek's ordered you to a Gulag camp in Moscow," Valery reaffirmed. "So what else can I do?"

"I suppose nothing unless we can avoid this Danil Prison, yet stay in the area?"

"There's no way without getting in more trouble."

Gerado gave him an assessing glance. "Don't forget I wrote an article about this prison. So I know what goes on." His voice was threaded with concern. "Men are in groups of five or six and if one of them does wrong, they're stripped naked and brutally whipped. And I've had enough whippings to last a lifetime, with my father whipping me with a razor strap when I was only five years old. And later, then those two soldiers in Minsk slamming me around...And what about Arina? She stands a good chance of being raped—""

"No." Mila stopped him. "That's where I come in. Each man has a woman, and Arina will be yours—"

"But I'll have to stake my claim on her." His voice grated harshly. "Which means we'll be having sex in a roomful of people."

Mila shook her head. A quick explanation appeared to be needed. "It's not as bad as it sounds. I hear the lights are out and the men and women are usually under a blanket." Her gaze sharpened. "And you know I'll be standing in the aisle to intervene, and make sure nobody touches her but you."

"Still, what happens if I chose not to have sex under these conditions?"

"Then somebody else will get her. It's the only way you can stake your claim."

"Gerado please"—Arina laid her hand on his arm. "We'll manage."

Mila also laid her hand on his arm. "Rest assured, no one will touch Arina but you."

"Which is as it should be. Yet, you can't stop me from getting a whipping. A painful thought that threatens to shatter me—"

"You won't be there that long," Ustin intervened.

"Doesn't matter. They'll know who I am and will take it out on me."

Valery pulled over and stopped the car. "If you feel that way then here are your choices. I can arrange for you to escape before you ever get to Danil Prison. But then, you'll never find Wallenberg. So you and Arina tell me what to do?"

Gerado looked at Arina. "I can't make that call."

Her body slumped in despair. "And I can't make a call that could possibly get you whipped."

Appearing to reflect, he thrummed his fingers on the car's door. "At the university I was taught that being a news reporter was often a risky job. Some of my classmates didn't like the idea and dropped out of the program. However, I stayed on. So I guess we'll follow your plan, Valery."

The airport was getting close, with a plane overhead, slicing through the night sky.

Gerado and Arina caught a glimpse through the windshield of several more planes. "They're flying low," she remarked. "Which is something I don't like."

"It's military."

The car slowed as it turned into the airport and headed toward a building with a line of windows and a wide door beneath them. Valery stopped the car at the door and flashed his badge at the policeman who was starting over to their car. The man quickly saluted. "May I help you, sir?" But Valery told him it wasn't necessary.

He then got out, opened the door, and held his hand out to Mila, Arina, and Gerado.

"I wish you well," Valery said, giving them each a hug. "And I pray you won't be in that prison very long." He paused, and feeling their eyes cutting his way added, "Mila and I will be talking." Then he turned to Ustin. "We've got work to do well into the night, so we'd best head out."

Ustin got back in the car, but Valery lingered a moment, dwelling on the risk he'd be taking tomorrow...*When I do, what I have to do.*

CHAPTER EIGHTEEN

Berlin
****The following morning at the**
Hotel Metropolitan**

Isabella was so worried about Gerado and Arina, she'd been unable to sleep.

"Bill and I are going down for breakfast, so join us, "Manuel urged.

"Even if I can't eat a bite..."Her voice trailed off.

"Doesn't matter. Join us anyway." He put his hand on hers to stop the trembling." I have a class to teach this morning, but I'll be back by noon, and then we'll have lunch together."

"What do you think's going to happen?"

"Arina is Valery's former mistress, and he treats Gerado like a brother. So rest assured, he'll protect them."

Isabella shook her head like she doubted it, but right now there was nothing they could do. "Will you call Valery for me?"

"When I get back. We need to give him some time."

Bill, adjusting his cowboy hat in the mirror, looked at Isabella and frowned. "The big thing right now is those Behl brothers," he blurted. "Who're apt to show up any time."

Someone pounded on the door, and Manuel hurried to open it.

"Max to the rescue." The young man's voice had a rasp of excitement, as he held up two large bags.

"What's in those bags?" Manuel asked.

"Some smoke bombs and tier gas."

Manuel shook his head at him. "I don't think that's legal."

"Neither are the Behl brothers," was Bill's reply. "Which is why I'm here. To save you!"

Isabella and Manuel rolled their eyes as if to say, '*We doubt that.*'

"I don't know if Bill told you, but my father's one of the owners of this hotel," Max bragged.

He went over and tapped on the adjourning room's door. "It's empty, so if those brothers show up we'll set off the smoke bombs in there."

Wide-eyed, Isabella and Manuel just stared.

"Great idea," Bill told Max.

Several moments passed before Manuel said, "We're having breakfast downstairs, Bill. Will you be joining us?"

"Indeed I will. But I'll just grab something, since my morning watch is about to begin."

Max deposited the two bags in the vacant room next door, then joined Bill as he boarded the elevator with Isabella and Manuel.

They ate quickly with Isabella having only a cup of coffee and a piece of toast.

"I'm going home to shower and change clothes," Manuel said. "But I'll be back here at noon, where we'll have lunch. And afterwards I'll phone Valery if he hasn't called."

Time seemed to move slowly for Isabella as the day progressed. *If Valery would only call.*

When to her surprise the phone suddenly rang in her suite. "Valery," she said, scrambling to pick it up.

"It's Ustin," came the voice from Kiev. "I called you because I thought Manuel would be teaching his class."

"He is. But tell me about Valery, Gerado, and Arina," she gasped anxiously.

"As yet nothing to tell."

"And Valery—where is he?"

"Don't know."

"And Marek?"

"He's back, but I don't know where he is. However, I do have some information about these coordinates your brother gave me. Do you have something you can write on?"

"Yes indeed." She reached for the notepad in her satchel. "But what have you discovered?"

"That the place is near the Finnish border, which can help us. But I'll read you what I wrote down from my findings."

"Then proceed."

Ustin cleared his throat, then began reading:

"Of course Bogdan Rodin's house never got built—though he owned the land until his death. And it's on this land where Wallenberg is being kept. A narrow, winding road goes up a hill to a Gulag camp for farming. But it's empty now, with everything planted, so the prisoners have been moved to another camp..In a gulley nearby is the house where Wallenberg is being kept. However, it doesn't have a twisted chimney...The grid records list Rodin as the former owner, and classify the property as a State Mental Facility. Which could possibly be a Soviet lie to keep people away. Something that could possibly make it a little difficult for my team to find the exact coordinates."

"But once I've found them, then it should be no problem to locate a map that leads to then." He lowered his voice. "And I think I can probably do it without Valery, even if he does have connections that make things go quicker."

"I'll get a hold of Manuel right now and read to him what you just read me," said Isabella. "But please—let me know something about Gerado and Arina."

"When the time is right, you will," Ustin replied. "Though for now, just hold off." He hung up the phone.

"Must tell Manuel right away, even if he's teaching," said Isabella. She dialed his office and Ernst answered the phone. "Can you get Manuel? I just had a call from Ustin, and it's urgent."

"He's in class, but I'll see what I can do."

So she waited, fidgeting nervously until Manuel took the phone. "My students are doing some research making it was easy for me to leave them alone for about fifteen minutes—but what's happening?"

"I scribbled this on the notepad in my satchel, so I wrote it down for you too."

"There's paper on my desk. And Ernst just handed me a pen. So go ahead and read it while I write it."

She'd began reading, but a little fast, with Manuel having to stop her several times and ask her to repeat.

"Once we get that map, we're there!" he exclaimed to Isabella. "So while we're having lunch, I'm open to suggestions on anyway we might be able to help Valery locate a map."

"Because you think Ustin or Valery can't?" she asked him.

"I think Valery's being cautious—"

"—I guess so, with Gerado and Arina under arrest."

"Isabel, stop it, please! You're assuming the worst. Since no one's confirmed your godson and Arina are under arrest."

***

Ernst had been listening to everything Manuel said. And after Isabella left, he read what he had written. So he dialed the Behl brothers the minute Manuel went back to his class. They were interested in what he had to say about the coordinates, the map, and Gerado and Arina possibly being under arrest.

"Damn it!" Ernst heard Vaiter shout. "We need that map!"

"Getting the coordinates for Soviet maps can often be hard to come by," Hermann shouted back. "And its my experience they don't like people having certain maps for fear they might use them to try and overthrow the government."

"Then what are we going to do?" Ernst asked. "Are things still going as planned today?"

"Yes. Even though that giant's hand was in North Carolina, it was a major clue. So we need the torn off copy of that painting with its cryptic message on the bottom, similar to the one on its top. Because who knows? It could possibly turn out to be some kind of another clue, that might help us if we have to track this fellow Valery. Which, without a map, we'll probably have to do."

"If I could come up with something as good as a map would you give me another American thousand dollars?"

"You're a hard one to deal with—but yes, we'll give you another American thousand dollars, as long as you come with us."

Vaiter grabbed the phone. "Ernst, don't forget, we'll meet you at noon outside the hotel with those two large packages you wrapped...with which we're baiting Isabella and Manuel."

"And I'll be waiting near the parking lot," he reminded, as Vaiter hung up.

Their conversation got Ernst to thinking. And he suddenly felt unprepared. *What if they killed Manuel? They'd mentioned he had a lot to pay for.*

But Manuel had always been good to him, and his aunt would have had money if she'd remained married to him. Though at times, she did mention Manuel slipped her some money.

This feeling of dread as to what they might do to him was beginning to weight him down. *Would they kill him? Or would they not? Probably not, since they needed a map from this Valery fellow, with whom Manuel was working.*

It seemed, trying to find ways to get money, had been Ernst's passion as far back as he could remember. Manuel gave him an allowance and paid for his piano lessons which, as he grew older, had provided a small source of income for him whenever he played with a small group. However, the money often went to his aunt, and she'd buy clothes and other things for him with it. But she was controlling, and always there to see where the money went. Manuel should have put his foot down about that, but he never argued with her.

Later, when he came of age, Manuel helped him get in the university, and gave him a small salary for being his office assistant. "My piano playing and my being his office assistant were two jobs in which I got to keep all the money. And never once did I give my aunt any," he gloated.

All seemed to be going well until two years ago, when he met Marie Ann at the university.

She was a young woman whose family was quite wealthy. And she was beautiful beyond words, with long, dark tresses flowing halfway down her back and melancholy, green eyes.

He'd admired her from the beginning, and when she began talking to him, he soon learned she did not look on him with disdain, because he had no money with which to take her out. And he tried to be careful and not do anything to encourage her, since she was clearly not his equal.

But as hard as he tried, his good intentions didn't last long. For it was she who began trailing after him, saying she liked the fact he was an archeology student.

Her goal was to become a novelist, and she'd once written a short story about an archeologist and won an award for it.

She was engaged to a Johann von Haggen, a man in his mid-thirties who had a thriving business in America...*And when she'd told me, I simply thought, Oh no! Oh no! Not a prayer for me—but I was mistaken.*

She found it interesting he was Manuel's "sort of" nephew. And he continued to find it interesting that his Aunt Eva, hadn't remained married to him. Manuel was from a moneyed family, in addition to the money he'd made being a successful archeologist. *'But he's away too much,'* his aunt would complain.

'Though he's making good money,' Ernst recalled he'd argued. *'Are you unhappy about that?'*

However, she never had an answer to the question.

She always seemed to be needing money, so what was her problem? And Manuel, though divorced from her, never failed to help her money wise.

Marie Ann was also impressed with the knowledge that the news reporter, Gerado Gerhart—the brother Hermann and Vaiter referred to as *Late Child*—was tied to Manuel's family. "I read everything he writes." She'd beamed with delight.

Ernst didn't have much to say about *Herr* Gerhart, and the way Isabella had taken him in. A war criminal's son who'd ended up with a great deal of money. Why had Isabella done this? It made no sense whatsoever.

"All I want is money, because it gives a man power." Ernst had scribbled in his notebook. "But I'd still love Marie Ann, even if she lived in *shantytown*, and hadn't a German mark or American dollar to her name."

Their affair was something that never should have been. They were aware of their differences, and did their best not to cross the line...with no kissing until it became unbearable.

When school wasn't in session they had picnics on Lake Wannsee, enveloped in awash of splendor from the translucent, noonday sun that flooded their hearts with a wistfulness of their dreams yet to come.

She would become a best-selling author. And he would be on digs, unearthing things like those twenty-five hundred year old Etruscan bullas in the university's showcase, It seemed innocent enough at first but then, things began going too far.

He wanted to know about this man she was going to marry, and she had nothing but kind words for him. *'He can give you things, I can't,'* Ernst recalled telling her. *'So go and be happy with him.'*

But she didn't. *'What we feel for each other is unexpected, Ernst. And leaves me without a clue as to what to do.'*

'What you're supposed to,' he'd remarked in a feeble *voice. 'Your family expects it.'* He took her hand and brought his lips to it.

If he was at a loss as how to explain his behavior around her, she was clearly at a loss explaining her behavior around him. A week passed when they didn't see each other, and he remembered being deeply grieved. Then, she came back to him, and that's when it began.

Since it appeared they could not be free to lead their lives as they wanted, they took matters into their own hands.

She bought the condoms, but there was a time or two they got carried away, and she turned up pregnant. Neither of us believed in abortion, so all she could do was move her wedding up and marry von Haggen.

It broke my heart and from that day forward I vowed, I'd never be on the outside looking in.

Marie Ann and von Haggen moved to America, and I never expected to hear from her again. Although. a year later I received a photograph from her of a tiny fellow with wisps of copper hair. A brief note read:

"Say hello to Cooper. He's my assurance that a piece of you will always remain in my heart.

Von Haggen in a good husband and father and never questions Cooper is not his own son. And even if he did, my husband has so much love in his heart for Cooper, I don't think it would matter. He often jokes, 'No one in your family or mine can figure out where little Cooper's red hair came from. But my answer to them is that it doesn't matter, because he's a gift from God, and we'll treat him as such.'"

When that note had come, Ernst had taken a week off from school, claiming he was ill. *I'm a father who'll never be able to hold his son and kiss him. My secret. That neither Eva nor Manuel ever need to know, because someday I'll have money and will control my destiny. And no one ever again will keep me from being close to those I love.*

★★★

In the hotel dining room, Isabella and Manuel were finishing lunch. "You're not eating enough to keep a bird alive," he admonished her.

"I can't help it."

"Yes *you* can. Because we don't know Gerado and Arina are in a Soviet prison." He shrugged, and shook his lead, like he was frustrated at being caught up in this location challenge. "And knowing they're in Valery's custody, they'll probably be at his villa."

"A place they could call us from."

"Not if Valery doesn't advise it."

"Manuel." She practically shouted his name. "It's not a safeguard."

A waiter approached to see if they wanted dessert, when Ernst suddenly appeared.

"What are you doing here?" Manuel asked, regarding him with a look of consternation.

"A call came at your office about two gifts being delivered to your hotel room. One is for you and the other for your sister." He nodded at Isabella.

"And you came all the way down here to tell me?"

"I thought it might be important."

"How'd you get here?"

"I took a cab."

"That must have been expensive—but here." Manuel reached for his wallet and handed him some marks. "This should pay for your coming and going."

"And I thank you," Ernst said, bowing slightly.

Isabella got up from the table. "Shall we go see who sent these gifts?"

"Definitely."

"Do you think Bill's up there?"

"No." Manuel stood up. "He and that young man, Max, are probably playing sheriff and deputy."

She glanced around the dining room. "Well, Bill knows that if he wants something to eat, all he has to do is sign the ticket."

★★★

"Gotta see the sheriff right now!" exclaimed a hotel guest at the reception desk.

The desk clerk looked at him, goggle-eyed. "We don't have a sheriff here. So mwhat'd you mean?"

"You *do* have a sheriff, "the guest insisted. "You've got wanted posters all over this hotel, and I just saw those two men pictured on them walk in."

Bill was standing at the end of the reception desk. "So our poster boys are here today—like I said they'd be. Which lets me know I'd better hurry and find my deputy."

The desk clerk opened his mouth, closed it, then opened it again, as he gaped at Bill with his cowboy hat and tin sheriff's badge.

Max wasn't far, and when Bill informed him the Behl brothers had arrived, the young man swung into action. "I got the smoke bombs and tier gas in a sack in that vacant room. So let's go!"

Once there, Bill could hear Isabella and Manuel talking, so he peeped through the keyhole. They were each unwrapping a large package. "What's in yours?" she asked Manuel.

"A silver tray that's shaped like a fish."

"And yours?"

She tore at some more paper before reaching into the box. "A silver tray in the shape of a shell."

"Any card that says who sent it?"

"Nothing. And yours?"

"The same."

"I think someone's made a mistake."

A furious pounding began shaking the door. "Another package for Frau Swanda," a voice called. Manuel rose. "I'll take care of it."

But when he opened the door, two masked men, each with a pistol, shoved one in his stomach.

They entered the room with Isabella shrieking, "Hermann and Vaiter!"

"We gotta get those bombs ready!" Bill pressed Max.

"They are—just need to light'um."

"Get over to that table—" Hermann ordered Manuel and Isabella. "And if you make a move you're dead!"

"Do what he says!" Manuel urged Isabella.

"Not on your life!" Bill mumbled from behind the door.

"Open your briefcase and give us the copy of that painting—or we're playing Russian roulette." Vaiter had his pistol pressed against Manuel's temple.

"Do it, Manuel!" Isabella shouted.

Manuel's hands shook as he opened his briefcase and handed them his copy of the painting.

"We've been wanting to kill Manuel for a long time, so why don't we do it now?" Vaiter suggested.

"Quick, Max," Bill exclaimed. "Get those bombs lit!"

"They are—"

"—but they're not smoking."

"Then give me your cowboy hat, so we can fan'um."

Bill was watching through the keyhole as the smoke from underneath the door began to rise and curl.

"Fire!" Max yelled.

Hermann turned to look. "By God it is!"

Vaiter ran toward the door. "Hurry! Get the elevator before it locks up."

Isabella grabbed her satchel, and Manuel his briefcase, before running toward the staircase.

"Those Behl brothers' are gettin' away!" Bill yelled, grabbing his cowboy hat. "So put the bombs out, Max, and meet me in the lobby with the tier gas."

Bill wasn't far behind Isabella and Manuel. And when they got to the lobby, the three of them practically collided with Hermann and Vaiter.

"Call the police!" Manuel ordered the desk clerk. "These men are robbers!" He pointed at them as they ran toward the parking lot.

Bill dashed after them, with Max joining him outside with the tier gas.

"When you fall in a hole you'd better not go to diggin'." Bill hollared at Hermann and Vaiter.

"Who's that idiot in the cowboy hat!" Vaiter yelled.

"Beats me."

Then, a young man's voice from a parked car shouted, "Wallenberg's former driver!"

The tier gas was working, but not being in an enclosed area, it was not exactly doing what it should have been doing. Which, unfortunately, meant Hermann and Vaiter were able to get in the car and drive off before the police arrived.

Isabella and Manuel had now joined Bill and Max. "By God, Bill, you and Max saved us."

"But they got away," Bill said angrily.

"Ustin's got my phone number," Manuel attempted to redirect. "So you and Isabella had better go with me to my apartment, where I'll find a way to make some room. Besides, I've got to call the university and explain I have a family emergency."

"He handed Max some money, the same as Bill was doing. "You've been a great deputy," he said, squeezing his arm. "And I, along with Manuel and Isabella, thank you."

"Much obliged." Max smiled. The gleam in his eyes shinning like a bagful of ripe oranges.

CHAPTER NINETEEN

**Earlier that morning at the Danil
Prison, near Karelia in the Soviet
Union**

It was close to six hours before the military truck pulled up at the prison. Then, at around five in the morning, the truck stopped abruptly with the guards driving it, getting out and flinging open its back door.

Arina and Gerado stepped out, followed by Mila who was wearing a khaki uniform and a hat, the same as guards. A rifle was also slung over her shoulder. "Remember, I'm their official guard," she remarked, to the two guards removing her paper from a small satchel. When two other guards joined them, bafflement rose on their faces, as she flashed her power badge showing her to be Valery Savin's wife.

"Do they need a shower?" one of these guards finally asked her.

"They had one before they came. And their scalps are clean and don't need anyone cutting or shaving their hair."

Arina, trembling, stared at the crude, shabby buildings in front of them that resembled the ghost towns, often shown in Hollywood's Westerns. The buildings had been built on a empty-looking, broad terrain with nothing in the distance but some faraway hills. The sky was a dull gray, and in the morning's light appeared to have no cloud cover. She thought it odd with the scenic Karelia so close, there wasn't one hint of beauty near this place.

Looking around, Gerado shook his head like he felt the same way.

A large fence resembling something from German concentration camps surrounded them.

"Makes me sick seeing a fence like that," Arina whispered to Gerado.

"I know the feeling," he remarked in a tense voice. "Even if it does lack the insulators showing it to be electrified."

Although, searchlights and watchtowers were scattered along the way, with armed guards inside them waiting to shoot any escapee.

Mila directed them to a gray, asphalt building, where they were ordered to line up behind three weeping, young women and two solitary-looking men, in front of what appeared to be the check-in counter.

A portly woman in a khaki uniform called out their names. And when Mila flashed her badge at her, she didn't seem surprised. "Every prisoner is a number. With each prisoner getting a numbered patch on a cord that is to be hung around his or her neck, so it's visible at all times. If you fail to do this, you'll be put in solitary."

Behind her stood four men, which from the nicer way they were dressed, appeared to be prison trusties who, more than likely, were senior prisoners holding high positions.

Their eyes examined the women from head to toe, but always returned to Arina. "That's the best-looking woman I've ever seen," said one of the men.

"And she's mine to fuck tonight" said another man, who appeared to be the leader of these men.

"No she's not!" Gerado yelled. "She's my wife!"

Mila quickly shushed him. "In case you didn't read my papers," she told the female guard, "my assignment here is to look after this couple until they're transferred to a political prison."

"Appears to be the way Valery wrote it, until he can get Marek straightened out," Gerado whispered to Arina.

"There's another good-looking blond woman here. And she's younger," said the leader of the trusties. "Like that attractive dark-haired female guard." He smiled at Mila. "When has any official like her, ever shown up in this place?"

"None that I can recall," replied the man's friend.

This trustee leader stepped over to this younger woman with her tear-drenched eyes.

"Here." He handed her a piece of torn cloth. "Dry your eyes and get ready to go to work at the prison's clothing shop. And remember, you women don't get whippings here. Marks on your bodies make you unattractive, so you women just get solitary confinement."

Valery and Mila warned us about the way these sex-driven men prayed on the female prisoners, Arina recalled, wondering if this young woman had ever been with a man? *Probably not from the fear In her eyes. Though maybe if I can talk to Mila, she'll be able to say something to her that will help to calm her.*

The large woman in the Khaki uniform summoned two guards near the check-in counter to each bring a basket filled with clothes. "One basket is for the men, the other for the women. It's prison clothing. So after you take the clothes off you're wearing—including your shoes—pick a shirt and slacks from the basket. Then, you'll put your original clothes in the basket. Some boots will be outside the shower in another basket, so take off your shoes, leave them, and put on the boots."

"But my people have already had showers," Mila reminded the woman. "So is there a place here they can change?"

"In the filing closet where we keep our records." She pointed at a door.

"Then you first," Mila told Arina.

"Let her have a basket so she can pick some clothes," Mila ordered the guard, holding the women's clothing. "And get her some boots."

She complied quickly. With Arina soon finding herself putting on a worn shirt with snaps down the front that had several missing.

The slacks they've given her had a few rips. They were made from a denim-like fabric much coarser than her blue jeans and looked like men's clothing. *'They're too tight and scratch me in places,'* she wished she could complain.

"If only I could keep my jeans, tennis shoes and socks," she remarked in a low voice, as she deposited them into the basket.

Outside the closet door, boots awaited her. And uncomfortable with her bare feet, she quickly slipped them on. They were a little large, but it didn't matter for now.

"At least my feet are covered," she remarked to Gerado, standing by the door.

"Don't worry," he told her. Mila's taking our clothes and shoes and giving them back when we leave."

"Whenever that is," Arina retorted, shifting closer to him. "Why do you think Valery's doing that's forcing us to wait here?"

The crease between Gerado's brows showed him to be knitted with concern. "Don't ask me *who*, but my gut feeling is someone has to die," he answered, his voice dropping in volume.

It didn't take him long to change. And when he reappeared Arina could see he was dressed in similar clothing. "Now for my boots," he said, a hint of disgust in his tone as he prepared to tug them on.

"Wake up call her is six a.m," the portly female guard informed them. "So I'll escort Mila Savin to the women's barrack, with the female prisoners...and our two male guards will escort the male prisoners to the bunker. Breakfast will soon follow."

"What crime or crimes did these people commit?"Gerado asked Mila before they left.

"From what I heard, each is a thief."

Arina shot back a miserable look. "Like us and my painting."

"Seems they've matched us together." Gerado shrugged, his expression reflecting hers. "And these clothes—God forbid the poor newcomers."

The portly female guard motioned Mila toward the door, who in turn indicated to the women to walk between them. Once assembled, the guard blew her whistle. "We'll wait at the bunker where you'll shower. And be quick—so you don't miss breakfast."

That appeared to spark fear, so they hurried with their ablutions. And as they came out, their guard pointed at what she called the newcomers' barrack, which was not far away.

"More crude-looking buildings," Arina murmured in a bewildered whisper.

As they entered their quarters, a trustee wearing a patch with a number, announced she was their block leader. She asked the names of the four newcomers and added them, along with their numbers, on the clipboard she held. Mila flashed her badge at her but, like the guard who came with them, she didn't seem impressed. Something Arina found peculiar for a trustee.

Single beds lined both sides of the room, with each having a mattress, sheet, and a blanket. The aisle in the middle was narrow.

The block leader walked the four women to the back of the room. "Pick yours." She pointed at four beds. Arina sensed the women were shy about picking them, from the way they're hesitating. *Like for some reason they're in awe of me.* So she took the bed next to the back wall, where a door reading *TOLIETS* opened from the aisle. "I'm taking this unpleasant bed because I won't be here very long," she muttered.

The other three women then began picking theirs. A bell clanged. "It's six-thirty and time for breakfast," the block leader reminded them.

Roll call followed, with everyone standing at attention in front of their beds. Afterwards, the block leader ordered the prisoners to make two lines and follow her to the mess building.

Something Arina recognized as a daily occurrence.

Since the portly female guard had vanished, Mila walked in back of the line.

But when they entered this mess building, there were two lines for female prisoners. One looked like it had some halfway decent food for those whose obedience indicated they'd earned the right to it. The other line was for the newcomers, who had been here only a month or two. This group was served a watery soup in an aluminum cup, and stale bread. "But no spoons," Arina murmured. So she passed hers to an older woman who had accidentally spilled some of her soup and dropped her bread in the doing of it.

The men and women here were segregated, but it didn't stop Arina from scanning the place in the hopes of trying to catch a glimpse of Gerado.

Finally she spotted him at a table with some men. He too appeared to be looking around for her, and when he spotted her, he nodded. She returned his nod, understanding that hand waves could possibly be viewed as suspicious.

Mila stepped over to her. "Gerado hasn't seen his block yet, but I was told at the check-in building where the men from it would be sitting for breakfast. And I whispered I wanted to introduce him to them when we got to the mess building, but he said he'd handle it."

"News reporters can be like that," Arina remarked, scanning the benches for a place to sit.

"Miss Guard, said one of the recently arrived prisoners to Mila. "We women are expected to sit on the benches lining the walls. However, the men get to sit at tables,"

"That's because the men mostly do manual labor," she informed her. "And women are clothes makers."

Another female prisoner asked Arina, "Is it true you're a violinist and being transferred to a political prison, when some official in a hospital comes out of a coma?"

"That's enough," Mila snapped. "No more questions."

It irritated Arina the way rumors about her were circulating this early after her arrival.

★★★

Gerado was also irritated by the rumors going around. *Not just about me but Arina too. How long before Valery gets us out of here?* he asked himself as he gazed at the soup in his aluminum cup. It supposedly had more substance in it than what the newcomer women were receiving. And he could see potatoes, cabbage, and several chunks of meat. They had no spoons. But with the bread they'd been given, which wasn't stale, it made it easy to dip the meat and vegetables from the soup, and drink the rest.

However, he didn't eat because he wasn't hungry. Mila had fed them in the back of the truck with bread, cheese, and sausages. Also, she'd provided fruit drinks and had insisted on several restroom stops along the way. Though the best thing she'd brought were two pillows, so they could stretch out on the truck's benches and get some sleep before they arrived at this terrible place.

Seeing Gerado wasn't eating, the prisoner sitting beside him, nudged him and asked if he could have his food. Which he gladly passed him.

"What's it like to be such a well know news reporter?" the prisoner asked.

He turned to him slowly. "What can I say? That it sometimes gets you in places you'd rather not be."

"Like here?" the man snickered.

"Indeed," agreed a robust man sitting at the end of the table. "Since it seems today's our day for punishment."

Immediately, everyone at the table got quiet. "Do we think they'll really do it?" asked a ruddy-faced man across from Gerado. "If the rumor circulating is true, then how can they beat us for a man they say committed suicide? And how'd he do it anyway? There's nothing in our block that would allow us to kill ourselves. Which makes me suspect our good block friend, Lucas, who was fragile and couldn't work as hard as we did, had a heart attack."

"What we all thought," said the man at the other end of the table. "But now we're getting a different story."

Gerado's knees began to twitch with uneasiness. "And that's the suicide one, isn't it?"

"Yes," answered the ruddy-faced man.

"By the way," said he robust man at the end of the table. "We know your name from the guards and the newspaper work you do, but mine is Rudy. And I'm the *unofficial* block leader, since there're only five of us in our small block...which I describe as not being big enough for a weasel— much less five men."

"The small block makes us easier to control," added another man at the table, whose name was Alexi.

After a long contemplation, Gerado informed them, "I once interviewed a man who had a connection with this place, and I ended up writing an article about it. So I'm aware of what goes on here." It was something he hated thinking about, but it didn't stop him from continuing, "They control the men here like they do the kids in orphanages. If one does something wrong, they're all punished—"

"With whips,"interrupted a man who called himself, Peter.

"And they view suicide as wrong," said Alexi. He gave a small shrug. "By the way, we know you're Otho Behl's son, and have probably been beaten by some who consider you to have tainted blood."

"By some soldiers in Minsk." Gerado answered. He was disturbed by this block mates suicide or death. *Will the guards use this as an excuse to beat my block mates to get at me?*

'Punishment for the sins of *the father.' I can still hear one of those Minsk soldiers say. Which are terrible words to have to endure.*

The ruddy-faced man known as,Boris, must have been reading his thoughts. "In case your worried about our punishment, we're not blaming you if we get beaten." A long pause ensued. With this man holding Gerado's gaze before he pointed out emphatically, "After all, you're here with that lovely violinist, Arina Pavlik, who's supposed to be Wallenberg's daughter. And if you weren't a good man, then she wouldn't have a thing to do with you."

"Yet, they put me with you at this very bad time—"

"Because we're short a man in our block," Rudy pointed out. "Does that ease your burden?"

"No," said Gerado, weighing what his next words would be. "Not if whips land on your backs because of me. Besides, how do we know one of the guards didn't use my coming as an excuse to kill that man? Because he couldn't work as hard as the others?"

"We don't. But if feeling guilty is making you question things, just know they'd have probably killed that man anyway."

"It won't be the first time they've done something like that." Boris breathed out, his eyes level under drawn brows as if recalling something similar.

Alexi gave Gerado a warm smile. "Having you around is like having a celebrity with us. And we know you'll be going to a political prison soon, which is the reason we plan on enjoying your company while we can."

"And I'm much obliged," Gerado said, feeling even more guilty that his block men were being so friendly and understanding toward him.

"We've all been whipped once or twice in this prison," said Peter. "And maybe it's hard to believe, but there is an upside to it."

"An *upside*?" Gerado repeated, shocked to hear a prisoner say something that.

"From the astonished look on your face, you look like you have some questions?"

"So many they'd easily fill a cinema screen," he didn't think twice about saying.

That brought chuckles from the men.

"Let me explain this *upside*," said Rudy, emphasizing the word. "We get the day off afterwards and medical cream for our cuts. And we still get our women, cigarettes and vodka if we want them. Plus, we get a week to work in the upholstery shop. Which is better than working outside, doing hard labor."

'But even so, being whipped is painful,' Gerado started to remind him, but deciding against it remained silent.

"Things could be worse."

Gerado didn't know how to respond to that, so when the men got up to return to their barrack, Rudy came over and took Gerado's arm. "That lovely dark-haired guard who came with you, appears to be looking out for you and your lady friend."

"She's trying—"

"But she can only do so much."

"Correct." Gerado agreed. "Since if we're to be punished, and it doesn't happen, then it appears this place is losing control over its prisoners. Something that spells disaster. And could possibly put us in a worse place than here."

That didn't seem to set well with his block men, but Gerado had said what he had to say, so that was all he could do.

When they were finally ushered to their barrack, it surprised Gerado not to see any guards. "Do you not have roll check here?"

"A few minutes after we wake-up," said Rudy. "But otherwise, as long as they're no problems, we're pretty much on our own."

"I guess so. Considering one mistake and you'll all be punished."

Their barrack was a fairly short distance from the mess building, and once they reached it Rudy explained to him, that their barrack was really one building which had been divided into two rooms. A wall separated them. And each room had a toilet now, instead of the buckets like there'd once been.

Gerado's jaw twitched at the thought of buckets. "Certainly makes it easier not having them."

When they got inside, five beds that had been made up earlier, lined one side of the room. Rudy pointed at Lucas's bed and told Gerado that it was his. It had a mattress, blanket, sheet, and a pillow.

"We're lucky," Boris said, "because we hear some of the women don't get pillows."

Surveying the room, Gerado's brows creased with disgust at his inability to do anything for these men. *It was certainly unfortunate for them...*"What do we do now?"

"Wait until someone comes and tells us," replied Peter.

"A...and if they punish us, I presume it happens here," Gerado said, struggling to get the words out.

"Yes." Boris pointed his finger at the floor. "We're made to kneel, naked, at the foot of our beds and two guards, one on each end, gives us twenty-four lashes with a riding crop."

Bile rose in Gerado's throat. *Same as I wrote*. And it's only a matter of time before these guards show up.

And sure enough at half past seven, three guards burst into the barracks. *'We're like trapped birds behind a fireplace screen, and they've come to light the fire—'* was what he would have liked to have said.

The two guards had their riding crops, but when Gerado's eyes snapped to the third guard, he saw he was holding something that resembled and SS man's swagger stick. *For me no doubt.* His spirit plunged. In his imagination an invisible ghost, like a heavy shadow, was prodding him down the spiral steps of a nightmare.

Each man began stripping off his clothes and when he was naked, he kneeled at the foot of his bed with his head bowed. Gerado had no choice but to do likewise. One guard stood close to the toilet door, with the other standing beside the wall. When the two guards met in the middle space they started over.

The air left Gerado's lungs the first time the guard struck him, but somehow he managed to catch his breath.

This guard then went on to the next man, and when the two guards met in the middle, they started over as expected. On the fifth stroke the other men were crying like children. Though it took three more strokes before Gerado joined them. *A whipping for no reason.*

This happened twenty-four times, with the third guard counting until it was over. Then, the guards tucked their riding crops back in their belts.

None of the prisoners moved. *They're as frozen as a sinking ship's rats that have leaped from it and landed on an iceberg,* was Gerado's impression.

But the worst was yet to come. The third guard brandishing his swagger stick, struck each man on his naked butt three times. Gerado bit his lips to steel himself. Though to his horror, this guard returned to him and struck him three additional times. "Nobody but your father and his friend did greater crimes against humanity," he said in a grainy voice after he was finished. "So this is in memory of what they did."

And he left. The two other guards mentioned a spray of blood on the floor and said something about wanting to leave, but they didn't until they'd put a jar of medical cream on each bed...*'Rudy, Boris, Alexi, Peter, all suffered because of me,'* Gerado mentally shouted. *'And this poor Lucas died.'*

His block friends were off the floor now, and had begun to rub cream on each other's cuts. But Gerado was unable to rise, until Rudy and Boris helped him up. "They really worked you over," said Rudy.

"With it feeling like blood is spilling down my legs." A silence passed as he released a long breath. "They worked me over because I'm Otho Behl's son...like I knew they would." His pain was so intense it couldn't have been worse if he'd been run over by a tractor—*that left me to die in a vacant field with my bones rattling.*

Flames now fluttered not just on his back, but in his stomach as well.

"Your medical cream, Gerado," said Rudy. "Stay turned on your side, and I'll rub it on you."

"This cream's a big help," added Alexi.

It did help to ease the pain a little. *Although, what I need is some morphine.*

Boris leaned over and covered him with his blanket. "Try and get some sleep, like we're going to do and—"

He stopped mid-sentence when the door burst open, and Mila walked in with a man carrying a large case, who presumably was a doctor. "I just learned what happened," she told Gerado.

"D...did you call Valery?" he stammered.

"I can't reach him. But at this point I don't know if he could have done much good."

The doctor began examining the men. "We don't usually get to have a doctor with us," Rudy told him.

"I know, but I'm here because of Mila Savin. And she's expecting me to check on Gerado Gerhart, so I might as well check on the rest of you."

"We need morphine," Gerado gasped.

"I've got it right here." Mila said, reaching into her pocket." Four tablets per man. Which should last awhile."

"Give it to them first, Mila," urged Gerado.

"If you say so."

Each man thanked her and remarked it was the first time they'd ever been given morphine.

"Hopefully, my Valery and I will be able to stop these whippings when the time is right. They're barbaric and give our country a bad reputation."

Nothing more was said, but the doctor examined each man and rubbed a cream on his cuts that was better than what they had. "What you have is old stuff," he remarked.

"That figures,"Gerado said, overhearing him.

"Will we still be able to see our women and get some vodka and cigarettes tonight?" Peter asked the doctor.

"I don't see why not, as long as you get some rest."

"I'm personally having lunch and dinner sent over," Mila announced. "So you won't have to go to the mess building."

Rudy smiled knowingly. "See, Gerado, there is an *upside* to all this."

"If you say so..." Not wanting to leave his bed, he turned to Mila, his gaze on her. "But how's Arina?"

"In the sewing room helping to put some men's slacks together. Which isn't easy for her. So I'm assigning her to work in the kitchen with me where we'll be putting together this special lunch and dinner for you and these men."

"Does she know what happened to us?"

"Not yet." Mila placed her hand against Gerado's brow. "The doctor says you have fever."

"I probably do."

"He's passing around some aspirin, so you should be fine."

"And I'll take all I can get..." Gerado groaned inwardly. "Though, tell me, how are the other prisoners here going to respond, when they hear about this special treatment we're getting?"

"They already know you and Arina are political prisoners, who'll be leaving shortly. So naturally a few perks have to be made."

"But still, you weren't able to stop us from getting the whippings."

"No. Which is the main reason the other prisoners probably won't make a fuss over these few perks."

"Like having a doctor and getting special food?"

"Exactly."

Undaunted, Gerado continued, "I still don't see why you and Valery couldn't have stopped this whipping."

"Only Marek could do it."

"Have we heard from him?"

"No word from him or Valery."

"Now that's strange."

"Very."

Gerado arched a brow. "And Isabella and Manuel. What do they think about my being in prison?"

"That you and Arina are in our custody and can't talk to them right now."

"I'm worried if Isabella hears about this she's liable to have a complete breakdown."

"Valery and I know." She gave his hand a warm pat." And we've been careful not to tell her much.

Also, Manuel is looking out for her."

"For which I'm extremely grateful."

Mila's eyes moved down the length of his body. "I need to get a better look at what they did to your bottom with that swagger stick. "

"Why?"

"Because Valery will be asking me. So I'll need to lift your blanket."

"Is it really necessary?"

"You got struck there more than the others, so Valery will be expecting a full report from me."

"I always thought I had a fair degree of modesty."

"You probably do. But what it comes down to is, you saw my breasts in my effort to save us. So now, I need to see your bottom to ascertain the visual extent of the damage."

Gerado was skeptical.

"A severe butt beating can bring on other problems, " she pointed out, like it was the only explanation he needed.

"Then I guess you leave me no choice," Gerado grumbled beneath his breath.

Her lips hardened. "The doctor's going to do some reflex testing. So when he puts his fingers on you, don't jump out of your skin."

"Rudy rubbed some cream on me, so hopefully I won't."

"By the way, don't forget you'll have to make love to Arina tonight, or someone else will claim her."

"How could I forget something like that?"

"Are you up to it?"

"If I get enough morphine."

"You'll have it," she assured him.

★★★

Gerado waited until after Mila and the doctor left, before he began mulling over the task facing him tonight. He was a broken man. Yet, in order to keep Arina from being raped by some undesirable prisoner—as sick as he was—he'd have to make love to her. And how would that go over with her? She was the love of his life, but he was sore from all of his whip cuts, so how could he send her spirits soaring...? He couldn't.

Of course his spirits would soar, but with his broken body and the way he ached for her, he'd probably end up wolfing her down.

They were so close to having made it in that hotel room. She'd loved Valery, but her heart was changing. *And she was beginning to love me instead of him.*

But if he made love to her tonight under these dreadful circumstances, it would be a disaster. And she'd probably write him off. Male prisoners would be fucking female prisoners with beds lined up against the walls. *A group of people having sex together in one room. With the lights supposedly dimmed...though I don't see it as helping that much.*

The men had been assigned women to ease their aches, with no love between them. Surely the women objected, but they were forced to endure it, And he'd be in a room with his beautiful, wonderful Arina where women, in effect, were being raped.

How could Arina ever forget these circumstances, under which they came together for the first time? Probably wouldn't. *And when we finally get free of this place, she'll simply walk away from me in an effort to forget. So, my having sex with her tonight to keep her from being raped, will destroy the relationship I've tried so hard to build.*

CHAPTER TWENTY

**** Kiev ****
Early-Afternoon

Marek had to die. Valery knew he had plans to kill Gerado and Arina, and also knew he kept a free room at a small inn located in a wooded area near the edge of the city. The innkeeper paid Marek for protection. Extortion money.

Whenever he wanted to be with Olga, his mistress, who was an attractive blond woman, Marek would visit the place.

Valery also was aware Marek had a key to this room and knew exactly where he kept it.

50, after he'd beat Mila badly, not once but several times, he decided to have a key made to the room. However, he waited until Marek was out of town, since it gave him time to study the exact position in which he'd left the key. So he could put it back without Marek suspecting it had been moved.

Today, fearing they'd be some of his hairs in this room Marek kept, Valery had a haircut earlier. And afterwards, he gave his servants the rest of the day and night off.

Ustin's sources claimed to know where Marek was at all times. "Eyes that move on the street," he referred to them.

This afternoon, when Marek had made plans to be with Olga, he gave her the exact time he would be at the inn.

Valery made a point of going to the inn early and parking in the wooded area where people weren't apt to recognize his car. His pistol had a silencer on it. A Makarov government issued pistol with no serial numbers so it couldn't be traced back to its agents, so forensic people thinking Marek's death a suicide.

And Valery made sure nobody saw him when he slipped in the inn's back door and went down the hall to Marek'sroom. His rubber gloved hands unlocked the door, then relocked it from the inside. Marek was paranoid about locks.

Valery then went to the closet in the room and opened the door. It surprised him to see it was filled with men's clothes, that were much too small to fit the portly Marek. There were greatcoats, shirts, trousers, and robes. Beneath them were boots and shoes, neatly lined up in a row. It made him recall how Arina had said Wallenberg was trying to trick the Russians by hiding in the closet with his boots looking like there were no feet in them. *The shoe trick. My boots will show like the other shoes, not aware a human leg is in them.*

While he was looking at the shoes, he heard the lock turning, and quickly got in the closet. It was Olga, and she'd come to prepare the room. Valery stepped from the closet, frightening her for a moment. He knew she didn't like Marek, and only went with him because she did not want her family harmed. *Sex under duress.* She had come to prepare the room and was wearing the driving gloves Marek had given her.

"You never saw me, Olga, but did anyone see you?" Valery asked.

She gave her head a sharp shake.

"And you parked you car in the wooded area, the way I'm told you do?"

She nodded.

"Then go back the way you came in and don't let anyone see you." He breathed out, not taking his eyes off her. "Your problems will soon be over."

The grateful look in her eyes told him she knew what he meant. "Be careful," he warned her. "And should you ever need anything come to me and Mila."

She looked embarrassed, even blushing a moment. Marek never treated a woman as an equal and never gave them any respect. "The good in my life is returning," she remarked in an even tone.

"As it should," Valery acknowledged. "But lock the door and leave before he gets here." He steeled himself. "Just make sure no one sees you."

"I doubt they will."

His eyes were pinned on her for a moment as she darted through the back door and hurried toward her car, which he surmised was not parked far from his.

Then, he went back into the closet and waited until he heard the lock turn again.

This time it was Marek. "Where in hell is she?" he snapped to himself, looking around.

He sat down and leaned back in a chair not far from the bed. "I knew I should have got rid of that sorry bitch."

His head was back *The perfect position*. So Valery, wasting no time, stepped from the closet very stealthy and shot him right in the brain. It was a distance of three inches, and so very quick Marek never had a chance to open his mouth again.

He'd been careful when he'd shot him, to aim the pistol far enough away so the powder wouldn't set the mattress on fire.

Time was not on his side and knowing that, he knew he had to work fast. So he lifted up the coverlet on the bed and pulled the sheet exposing the mattress. Then, stepping back five feet he fired within a foot of the mattress.

Even wearing gloves, he wasn't taking any chances. Which is the reason earlier at his house, he'd taken the pistol apart, cleaned it, and wiped it off. That way no prints would show inside it.

Growing anxious, he went over to the bed, and pulled the coverlet and two sheets back. There was a hole in the mattress, but no burn marks on it. *No residue*. Nobody will ever know the mattress was shot.

He took the mattress sheet cover and folded it over in a hospital fold, then took the top coverlet and sheet and folded them so it looked like the bed was made.

Once again the bed is neat, the closet door shut, and soon this room will be free.

The next thing he did was to take Marek's right hand and press his finger on the pistol's slid...like he'd used it. His arm was now hanging down, the pistol on the floor, the residue on his hand and sleeve testifying he'd killed himself.

"With all residue gone from me," Valery said, careful to lock the door before leaving.

He was also careful when he left to make sure no one saw him as he headed toward his car in the wooded area.

He started the engine quickly, and heading out was soon on the highway. The perfect opportunity to take the room key he'd had made and throw it in a bar ditch. Which he did.

When he finally got to his villa, he shut the garage door and stripped out of his clothes. He put on a robe he'd left there and took his garments to the fifty-five gallon drum he had out back.

It contained the thermite bomb which was meant to destroy the government papers, that Marek didn't want anyone to see.

So taking the garments he'd worn, he placed them in the drum, with the thermite bomb on top of them. Then pulling the pin he walked away.

Forty-five seconds passed before he looked in the drum to see nothing but fine, white powder.

He then hurried into the house and showered, pouring bleach up to his elbows.

After he washed it off he put a cream on his skin, so the red from the bleach wouldn't show.

The hardest part would come now, when he had to wait until someone discovered Marek's body.

He went to his office and phoned Ustin, but didn't mention what had transpired. *Like he wasn't smart enough to know?* He pressed him about the map. How soon before he could get it?"

"Right away. I'll make a few calls and you should be able to go and get it in less than an hour."

It wasn't the time to remind him that he'd been designated to fill Marek's position if something happened to him. After all, he was his son-in-law. Still, he would never tell Mila how her father had died, even if she probably wouldn't have minded...No one would ever know, not even Ustin—*though my gut feeling keeps telling me Ustin does know.*

The information with which Ustin provided him had aided him in Marek's murder...or *suicide*.

And picking up the phone, Valery began making some additional calls, with the map he was seeking turning up quickly. "Surprise. I've found it," he told Ustin on the phone. "Arina will be overjoyed, so go get it." He gave him the address of where to go.

"Congratulations. You did better than I did," Ustin said. "Though before I left the office, Mila called you with a message and was surprised you weren't there with me."

"I had important business," Valery lied, not wanting to tell him he feared if Gerado and Arina were abused at the prison, Mila would tell him. *It will upset me. And I have to stay focused until Marek is officially declared dead.*

Ustin came to his office with the map. "Don't mention it to Mila if she calls again," Valery told him.

"Because she's apt to tell Arina. Getting her hopes up in our search for Wallenberg."

"Whip cuts...Gerado's situation...Mila told me about it on the phone," Ustin informed him. "But I asked her not to tell Arina until she talked to you."

"Good thinking," Valery praised him, feeling awful over Gerado's whip cuts. He didn't believe it would happen to him this soon. *But I was wrong. And if there's a way to make it up to him, I'll do it. But how can I for something like that?*

The phone rang, and Ustin answered it. "Mila's calling again," he whispered, putting his hand over it. "And she wants to talk to you because her father's not returning her calls."

"You know what to tell her."

"When your husband learns where your father is he'll call you back," Ustin said.

Valery wanted to talk to her, but the time wasn't right. Strangely, he was beginning to love Mila, and could now sleep more than three or four hours a night. The sleep helped ease his heartbreak over Arina, and the rest of his grief concerning her.

They were soul mates, and he'd always love her—no matter how brief their relationship had been.

But then, Mila would always love Nicky.

Happy days and memories of Arina would sustain him into thinking he'd done the right thing for her.

'*His graciousness*', she'd referred to him, when he talked about helping her get to Italy.

He'd been so long without anything or anyone. But now he at least had Mila. A great good in *his* life, with Gerado being there for Arina, and a great good in *her* life.

It concerned him that Moscow kept such a firm hand on Danil Prison. However, Marek, though living in Kiev, did have the power to ease the situation at the prison, since it was one for which he was responsible.

If it came down to it, getting Arina out of the Soviet Union and over the Finnish border with Gerado would be his way of parting with her. Recalling he'd told her that being at Danil Prison would make it easy for him to do it without risking himself.

But what about Wallenberg? With Marek dead Valery knew he'd have to be careful about helping her find her father. His new position would prompt other high-ranking Soviet officials to look over his shoulder. *'Will he be as strong as Marek?'* they'd ask among themselves. *'Or will he turn out to be a weakling?'*

And he would deeply regret Arina couldn't be able to visit with Wallenberg for very long. A *hasty departure will be required, so her visit won't flash back on me*, Valery had to keep reminding himself.

Of course his heart would cry for Arina making him wonder if anything would ever change the way he felt for her? He doubted it.

The words on the painting's back about the path leading to Wallenberg were touching. But once this was accomplished, the path that had bound his heart to Arina's would be blocked—if it wasn't already—with no sign of an exit.

Marek had caused all this, and part of him wished he could tell the truth to Mila about what happened to Marek, but he couldn't do it even if she despised her father. *Why? Was it because he'd known people who despised their parents, but when they'd died had shed tears over them?*

It made him wonder if at some point they were hoping to establish a better relationship with them? An opinion he'd once heard a woman voice.

He wished he did not know these things, like he wished he did not know what had happened to Gerado today.

Suddenly, the phone rang, and Ustin picked it up, identified the person, and handed it to Valery.

"Marek's dead. And it appears to be suicide," the coroner's voice said on the other end. "Though we have to make certain."

"Then do it quickly," Valery pressed. "His daughter's my wife and on a special assignment at Danil Prison, and we need to know for sure before I call her."

The coroner appeared to understand, so Valery waited again.

An hour passed, then another until the call came that confirmed Marek's death was a suicide.

Ustin showed not a flicker of surprise. *'And you, Valery Savin, are now in charge,'* he looked like he wanted to add, but didn't.

Mid-afternoon tomorrow Valery planned on flying to the civil-military airport near Karelia, and getting a military truck with a phone. He would then make the drive to Danil Prison where he would pick-up Mila, Gerado, and Arina. "I'll hand the prison officials written orders for Gerado and Arina's release. And with the aid of the map I have, we'll find Wallenberg's location."

But what about Isabella, Manuel, and Bill? He'd call them tonight and tell them to take a morning flight to St. Petersburg. There was a train station close to where Wallenberg supposedly was, so he'd advise them after their flight, to take the train. It was a long ride, but once they got their times straight, then he'd meet them at the station in his truck with its phone, uniforms, and pistols.

He'd also have everything packed in their suitcases from their Kiev hotel rooms, which he'd take with him on the plane, and later put in the truck. *And I'll be sure to pay their hotel bill, which is the very least I can do for them.*

Manuel and Bill had once been close to Wallenberg and were anxious to see him. But Isabella, poor Isabella. *How will I ever explain to her about Gerado's whipping?*

He continued to be worried about that—and Hermann and Vaiter in Berlin. They were clearly getting information concerning Wallenberg's possible location from someone at Manuel's university. A spy. Something Ustin's people were doing their best to learn who it was. *'In fact, they've double-checked their suspect so many times, they've lost count,'* Ustin would say. *'And even if those Behl brothers don't have a map, it won't* matter.'

Of course not. They'd learn from their spy source about the flight Isabella, Manuel, and Bill would be taking, in addition to their train ride.

"The Soviets need to stop those Behl brothers, so let them come," Valery blurted, voicing his opinion to Ustin.

He continued to maintain that the closest name at the university with which his sources could come up with was, Ernst Weir. Manuel's student assistant he'd helped raise.

Sadly, though Ustin knew Manuel would never buy the story. *'It couldn't be Ernst,'* he'd insist.

'And if it is, I demand a motive.'

'You have to find a motive in order to prove it's Ernst.' Ustin had told his people. But as yet, they hadn't been able to do it.

What possible motive could Ernst have? An unanswered question which was taking a great deal of time to uncover.

Yet, Ustin's people were convinced this spy had to be Ernst Weir—though proving it was another thing.

Valery knew that if Manuel, Isabella, and Bill made the long trip by train to the small station near Karelia, it would enable them to be on the lookout for a *tracker*. People getting on and off at the various stations, with someone working with Hermann and Vaiter sure to turn up. And Ustin agreed with that.

"It will also make it easier for me to contain the situation," Valery told him, "if they take the train. And for time being I'll name this tracker, *Seldte*...the man believed to be a former *kommandant* of a sub-camp, who's said to be a friend of the Behl brothers." Valery pivoted in his chair as he gazed at Ustin "Your sources said he was once a tracker for the SS. Though on short notice they don't seem to be able to get a current picture of him."

"They've certainly tried."

"I realize that." Valery's throat tightened. "But how will these Behl brothers be able to connect with *Tracker Seldte*, Manuel will probably ask me?"

"And your answer?" Ustin asked after a brief contemplation.

"They'll drive a truck with a phone on a narrow part of the border where Russia and Finland merge. Then head to the train station."

This narrow border was one of several disputed boundaries which wasn't clearly marked, with many people residing in small towns thinking they living in Finland, when to their surprise, they were either living in Sweden, Estonia, or the Soviet Union.

It required a visa to enter the Soviet Union, and Hermann and Vaiter would likely have sources connected with the Russian mafia—as Americans called it—which would allow them to purchase guns. *The whereabouts of these people we'll learn from the Behl brothers, before Gerado, Manuel, and I take care of them with the guns in my truck.*

Valery got angry each time he thought of how the Behl brothers were attempting to abduct Wallenberg. *Twenty-two years was too long for Wallenberg to be a Soviet prisoner. With the only reason being he was trying to procure some financial aid for Jews who'd survived the war...*It was a remorseful thought that never stopped pounding his brain.

And though Wallenberg might have seen other members of his family, the last time he'd seen his daughter was when she was six years old. Yet, if they'd known, his family probably would have refused to recognize her as his daughter. *'He was not married to her mother,'* he felt certain they would say. *'So how do we know who she really is?'*

But if Wallenberg and Arina could just spend a few minutes together, it would make his life and hers so much better...A much needed closure.

"And as for Hermann and Vaiter," Valery said, thinking aloud as his anger continued to rise. "How dare those neo-Nazis enter the Soviet Union after what Hitler did to Russia. However, once I take care of them, those in charge here, will be so impressed I'll have the power to civilize Danil Prison, with Moscow not uttering a word."

It was stupid of Marek to imprison a well known news reporter and not attempt to stop his whipping. The West called the prison brutal, with news articles about it spreading all over Europe and America. *Clear evidence Marek had some brain damage. And not just from his fall, the day before his suicide.*

"This brutal prison needs to under go a change. And I'm the person to do it," Valery murmured, practicing his monologue to the attentive Ustin. "Moscow looks quite bad to a good portion of the world. Which is something we need to put more effort into correcting, with my instincts telling me it'll make it easier for most citizens, including me, to survive in the Soviet Union."

"Isn't it time to call Mila and let her know about her father?" Ustin asked, intruding on his monologue.

"Yes. And Olga," Valey added. "But you call her for me after I'm finished with Mila." He picked up the phone and dialed the Danil Prison.

"Mila's overseeing the mess guards and kitchen help," an attendant at the prison informed him. "But I'll send someone to get her."

Time passed, a lengthy amount, until Mila came on the phone. "Valery, where've you been?" she probed eagerly.

"I...it appears your father committed suicide in his small room at the inn," he answered in a voice shakier than he would have liked. "So I was waiting for a report from the coroner before I called you."

"Well now, isn't that something," she remarked in a tone of astonishment. "What do you suppose took him so long?"

Her reaction gave Valery a cold sweat. Why it did, he hadn't a clue? He shouldn't have been shocked, but he was...Still, considering the way Marek had slapped her around, what could he expect her to say?

From his experience when a family member died, if any other member felt hostility toward that person, they saved their comments until after the funeral.

Mila then asked if Olga was with her father, and Valery lied and said, to his knowledge, she'd never shown up.

"She was late at times and my father usually slapped her for not being on time," was her response.

Valery knew all that, which was one of the reasons Olga couldn't stand Marek. And she tolerated him only because she needed money for her family. "I'm sending her some money. And when things settle down, I'll find a job for her," he told Mila.

"And I'll help you," she volunteered. "But what about my father's funeral arrangements?"

"Nothing yet. "

"Then tell them to hold off until I return."

"We'll do. However, I have the map we need. And I'll be coming to the prison tomorrow in a military truck, with a phone, to pick up you, Gerado, and Arina. So stand by and wait for my calls, in order to get our times straight."

"How'd you come by the map? "Mila asked. "If I may be so bold as to inquire."

But he didn't answer, fearing someone might be listening. "We'll talk tomorrow, just know it appears we've found our man—"

"Did Ustin tell you what they did to Gerado?" she a broke in, before he cut her off.

Immediately, tears misted his eyes. "He did," he replied, regretting he couldn't have shown a more solemn reverence for Gerado's abuse.

Mila then began discussing tonight's situation, when the male prisoners came to have sex with the female ones. She was concerned because Gerado was worried. It seemed he and Arina hadn't been able to finish what they'd started at the hotel. And would be forced to have sex under duress...like some of the female newcomers being forced to have sex with men who'd picked them. Which was nothing short of rape...And Gerado was to have sex with Arina—their first real time—under these conditions.

She then recounted what Gerado had told her about fearing Arina wouldn't want him after this. And he understood he'd have to be *her man* here in the prison, or some other man would claim her. But with all the pain he was in from his whip cuts, he continued to worry he wouldn't be able to pleasure her like he knew he should.

Valery couldn't bear to hear any more. "I have to go now, but I'll call you when I'm in St. Petersburg." And he hung up.

It was obvious something had to be done for the pair, but what? Valery knew Arina was attracted to Gerado and was trying to reach out to him. *She's doing it because she and I can never have each other.*

And if a woman feels like that, and the first time she and her new man make love is in a roomful of people having brothel-type sex, what will be the effect on someone like Arina?

Had this ever happened before? Probably. Even if he hadn't heard of it until now.

So what will Arina do? Will she turn away from Gerado, in an attempt to forget the dreadful circumstances under which they'd been forced to have sex? Such unpleasantness could blotch a blooming love. And if it happened, what then?

Arina probably wouldn't leave the Soviet Union, raising the question if Mila and I could be happy if Arina remained in Kiev...? No. It would damage our relationship because if Arina stayed in Kiev, then what? I wouldn't be able to stay away from her—

"There's a call on the phone in the other office," Ustin interrupted, returning his wandering mind to the present. "Shall I take it?"

"Who's it from?"

"One of my sources in East Berlin, who's discovered something about Ernst, and a relationship he had with a wealthy girl while she was a student at the university."

"Then you'd better take it."

PART 3

WINDFALLS

CHAPTER TWENTY-ONE

*** Berlin* ***
Early evening the same day of
Marek's death

When Manuel got back to his apartment with Isabella and Bill, he locked the door, before calling the university about his family emergency. They understood.

Then he called Ernst in his office and explained the problem. "I'll do whatever you need," he offered.

In the background at his apartment, Bill was saying he'd left his canvas tote bag with some clothes in it at hotel. Fortunately, Isabella had grabbed her satchel, when Manuel had grabbed his briefcase.

Manuel's apartment was close to the university, so he told Ernst if he'd come over, he'd give him cab fare and the key to Isabella's hotel room. Luckily,there hadn't been a real fire, just those smoke bombs. Also, he told him about the mysterious gifts he and Isabella had received. "Two silver trays. One shell shaped, and the other fish shaped. So bring them too."

Ernst agreed to everything Manuel wanted, and by taking a cab he was back in no time and sunk on the room's, dark leather sofa watching television.

Upon his arrival a call came to Manuel from Ustin. He informed him that Marek was dead, Valery had a map, and that Mila, Gerado, and Arina would be meeting up with him at Danil Prison late tomorrow afternoon. "Valery's now in charge. And Gerado and Arina are no longer prisoners."

Manuel motioned at Isabella to put her head on one side of his shoulder and Bill on the other, so they could listen.

"Great news!" Manuel exclaimed. "But where do we meet up?"

"At this train station tomorrow. Valery will be in a military truck with a phone. So call him from the *kiosk* phones from time to time, whenever the train stops." He gave him the time and number of the train they were to take, and the station where they would get off. "Also, Valery wants you to take the plane to St. Petersburg, then the train—"

"That's a long train ride," Manuel intervened.

"I agree, but it's necessary. The Behl brothers will have a tracker that you, Isabella, and Bill will try to spot. It's their failsafe method because without a map this tracker, in constant surveillance, is like these Behl brothers have their boots on the ground. With the only way they can locate Wallenberg is by following Valery."

"But how will this tracker know what plane and train we'll be on, when we don't even know?"

"Because of Ernst. Let him make your reservations," Ustin said in a coolly impersonal tone. "That way he'll get details, enabling Valery to stop those *damned* Behl brothers."

"But it can't be," Manuel whispered into the phone. "Why would Ernst do it?"

"Once I learn the details in the next half hour, I'll let you know. But is this young man here with you?"

"He's seated on my sofa. Since it appears he and his aunt had a falling out yesterday over some money he borrowed from her and hasn't repaid."

"Money is part of his motive, as you'll soon learn. So have him make the reservations for you, Isabella, and Bill. Also, mark my words, the Behl brothers will be taking him with them, as they trail you to Wallenberg's."

"But why would they take Ernst?"

"They're going to kill him to keep from paying him the American money they've promised him."

"The boy I helped raise," Manuel murmured in a soft voice. "How very sad. Even if I do still believe there's a mistake."

"You'll understand there isn't when I call back."

Isabella grabbed the phone. "I tried not to think about it, but feared all along he'd be the spy—but Gerado and Arina, what about them?"

"You'll be meeting up with them tomorrow evening. And if there's something you need to know, about anything that happened at the prison, let them tell you."

Her face went grim. "Doesn't sound good—"

"Manuel needs to give me the exact reservation information, so I'll be calling you back," remarked Ustin, before hanging up.

"I deeply regret the spy was Ernst," Isabella whispered to Manuel.

"Enough—we'll talk later." His eyes then snapped to Ernst. "If you'll make these plane and train reservations at these times for Isabella, Bill, and myself, I'd appreciate it." He scribbled some information on a notepad and handed it to him.

Ernst grabbed it eagerly. "I'll do it now, but do you think you'll find Wallenberg?"

"Valery's meeting us with his map, so we should. And by the way," Manuel continued, "It's crowded here, so why don't you spend the night in the hotel room we still have?"

"I'd love it."

"And I'll call the desk and tell them to put anything you want to eat on my bill."

"Why that's the best offer I've had all day!" he exclaimed, his excitement at a fevered pitch.

He made the reservations, then handed them to Manuel who gave him some money for cab fare and also some extra. "Give this to Eva, and you can repay me with the money you'll make when your music group plays again."

Ernst thanked him before sprinting out the door.

Several minutes passed before Manuel phoned Eva and informed her where Ernst would he spending the night. All he said. Still, why did he wait to tell her about Ernst being a suspect? Was it because some of the brightness in his life would be spoiled if the spy turned out to be Ernst?

Finally, he called her again and told her what had happened at the hotel with those Behl brothers.

"Does Ernst ever talk about them, since he knows about them through me?"

Eva's anger overflowed. "He played the piano for them at a party, and I wasn't happy about it!

Did he ever tell you?"

"No." Manuel disliked the way she was arousing his concerns even more. *I'm still not ready to face the truth.*

And changing the subject, he provided her with the departure times and reservation numbers of his plane and train trip tomorrow.

She asked why the train ride, but he didn't answer the question.

"The Behl brothers tricked us with gifts," he explained. "And when we opened the door for a third one, they entered with guns pointed at us."

"What kind of gifts?" Eva pressed.

"A silver fish tray and a silver shell one."

When he said it, she let out a loud shriek. "I have two trays like that!"

"Then come see if those two trays are yours, and I'll reimburse you for cab fare."

"My instincts tell me the truth's about to surface," Isabella remarked, looking Manuel square in the eye.

"Let's hope not."

Bill got up from the sofa and came over to her. "Don't worry, Miss Isabel, those two brothers may have got away, but I'll get' um next time."

Ten minutes passed and someone banged on the door. "Probably, Eva," said Manuel. "Since her new apartment's only three miles away."

He got to the door as quickly as he could and began fumbling with the doorknob's tricky lock.

"Manuel," Eva hollared. "I've got something to show you!"

"Just a minute," he hollared back, before finally getting the door open." I need a new lock."

"Yes you do. "She removed a letter from her purse and handed it to him. "There was a knock on my door after we talked. And when I went to open it, this was taped to it."

It had money in it, but also a copy of a note from a young lady, Marie Ann. Plus there was a copy of a picture of a baby with red hair. The note scribbled at the bottom read:

"I will never again be so powerless that I can't hold my son. And money is power, and the Behl brothers are paying me two thousand American dollar. So I'm going with them."

Manuel knew Eva needed comfort, but having been victimized by someone he'd trusted, he was too drained to offer any. *I feel like I've fallen into a trench. Which is a difficult concept for me to understand, when I've done so much for Ernst.* He felt so remote, he allowed several minutes to pass before he asked Eva, "Did you call the hotel?"

"I did. And he's not there. In fact, I even had him paged."

Manuel released a deep sigh. "He seemed so excited to spend the night there."

Eva was clearly exasperated. "Well, apparently he changed his mind—"

"May I see the letter, Manuel?" Isabella broke in lightly.

He handed it to her, and there was a tear in her eye when she saw the picture of the baby.

The phone rang, and he picked it up. It was Ustin again whose sources had given him the same story as was in Eva's letter.

"Just like we suspected and feared," Manuel remarked, with an unabated weariness as he put the phone back on its rest. "If he'd just told us. I would have helped him financially."

"I know," replied Eva. "And I would have stood by him and not allowed this happen. "She went over to the two silver trays sticking out of a box in front of the bookcase. "These are mine." She picked one up, then the other. "Can you believe he actually used these to trick you into opening the door for those brothers—"

"Who shoved a pistol in my stomach."

"Ernst is certainly in deep with those two," said a remorseful, looking Bill, from across the room.

"And they're apt to kill him," Eva sobbed, tears sliding down her cheeks.

Manuel blotted her eyes with his handkerchief. "Valery and all of us will be meeting up with them near Karelia. And we'll stop them."

Eva's eyes narrowed. "And Ernst, will the Soviets take him prisoner?"

"He's part of it. So *yes* they will."

"And put him in a Russian prison where he'll die?" Her expression was surprisingly stoic.

"Not necessarily." Manuel tucked his handkerchief in his pocket." Since there're various kinds of prisons in the Soviet Union,—but we're getting ahead of ourselves."

Isabella came over and gave Eva a hug, followed by Bill. "We'll find him and keep him safe," they each vowed.

"Why don't we go to the hotel?" Manuel suggested. "And we'll be there if Ernst shows up."

"But Eva declined. "It still might not be safe for you."

"A chance I'm willing to take, if I can keep him from leaving the country with Hermann and Vaiter."

What had he expected her to say? After all, she was a ghost from his past. They'd only been dating a month before they married. Not much time to get to know each other.

Another four months passed before he had to go on one of his digs, which was bad timing for a newly-wed couple. He had a doctorate in archeology, yet he seemed to be lacking in common sense or he would have figured it out.

Shortly after he and Eva had married, he recalled her sister had given birth to Ernst.

Eva was an attractive, part-time secretary, but she'd quit her job after they'd married. On the other hand, her sister continued to work, claiming her husband said they'd need more money with a new baby. So it came a no surprise little Ernst was frequently dumped on Eva.

Manuel lost count of the number of times he held the baby, while Eva prepared his bottles. His fingers would stroke Ernst's reddish-wisps of hair, and the little fellow would coo...And when the assignment for his dig came, he regretted he had to leave Ernst as well as Eva. But they needed money, with archeology paying well. And *yes*, he was from wealthy family, but his father had deemed him a spendthrift and had set it up in a trust that made it impossible to draw on until he reached a certain age...which had only been a few years ago.

One of the reasons he and Eva would probably not remarry, even if they'd talked about it.

Then, the unthinkable had happened; Eva's sister was killed in an auto accident.

And her sister's husband didn't like the idea of taking care of Ernst and dumped him on Eva, before he disappeared out of the country.

It was shortly after that Eva divorced me, Manuel recalled. *She needed money, so why?*

Because of Ernst he didn't neglect her, paying for a lady to take care of him while Eva resumed her part-time job. Something that always made him wonder if she wasn't looking for a wealthy man to marry? And for awhile she did have a rich boyfriend, but it ended badly.

Ernst became my ward, and whenever Eva said he needed something, I'd provide it—

Manuel felt himself tearing up and removed his handkerchief again. The really sad thing is that Ernst was off to a great career. Yet, with the aid of the Behl brothers, Ernst was marked for annihilation.

'*It's as if they've glued my nephew to a collapsing sidewalk,*' he would have liked to have said, but knowing it would upset Eva, kept his mouth shut.

CHAPTER TWENTY-TWO

*** Danil Prison* ***
Later, the evening of the same night
before the departure of Isabella,
Manuel, and Bill for Karelia.

"Do I know what I'm doing?" Gerado asked himself. In half an hour, at eight-thirty p.m. for forty minutes, he'd be with Arina in a roomful of people having brothel-type sex.

'At least the lights will be outside of the barracks,' Rudy had told him. *'Even if searchlights shine on each one.'*

Circumstances being what they are, Gerado knew darkness was much better than light with the faces of these unfortunate women not able to be seen, as they had forced sex with men they either disliked or detested.

But I'll be able to see Arina's face, since she won't be hiding under a blanket like Rudy says many of the newcomer women will try to do.

And when I see her face, with some of these women screaming and shouting they're being raped, her eyes will tell me part of her heart is still tied to Valery's. And this physical contact we have tonight obviously won't give her any pleasure—and barely me—with all my whip cuts. So Valery wins.

Why, when they'd met, did their attraction for each other have to be complicated with Valery?

The damage was already done before I entered her life or was it? At the hotel it might have been undone had those secret police not stomped into the room and arrested them.

The way history was taking it toll on them was like the sun had set between Arina and him.

Why did it have to be like that? he continued to question. With many who were running the Soviet government so mean-spirited, they'd take a kindly man like Wallenberg and imprison him for life?

But if they hadn't would he have ever have met Arina? Strange as it may seem, he believed fate would have found a way to bring them together in a more gentle time. But history had turned on them; the poles had shifted... *Forgetting to tell Arina's heart that, regardless, she and I were meant for each other.*

And nothing anyone could do or say would stop him from believing it, despite the fact his and Arina's lives had taken a turn that upset the boundaries of what was meant to be for them.

Like a fish leaping above the water...questions inviting answers... continued to surface in Gerado's heart. Although, just when an answer was about to come, this fish would return to the very dark depths of its ocean.

Tears slid down his cheeks. If his blood wasn't tainted, he wouldn't have these whip cuts.

And to spite the morphine, not be in such pain. Then, he'd be able to give Arina so much pleasure she'd want her life to be with him...*But my tainted blood has set me on fire, burning me inside and out; the same as the victims' in the camps.*

It hadn't seemed to matter that an angel had taken pity on him and dropped him in is mother's womb...with this angel also taking pity on Mila and him, when they were stranded on that very dark, country road.

If this angel could do all that, then why couldn't he do something about my tainted blood, and my love for Arina?

Instead he'd given him the cryptic message, *'When the time comes, you must let go of things that aren't meant to be.'* That had to mean Arina; the one person with whom he couldn't say good-bye.

Something he should have reminded this angel but didn't; *all I want besides Arina is to be free of my tainted blood. And the gathering dark, rain clouds that surround me because of it.*

He'd lost count of the number of times he'd envisioned himself standing at one of the camps holding an umbrella, as the fiery rain from the crematoriums poured down on him. *Dusting my soul with the ashes of the slain victims' hearts; ashes meant to taint my blood.*

★★★

"Gerado." It was Mila's voice, and when he looked up she was approaching his bed.

"What brings you here? I thought we were meeting in the barrack, where you're supposed to be looking out for Arina."

"We are. It's just I had to come to see if you're prepared."

"If you mean do I have any condoms, I don't."

"They don't use them here."

"Then what keeps the women from getting pregnant?"

"They're fitted for diaphragms, which I realize is old-fashioned birth control method."

"And Arina? Was she fitted?"

"Not enough time," Mila said, shaking her head.

Disgusted, he turned away. "And if I get her pregnant?"

"Hopefully, with the stress you're both under, you won't. But if you do, then you'll have to work it out."

He was flustered by all these regulations. They made no sense. "Will any of these men here in Arina's barrack be with me when I'm forced to have sex with her?"

"I've checked, and they'll be in different barracks."

"And I presume all of us men will be given some vodka and cigarettes?"

"Do you want that?"

"Hell no!" he said firmly. "They punish us with whips. Yet give us women, vodka, and cigarettes. A concept that defies my understanding."

"Normally it would, but good workers are needed. And if they work hard they get women and vodka.

However, as you know, if someone in their barrack makes a mistake they're all punished."

"This prison is an outrage."

"Because it's like some in Siberia after the Second World War—"

"A different time, a different place," he interrupted with the reminder. "Which doesn't exactly fit today's world. Soviet Union or otherwise."

"I agree." She nodded gloomily." Though it seems this man who took over this prison had worked in a Siberian one. So he modeled this one after it. And to this day, no high-ranking Soviet official has objected."

Mila took Gerado's hand and pressed it against his chest. "Your heart is beating so fast it brings to mind an elephant gone berserk. Which lets me know your frissons of fear about tonight are spiking with each passing moment. And you're afraid about how Arina's going to end up treating you. Because you love her—but she loves Valery, and he loves her. Another convoluted mess my father helped bring about. But I'll talk more about him later. Anyway, you think tonight in this ugly prison after you and Arina copulate for the first time, it will be over for her. And with many women it would, because they'd find the situation as unpleasant as having to squat over that hole in the Kiev prison's oriental restroom. Making it difficult for them to look beyond into the future, and question whether or not one really exists, after having sex with a man they detest—"

"Exactly."

"Some of the newcomers will scream and fight these men tonight, but in the past, when other women arrive, the men usually retire these women in favor of the newcomers. And then, for those retired, a glimmer of a future should begin to reappear."

"It's terrible women have to put up with something like this."

"It is. Though change is coming, and things will soon get better. But just so you'll know the two newcomers in beds by Arina's, tell me they've never had sex. So I've promised them, I'd hold each one's hand while it's happening and ask the men to be considerate of them."

Gerado chastised himself for being so helpless. "All you can do, Mila, but did you tell Arina about my whip cuts?"

"I didn't think the time was right." Her voice was subdued. "So you'll have to tell her, but only after I've had a brief talk with the two of you."

"Still, I keep wondering why I couldn't appear to adjust my clothes and crawl in bed with her. Since I now know the room will be dark, and we could pretend we're having sex?"

"Because in my opinion you need to finish with Arina what you started in the hotel or otherwise—"

"What?"

"Arina and I have talked briefly. And I think she'll surprise you. Nicky guided me to Valery—if you can imagine. Which gives me reason to believe something similar will happen between you and Arina."

"Cryptic talk," he replied sullenly.

"I know. But you'll have to wait and see. Since only Arina can tell you."

"And you really think, whatever this is, will happen between Arina and me?"

"I've got some wonderful news that I've been waiting to share with the two of you—so *yes*."

"Which is what? That Valery or Ustin's coming to smuggle us out of here and get us into Finland?"

"Better than that. You'll get the good news first from me. Then Arina will get the bad news about your whip cuts, from you. Which should ease matters between you. So follow me. The forty minutes is about to start for these men who—think they're going to die if they don't have a woman."

The fact he hadn't seen Arina since early this morning, made him eager to see how she was doing. After being in this place he doubted the brightness, reflected in her eyes was still apparent. And he suspected her beautiful gold eyes, the color of an angel's harp in a Gothic painting, had probably darkened with the pain surrounding her.

★★★

When Gerado and Mila reached Arina's barrack, two guards outside stood behind a table with vodka, paper cups, and cigarettes. "The women complain the men always smell like vodka," Mila informed Gerado.

She reached for a paper cup and poured some vodka into it. "Gulp it down. It's just a small amount which should help to ease your nerves and pain."

"Will it mix with my morphine?"

"Don't worry about it." She lifted a hand to calm him.

It tasted good, so he asked her to pour him another. Which she did.

They then went inside the dimly lit barracks. "When the lights go out it'll be pitch dark," Mila reassured him.

The other women appeared to be trying to sleep, their feet and heads covered with their blankets.

Bewildering—to say the least. "Don't they know who's coming, Mila?"

"There are a few nights the men don't show, so there's always hope for them."

"But tonight just couldn't be one on them—now could it?" Gerado replied, in a tone heavy with sarcasm.

"Arina's bed is next to the back wall." Mila pointed. "Beside the door marked *TOLIET*, where it smells sometimes—so I'm told."

"I'm sure it does."

When Arina saw them she stood up. She was wearing a flimsy off-white garment that buttoned down the front. However, it had some buttons missing. "I found that for her in some discarded clothing," Mila informed him.

Gerado went over to her and took her hand. "Are you ready, if not—"

"Remember what I said, Gerado," Mila intruded. "So you sit on the edge of the bed and let me talk, since you'll like what I have to say."

He obeyed her without question. "To begin with, my father's dead—a suicide. And Valery's now in charge."

Shock struck Gerado like a bow string in the middle of a lightning storm. *So this is what Valery meant by waiting...He had to wait to kill Marek and make it look like a suicide. Something* only *someone very clever could pull off. Which Valery most certainly was.*

Arina looked as dazed as Gerado felt. "What do we say, Mila? After all, he was your father."

"As little as possible," she insisted archly. "Now the other thing I'm here to reveal is that Valery will be picking us up here late tomorrow afternoon. He has a map he believes will lead us to Wallenberg."

Arina gasped, putting both hands together and bowing her head as though offering a prayer of thanks. "I knew somehow he'd find one."

"Still, we'll have to be careful," Mila warned. "Because getting to him won't be easy."

"What about Isabella, Manuel, and Bill?"

"We'll be picking them up at a small train station nearby...a long journey but a necessary one with lots of stops and starts. Because they're looking to identify this Tracker Seldte—we're calling him—that the Behl brothers have traveling on the train. And this man will be spying on Isabella, Manuel, and Bill in order to verify Wallenberg's location, when the train arrives at its final destination."

"My sorry brothers," Gerado spat.

"As sorry as they come," Mila agreed.

"And who told them...? Why Manuel's student assistant, Ernst Weir," he replied loudly, answering his own question. "A young man my gut feelings told me sided with my brothers for money."

"A...and you found that out how?" Mila stammered, the aghast look on her face making it seem her mind was frozen for a moment.

"Ernst, seemed the most logical person, Isabella remarked to me a time or two. But Manuel refused to believe her."

"The last phone call I got from Ustin," said Mila, attempting to capture her composure." I learned Ernst, supposedly, is coming with your brothers."

"If they're planning to abduct Wallenberg those Behl brothers will have guns or pistals," Arina reminded, a possessive desperation in her voice. "So how will they get them into the Soviet Union?"

"They'll cross the border where Russia and Finland overlap, and get them from the Russian mafia—as some of us refer to it. Then these Behl brothers will pick up Tracker Seldte at the train station, and they'll wait to see who gets in Valery's truck. And once they do that, they'll follow us to Wallenberg's. He's expecting gunfire with the cowardly Ernst—as Ustin refers to him—getting killed. And if he isn't, Valery will probably threaten him with a beating unless he identifies the location of these mafia criminals in our country."

Gerado tendered an agreeing nod. "Will we be shooting?"

"We'll each have a pistol and be wearing the Russian uniforms Valery is bringing. Since he suspects only the military will be allowed to see Wallenberg."

"That leaves the Behl brothers out. Though they'll still be attacking Russia in a manner of speaking."

"Oh yes," said Mila, putting her hand on the sleeve at Gerado's elbow. "Also, at your hotel in Kiev, Valery and Ustin packed all of the things each of you left there, and Valery is bringing them along."

Arina took a quick, sharp breath. "Did he pay the hotel bill?"

"He did."

"Then I owe him," Gerado spoke in all honesty.

Mila shook her head vigorously. '*Under no circumstances*—'to use his exact words."

A sudden crashing noise with the women bolting up, revealed the shouting men shoving their way into the barracks. And though the women knew what to expect, it didn't keep several of them from shaking and screaming.

Gerado shot up, so the men would see Arina was his. "We got sidetracked," Mila said, shifting toward him. "And you didn't tell Arina about your cuts. So do it now while I tend to these two newcomers. She moved between their beds and grabbed hold of each young woman's hand.

"There's that pretty one I saw earlier. "A burly man, who appeared to be a block leader, pointed at Arina.

He quickly stepped over to her, motivating Gerado to remain standing.

"What's the matter?" the man asked. "If you're not gonna take her, I will!"

"I'm taking her," Gerado shouted, ripping off of his clothes...*Never mind about my whip cuts. It's too late to tell her about them.*

The dim lights clicked off, but not soon enough, and Arina got a good look at them before darkness enveloped the room. "Gerado, what happened!" she exclaimed in a shout as loud as his.

Fear igniting him, he pushed the flimsy garment she was wearing from her shoulders. Then he got on top of her. "If I don't take you that block leader man will. And I know you won't get any ripples of excitement, from me, but I'll make it up to you." And with his chest thundering against hers, he plunged into her with reckless abandon.

Tremors of need seized him, buffeting him with delicious sensations that drove out every thought.

And he lost control, pleasuring himself but not pleasuring her.

He'd staked his claim, but it was rape to him...*I'm forcing myself on the woman I love, who will soon be lost to me...with my ending up spending my whole life trying to win her back, but not succeeding.*

Mila was talking in a loud voice to the two young men, who'd selected these girls earlier. They didn't look to be much older than the girls. "It's their first time, boys. So please try and be careful with them."

Why couldn't he have been careful with Arina? "I...I'm so very sorry." Gerado's voice broke.

"Say no more. "She laid a finger against his lips. "Just being joined with you finally is pleasure enough for me. Besides, you've been so brutally whipped, that anyway I can satisfy your hunger I'm pleased to do it." A feeling of great sorrow appeared to overcome her. "So let's go again when you're ready. And don't worry about me. Enjoy yourself."

She couldn't be saying that, could she? It was clearly his imagination... had to be.

Gently, she pressed her lips against his forehead. "You're in pain I can tell, so don't hesitate to give yourself another surge of excitement before our forty minutes is up. But how do you feel? Is the morphine helping?"

"A little. But how I feel is like the time I stopped a neighbor boy, who collected butterflies, from chloroforming a beautiful peacock one in a jar. I paid him an American dollar to give it to me. Which he did. And then I rushed home, opened the jar, and released the butterfly. But it fell on the grass with its wings spread, like me at this moment, having lost its ability to fly."

"That's so very sad." She rested her head against his chest. "But we're free tomorrow, and then we'll be rid of this suffocating environment. So take me again—"

"Boys," the block leader interrupted in a loud voice. "If you can't get it up in forty minutes you got no business fucking."

"It'll have to be another quick one." Gerado sighed, raising his head.

"Better that than nothing," she reminded, adding, "One of the things I love most about Valery is that he brought us together—"

"Like the deceased Nicky brought Valery and Mila together."

"Correct." Arina's hand touched his organ, and bursting with love for her, his hunger got the best of him...It was more than he could stand. And quickly entering her, he now had no fear that his erotic assault would make her think him a poor lover for having to hurry with his completion.

★★★

Berlin
Later That Night

Ernst watched from the staircase in Hermann and Vaiter's home as *Herr* Danner, their tracker, modeled the outfit that he would wear on the plane and train tomorrow. It was a disguise Danner had used several times when he was working for the SS.

He turned around, showing off his outfit. "Do I look like a priest?" he asked Hermann and Vaiter.

Hermann looked him over from head to toe. "Black suit, black T-shirt, white clergy collar, black hat, and black shoes and socks. I'd say it's perfect."

Arms crossed, Vaiter regarded him with a critical expression. "It's perfect except for your Bible.

"Which is right here," Danner said, reaching on the coffee table for it. "It's an old one. A Catholic Cannon that had belonged to my grandmother."

"Your outfit should convince Isabella, Manuel, and this Bill fellow—Wallenberg's former driver—that you're not the tracker."

"It will. And I intend on making friends with them, so they'll not believe me to be the tracker."

"Still, why is a priest in Russia?" Ernst asked from the staircase. "When religion is not supposed to be discussed in that country."

Danner wheeled around and in a condescending tone replied, "I'm telling them I'm working out of the Vatican Embassy, Ernst. And the Russian government has asked the *Holy See* for questions concerning religious history—does that answer your question?"

He regretted he'd asked and returned to the guest bedroom where he was spending the night...But he had trouble sleeping. Tossing and turning. He would get up early tomorrow with the Behl brothers, Glasen, and Ackert. And the five of them would be taking a plane to a small Finnish airport near the Russian border. He was anxious about the trip, and the fraudulent visa Hermann had given him. Would they get into Russia without a problem, in the truck Vaiter had procured for them at the Finnish airport? Probably so. Since Vaiter was supposed to be the expert when it came to sneaking into Russia.

"And also getting pistols," Ernst declared to himself. "But something's holding me back, making me wish I weren't going with them."

CHAPTER TWENTY-THREE

The train station was filled with soldiers, business men with briefcases, farm-looking women carrying baskets, couples with small children, and stylish French and American tourists, with a female guide, snapping pictures. A collection of people heading to either Russian cities, the countryside, or the scenic Karelia. A good many of these people on the train were women.

"But it's a man we're looking for," Isabella murmured. "Which, with all these women, should make it easier to spot our tracker."

Manuel agreed.

She, Bill, and Manuel were dressed in jeans and denim jackets and wearing boots. At the last minute she'd purchased a pair at the Berlin airport and tucked her tennis shoes in the large cloth bag she was now carrying. The bag was valuable because it also held Manuel's Polaroid camera in its small case—in addition to ten rolls of film.

Isabella hadn't ridden a train in a good while, nor had Manuel. And Bill said he couldn't remember the last time he'd been on a train.

This particular train was like a commuter train, with only three passenger cars and the rest freight ones.

"Another reason it'll be easier to spot our tracker," she remarked, taking a wine-colored, cushioned seat next to a window near the back. They'd asked Ernst to request the back for them, when he'd made their reservation because it was less noisy.

Bill was already in the aisle seat on the row in front of her and his cowboy outfit was bringing stares from the passengers, "What time is Valery supposed to get his military truck?" Manuel asked, resetting Isabella's thoughts as he plunked down beside her.

"He said around three this afternoon."

"You told me last night, but I couldn't remember since Eva was so upset."

"And you were too."

"I know. Though I do recall you said something about Valery calling ahead."

"He called ahead and ordered his truck at the civil-military airport and made them give him the number of the phone in it. And Ustin then called and gave it to me. So when it's closer to the time, we'll be able to call Valery from a *kiosk* phone at a station where the train makes a stop."

Manuel sighed, looking out the window as more passengers boarded. "We're all sure running up a lot of long distance phone bills."

"Doesn't matter, we have the money to do it."

"I'm certainly glad you handled things, since Eva wanted to come with us."

"It's dangerous," Isabella found herself reminding. "And she has no business."

"What I told her."

"Do you think we'll be able to save Ernst, like I feel certain you assured her we would?"

Manuel drew an audible breath, then released it. "We'll do everything we can."

Several more passengers boarded, before the train began to move. "Running late," the conductor shouted. "So hurry and grab a seat."

In the front excited tourists laughed, with their talk rising and falling, bringing to Isabella's mind tourists she'd seen on the Italian Rivera. '*The one who can get the farthest wins they prize,*' they'd joked, having fun chasing the an ebb tide's flow as it receded from the shore...*like our train is now receding from the station.*

The train lurched forward, shaking everyone slightly. "Almost as good as a carnival ride," shouted a young girl, laughing.

"We're starting to move, even if it's slow," said Bill, glancing from left to right.

But to everyone's surprise it stopped suddenly, On the station platform an older man, wearing a black hat, was hurrying to board. The conductor looked as if he'd been waiting for him and stepped down to give him a hand.

Isabella turned her head to get a better look at the man as he stood with the conductor in the corridor of the train. "W...why that man's a priest, Manuel."

"Who?"

"The man the conductor appears to be escorting to the seat behind us."

Manuel craned his neck. "Why by God, he is. And in Russia of all places."

The train lurched forward again, continuing to move slowly, until it rounded a corner with two large sheds on each side. Then, it picked up speed.

As its rhythm became more even, Isabella allowed her thoughts to flash from the priest to Gerado.

She'd read the article he'd written about the Danil Prison last year and knew how the prisoners were whipped, and the brothel-type sex that went on in the place. Those evil people had whipped Gerado. There were too much mystery surrounding him whenever she'd asked about him...and *no* answers were answers.

His job required traveling, but like as had been mentioned, wherever in the world he was, hardly a day would pass he wasn't in touch with her. Though this time, they weren't even allowed to talk to one another.

And as for Arina, being forced to have sex with him in such a terrible place, how would she react? *'I won't think about it. Can't think about it,'* Isabella caught herself before saying.

The priest tapped Manuel on the shoulder, and he turned. "I'm Father Muller, and my apologies to you fine folks for my being late, but a telegram was sent to me at my hotel that required my immediate response. So I phoned the station and informed them I was coming and would like the back passenger car, because it was usually less noisy. And since I'm here at the request of the Russian government, they allowed it."

"Interesting the Russian government is expecting a priest."

"They know their time is coming. The Berlin Wall will soon fall and the borders of the Iron Curtain countries will be opened, with religion returning to Russia."

"And when is this supposed to take place?"

"Most likely in the next decade. So the Russians are getting prepared."

Stretching, Manuel stood up in the aisle and raised his arms above his head. "Did you hear that, Isabella?"

"Gerado mentioned it to me once or twice. And said when it happened he wanted to be sure and cover the story."

"Yahoo!" Bill shouted behind her.

The startled priest stood up, then sank back down. The train was beginning to rock. "Is that an actor you've got traveling with you?"

"W...well," Manuel sputtered, taking a step forward before swinging back around to Isabella. "How about you answer that question?"

"Be glad to." She offered a brief smile. "Cowboy Bill is a very fine actor."

"And your names?" asked Father Muller, moving to the vacant seat across the aisle from them.

They introduced themselves, apologizing for not having done so sooner.

"I didn't get much sleep last night." Manuel yawned, plopping himself in his seat.

They were speaking in German and since they were hunting a German tracker, Isabella's curiosity was aroused. So she boldly asked this priest, "Where were you during the war?"

"In Spain. Where the Vatican assigned me."

"And you?"

"Paraguay," she answered in a clipped tone."

"Then you missed all the action."

"Thankfully. Since Manuel and I are Jewish."

"And you're living in Germany now?"

"Italy."

He stalled a moment, staring at her unflinchingly before remarking, "A great change is coming in the Soviet Union, so you won't have to worry about your Russian -Jewish friends—if you have any—being rounded up and made to live in Siberia."

"I don't have any Jewish friends in this country."

"Then you're a tourist coming to visit Karelia?"

There was an air of arrogance in this priest. Yet, just when it would slip out, he'd cover it with a smile, making her suspect he knew the answers to the questions he was asking...Part of a name was beginning to form in her mind. *So just keep talking, and it'll come to me where I've seen it.*

"My godson, Gerado Gerhart, the newsman, is getting out of a Russian prison today," she informed him.

The Father looked shocked, with his mouth dropping open like an actor's onstage might, if he'd just received some unexpected news. "I've read many of his articles, and recall reading one that might have offended the Russians."

"It's not about that."

"Which raises another question. Why did you take in a war criminal's son and his mother when you were Jewish?"

Now there was a slip, which she likened to the bones of a missing person's body suddenly becoming visible. *Since* I *didn't mention taking in his* mother...*But just keep asking questions, Father, and you'll hang yourself—if you are who I suspect you could possibly be.*

"They were being abused," she answered. "And though my husband and I were Jewish, we took Gerado to a protestant Church, and he would go to Temple with us sometimes."

"Did you celebrate Jewish and Christian holidays together?"

"We did."

"Strange *Herr* Gerhart never became a Jew."

"There were many Jews who looked on him as having tainted blood because of his father, so it wasn't encouraged."

Another flash. This time it was strong...like she'd been doused with a bucket of water from a splashing fountain, as the memory of a worn photo in Gerado's album came to mind. There was a fireplace, in what looked to be an expensive home, with three pairs of eyes in front of it, staring at the world with disdain...The names Hermann and Vaiter were at the bottom of this photo as was this fellow's called *Dan.* It was the first part of a name, with the last having been smudged out. And these men were holding a sign: WHO DO THESE DAMN JEWS, RUSSIANS, and GYPSIES THINK THEY ARE?

Dan Muller is this phony priest's name...No—that can't be right. Because part of the name seems to fit and part of it doesn't. Still, I'm getting closer.

As the train picked up speed, its even rhythm appeared to develop more of a swaying or rocking motion. But it didn't seem to stop three American women from going over to Bill and asking if they might take his picture.

He beamed with pride. "By all means, "he said standing up and gripping the back of his seat, since the one behind him was vacant.

"You speak good English," one of the ladies complimented him. "How'd you learn it?"

"From Hopalong and the Lone Ranger on the television."

The women applauded him. "Now that's really something," remarked the youngest looking of the women, like she couldn't believe it.

It was starting to rain, and clutching her camera another of the women stepped two seats behind Bill and began snapping pictures of some buildings. "The weather's getting worse, so I'd better take them while I can still get some good shots."

"Yes, you should," said Bill. "Because those raindrops that are starting to splatter the windows are fat like me."

That brought a chuckle from each woman.

The conductor, coming down the aisle, urged them in English to return to their seats.

"How long before we start seeing some countryside?" Bill asked him.

"About another hour, but please take your seat."

"I've got to take some Polaroids," he said, looking like Hopalong getting ready to saddle up and ride. "And it can't wait."

Once the conductor left, Manuel told Bill not to worry, and motioned him to scoot over so he could take the aisle seat next to him.

"It's two hours before we stop again. Which should give you plenty of time to photograph the passengers in the three cars."

He slid the camera's strap over Bill's neck. "Your Polaroid intrigues me," he said. "And I'm certainly glad you showed me how to use it on the plane."

"It's a valuable camera."

Seeing that the aisle seat next to Isabella was now vacant, Father Muller took it. "Having lived in Paraguay makes you an interesting lady. Since I've always wanted to visit that country."

"It's not the best place to visit with the large group of neo-Nazis living there."

"And that's a pity."

The familiarity about this man continued to disturb her. Of course she'd never met him, yet the youthful image of a man called, *Dan*, in Gerado's photo album kept trying to surface.

Arrogance. And this priest had the same air of arrogance, he kept trying to cover with a smile.

Gerado's mother had brought the photo album with her. *'I don't want it, but my son may want it some day,'* were her words.

Which he did. *'I'm a newsman, and I've got to keep track of what's going on with some of these wicked people in this album,'* he'd tell Isabella.

And hoping to help Gerado, she'd often looked at this album, which was filled with images of threatening people who were still living.

Caught up in her thoughts, she almost didn't hear Father Muller when he said politely, "I need to be excused, but we'll talk more when I return from the restroom."

Manuel must have heard him because when he left, he took his vacated seat. "What the hell's the matter with you, Isabella? I heard you talking and you were telling a complete stranger everything about us."

"He's the tracker, and if I keep talking to him, his full name will eventually come to me."

"This is ridiculous!" Manuel snapped. "That priest almost didn't make this train—and trackers don't work like that!"

"He's clever. Besides Gerado has a book on body language I read, and this priest is giving me some signs that tell me he's not who he says he is. Particularly, when he slipped up and said I took in Gerado and his mother. Someone I never mentioned. So for all he knew I left her in Paraguay."

"A logical assumption on his part. If you took the child, you'd take the mother."

"Ernst, was a logical assumption too," she pointed out in reply. "Though we seemed to have overlooked it."

Manuel's face twisted with a mixture of disgust and disapproval. "That's enough. All we need to do it identify the tracker—*not* get his name."

The Father was coming down the aisle, so he got up and resumed his seat next to Bill.

Isabella didn't tell Manuel that when he was trying to calm Eva, she'd talked to Ustin. She wanted to talk more about Gerado and Arina, but he assured her they were doing fine, before sidetracking the conversation. *'Valery just called and, if possible, he wants the tracker's name,'* Ustin had said. Explaining rumor has it, he's one of those three former *kommandants,* whose working with the Behl brothers. A man who was said to have ordered his uncle, a Russian prisoner of war, shot to death.

'And if they hadn't killed him, then I wouldn't have had to go to that terrible orphanage after my parents died,' were Valery's exact words. *'So if this is the man—and he's not killed in our exchange of gunfire—then I'll see he takes a trip to the wall...But I need his name!'*

'It'll be hard enough to identify this tracker, much less get his name,' Isabella had been *about* to say, when Ustin murmured, *'Valery was told this man had a palm reading from a woman, who saw a tiny mole at the bottom of his left little finger. And when he asked the meaning, she was said to have told him he had a bad reputation in business. Words that made him so angry, he ordered her killed.'*

Isabella knew that if it was tiny, it would be difficult to see. But still, she'd try. Her intuition telling her that first she needed to learn Father Muller's real name.

Manuel and Bill summoned Isabella to go with them and snap some pictures. The front of their car had some empty seats, and Bill had Isabella sit in one. It looked like he was taking a picture of her, but he was actually taking a snapshot of every face in the car. Then he took a picture of Isabella. In the two other cars they did the same thing.

They were due to stop at the next station in less than an hour and would have time for a brief lunch at the station's *kiosk*. New passengers would be boarding, with others disembarking.

Isabella wasn't concerned. *I know who the tracker is, and I'm calling Ustin from the station to see if his sources can come up with the man's full name. He can do that while I'm making sure Father Muller has that mole on the little finger of his left hand. And how will I do it? I'm treating him to lunch.*

CHAPTER TWENTY-FOUR

Isabella's lunch offer was immediately accepted by Father Muller, and when they got off at the station, they headed toward the *kiosk.*

Chicken wrapped sandwiches and feta cheese pastries was about all the *kiosk* had to offer, so that's what they ordered.

"And what do we drink, Isabella?" Manuel asked.

"Why Russian tea, of course."

The man at the *kiosk* didn't seem very happy about her request. But she gave him a good tip and asked him to put it in a pot and bring some cups.

The only place they could all sit was at a plastic table with some plastic chairs. Isabella made sure to sit on Father Muller's left side, and when she began pouring the tea for everyone, she fumbled and poured some on Father Muller's left hand. "Oh!" she hollared. "Look what I've gone and done!" She grabbed his hand. "I've burned you, let me see." The mole was there.

"It's all right, it could have been worse," he assured her.

She reached for her satchel. "I may have some cream that should help." But he stopped her. "I'm fine so leave it alone."

When they finished lunch, Isabella hurried to the telephone *kiosk* and dialed Ustin.

"Valery didn't have his truck yet. So wait to call him later this afternoon after he's picked up Gerado and Arina. Which should be around four or five."

"We have a train stop at that time"

"Of which I'm aware."

She then proceeded to tell him about the priest. "He's the tracker. His name is Dan *something,* and he has the mole."

Ustin was elated. "I'll tell Valery as soon as he calls me. And in the meantime I'll try and learn our good Father's name—"

"By the way, in case word hasn't got out yet, Ernst, Manuel's nephew is with Hermann and Vaiter."

"I'll be sure to point that out to him," Ustin promised before hanging up the phone.

Passengers were boarding the train, so Isabella rejoined Manuel, Bill, and Father Muller. Everything was falling into place.

★★★

* * Earlier That Day in the Soviet Union* *

Ernst was surprised when Glasen and Ackert pulled back the truck's canvas. "We're here," he said, as Hermann stopped the truck in a wooded area in front of a large, log house with a wide porch, that reminded Ernst of a vacation retreat. It wasn't what he'd expected. There was a spacious lawn surrounded by a chain link fence with wire at the top that was pointing out, not in. A large garage—probably a four car one—was in back.

A heavy-framed man with a black mustache opened the door for them. The man spoke German and appeared to know the Behl brothers, having undoubtedly done business with them in the past.

So, after trading handshakes, Vaiter excused himself to go check the oil and water in the truck. Inside, the house had the basic furniture: a dark sofa in front of a television, several chairs, and a dining table and chairs near the kitchen. A door that said RESTROOM was next to the kitchen. "Odd place to have it," Ernst mumbled. He glimpsed three bedrooms off to the side. *Why wasn't the restroom closer to them?*

A short, dark-haired woman was chopping up some vegetables at the kitchen sink that she was adding to a pot of soup. It reminded Ernst of his hunger. '*We didn't have any lunch,*' he'd told Hermann earlier.

'*There was water, cheese, and bread in the back of the truck,*' Vaiter had spoken up. '*So if you didn't get any then that's your problem.*'

'*But Glasser and Ackert ate it all up,*' he'd informed him. '*And never offered* me a bite.'

Vaiter had stared at him with a crooked smile. *'What did I just say? If you didn't get any, then that's your problem.'* Those were his words before he had headed out the door towards the garage.

More and more Ernst was regretting he'd come. *But if I hadn't they weren't going to give me my money. What then?* He was frightened by the mere thought. *What if they didn't give him his money?* His aunt had warned him they were bad people and to stay away from them. *Maybe she was right.*

Hermann, Glasen, and Ackert were in the restroom with the mustached man. Something that made no sense to Ernst.

"Anyway I'm hungry." He went over to the dark-haired lady and pointed at the soup pot. "Might I have a bowl?"

She obviously didn't speak German, so he rubbed his stomach and pointed at the soup pot. "No ready."

Well, she did know a few words. "Doesn't matter I'll take it anyway I can get it."

She understood that too, and poured him a bowl, which he quickly devoured.

Holding pistols Hermann, Glasen, and Ackert came back later from the restroom with the mustached man.

"Is the soup ready?" the man asked the dark-haired lady.

She nodded it was.

The men sat at the table, reserving a seat for Vaiter with a pistol in his chair. "He'll be back when he finds the right vehicle," Hermann said.

"No place at the table for *me*," Ernst muttered. "Good that lady gave me some soup."

Hermann complimented the mustached man on how clever he was to keep the guns hidden in a secret panel close to the restroom and kitchen pipes. "If I'm searched with metal detectors," the man said, "those pipes are expected to be there, so no one will be any wiser."

Vaiter came in and took his seat. "We've both got phones in the vehicles now, so we'll be talking to one another."

Ernst flipped on the television. *Forget the money, I need to get away from these men. But how, when I'm in the Soviet Union?* Suddenly, something told him that it didn't matter, just get up and leave. *They plan on killing me to keep from paying me.*

The road they drove on curved around, and there was some traffic. If he could hitch a ride, then maybe the driver could take him to a phone where he could call someone for help. But who would he call in the Soviet Union? He recalled some talk he'd heard from Isabella and Manuel during their phone conversations. Valery Savin's wife was at the Danil Prison with Gerado and Arina, and they were supposed to be freed today. If he could get a call through to her, then maybe she'd help him. *Worth a try anyway.*

Everybody was busy talking at the table and weren't paying him any mind, so it made it easy for him to slip out into the woods. The road wasn't far, and several vehicles passed before he could wave at them. But when he saw a truck loaded with baskets of vegetables, he practically stepped out in front of it. The driver, a man with blond hair and large eyes, stopped and began asking him questions in Russian. Ernst tugged at the door, and the man opened it for him. He spoke no German, so Ernst began pantomiming his need for a phone. "Some men back there are trying to kill me...Shoot me!" He played dead for a moment.

The man seemed to clearly understand those words, because his response was, *Schwester* in German, and *Sister* in English."

He continued down the road until he stopped in front of a small, A-frame house in a rural area. A fence with lots of chicken wire surrounded it. "*Schwester* here." The man pointed at a blond-haired woman standing in the front door.

Ernst doubted she'd have a phone, but to his surprise, she did. "Use phone," Ernst told her, because like her brother, she didn't appear to speak German. Danil Prison was probably at least two, maybe three hours away and would require a long distance call. *Money I don't have and these people look like they don't have it either...Valery Savin. Wasn't he supposed to be some high-ranking official in this country?*

He said the name and when he did the woman's eyes gleamed with a spark of light, the same as her brother's. Ernst picked up the receiver but before he dialed, he looked at the woman for approval. "Danil Prison, Mila Savin," he told her. "And I'm Ernst Weir."

The woman took the receiver and began dialing. The wait before Mila came on the line wasn't long. Their conversation in Russian was short, and the woman put the receiver back and said something to her brother that sounded like three one hundred American dollar bills.

Immediately, he gestured at Ernst. "Igor," he said pointing at himself. "And Sofia" He took her hand, before turning to Ernst. "Danil Prison." He gestured at his truck.

Ernst had trouble believing he was really being driven there. He'd made it and for time being had managed to escape from Hermann and Vaiter.

It was a several hour's drive, and when they pulled up at the prison's gate, Igor mentioned the name, Mila Savin, to the guard. "I'll call her and tell her your here. And she should be in the entrance room of that asphalt building just ahead of us."

By the time Igor parked in front of the building, Mila was standing outside. Ernst had never met her, but was he ever glad to see her. "You must be *Herr* Weir," she said. Then snapping her head around to Igor, she reached in her pocket and handed him what was obviously three one hundred American dollar bills.

He was so grateful he bowed.

"Tell you and your sister I appreciate your bringing Ernst to me."

He bowed again, promising her he would. Then he got back in his truck and started he engine. Ernst waved at him as he headed out, and he waved back.

"Well, Ernst, I phoned my husband, and he's certainly glad you're with us. Manuel was quite worried."

"Does he know?"

"He will when Isabella phones Valery from the next train stop."

"I've certainly been stupid."

"We'll discuss that later."

Gerado and Arina, once again outfitted in their jeans and tennis shoes, were seated inside this gray building at the check-in counter, waiting to check out.

Arina even had her tiny gold violin, that Mila had kept for her, pinned to her denim jacket.

"Been awhile since we've seen each other, Ernst, "said Gerado, stepping over to him. He motioned Arina to join them. And when she came over, he introduced her.

"I know you must think I'm terrible, which I am," Ernst began—

"We 're expecting trouble," Gerado cut him short. "So no talk about it now."

"Have you had anything to eat, Ernst?" Mila asked him.

"Just a bowl of soup."

"Then we'd best go to the kitchen and grab us a bite, since it'll be another hour before Valery shows up."

Gerado and Arina reached for their cloth bags that held their prison boots, before following her and Ernst.

They decided on beef kebobs and potato salad, with Russian tea to drink. "Do the prisoners eat this good?" Ernst asked Mila.

"No, but the guards do."

They ate quickly and were soon back at the check-in counter where the phone was close. Mila checked her watch. "Valery should be calling soon."

Which he did.

"Ernst got away from Hermann and Vaiter and is with us," were her words.

"How in hell did he manage that?"

"He was running away, and a truck driver picked him up. Fortunately, Ernst remembered our names and the prison, from all his spying. And the driver's sister called me...I promised this driver the three hundred American dollars you gave me for emergency...*Stash* money...if he'd bring him to me. Which he did."

"What a stroke of luck. But would you mind putting Ernst on the phone?"

She handed it to him. "My husband wants to talk to you."

"Probably to tell me I have to remain here in prison."

"No. He has a question."

"I'm sorry for everything, *Herr* Savin," Ernst apologized.

But he said nothing other than, "Do you know the name of one of Hermann and Vaiter's men whose name is similar to *Dan*?"

"Danner. And he's disguised as a priest."

"What I suspected."

"And what does the truck look like they're in?"

"It's a dark brown canvas one. And they got pistols from some Russians who keep them hidden behind some plumbing."

Mila took the phone. "How long before you get here, Valery?"

"Less than an hour. Which is around the time of Manuel and Isabella's next train stop."

"They'll be happy to learn Ernst is with us."

"Manuel gave me Eva Weir's phone number. And though it's not over yet, I'm going to call her and let her know we've got her nephew."

Mila put her hand over the phone. "He's calling your aunt, Ernst."

"Then please thank him for me."

She did, and Ernst turned to Gerado and took a seat by him. Arina was on the other side.

"This is my son, Cooper." He handed him the picture. "Though I'll never be able to see him, which the reason I did what I did for money."

Arina gazed at it, then Mila. "He's got your red hair," she commented before returning it.

Gerado looked like he wanted to add something, but didn't.

Ernst flashed him a tight smile. "You know some would view us as first cousins. Did you ever think about that?"

"Once or twice maybe. We weren't around each other very much."

"And you're so well known, it's like we didn't have much in common."

"I sense you want something from me, Ernst, so what is it?" Gerado asked, gazing at him intently.

"For you to help me get some pictures of my son, as he grows up."

"Now that's one I didn't figure," he breathed, awed. "So just exactly how am I supposed to do it?"

"Little Cooper's mother, Marie Ann, wants to be a writer. And she loved your writing and read everything you wrote. So if you could become friends with her and help her get something published, I feel certain she'd give you some pictures of little Cooper as he grew older."

Gerado shifted his attention to Arina. "What do you think?"

"That we probably should ask Valery."

"I agree," said Mila, launching herself toward Ernst. "Because as you've probably already figured out, you'll be spending time in a Soviet prison."

"Like this one." Ernst covered his face with his hands. "I read Gerdo's article about it, and the things they do in this place are terrible. So I guess I was wrong not to let Hermann and Vaiter kill me."

"No." Mila's voice was firm. "You'll be in a political prison like Bill, which is a big difference."

"It is," Gerado agreed. "And I'd like you to have some pictures of little Cooper as he grows older. However, there is a risk."

"A risk?" Ernst glared at him. "What kind?"

"A strong one in this delicate situation." Gerado paused briefly before venturing into his explanation. "I'm sure Marie Ann knows my connection with you, and she might think it strange I'm suddenly offering to help her with her writing. She'd probably take me up and possibly send pictures… Something that concerns me because she could be taking a risk. Her husband believes little Cooper is his son. And if he starts investigating me—and Manuel—a picture of you might turn up. 'Redheaded like little Cooper,' I can imagine him saying. 'The dots are connecting…' Now her husband loves little Cooper and that's the important thing. So we can't afford to do anything that could possibly drive him away."

His illusions shattered, tears rolled down Ernst's cheeks. "I wanted some pictures badly, but if I can't get them, then I guess it's another reason I should have let Hermann and Vaiter kill me." He said it like someone unwrapping the gift of a honey jar in the middle of the night, and lifting it to a candle…only to discover it was the light, mild flavored kind, that most people didn't enjoy.

Arina and Mila appeared to think about Ernst's picture request carefully, the same as Gerado. And after a long silence, he told him, "Isabella is great at handling delicate situations. Which in this case, I feel Manuel and Eva will be standing by to assist her. So with these three working for you, I'm optimistic they'll be able to get the pictures you want so badly—just give them some time."

"I'll do my best."

★★★

More than half an hour later, Gerado saw Valery getting out of his olive-drab canvas truck.

Mila's eyes radiated delight. "Valery's your official check-out and soon you and Arina will be free from this dreadful place."

Gerado was overjoyed. "That makes me feel as excited as a group of onlookers watching a soaring geyser touch the sky."

"Well said." She burst out laughing. "Since it would take a talented newsman to describe it like that."

The desk workers and guards, the same as in Kiev, acknowledged their respect for Valery, by either saluting or bowing.

He handed his official papers to those at the desk, and they began the process that would liberate Arina and Gerado. "Certainly good to have a high-ranking Soviet friend," he acknowledged for both of them.

"Valery." Arina touched his sleeve in a grateful way. "We couldn't have made it without you."

"I'm doing all I can..." His eyes drifted over to Mila. "Ustin's given Isabella the truck's phone number, and she's apt to call any minute. So, if you don't mind I'm headed there now."

Gerado's attention was focused on the truck. "May I go with you and Mila?" he asked, rising.

"Absolutely." Valery nodded.

In less than ten minutes Isabella called from the station's telephone *kiosk*. "Great news!" said Mila, smiling at the receiver as she switched it to her other ear. "That priest Danner is the tracker, and Ernst is now with us."

"Wonderful!" Isabella exclaimed. "Does Eva know?"

"Valery said he called her."

"Manuel's got his head on my shoulder, listening," Isabella informed her. "So I'm handing the phone to him for a moment."

"How'd all this come about?" he asked in a voice close to a shout.

"A long story."

"Allow me, please," said Gerado, taking the phone from Mila. "Isabella, is this really you?"

"Gerado!" she exclaimed, giddy with excitement. "I want to know everything."

"Later. Valery's headed toward me making hand signals he needs the phone again."

"Then give it to him."

He began talking to her and getting their times straight. "It'll be dark when I get there. But on the station platform Ustin tells me there's a small alcove with a bench close by, that a person can see from the parking lot. So make an effort to be there if our times don't quite match."

"We'll do our best."

He handed the phone back to Gerado. "Hugs and kisses from your godson."

"And always hugs and kisses to my little boy." She hesitated briefly. "Mila tells me Valery's got pistols and Soviet uniforms in the back of his truck. Which we'll need to wear in order to see Wallenberg."

"And Hermann and Vaiter with their neo-Nazi friends will be following us," Isabella added in a remorseful tone.

"Valery's looking out for us and will do whatever needs to be done," Gerado reminded, reaching out to her in a counseling voice.

"I know. But why pistols and not submachine guns?"

"Because it's a small group with pistols we're up against. And most of our people haven't had the necessary training to fire submachine guns."

"Pistols would suit me just fine."

"Just remember, my sweet Isabella, Valery will be there for us, and we for him. But just be prepared," he cautioned before hanging up, "if something unexpected happens."

CHAPTER TWENTY-FIVE

When Valery pulled up, Isabella, Manuel, and Bill were seated on the bench in the alcove. "Any sign of Danner?" he asked, going over to them.

"It seems he's disappeared," Isabella answered.

"I feel certain Hermann and Vaiter are parked not too far from the woods near this station, watching us."

"That's to be expected," Manuel remarked bitterly.

Valery motioned them to follow him to his truck where Mila was waiting to pass out their pistols. A small ladder was propped against the truck's back, so it was easy for them to climb in it.

Manuel introduced himself to her and thanked her for taking care of Ernst.

"I'm so very sorry I did what I did," Ernst apologized.

"Certainly unexpected," was the chilly answer Manuel gave him. "When my graduate gift to you next week was to pay your living expenses your first year in Canada."

The utter, utter surprise on Ernst's face was followed stains of grief.

"He's been kicked full circle," Valery murmured.

He was standing close to the ladder, watching everyone, as they began putting on the brown Soviet uniforms over their clothes and slipping on the Russian boots and hats, he'd been lucky enough to get for them.

"I never thought I'd be wearing a Soviet uniform," Bill remarked. "But if that's what it takes to see Wallenberg, then I'm more than happy to do it."

Isabella and Gerado exchanged hugs and kisses before climbing up. Then, she hugged Arina. "Take a look at his whip cuts," she said, pulling up his shirt.

"God in his mercy!" She was clearly appalled. "I knew, but I didn't want to know. And by all means he's going to a hospital in Finland, once we cross the border."

Arina agreed.

"Guess I have no choice." Gerado replied with a glum expression. "Though I'm not the first reporter to get beaten up. And surely won't be the last."

"Keep a look out for a dark brown truck," Ernst said, peeking through the canvas.

"Which I'm sure Valery will be doing once we get moving," Manuel returned.

"Are you excited, Arina?" Valery asked, smiling at her eager face.

"So much that I fear I'm going to pass out."

Gerado also smiled. "If you do, it'll be in my arms...But by the way, if I got you pregnant in that terrible prison would you marry me?"

A train rumbled in the near distance. "I'd marry you if I weren't."

It was obvious he was suddenly swept with happiness. "Then it's a done deal." he shouted above the noise. "Though I would like to ask Wallenberg for his blessing."

Her hand reached for his. "He'll give it. There's no doubt in my mind... because I suspect he knows we're coming."

"How? From the writings on the back of your painting?"

"Considering the writing was from an angel, there couldn't be any other way."

"There's a group of Russian soldiers training for night combat in the interior of those woods." Valery pointed out, shooting a glance in their direction. "And I don't think we'd create an interference because the sound of pistols doesn't travel that far. But even so, Hermann and Vaiter are watching us. And where those two are concerned anything could happen. So it might be a good idea if we leave."

Arina's eyes widened with excitement. "I'm for getting out of here and into my father's arms as quickly as possible."

Bill leaned over and put the small ladder back in the truck.

"Then into the cab we go," Valery said, sliding his arm around Mila.

He started the engine quickly, and turning around, began heading down a dark road his map showed leading to the coordinates he was seeking. The road was strangely silent.

Soon he saw the brown truck in his rear-view mirror. "We're being followed as expected," he told Mila. She snapped her head around to look.

The brown truck passed them when Valery turned onto a narrow, winding road and into a vacant Gulag camp. All had been planted with the prisoners going to another camp.

As had been previously noted, grid book records called it a State Mental Institution in an effort to keep people away.

Two brown suited, uniformed guards were at the gate. Valery flashed his badge and explained trouble was brewing from neo-Nazis headed their way in a brown truck.

There was a house in a gulley and these soldiers called it and informed the housekeeper about Valery's group and the people in the back of his truck.

There were several small apartments in back where the guards said a maid, housekeeper, nurse, mechanic, and cook resided when they weren't working in the big house.

Valery asked the guards if he knew who lived there. They didn't but noted that occasionally a bald headed man, sometimes wearing a hat, would be driven out and taken somewhere.

The path the painting had mentioned led to the front door, and the housekeeper opened it and let us in.

The dying Wallenberg was in bed and a doctor was with him. He told them what they'd guessed; Wallenberg had been expecting them claiming an angel had sent him a dream.

★★★

Now I must stop here. No one must ever know we found Wallenberg and what transpired. I will put it in my journal and put it behind one of the bricks around Isabella's fireplace. And when we are all gone from this earth and there's another Soviet regime, then the world will know…The angel was right when he said I must let go of things not meant to be…Meaning Wallenberg and not Arina.

The archive of Gerado's Journal:

When we arrived we discovered Wallenberg had a celestial journey to make. He was dying—perhaps any moment. Yet, here we were, the Wallenberg people: Arina, Bill, Manuel, Isabella, Valery, and Mila. "The painting," Wallenberg said, "was an unexpected path that brought you home to me."

Ernst stayed in the background. He was to do time in a political prison and after he got his doctorate in archeology with the books Manuel would send, then Valery said he would be free to go.

Wallenberg gave his blessing to Arina and me and mentioned he felt we'd have two sons.

Word had somehow reached Wallenberg about Sana and her imposter *Wallenberg* friend. The pair had made it to Israel, with Kato Orman sending a letter to Valery.

Money was being raised and put in Swiss banks to bribe the Soviets to release some of its Jews and send them to Israel. Mention was made how this imposter now wanted to at least pretend Arina was his daughter, and that she would pretend he was her father. Something Wallenberg encouraged, since he wouldn't be around much longer.

That's when I, Gerado Behl, knew what I must do. Raise money to put in those Swiss banks. And with Arina's violin playing and my newspaper contacts, it was the logical way to do it.

'*You have fulfilled my mission*,' Wallenberg told me."

That brief night the joy, the beauty all of us shared was incredible. Arina and I played our violins. Two songs. A perky gypsy one and a melodic one.

But when Mila and Bill went with the housekeeper to put our violins back in the truck, that's when the trouble started. The Behl brothers and their three friends were now in a black truck...two trucks, wouldn't you know, which didn't surprise me.

They'd taken the two guards, tied them up, and put them in the guardhouse. Then stormed through the front door of Wallenberg's dwelling, prepared to take him prisoner...though he'd already passed.

Later, I leaned the housekeeper gave Mila the keys to the house's van. *'We'll follow those damn Behl brothers!'* Mila had said.

Wallenberg having passed wasn't able to be moved at present, but it didn't stop Hermann and Vaiter from taking me, Arina, Isabella, Manuel, and Ernst prisoner. They planned on killing us in the woods, but with the Russian soldiers in training there, they decided against it. Isabella suspected Danner had seen the battered-looking boxcar left on the rail track in use, so that gave them the idea to take us there. 'Wouldn't a locomotive hit it?' she asked me.

Yes, but I don't think the Russians cared…An easy way to get rid of it, because usually these locomotives just kept moving after the boxcar was shattered.

Mila and Bill were prepared to fight at long range…Luckily, our boxcar had a hole in the roof and some crates on the floor, even if its doors were shut tight.

On a side track not in use was another boxcar with my brothers and their three friends on top ready to shoot us if we tried to climb out. Which of course, we did…with Mila and Bill covering us. There was a shoot-out. Mila and Bill exchanged fire with my brothers and their SS friends. And believe it or not Mila and Bill killed them all.

Suddenly, there was the scream of a locomotive whistle on the track that threatened to tear the boxcar apart.

Arina, Isabella, Manuel, and I made it out safely. Although, Valery insisted Ernst go before him, but he refused. Finally, Ernst agreed because Valery told him that regardless of his previous actions, he'd realized his mistakes and would now have the ability to help make the world a better place. Something Ernst wanted to do to atone for his actions.

The locomotive hit the boxcar while Valery was in it. We were horrified. But then there was a freeze frame, making it seem like time stood still for a moment…*A miracle—a blinding white light.*

The boxcar was shattered, but Valery was on the ground away from all the debris.

The locomotive kept moving.

The angel had lifted Valery, taking his hands so that his palms were silver.

'*But fading!*' Mila cried, urging Valery to make a furtive sweep down my back because his hands would heal my whip cuts.

Which naturally he did—So this is the way it ended.

Valery and Mila were as anxious for children as Arina and I. And we agreed that one day our children would play together. Valery said Mila would also be his assistant and the '*new sheriff*' in town. And Bill urged her to give him a kiss. Something she had no problem doing.

Manuel, Isabella, and Bill agreed to do what they could for Ernst at the political prison. And also, help me and Arina with our attempts to get many Jews out of the Soviet Union and satellite countries.

In the end all would go quite well.

Arina and Valery were soul mates and, to a degree, would always share their feelings. Although, Valery loved Mila and Arina loved me. "But you'll always hold my heart, Gerado," she declared.

According to what she said, hers and Valery's soul mating was a wedding of their hearts. Valery lifted her heart to have a better life with me, which she described—to my great joy—as living with an extraordinary human being in the western world.

And Valery said Arina lifted his heart to take advantage of Mila, the wonderful wife he already had, but had failed to recognize.

★★★

Looking back I realize ours was a journey of acceptance to better the lives of those involved and to discover, the format to a puzzle which was the canvas of God's work. We at Wallenberg's were all affected in a way that created a positive outcome for us. And, of course, one outcome in particular was soliciting money to help get many of the Jews out of the Soviet countries…Something we came to appreciate when we saw how the men and women who'd moved to Israel, helped to cement the growth of a better future and freedom in the world.

As a newsman I recall an article with which Wallenberg's housekeeper presented me. It was an article about how many of the children of war criminals had taken up with God…Missions had to be accomplished: some were archeologists, while others were newsmen and priests.

The article read that in light of the cruelty their parents had inflicted on the world, the children made a point of attempting to be like a blessing from God. Something I tried hard to be...And the discoveries I sought to make during my time on this earth, I came to view as being a path which would lead those coming after me, to uncover some extraordinary truths...Guides to a better, more caring world that would enhance the human condition and help erase much of the darkness our fathers had so brutally put upon it.

THE END

AUTHOR'S NOTE

The ashes of the six million who died will always be with us. And my eyes blur with tears at the thought, as I wonder...*What if my father had been a war criminal? And if so, then how would I have coped with such knowledge?* Questions that led me to research and learn, that the majority of these innocent children, sired by war criminals, suffered persecution like Gerado. One in particular was severely beaten three times. "Tainted blood," they were said to have with most, like Gerado, wanting tears shed only for the six million who had died.

Nevertheless, my intention with this novel, set in the 1980's, became for me another way to remind us—least we forget—that the prejudices and persecution these children suffered were from people too blind to see that such feelings underscored how the Nazis felt about those they deemed to be inferior.

Eisenhower ordered historical photos and films taken of the concentration camps because he said the day would come when people would deny these events...Let us hope it never does.

DISCUSSION QUESTIONS

1. Arina had a lot of high-ranking Soviet officials chasing after her. Were you surprised when she took to Valery so quickly?

2. Do you believe in love at first sight? Arina, Valery, and Gerado each claimed their experience, making it seem fated. A strong notion. What finally allows Arina to let go of Valery and move into a future with Gerado?

3. What do you think about the abuse Mila suffered from her father? Do you think Gerado did right to encourage her to warm up to Valery, her husband?

4. Were you surprised at the male bonding between Valery and Gerado, despite their opposing circumstances? What do you feel caused this?

5. Should Ernst have gone to a regular Russian prison like Danil, rather that a political one? Give your reasons for or against it.

6. Was Cowboy Bill completely unexpected in this story? Explain your reasons.

7. What is your opinion about Isabella becoming godmother to a mass murder's son? Would you have done the same thing if you'd been in her position?

8. Wallenberg said he'd either be a Russian guest or a prisoner. Not a surprising reversal of fortune when he became a Russian prisoner. Should he or should he not have tried to get money from other sources in order to help the Russian Jews? What about Wallenberg's family? Did they do the right thing to

continue their relationship with the Russians when Wallenberg
became their prisoner?

9. Gerado and Arina followed a path leading to Wallenberg.
    Were you taken aback at the way everything interplayed?
    What caught your attention in particular?

10. Do you believe this journey to find Wallenberg was really a
    path for the people involved to discover the puzzlement to
    the canvas of God's work? Give your reasons why this could
    be true.

11. *The Plight of the Gatekeeper's Son* is divided in three parts—
    "Expectations," "Paths" and "Windfalls." Why do you believe
    Kymberly Hastings structured the novel this way? How did
    each of these parts contribute to the overall view of the novel?

www.ingramcontent.com/pod-product-compliance
Lightning Source LLC
Chambersburg PA
CBHW030810210726
48290CB00002B/519